THE CTHULHU CASEBOOKS

SHERLOCK HOLMES
and the Sussex Sea-Devils

ALSO AVAILABLE FROM
JAMES LOVEGROVE AND TITAN BOOKS

THE CTHULHU CASEBOOKS

Sherlock Holmes and the Shadwell Shadows
Sherlock Holmes and the Miskatonic Monstrosities

THE NEW ADVENTURES OF SHERLOCK HOLMES

The Stuff of Nightmares
Gods of War
The Thinking Engine
The Labyrinth of Death
The Devil's Dust
Sherlock Holmes and the Christmas Demon (November 2019)

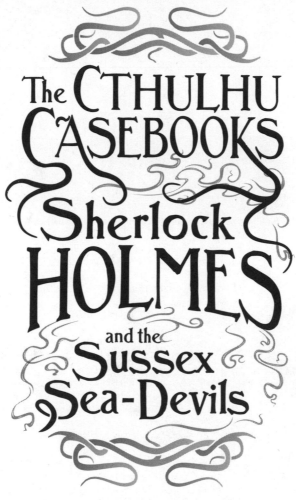

The CTHULHU CASEBOOKS

Sherlock HOLMES

and the Sussex Sea-Devils

JAMES LOVEGROVE

TITAN BOOKS

The Cthulhu Casebooks: Sherlock Holmes and the Sussex Sea-Devils
Hardback edition ISBN: 9781783295975
Paperback edition ISBN: 9781785652936
Electronic edition ISBN: 9781783295982

Published by Titan Books
A division of Titan Publishing Group Ltd
144 Southwark St, London SE1 0UP

First edition: November 2018
2 4 6 8 10 9 7 5 3 1

A CIP catalogue record for this title is available from the British Library.

Printed and bound in the United States.

SO WE COME TO THE THIRD AND FINAL VOLUME OF *The Cthulhu Casebooks*. Here we find Sherlock Holmes, now in his late fifties, still engaged in his secret war against hostile cosmic forces whose existence alone gives the lie to the notion that mankind is in any way a superior species and has a meaningful place in the order of things. We humans are not blessed, not special. That is the disquieting message that comes from these texts and likewise from the writings of my distant relative and near-namesake H.P. Lovecraft. We are, in the eyes of certain godlike beings, little better than cattle. Their unholy divinity proclaims that we live in a godless universe – a universe in which capital-G God isn't the adoring super-father the Bible says, more like a deadbeat dad who wants nothing to do with his "children".

At any rate, some of the action of this book, *The Sussex Sea-Devils*, takes place in the vicinity of my hometown Eastbourne. It is well known to readers of Dr Watson's published oeuvre that Sherlock Holmes retired to that part of Sussex in 1903 to take up the study of beekeeping, among other occupations. His rural retreat is described, in Watson's preface to *His Last Bow*, as "a small farm upon the South Downs". In "The Adventure of the Lion's Mane" we get a little more detail, although not a lot: the house is a "villa [...] commanding a great view of the Channel". Its location is generally reckoned to be within a few miles of Eastbourne.

My own house lies at the westernmost edge of that town, within easy walking distance of the only building in the area that matches the above description in every part – a flint-walled smallholding set back from the road leading from Beachy Head to Birling Gap. (I often pass it when out exercising my dog.) It's a windswept, slightly austere place, and I can easily imagine the great detective tending to his beehives in the lee of the shrubbery that forms part of the property's perimeter.

My genealogical links with Lovecraft may be tenuous, each of us perched on wide-apart branches of the family tree. However, my geographical links with the Sussex coast, where I was born and have lived most of my life, are deep-rooted. I have chalk and grassy downland in my bones. The crunch of pebbles underfoot, the bluster of a salty breeze, the hiss of surf, cloud shadows racing across the sea, smooth green undulations of hill – these are the things I think of when I think of home. For which reason I feel a stronger than usual connection to the story told within the pages of this typescript.

The other town that features prominently in *The Sussex Sea-Devils* is Newford. It's an odd little place that hunkers beside a shingle beach between two frowning brows of cliff, a few miles due west of Eastbourne. Newford is best defined by what it is not. It isn't a thriving port, although fishing boats and pleasure yachts do put out from its tiny harbour. It isn't scenic enough to be a holiday destination, despite a handful of bed-and-breakfasts and a single, forlorn-looking hotel. It has very little to offer in the way of historical significance other than a couple of concrete pillboxes and the remains of a gun emplacement dating from the Second World War, all gazing towards France with a somewhat wistful air as if pining for the glory days. Otherwise it is simply a warren of narrow streets that revolves around twin hubs, one spiritual, one secular: a medieval church with a crooked spire and a small pedestrianised shopping precinct built sometime in the 1960s where the retail units sell nothing anyone in their right mind would want to buy (but at least sell it cheap). There's a railway station, sitting at the end of a spur on the Hastings-to-London line, but trains are a rare sight at this one-track terminus, calling in only four times a day, half as often on Sundays. Buses may stop along the high street; I don't know.

What Newford has is mystery. Specifically, it has rumours of strange amphibian humanoid creatures who have been visiting the spot since the Iron Age or earlier, back when – according to the archaeological record – there was nothing there except a tiny cluster of huts, barely even a settlement. The creatures, known as Sea-Devils, are said to emerge from the waves at night, usually after a fog has rolled in, and roam the streets. Their arrival is customarily presaged by eerie lights glowing in the sea some distance offshore.

On such occasions you may, from the sanctuary of your home, hear the soft, moist *flap-flap-flap* of webbed feet on tarmac. If you have any sense, you will keep the door locked and the curtains drawn and not venture outside. Some local historians even claim that Sea-Devils and inhabitants of Newford have interbred in the past and that descendants of the two commingled bloodlines still live there. They have a distinctly piscine look about them, these hybrids, and seem to walk awkwardly on land, but are often skilled swimmers. For proof, one might consider the statistically high incidence of Newforders who have achieved success in aquatic athletics, amongst them an Olympic breaststroke silver medallist and two cross-Channel record holders.

I can't comment on any of that. I do know that the town council did attempt once to capitalise on this piece of folklore. Not far from the aforementioned shopping precinct stands a statue depicting a Sea-Devil. Erected in the seventies, it is sculpted in the Elisabeth Frink style, a thing of rough, pitted bronze with etiolated limbs and a rather sombre air. Its eyes are bulbous. Gills flare upward from its neck. Its broad mouth has drooping, pendulous lips that remind me of the actor Alastair Sim at his most lugubriously disapproving. Coincidentally – or not – many Newford townspeople I've seen have a similar look about them.

The figure was intended as a tourist attraction, something to put Newford on the map. Curiosity seekers and students of the esoteric were supposed to come to the town in their droves in order to learn more. Cryptozoology – and the paranormal in general – was big in the seventies. It was hoped that Sea-Devils would become Newford's Nessie and that Newford itself might gain the cachet of the Bermuda Triangle or Area 51. You can never underestimate the optimism of municipal councillors.

Nothing came of it, of course. The statue is now splattered with guano and more often than not someone will have lodged an empty can of lager on its head – or, more amusingly, an empty can of the energy drink Monster. It's become a running gag. Seldom does the statue go uncrowned.

Having read *The Sussex Sea-Devils* (and edited it for publication), I feel I now know a little bit more about Newford and its putative amphibious guests. I also know a little bit more about Sherlock Holmes's later years and consequently feel greater awe for his accomplishments than ever before, as well as greater compassion for the man himself. If everything Watson says in this book is to be believed, then the great detective fought valiantly to keep the world from harm and paid a steep price for it. Over a century on, we owe him far more than we realise.

J.M.H.L., EASTBOURNE
November 2018

IN MY PUBLISHED WORKS I HAVE GIVEN THE impression that Sherlock Holmes's retirement in Sussex was for the most part an easeful and contented one. I sketched a portrait of a man enjoying a rural idyll interrupted now and then by the call of duty. The beekeeping, the monographs, the smallholding overlooking the sea; what could be more desirable for a city gent whose hurly-burly is done and whose battles, if I may continue my paraphrasing of Shakespeare, have been lost but largely won?

It was not really so. For Holmes, as for me, the battles were still very much being fought. To all intents and purposes my friend did give up his practice as a consulting detective in 1903. By then he had successfully resolved a few non-supernatural cases for certain very high-born clients who were so unstinting in their generosity that he was left independently wealthy. No longer did he need to pursue the tawdry, mundane enquiries that furnished a dribble of income or to rely on contributions out of my pocket. He was, in a sense, free.

Prior to this newfound liberty Holmes had numerous interactions with R'luhlloig, the god formerly known as Professor James Moriarty. R'luhlloig had declared war on Holmes in 1895, as I have related in the previous volume of this trilogy, *The Miskatonic Monstrosities*. In the eight years following, the two of them skirmished often, the so-called Hidden Mind having taken it upon himself to badger and beleaguer my friend persistently.

Some of these clashes I have chronicled amongst my fictionalised accounts of Holmes's exploits, in disguised form. Readers familiar with "The Adventure of the Creeping Man", for instance, cannot possibly suspect that the awful transformation undergone by Professor Presbury, the famous Camford physiologist, was induced by exposure to spores from a fungus hitherto unknown to botanical science and believed to come from space, the properties of which caused him to regress to the state of one of our primitive ancestors. Nor is it common knowledge that Godfrey Emsworth, the blanched soldier from the story of that title, was suffering from a curse inflicted upon him by a tribal wizard in South Africa, which resulted in his succumbing to a gradual necrosis of the body, a kind of living death. As for the lion that allegedly mauled Mrs Ronder, wife of the celebrated circus showman, suffice it to say that the beast was, in truth, no lion.

The presence of R'luhlloig lay behind the three above-cited examples and behind many another, like some deep organising power. Able to insinuate his consciousness into that of any susceptible person and influence his host's behaviour, R'luhlloig would set up a teasing conundrum liable to be brought to Holmes's professional attention, whereupon he would spring a trap, in the hope of snaring and killing his prey. Several times he almost succeeded. The caveman-like savagery of Presbury, the traumatised psychosis of Emsworth, and a leonine monster that can only be called a were-cat – all placed Holmes and me in direct mortal danger. Happily we were able to outwit our lurking foe's machinations each time, but not without cost. I have more than a few ugly scars upon my body which bear testimony to that.

By 1903, however, the frequency of such cases had tailed off, prompting Holmes to feel that he could move out of London, away from the hub of things. He did not abandon altogether his investigations into crimes that had a basis in the occult and the eldritch; it was just that fewer of them came to his notice. He and I concomitantly saw less of each other. I remained in Marylebone, enjoying my practice and the less hectic pace of life which distance from Holmes brought. For both of us it was a respite. Neither of us, however, believed it to be a cessation of hostilities. That, indeed, was a common topic of conversation whenever I went down to Sussex to visit him. "One knows the difference between a pause and a halt, Watson," said Holmes, "and this is surely the former. We are in the trough between two waves, and the next wave, I fear, may be the biggest and most powerful we have yet faced."

Herein I recount the breaking of that wave: Holmes's final, fateful and I will say *fatal* encounter with R'luhlloig, which occurred in the autumn of 1910.

By that time the seeds of the recent global conflict

had already been sown, ready to burst forth four years later and bear terrible, bloody fruit. The great European imperial powers had already come to the brink of war in 1906, over Morocco. The aftermath of that crisis led to a strengthening of alliances on two sides, with Russia joining the *entente cordiale* that existed between England and France, and Germany, feeling ever more isolated and belligerent, forming a tripartite coalition of its own with Austria-Hungary and Italy. Opposing positions were becoming ever more firmly entrenched thanks to a succession of diplomatic rows and political moves seemingly designed for no other purpose than to antagonise, such as Austria-Hungary's annexation of Bosnia and Herzegovina in 1908.

A fevered atmosphere, fraught with hostility and mistrust, gripped our nation, as it no doubt gripped our neighbours. People could not help feeling a sense of ineluctable doom, like an anchor dragging at their hearts. The march to war seemed inexorable. It was a question not of *if* but *when*.

Few could have had any inkling that another war, one of hellish, cosmic proportions, was already underway.

J.H.W., PADDINGTON
1928

CHAPTER ONE

Things That Move in Darkness

UPON ARRIVING AT SHERLOCK HOLMES'S FARM IT did not take me long to ascertain that nobody was home. The sun was setting and the air was growing chilly, but no light shone in any window, nor did I glimpse the flicker of a welcoming hearth fire as I strode up the front path. Above all, the house had that markedly desolate air that a building exudes when it is uninhabited, like a body from which life has fled. It came as little surprise when my knock at the door went unanswered.

I was irked, to say the least. Holmes and I had planned this visit a fortnight ago, and he had confirmed the arrangement by letter just yesterday, saying how much he was "looking forward to seeing dear old Watson tomorrow evening" and how he had made every provision for my stay to be "a comfortable and leisurely one". I had told him, to the hour, when he should expect me. Yet he was not here.

I fancied that he had been delayed by some urgent domestic errand and would show his face presently. Yet at the back of my mind lay the possibility that there might be some more ominous reason for his absence.

Quashing the thought, I watched the dog-cart that had brought me hither from the station trundle off along the narrow, winding lane that led back to Eastbourne. I rather wished I had bidden the driver to stay, but it had never occurred to me that I might end up stranded.

I resolved to make the best of it and wait. I would allow Holmes thirty minutes. If he was not back by then,

I would walk to the nearest village and find lodging at an inn. I dared not leave it much longer than that, with the daylight fading rapidly. Blundering around the Sussex countryside after nightfall was not a prospect I relished.

Seating myself upon the doorstep, I took in the view. If nothing else, Holmes's smallholding was wonderfully well situated, the very definition of splendid isolation. There was not another building in sight save for Belle Tout, the decommissioned lighthouse that perched on the clifftop some half a mile away. The English Channel scintillated before me in the sun's golden gleam like a vast, million-faceted blue gem. A breeze blew across the grassland and made the bushes which encircled the property – blackthorn and gorse, primarily – shiver as if with delight. Gulls mewed, diving to and fro above their cliffside roosts, and the bees in Holmes's hives burred drowsily.

I felt drowsy myself after the journey down from London, and indeed I must have nodded off for a spell, because all at once the sun was gone, the sky was dark and a crescent moon was rising. I sprang to my feet, cursing my own folly. Now I would have to do precisely what I had hoped not to and find my way to some overnight accommodation with barely a glimmer of light to see by. The glow from Eastbourne's streetlamps limned the brow of Beachy Head in a radiant halo, but all this did was make the darkness of my immediate surroundings seem deeper.

I was about to pick up my travelling bag when I heard a faint rustling noise. It came from one of the larger outcrops of blackthorn nearby, and at first I assumed there must be a hedgehog or perhaps a fox grubbing around in the undergrowth. When the noise came again, however, it seemed to me that it was generated by a much bigger animal. Moreover, I sensed something decidedly furtive about it, as though the creature was taking pains to conceal its presence, if without success.

Immediately I was on my mettle. Three decades of sharing adventures with Sherlock Holmes had taught me to take nothing at face value and be suspicious of everything. If instinct was telling me to beware, then I should heed that instinct. In particular, I knew to exercise extreme caution around things that moved in darkness, and there was a great deal of darkness in the shadows of that blackthorn bush.

I groped for the clasp of my bag, undid it, and delved a hand inside, seeking my Webley. I had brought the revolver with me in spite of the fact that I was on a purely social engagement. Seldom did the weapon leave my side and never did I carry it unloaded. I never knew when I might need it, and I needed it more often than I liked.

Whisking the gun out, I cocked the hammer and issued a challenge.

"You there. I know you're hiding. Come out, whoever you are, or else."

For a moment I felt somewhat foolish. Perhaps it was just an animal after all, in which case I was barking threats for nothing.

Then a figure arose from beneath the bush. Silhouetted against the sky, it was a man clad in some sort of black hooded robe. I could not see his face but he was clearly looking at me.

"I thought so," I growled. "Who the devil are you? What were you doing in that bush? Creeping up on me, I'll be bound."

Answer to my queries came there none. The man simply stood in sombre silence. He was some sort of monk, as best I could judge. The black robe hung to his feet and had long, flaring sleeves that covered his hands.

"One last chance," I said, gesturing with the pistol in such a way that he could have no doubt I would use it. "Speak up."

The monk's continued stillness and silence were unnerving. I began to wonder if this was not a mortal being at all but some undead thing. His refusal to acknowledge my interrogatives in any way was signally revenant-like behaviour.

I advanced towards him, gun to the fore, determined to get to the bottom of the matter. All I had to do to establish whether or not he had physical substance was grab him.

Calmly he held his ground, and only when I was within arm's reach of him did I perceive that he was not alone. Two other men, robed identically, emerged from the cover of the bushes, one to either side of me.

They were quick, these two, catching me unawares. One seized my right wrist in an iron grip, wresting the Webley out of my hand. I was too startled to prevent him. The other snaked an arm around my neck, securing me in a chokehold.

I, of course, did not take kindly to this rough treatment and fought back. I like to think I gave a good account of myself. I aimed a few hearty kicks at my attackers, and flailed with my fists. They were strong, however, and quite implacable in their resolution to subdue. The one who was choking me had little intention of letting go, no matter how hard or often I struck him with my elbow. I could feel myself growing lightheaded as the pressure he was applying took its toll. Blood was not reaching my brain nor air my lungs. I struggled harder, but in vain.

Next thing I knew, I was on the ground, semi-conscious, with my hands fastened tightly behind my back with rope. The three robed men were talking amongst themselves. Their voices came to me mutedly through my fog of grogginess, as if from an adjoining room.

"It's not him, is it?" said one. "It's not Sherlock Holmes."

"I seen Holmes last Tuesday, in Eastbourne," said another. He spoke, like his comrades, with a heavy Sussex accent. *Seen* was pronounced *sin*; *Tuesday*, *Toosdee*. "This fellow's the same age but a bit shorter and a lot stouter. Also, Holmes is clean-shaven."

"So what's he doing at Holmes's house?"

"How should I know? All I know, brother, is Holmes isn't here and we've got the wrong man."

"Well, we can't let him go. Not now. Whoever he is, he's not going to amble away all meek and quiet-like, not after this. He's going to go straight to the police, isn't he?"

"Are you saying what I think you're saying?"

"We can't let anything interfere with the ceremony. Tonight's our moment. The stars are aligning. Kl'aach-yag awaits. We won't get another chance like this, and we can't afford for the slightest thing to go wrong."

"Then we kill him with his own gun and toss the body into the sea. There's nobody for miles around to hear the report. We're planning at least one death tonight. What's another?"

"A sacrifice is one thing, murder quite different."

"It's a fine distinction."

"Here's my idea. We take him with us. It's what we were going to do with Holmes anyway, as per Brother McPherson's instructions. Brother McPherson can make the final decision."

I gathered that this Brother McPherson was the three men's superior. They all seemed quite pleased at the thought of abdicating responsibility to him.

"What do you think, brothers?" continued the one who had made the suggestion. "Is my proposition acceptable?"

The other two assented. "You know him best, Brother Murdoch," said one. "If that's your advice, I see no objection."

So it was that I was hauled to my feet and marched in no gentle fashion down the front path and onto the lane. I had no notion what was to become of me but I could only think that some dismal fate lay in store.

And where, I asked myself despondently, *is Sherlock Holmes?*

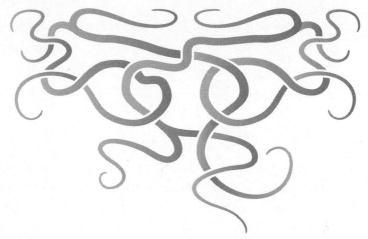

CHAPTER TWO

The Brotherhood of the Pulsating Cluster

A FEW HUNDRED YARDS DOWN THE LANE, WE CAME to a lorry that was parked on the verge, screened from view by a stand of hawthorn trees. By the thin moonlight I could see that it had seating at the front for two and, at the rear, a long wooden bed with shallow raised sides. It was normally put to agricultural use, if the mud-stained tyres and the straw-strewn planks of the bed were anything to go by.

I was made to clamber into the back and lie prone. One of the robed men – the one the others had referred to as Brother Murdoch – volunteered to keep guard over me and persuaded the man with my revolver to surrender the weapon to him.

"He may be tied up but you never know. He's a tiger, this fellow, for all that he's old. Makes sense for me to have the pistol, just in case."

As Brother Murdoch joined me in the back of the lorry, one of his colleagues sat behind the steering wheel while the other cranked the starter handle. After a couple of attempts the engine thundered into life. The third man climbed aboard and we were on our way.

We drove for a good half an hour at the pace of a man walking briskly. The lorry's jolting, roaring progress was hardly conducive to marshalling my disordered thoughts, but I was able to piece together a vaguely coherent picture of my situation. The robed men must belong to some kind of cult, if their talk of a ceremony and a sacrifice was any clue. Moreover, they appeared to venerate one of the profane entities with which Holmes and I had had continual dealings over the past thirty years. The name they had mentioned, Kl'aach-yag, was not familiar to me, but then the sky-spawned gods were numerous and nobody had yet compiled a comprehensive list. Moreover, new ones were being spawned all the time, for these creatures paired off, mated, and birthed offspring just as humans did. Kl'aach-yag, translated from the R'lyehian, meant "The Pulsating Cluster", which, though grotesque-sounding, was not unusual as such appellations went.

Several times I strove to get a look at the face of Brother Murdoch, but all I could distinguish within the hood was a whiskery chin and the glint of eyes reflecting the moonlight. He seemed utterly serious about his duties. The pistol did not waver, however much the lorry bounced and lurched. I had the impression that he would not hesitate to shoot if I attempted to escape – not that I was in any real position to do so.

Eventually the lorry descended through a series of sinuous bends and pulled up at the edge of a beach. Brother Murdoch indicated, with a wave of my gun, that I should get down from the vehicle, and the four of us commenced walking along the shore, just above the high tide line, which was marked by skeins of dried-out bladderwrack. Pebbles clattered under our feet, clumps of sea kale rustled in the wind, and the waves seethed. While I had far from abandoned all hope of extricating myself from my predicament, I could not yet see how I might. An opportunity would arise, I assured myself. All I had to do was bide my time.

At the base of a particularly tall and craggy run of cliff we came to an opening in the rock with a tunnel beyond, which I presumed led to a cave. A cultist was waiting outside to greet us, a lit torch in his hand.

"Is that him?" he enquired. "The pestilential Holmes?"

"No. Someone else. Holmes wasn't at home but we found this fellow instead."

"A friend of his?"

"Not sure. We're hoping Brother McPherson will know what to do with him."

"Brother McPherson has much else to think about right now. All you had to do was nab Holmes. Now you've made things more complicated."

"It's not our fault. The fellow drew a gun on us."

"Well, on your own head be it, brother. Let's go in. It's nearly time."

The man with the torch led the way down the tunnel, we four following in convoy, I second to last and Brother Murdoch bringing up the rear. It was just about tall enough that we did not have to stoop but so narrow as to permit us to walk only in single file. The air within was rank with the smells of rotting seaweed and brackish water, although I detected another odour as well, one that was both fainter and fouler. We travelled for some fifty paces on a downward incline, until all at once the tunnel debouched onto a sizeable cavern.

Torches were arrayed all around the cavern's periphery, lodged into clefts and revealing rugged chalk walls that curved inward to the ceiling. The air was moist and humid, and there were dozens of slimy green rock pools dotting the floor. The foul smell was stronger here, almost a stench, redolent of decay and putrescence.

A further four cultists were gathered near the cavern's centre, making a total of eight in all. Although I could not see their faces, these men stood in attitudes of expectancy and, I thought, apprehension.

In their midst was a fifth person, a girl, and the sight of her stirred indignation in my breast, for she was clearly not there of her own volition. She was dressed in ordinary day clothes, and she blinked around dazedly, uncomprehendingly, swaying somewhat. She could not have been more than eighteen or nineteen, and would have been quite beautiful if her demeanour were not so haggard and lost.

When she saw me she tried to say something, but only a stumbling confusion of words came out. Perhaps, because I too was not attired like one of the cultists, she thought me an ally, a potential saviour. Her inarticulacy, and the general lassitude of her bearing, suggested to me that she had been drugged to keep her docile.

My blood boiled. The girl must be the sacrifice I had heard mentioned – a human sacrifice. Tonight's abominable ceremony was to entail taking the life of an innocent young woman in order to appease Kl'aach-yag and curry the god's favour.

I was unable to keep from venting my anger. "Blackguards!" I exclaimed. "Vile heathens! Let her go this instant. If you want to make an offering of someone, why not me? Spare her."

One of the sinister congregation broke away from the

others and approached us. In cultured tones he asked my captors to explain who I was and why they had brought me thither. They, as they gave their account of events, addressed him as Brother McPherson, but I had already inferred his identity from the air of authority he assumed.

"Then Sherlock Holmes remains at large," McPherson said. "Dash it all! I should have dealt with him when he came snooping round my house this morning. He all but accused me of abducting Maud and told me he would not rest until he had ascertained her whereabouts."

At the word "Maud" the girl moaned and mumbled. I could only assume she was responding, albeit incoherently, to the sound of her own name.

"He also vowed that he would turn up concrete proof that I was connected with her disappearance," McPherson continued. "If only I had had the opportunity to strike him down there and then, and have done with it. I am sure he is dogging our footsteps even now. Oh well. It is too late for him. The hour is upon us. Kl'aach-yag shall have his offering, and by the spilling of my Maudie's blood we of the Brotherhood of the Pulsating Cluster shall receive all that we desire and deserve, courtesy of our great god. Is that not so, brothers?"

The other cultists gave voice to a low rumble of assent.

"Then gird yourselves. We are all here now, a full complement, and the heavens are in an auspicious configuration. Let us summon Kl'aach-yag from his realm. By evening's end each of us shall have his deepest, dearest wish granted, bought at the price of Maud Bellamy, whose value is made all the rarer by the love I bear for her and she for me."

"You fiend!" I cried, giving such a violent start that two of the cultists guarding me felt obliged to seize an elbow each and hold me back.

McPherson shrugged his shoulders complacently. "Rail away, old man, whoever you are. It will make no difference. Where Maud is going, you shall soon be joining her."

"Untie my hands and we'll see about that."

McPherson, untroubled by my threat, turned and sauntered back to Miss Bellamy. He produced a long, sharp knife from the folds of his robe. I strained, hoping to free myself from the clutches of the two men detaining me, but in vain.

The other cultists fanned out in a semicircle, and a solemn chant began. McPherson intoned certain phrases in R'lyehian that I knew to be ritual invocations, and his brethren duly echoed them, like the call and response of some blasphemous catechism. The torchlight seemed to dim as the chant grew louder and more impassioned. The climax came as eight voices called out in unison, *"Iä, Kl'aach-yag! Iä! Iä!"*

In the rock pools something stirred. The slimy surfaces began to ripple and swirl.

At the same time, I felt a hand tugging surreptitiously on the ropes that bound me, and a voice – a voice I knew so well – whispered in my ear.

"Be ready, Watson, old friend. When I act, act with me."

CHAPTER THREE

A Glaucous, Slobbering Blob

FROM ONE OF THE ROCK POOLS, THEN ANOTHER, then all of them, gelatinous shapes emerged. Each consisted of a transparent hemispherical hub fringed with tentacles, transparent too and delicately thin, almost threadlike. They were jellyfish of some sort, their bodies ranging in size from a man's clenched fist to a football, and they propelled themselves from the water onto the cavern floor with a squirming, rolling motion that was quite revolting to behold. They came out in disorderly processions, the faster crawling over the slower, and such was their number that I could only assume the rock pools were not shallow cavities like the ordinary seaside variety; they were, rather, the mouths of wells that sank some way into the earth, possibly all connected to a single reservoir below, the creatures' communal home.

Appalled though I was by the sudden bizarre manifestation of the mass of jellyfish, I was feeling some measure of relief too, even delight, for the voice that had just whispered to me belonged to none other than Sherlock Holmes. He was masquerading as a member of the Brotherhood of the Pulsating Cluster, the one known as Brother Murdoch. He also happened to be one of the pair currently restraining me. I now had a clearer view of his face and could see that lumps of theatrical putty altered its contours and a lush beard adorned the chin, presumably false. The eyes, however, with their keen gleam, were unmistakable.

Holmes had deftly loosened my bonds, and he was armed with a weapon. All at once, things were not looking so rosy for the cultists.

The jellyfish migrated to one end of the cavern, where they began massing. They climbed onto one another, entangling together to form a large, bulbous agglomeration of pulpy bodies and stringy tentacles that stood taller than a man. The foetid smell they exuded was noisome indeed, like something from the pits of Hell. Several of the cultists gagged and retched, although not McPherson. He brandished the knife with great glee. As for poor Maud Bellamy, whatever wits she still retained were fast deserting her. Her eyes rolled in their sockets and mewling, strangulated cries of maddened despair escaped her lips.

The assembled jellyfish were now moving as one, throbbing as though animated by a shared heartbeat. Somehow, as they clenched slipperily together, they produced a noise that constituted speech. Each syllable was a loathsome wet suck, like a gourmand smacking his lips, yet intelligible nonetheless – assuming one was conversant in R'lyehian.

"Give it to me," said Kl'aach-yag, the Pulsating Cluster, a single being composed of many. "Bring me my food, that I might gorge upon its sweetness and gain sustenance."

One of the cultists dragged Miss Bellamy forwards, under guidance from McPherson.

"Force her to her knees," the leader of the cultists said. "Quick about it, brother. Yes. Now draw back her head. That's it."

The girl's neck was thus exposed, and McPherson

held the knife beneath her chin, its cutting edge upward. He was going to slit Miss Bellamy's throat as though she were a heifer at the slaughterhouse.

"Now, Holmes?" I hissed. I could not believe my friend was willing to delay a moment longer.

"Now," he confirmed.

I lunged sideways, barging my shoulder into the cultist on my left and knocking him flat. Meanwhile Holmes, on my right, took careful aim with the Webley and fired.

The bullet struck McPherson in the arm. The impact spun him round and with a yelp of pain he collapsed, dropping the knife.

At the sound of the gunshot everyone else in the cavern froze. Even Kl'aach-yag ceased his avaricious, masticatory jabber.

"Quick, Watson. The girl. Get the girl. I'll cover you."

I darted towards Miss Bellamy, the ropes tumbling free from my hands as I went. One of the cultists stepped into my path to intercept me. I handed him off as a fly half might an opposing three-quarter coming in for the tackle. I was not a young man any more, far from it, but I could move with alacrity when the occasion called and I had lost few of my rugby skills. The cultist who was holding Miss Bellamy also tried to waylay me, but Holmes saw him off with a well-placed round that ricocheted off the cavern floor just inches from his feet, sending up a spray of chalk fragments.

I took the hapless girl by the shoulders and hauled her away from the glaucous, slobbering blob that was Kl'aach-yag. As we reached Holmes's side, McPherson reared up from the ground, bellowing with rage. His wounded arm hung useless by his side, but he now held the knife in his other hand.

"Bring her back! Damn you, I have waited months for this. Maud is practically my fiancée. Kl'aach-yag knows how much it means to me to let him have her. He will not be denied his wishes, and neither shall I!"

"No," said Holmes. "He will not." He switched to R'lyehian. "Kl'aach-yag, where you have been deprived of one feast, take another. I offer you Fitzroy McPherson, science master at The Gables school and as black-souled a rogue as ever drew breath."

McPherson was not, it seemed, as fluent in that ancient, alien language as either Holmes or me but he recognised his own name and grasped the import of the rest. He swivelled to face Kl'aach-yag. Blood was pouring from his arm and dripping onto the floor, stark red against the white of the chalk.

"No, no, do not listen to him, o mighty one," he protested, gesturing at Miss Bellamy. "I am not to be the sacrifice here. She is. *She* is."

The god, however, appeared to disagree, for all at once a score of tentacles shot out, ensnaring McPherson's limbs. McPherson screamed and slashed at the tendrils with the knife, but for every one he severed, another snaked out to take its place. Soon he was wrapped in a web of the fleshy extrusions and Kl'aach-yag was slowly, inexorably drawing him closer, like an angler reeling in his catch. From the anguished way McPherson cried and writhed, I could only assume the tentacles sported venomous cysts, which were stinging him through his robe. He was alive to the horror of his position and aware that there was nothing he could do to change it.

Finally he was pressed bodily against Kl'aach-yag, and individual jellyfish began oozing over him, covering him and subsuming him into their collective self. His screams took on a sobbing, plaintive timbre and then were silenced as Kl'aach-yag absorbed him entirely. Thereafter all I could do – and the same was true of everyone in the cavern – was watch him suffocate in the god's interior, his movements becoming increasingly feeble and spasmodic until they ceased altogether.

Then, with almost indecent rapidity, McPherson's lifeless body began to disintegrate. Kl'aach-yag was digesting him. Skin melted away to reveal muscle, sinew and vein, which in turn liquefied to nothingness, leaving just bare bones. I was put in mind of my anatomy lessons at medical school, although here the dissection of the cadaver took less than a minute rather than being prolonged over the course of several sessions.

When McPherson was a mere skeleton, Kl'aach-yag dispersed, dividing up into his discrete jellyfish components, which squelched back to the rock pools and slipped in. The bones clattered to the floor.

The remaining members of the Brotherhood of the Pulsating Cluster stood around, seeming stunned and at a loss. Holmes, keeping the revolver levelled, indicated to me that we should beat a retreat, along with Miss Bellamy. I went ahead, escorting the girl back up the tunnel to the beach. Holmes followed, walking backwards. Had any of the cultists got it into his head to come after us, he would doubtless have had a bullet sent his way and been encouraged to rethink. In the event, I suspect all of them were too shocked by their leader's grisly demise to stir themselves to action.

At the cave entrance Holmes let out a loud, shrill whistle. Shortly, a contingent of the Sussex Constabulary appeared, wading ashore. It transpired that the policemen had been in a rowing boat anchored some way out to sea, awaiting Holmes's signal.

"Here is Miss Maud Bellamy, Inspector Bardle, as promised, safe and well," my friend said to the senior-ranking official. He had by now divested himself of his facial disguise. "See to it that she is returned to her family home in Fulworth and receives medical attention as soon as possible. You will find some rather perturbed fellows within the cave, all of whom you may arrest for conspiracy to commit murder. Their ringleader is no longer in any fit state to face trial, more's the pity, but the rest of them will, I have a strong suspicion, come quietly. You may also wish to send officers to The Gables school, where they will find a mathematics teacher, name of Ian Murdoch, trussed up and gagged in his lodgings. He likewise should be arrested. And then, Inspector, if I might make a recommendation, you should requisition a few sticks of dynamite, blow up the entrance to that cave, and seal the place off forever."

CHAPTER FOUR

Holmes's Own Personal Ambrosia

LATER, AS HOLMES AND I SAT IN HIS SITTING ROOM WITH glasses of brandy, my friend tendered a fulsome apology.

"I am truly sorry, Watson, to have embroiled you in this affair. Time was pressing and I could see no alternative. In the event, your unwilling involvement was a blessing in disguise. Access to your revolver gave me an unassailable advantage."

"Why did you not warn me beforehand that you were in the throes of an investigation?" I asked. "A short telegram was all it would have taken."

"Until this morning I had no idea that a crisis was in the offing. A game was afoot but I did not appreciate that its dénouement was quite so near. Then, shortly after breakfast, old Tom Bellamy, Fulworth fishery magnate and Maud's father, came to me, entreating me to look into the sudden disappearance of his daughter. She had gone out for her daily constitutional and not returned. His immediate thought was that she had eloped with Fitzroy McPherson, her fiancé. Bellamy disapproved of the engagement and had made no secret of the fact to both parties. Maud was not only considerably younger than her intended but, as heiress to a small fortune, of considerably greater means than a mere schoolmaster. Bellamy feared that money rather than love was McPherson's primary motivation. He asked me to pay a call on McPherson."

"Why not go himself?"

"He said he could not trust himself in McPherson's

presence, especially were he to find Maud with him. He might give in to his more bestial instincts. He knew I would be more circumspect and tactful. He knew, too, that I was a friend of McPherson."

"You were? That monster?"

"Well, 'acquainted' might be more accurate. I happen to be on very amicable terms with Harold Stackhurst, headmaster of The Gables. Through him, McPherson's path and mine have previously crossed on a couple of occasions, in a social context. The same goes for Ian Murdoch, a mathematics teacher at the school."

"Whom you impersonated this evening."

Holmes nodded. "As it happened, I was only too happy to accede to Tom Bellamy's request to act as go-between, for I already had other reasons to think that McPherson was not on the up and up. Over a glass or two of wine at the dinner table McPherson was wont to become a touch garrulous, and in my presence he once let slip a reference to non-Euclidean geometry during a general discussion of architecture. He averred that while it is possible to build structures upon non-Euclidean lines, the effects of hyperbolic angles and curvature tensors upon the human brain, when experienced on a monumental scale, might well induce psychosis and madness."

"As is said to be the case with the lost city of R'lyeh, home to Cthulhu. To walk its streets is to court insanity."

"Quite so. That gave me my first inkling that there was more to McPherson than met the eye. I then inveigled my way into visiting him in his study at the school, ostensibly to discuss a subject of mutual interest, chemistry. One can tell a great deal about a man from his study, especially its bookshelves, and McPherson's proved to be quite revelatory. Squirrelled away amongst the expected scientific textbooks were English editions of the *Pnakotic Manuscripts*, *De Vermis Mysteriis* and *Daemonolatreia*, to name but three."

"No *Necronomicon?*" The bookshelves of Holmes's own study were replete with countless similar such volumes, including not one but two copies of that dread tome whose name I had just mentioned.

"No, thank goodness," said Holmes. "I steered the conversation around to esoteric cults, whereupon McPherson, thitherto genial and expansive, became cagey. I said that up and down the land one found bands of acolytes in thrall to strange old gods. I considered such people a menace to themselves and to the public at large, for they were dealing with forces they could neither comprehend nor control. McPherson was quick to dismiss them as cranks. 'Anyone can don robes and light torches and chant a bit of mumbo-jumbo around a makeshift altar and think they have contacted gods,' he said, 'just as anyone can buy a Ouija board and hold a parlour séance and think they are communing with the spirit world.' His contempt struck me not as that of a rational man scorning superstition but rather that of a professional sneering at amateurs."

"The gentleman doth protest too much, methinks."

"Ha ha! Yes. Thereafter I began taking careful note of McPherson's habits and his comings and goings. He had several associates in town with whom he would meet regularly at pubs and other such places, amongst them

Ian Murdoch. I got the clear impression that they were cronies, and by eavesdropping on their conversations, in a variety of disguises, I was able to glean certain references that gave me cause for concern. You know the sort of thing. Then, three days ago, while shadowing McPherson around Eastbourne, I saw him enter a costumiers on Cornfield Terrace, from which premises he emerged laden with bulky parcels. I went in straight afterwards and, acting on a hunch, asked the rather satisfied-looking shopkeeper whether he had anything in the monastic or ceremonial line. The fellow was not slow in admitting he had just fulfilled a lucrative commission in that vein. 'Eight sets of black robes for a play about the history of the Benedictine Order,' he told me. 'A new production they're putting on at the Royal Hippodrome later this month, so the customer said.' One rarely thinks about such mundane, practical details when it comes to investigating occult crimes, but sometimes they can prove pivotal."

"Cultists need robes, after all."

"Absolutely, and now I had evidence that McPherson, Murdoch et al. might well be planning some sort of rite, although I had yet to establish its nature or level of seriousness. So it was that, this morning, with Maud Bellamy having gone mysteriously missing, matters seemed to be coming to a head. Confronting McPherson at the school, in part-compliance with Tom Bellamy's request, I implied heavily that I knew he was responsible for the girl's abduction. I did not know anything of the sort, of course, not with any certainty, but I hoped the bluff would constitute a viable threat and McPherson might think twice about whatever heinous misdeed he had in store. His intemperate response led me to believe that he was not going to back down."

"You should have beaten the villain until he was black and blue."

"Under what pretext, Watson? What if I was mistaken about him? What if Miss Bellamy had fallen foul of some other agency? That seemed unlikely, mind you. It was surely not coincidental for her to have disappeared when her fiancé was, to my way of thinking, a very shady character and up to no good. McPherson and she could easily have arranged an assignation, whereupon he subdued her, perhaps with chloroform, and spirited her off to some hideaway. Yet I had no idea where she was and could not conclusively link the one thing with the other. My only recourse was to infiltrate McPherson's operation."

"By disguising yourself as Ian Murdoch."

"Having first taken the precaution of going to Murdoch's lodgings and putting him out of action," said Holmes. "I then compelled him to tell me where and when he and his fellow cultists were meeting."

"Compelled?" I said with a note of irony. "By what method? Magical or physical?"

"Physical. I was pressed for time."

"And just how much physicality was required?"

"Not as much as you might expect. Murdoch – altogether less wily and obdurate than his friend McPherson – was rather cowed by the ease with which I overpowered him and readily gave up the goods. Events were moving fast. I telephoned Inspector Bardle. He is a sound fellow and we have had some dealings in the past which have redounded to his advantage. I told him what was going on and he agreed to have officers in a boat offshore, ready to pounce when I gave the signal. I then set about making myself up to look like Murdoch, who is, by good fortune, of approximately my height and stature. I did a fairly good job of it, all said and done, right down to the bushy beard and the somewhat crooked nose; and I was able to mimic his mannerisms and even his Sussex burr – he is a local, born and bred. In short, I could pass for him, especially in the dark and when swaddled in borrowed robes. I turned up at the prearranged rendezvous point, where I was met by two of his brethren. It was then that I learned that our first port of call was to be my own house and the first item on our agenda ambushing Sherlock Holmes and taking him captive. And that, Watson, is where you entered the picture. I am glad, by the way, that you refrained from shooting me. That would certainly have put a crimp in my plans."

"And I am glad that you inveighed against killing me."

"That would certainly have put a crimp in yours. In fact, I was overjoyed to have my Watson beside me as I tackled the Brotherhood. It was just like old times."

I sighed ruefully. "Maybe, but I am not as young as I used to be and I am feeling the effect of my exertions earlier. My shoulder aches from lying tied up in the back of that lorry and I fear I may have pulled a tendon in my leg charging across the cave to reach Miss Bellamy. You on the other hand, Holmes, look hardly incommoded at all after the late shenanigans. Indeed, if I may say so, you look positively vigorous, and not just tonight. Every time I come to visit, I note how immune you seem to the effects of age. There is scarcely a grey hair upon your head nor a line upon your face, and I spy no sign of bodily infirmity anywhere. It is quite vexing how youthful you remain, even as I decline into decrepitude. What is your secret?"

"Honey," my friend replied simply. "The honey I harvest from my hives. It is a most remarkable substance, full of healthful enzymes and sugars. Your ancient forebears in the medical fraternity used it to treat wounds, did you know that? I myself have found it efficacious in boosting my levels of energy, far more beneficial and less harmful than cocaine ever was. I would go so far as to deem honey my own personal ambrosia, conferring longevity upon me as that selfsame nectar did upon the Greek gods. Then, of course, there is the sea air, the revitalising properties of which are well documented."

"Perhaps I too should retire to the coast and keep bees," I said. "But I am afraid I am too much the inveterate Londoner ever to quit that great city for good. I would miss it, even if it would not miss me. What is one fewer inhabitant to a place that boasts nearly seven million of them?" I stifled a yawn. "Well, you may not be exhausted, Holmes, but I am. I think it is high time I took myself off to bed."

*

I slept soundly and dreamlessly, albeit not for long, because my slumbers were intruded upon by the shrill clangour of the telephone in the hallway sometime during the small hours. I heard Holmes go down the stairs to answer the device.

"Hello. Sherlock Holmes speaking. Yes, operator, I will take the call. Hello? Mycroft? Yes, it's Sherlock. Slow down, Mycroft. Repeat that again. Mycroft! You must calm yourself, I can hardly make out what you are saying. Talk sense. Mycroft? Mycroft, whatever the matter is, listen to me. I urge you to stay put. Do not go anywhere. Do not do anything rash. I shall be there as soon as humanly possible."

I emerged from the guest bedroom as Holmes was replacing the receiver on its hook. He looked puzzled and not a little anxious.

"Your brother," I said. "What did he want?"

"I cannot tell you. Mycroft was… 'babbling' is the only word for it. Completely incoherent. I could not make head or tail of anything he said. Mostly he just spoke my name over and over."

"Gracious! Do you think he may have taken ill?"

"I do not know what to think," Holmes said tersely. "I know only that I am getting dressed and going up to London post-haste."

"And I am coming with you. If Mycroft has succumbed to brain fever or, God forbid, a stroke, he will need my help, as will you."

"I shan't argue with you, Watson. I shall ask you only to hurry."

CHAPTER FIVE

Tragedy on Pall Mall

WE WALKED TO EASTBOURNE BY THE COLD GREY light of dawn and caught the first train bound for London. We reached Victoria station shortly before seven o'clock, whence a hansom ferried us towards St James's. Mycroft's business never took him outside that area, which incorporated his two principal stamping grounds, the Diogenes Club and the Palace of Westminster, as well as his apartment.

It was still fairly early and the streets of the capital were unfrequented. However, as the cab turned onto Pall Mall, I spied a small crowd ahead, a score of people milling outside a townhouse. They were gathered about some bulky, huddled object that lay on the pavement in front.

A little worm of dread squirmed into life within me. I knew the townhouse in question; it housed Mycroft's rooms. I hoped against hope that the object on the pavement was not what I thought it was.

Holmes had seen it too. Before I could say anything, he flung open the hansom's doors and leapt out while it was still rolling. He sprinted over to the crowd and shouldered his way through to the middle.

I shall never forget the howl he gave then. It echoed along the street, an ululation of purest agony.

I hastened to join my friend. Holmes had sunk to his knees. His head hung.

Before him lay the mortal remains of Mycroft Holmes.

I am hesitant to describe the condition of the body.

It was horribly mangled. Blood encircled it in a gory halo; some had splashed as far as the steps of the house next door.

The ample frame was undoubtedly Mycroft's, and the head, though far from intact, was recognisably his too. I will add no further detail save to say that the great brain of the man, considered to be superior even to that of his younger brother, was no longer fully contained in its casing.

Feelings of shock and incomprehension threatened to overwhelm me. I had found Mycroft Holmes overbearing at times, even arrogant, to a still greater degree than Sherlock Holmes himself; yet I had known him to be an honest man and a towering intellect, not to mention a powerful ally in the fight against evil, and had grown to admire him for those qualities. To see him destroyed so violently, so totally, was a startling, sobering sight indeed. I struggled to master my emotions, for to succumb to them would hinder me from giving Holmes the support he now must need.

Holmes himself was doubtless undergoing far worse an inner torment than I. It showed in the way his face had gone ashen and his lip trembled. For perhaps the first time in his life he appeared on the verge of weeping. I placed a consoling hand upon his shoulder but he shrugged it off. By some supreme effort of will he steeled himself and stood up. Addressing the crowd, he said, "Which of you found him? Anyone? Speak up."

A hand rose. "I did, sir." It was a postman. He looked almost as shocked as Holmes. "I was doing my round when I came upon… this. That was quarter of an hour ago. I've sent for a constable but none has come as yet. He's known to you, I take it."

Holmes ignored the remark. "How long had he lain here before you happened along? Tell me."

"I really can't say, sir."

"Try, man. Try. Was the body still twitching? Were the bloodstains fresh?"

"Holmes." Gently I took his arm. "Leave the fellow be. There's no point bombarding him with questions. He is no expert in such affairs. Permit me to conduct an examination. I might be able to provide the answers you seek."

Mycroft's skin was still warm to the touch. The blood was viscous and tacky, only partially congealed. Raising Mycroft's forearm and observing the flexion of the wrist told me that rigor mortis had not yet set in.

"I estimate he has been dead between half an hour to an hour," I said.

"Be more accurate," said Holmes.

"I cannot. Does it matter? We came as quickly as we could. There is nothing you could have done to prevent this. To think that you might have is to torture yourself needlessly."

Holmes appeared to ponder the matter. I sensed a maelstrom of emotion churning beneath the surface, only just held in check.

"You may well be right," said he eventually. "But just because I did not prevent it, that doesn't mean I cannot do something about it."

"Now that's the spirit," I said. "What course of action do you propose?"

Just then a constable appeared and took charge of

the scene. The first thing he did was shepherd the crowd of ogling onlookers, whose numbers were growing, away from the source of their morbid fascination. Then he demanded that someone fetch a blanket with which to cover the body. He was peremptory and officious, but in the circumstances that was just what was required.

Holmes, meanwhile, had stepped into the road and was peering up at the house.

"He fell, obviously," he said, partly to me but mostly to himself. "But none of the windows of his rooms stand open. Besides, he resided on the first floor and a fall from that relatively low height would not have caused the… devastation we have seen. It is more likely that he plunged from the very top. There is a balustrade up there that is low enough to straddle easily, and access to it may be gained via the attic, whose windows are inset into the mansard roof. What must be ascertained is whether Mycroft was the sole actor in the deed or had assistance."

"In other words, was it suicide or murder?" I was perversely glad to see my companion resorting to logical analysis. Grief would unman him completely if he allowed it to. For now, it was better if Sherlock Holmes the detective came to the fore and Sherlock Holmes the newly bereaved brother took a back seat. While the evidence was still fresh, Holmes stood a greater chance of getting to the truth.

"Excuse me. Mr Holmes? Mr Sherlock Holmes?"

The speaker was a slender, dapperly dressed fellow whose face I recognised, although it took me a moment to place him. He was the secretary of the Diogenes Club, the premises of which lay practically across the road from

Mycroft's rooms. He kept his gaze studiously averted from the blanket-covered corpse.

"Yes?" said Holmes. "It's Unthank, isn't it?"

"Your servant, sir." Unthank wrung his hands, gravely apologetic. "My sincerest condolences. It is a terrible loss. A terrible loss to us all. A heavy blow – one amongst several."

"What on earth do you mean?"

"I have just this minute arrived at the Diogenes, but I have been up half the night," said Unthank. "I wish I could say I was surprised to discover Mr Holmes – that is to say, your brother – has met his end. I really wish I could."

"There have been other deaths tonight?"

"The news is grim. Telegrams and telephone calls have been winging their way to and fro. I can hardly believe I am saying this, but six of our members have gone to their great reward during the past few hours."

"Six!" I exclaimed.

"Seven now, the senior Mr Holmes being the latest addition to the tally and, I pray God, the last. It is, not to put too fine a point on it, a massacre."

"Their names," Holmes said. "Who are they?"

Instead of replying, Unthank consulted his watch. "You should come with me. There is a tradition to be observed and every member of the club who is able is on his way. You, as Mycroft Holmes's close kin, are entitled to attend. Afterwards, if you still have any queries, I shall do my best to oblige."

CHAPTER SIX

Breaking the Silence

THE QUEEREST CLUB IN LONDON WAS EMPTY WHEN we entered, but within a scant twenty minutes it teemed. Members packed the main lounge and, as ever, not one word was uttered. The members of the Diogenes maintained their habitual silence, in accordance with the club's golden rule. Yet upon the faces of all, sorrow was writ large, so patently apparent it hardly needed articulating aloud.

Once Unthank had determined that there was a full complement and no one else to come, he tapped a small bell. Its chime hung sonorously in the air and, when it faded, the secretary spoke a name.

"Milton Goldsworthy."

In unison, the club members repeated the name.

"Sir Alexander Chalfont-Banks."

Again, the name was echoed by all present.

So it went for a further four names – a peer of the realm, a general, an industrialist, a press baron – until the seventh and final one came.

"Mycroft Holmes."

The response this time was louder, I thought, and more heartfelt than any of the previous, perhaps in recognition of Mycroft's stature both as a pre-eminent member of the Diogenes and as a linchpin of the nation's government.

Unthank rang the bell again, and the club members, without another word, dispersed.

It was a strange ritual even by the standards of the Diogenes, but I found it extraordinarily moving all the same. In an establishment where silence was mandatory, the formal breaking of that silence carried great weight. As when a geyser bursts up from a previously placid pool, it suggested deep pressures below being vented.

Sherlock Holmes, for his part, grew steadily more sombre as Unthank announced the roll of the dead. He remained so as we repaired afterwards to the Stranger's Room to wait for the secretary, who busied himself seeing people out.

"No two ways about it," Holmes confided to me, "this is enemy action."

"Enemy action? How so?"

"The seven names, Watson. The seven dead members. What do they have in common? Come on, one does not have to be the sharpest of wits to divine the connection."

"They…" I began. Then I saw it. I could have slapped my forehead in exasperation. How slow I had been on the uptake. I blamed tiredness and the misadventures of the night before. "They all belong to the Dagon Club."

"Correction: they *are* the Dagon Club. The seven of them – Goldsworthy, Sir Alexander, Mycroft, the rest – together constitute the entirety of that august, clandestine body. And now, in one fell swoop, all seven are dead. That betokens a concerted effort on the part of some opponent."

"R'luhlloig?" Always whenever mentioning the name of the godlike being that had once been Professor James Moriarty, I found myself lowering my voice somewhat. "Could he be behind it?"

"Given that he has been behind so much else these past few years, it would not surprise me. The Hidden Mind's conspiracies are persistent and manifold. He is a disease that cannot be eradicated. The infection is stemmed in one place, only to crop up in another."

"If it is him, then this is not simply another outbreak of his evil. It is a veritable epidemic. Until today, you and he have been skirmishing. Now there has been a significant escalation of hostilities. And all the while, R'luhlloig continues to wage war on the ethereal plane as well, leading the Outer Gods in repeated harrying assaults against the Old Ones. You have been keeping abreast of that conflict. How goes it? Has it stepped up too? The last I heard, the Old Ones were not faring so well."

Whatever reply Holmes might have been about to make, it was interrupted by the entrance of Unthank into the Stranger's Room.

"Again, Mr Holmes, my sympathies," said the secretary. "What an awful day this is. No doubt you are keen for me to furnish details of all the deaths."

"If you would be so kind."

"It would appear that each of the seven men committed suicide. Your brother… well, you saw with your own eyes the aftermath. He must have thrown himself from the top of the house."

"I intend to substantiate that theory, or otherwise. What of the others?"

"Milton Goldsworthy, the prominent financier, drowned himself in his fishpond shortly after 11 p.m. His wife found him lying face down in the water. All attempts to revive him proved futile. He was the first. Around midnight, came news of Lord Cantlemere. Dead at the foot of the staircase in his Kensington mansion of a broken neck. Cracked spindles along the banister attest to his having tumbled down the stairs."

And so it continued, death after death, a grim litany. One man closed all the windows in his library, stopped up the gap beneath the door with his jacket, and switched on the gas jets without lighting them. Another stabbed himself through the eye with a carving knife, piercing his brain. A self-inflicted hanging. A wrist-slitting.

"Seven suicides," Unthank concluded, "all within the space of a few hours; the one significant factor linking them is that all seven men were longstanding members of the Diogenes."

Not even the club's secretary knew of the existence of the Dagon. That subset of the Diogenes was a discrete entity, a secret conclave that nested within the larger club like one Russian doll within another. Its seven members, under Mycroft's aegis, had dedicated themselves to restricting knowledge of the activities of the gods and their worshippers and suppressing any reportage of same. Thanks to the Dagon Club, the ship of civilised society sailed on, serene and largely oblivious to the dark forces that swirled like icy undercurrents in the waters around it.

"Were there any precursors to the deaths?" Holmes enquired. "By which I mean did any of the seven behave at all erratically or atypically in the hours leading up to the act of self-destruction?"

I could tell he was thinking of his telephone conversation with Mycroft.

"Now that you mention it, yes," said Unthank. "Mrs

Goldsworthy told police that she heard her husband shouting loudly a few minutes before she found him dead. She had already taken herself to bed when the ruckus began, and she confessed that she thought it was the consequence of too much alcohol. Mr Goldsworthy, for all his many virtues, was fond of the bottle and apt to fly into a mindless rage when inebriated. Never here, of course. The Diogenes would not tolerate such misconduct; he would have been blackballed. At any rate, his wife – his widow, I suppose I should now say – assumed he had succumbed to one of his drunken fits and it would pass. Even when she heard him thrust open the French windows and dash into the garden, she elected to pay it no heed. Only when things then went abruptly, ominously quiet did she venture downstairs to check on him."

"Were there similar circumstances in any of the other cases?"

"In one other that I know of. Sir Alexander Chalfont-Banks, before he hanged himself from a newel post of the minstrels' gallery in his house, screamed non-stop for ten minutes, so his domestic staff claim. They were quite terrified by the noise he made, and his valet and his butler both remonstrated with him, to no avail. Sir Alexander seemed to have been overcome by a terrible mania and was resistant to all efforts at placating him. He then rushed to his bedroom and emerged a minute later with a dressing-gown cord fashioned into a noose, slung around his neck. His servants were not quick enough off the mark to prevent him attaching the other end of the cord to the newel post and leaping from the gallery."

"That shows a definite determination," Holmes remarked. "I am wondering, you see, whether there was some precipitating cause that sparked the suicides, some catalyst common to them all."

"Now it is interesting that you should say that," said Unthank. "I don't know if it is germane or not, but both Goldsworthy and Lord Cantlemere received parcels yesterday evening by the fourth postal delivery."

All at once Sherlock Holmes was quivering like a greyhound that has picked up the hare's scent. "Parcels? What sort of parcels?"

Unthank shrugged regretfully. "I do not have much more information than that. Mrs Goldsworthy mentioned a parcel to the police, in passing, and they in turn mentioned it to me. Lady Cantlemere told me personally – for I spoke to her at some length on the telephone – that her husband took receipt of a 'small parcel' around nine o'clock. She would not have remarked upon it at all but for the fact that he seemed bemused by its arrival."

"He had not been expecting it."

"Just so."

"Who was the sender?"

"Lady Cantlemere did not know. His lordship did not open it straight away, for the family had guests over for dinner. Only after they had departed did he go to his study with the package. It was perhaps ten minutes later that he took himself to the head of the stairs and hurled himself down."

"Now listen, Unthank," Holmes said urgently. "I wish you to contact the other households – apart from my brother's, for I shall handle that myself — and ask whether the deceased received parcels before their deaths."

"You believe the other five received similar packages?"

"Where there are two, why not all? I should be grateful if you would do me this favour, and immediately."

"Out of respect for your brother, and of course for yourself, Mr Holmes, I shall."

"And, Unthank?" Holmes added as the secretary was on the point of leaving.

"Yes?"

"It would perhaps be best if you were to warn everyone concerned not to touch the parcels. They should leave them well alone."

"My goodness me, yes. If I read you rightly, there may be some direct connection between the parcels' contents and the suicides. A poison, perhaps, or a drug, or a gas, still potent. Yes, yes. I shall do exactly as you say."

*

Holmes paced the carpet of the Stranger's Room for a full half an hour as we awaited Unthank's return. Such was the intensity of his agitation and the depth of the scowl which etched his brow that I refrained from speaking. I feared triggering an intemperate outburst should I intrude upon his ruminations.

When the secretary came back, he quickly confirmed Holmes's inference. Parcels had indeed been delivered to the four other Dagon Club members as well as Goldsworthy and Lord Cantlemere. All six packages were, Unthank had ascertained, identical. Each consisted of a cubic cardboard box measuring eight inches per side, wrapped in brown paper. Each had been opened by its designated recipient and now lay empty, its contents unknown.

"And here is the really curious aspect of the whole thing," Unthank said. "I was as thorough as could be and enquired in each instance the name of the sender. I presumed it to be written somewhere on the wrapping. Sure enough, I was able to confirm that all six came from a single source."

"A-ha," said Holmes. "Now we are getting somewhere. Who was it?"

"I am afraid to say," Unthank replied, "none other than Mycroft Holmes."

CHAPTER SEVEN

Mycroft's Final Steps

BY THE TIME WE CROSSED BACK OVER TO THE OTHER side of Pall Mall, Mycroft's body had been removed. An ambulance must have come to transport it to the mortuary while we were in the Diogenes. Outside Mycroft's house a pair of maids were on hands and knees, scrubbing the pavement clean. Their faces registered an understandable disgust as they went about their gruesome task.

The page, to whom Holmes was known, readily admitted us into the house. Nor did we have any difficulty gaining access to Mycroft's apartment, for the door stood ajar.

Before we entered, however, Holmes set out to prove that his brother had indeed jumped from the balustrade at the top of the house. Sure enough, there was spoor to follow, albeit faint. On one of the stair risers there was a fresh scuff mark left by boot polish. From its distinctive oily texture Holmes identified the polish as Day & Martin's, the brand of blacking which Mycroft favoured. An attic window was wide open and a tiny scrap of thread was caught on one edge of the casement. Holmes affirmed that the thread was the same kind of worsted wool from which Mycroft preferred his suits to be made. It must have become detached as Mycroft was heaving his bulk through the narrow window. Another boot-polish scuff mark on the balustrade put the matter beyond all doubt. We had traced Mycroft Holmes's final steps.

In the apartment itself there was a notable amount

of disarray. Normally Mycroft was meticulously tidy but cushions were scattered across the floor, a curtain hung askew from its pole, partly torn off its rings, and a dining-table chair was overturned. Furthermore, a glass of red wine lay on its side on the table, its spilled contents having soaked into the rug below.

Beside the glass sat a cardboard box, lid gaping wide. Its dimensions matched those of the boxes described by Unthank. Nearby was a crumpled sheet of brown paper that had in all likelihood served as wrapping.

One could easily imagine the scene. Mycroft, after pouring himself a hefty helping of claret, had settled down to unwrap the parcel. No sooner had he opened it than *something* happened. The glass was knocked over, then the chair, or vice versa.

Holmes picked up the paper.

"Holmes," I said. "Should you not be careful? Unthank mentioned poison and you did not disagree with him. What if the paper is impregnated with some substance which drives anyone who comes into contact with it mad – mad enough to kill himself?"

"Then the postmen who delivered the seven parcels and everyone who handled them at the post office and the sorting office would have committed suicide too," Holmes replied. "Such a rash of mortalities within a single profession would be public knowledge by now. We would have seen headlines about it blaring from the front pages of the morning editions on the newsstands at Victoria. Since no such report has been forthcoming, I feel I can touch the paper with impunity."

He smoothed out the creases in the paper and studied the handwriting on it.

"The addressee is Mycroft, obviously," he said, "and just as obviously he is not the sender, unlike with the others."

"Who is this one from, then?"

"Lord Ichabod Cantlemere. See? And here is the sender's address: 17 Kensington Palace Gardens, SW. That is, I believe, his lordship's town residence."

"But Cantlemere no more sent this parcel than your brother did the others," I said. "That must be your thinking."

"I would need to examine the other parcels to confirm it, but yes, that is my thinking. The very fact that six of the parcels are purportedly from Mycroft and the seventh, this one, is purportedly from Cantlemere is more than a little suggestive."

"How so?"

"Mycroft is" – Holmes corrected himself – "was the de facto head of the Dagon Club. Lord Cantlemere, who was rather of the old regime but as excellent and loyal person as you could hope to find, was the second-in-command. There were no formal rankings, but that was how it fell out. Therefore Cantlemere and the other five Dagon members were unlikely to question a parcel that appeared to come from Mycroft, even if it was unexpected, since he was their captain. By the same token, Mycroft was unlikely to question a parcel that appeared to come from his lieutenant. The sad truth is that these seven men trusted one another implicitly and this, in the event, proved their undoing."

"Would they not have known one another's

handwriting and thus realised that the parcels did not come from the alleged senders?"

"Men like that have secretaries to address correspond-ence for them."

"So somebody sent all seven parcels under false pretences," I said, "using in each case a sender's name that was a certificate of bona fides."

"It is all but certain."

"Do you have any idea who it was? Does the packaging itself afford any clues?"

"Several," Holmes said, brandishing the wrapping paper. "Above all, the handwriting bears some singular features which…"

His voice trailed off as he scrutinised the writing once more. He held the piece of paper up to his nose and took a long, hard sniff. Then, still not expounding further on his last remark, he turned his attention to the cardboard box itself. This he approached with greater circumspection than the paper, examining it close up from all angles without physically handling it. I watched him while at the same time feeling disquiet at being in an apartment whose occupant was so recently deceased. It seemed somehow a kind of imposition to be breathing the air from which Mycroft Holmes had drawn his last few breaths and to look around at the fine furniture, décor and *objets d'art* which he had spent a lifetime accumulating and appreciating but would now never again enjoy.

"Ah!" Holmes said with a note of dark satisfaction. "Observe, Watson, the tiny, almost undetectable scratches here and here in the box's interior, as of claw marks; and in the corner here the signs of gnawing, as of minute teeth. This is telling indeed."

"A mouse?" I hazarded. "Some other kind of small rodent? Or a lizard maybe."

"Would that the marks had been put there by so innocuous a creature."

"Would that I had not feared you were going to say that. What do you suppose it was?"

"Something rather terrible, if I do not miss my guess. Something I have read about but consider myself fortunate never to have encountered in the flesh. Something, what's more, that I—"

He halted mid-sentence, fixing me with a very intent stare.

"Watson. Do not move a muscle. You are in perhaps the gravest peril you have ever known."

CHAPTER EIGHT

What Was in the Box

NATURALLY I DID JUST AS I WAS TOLD. HOLMES WAS in deadly earnest. I did not doubt for one second that what he said was true.

"Holmes…" I whispered.

"No. Don't even speak. I am going to walk over to that writing desk there and fetch a paperknife. I shall keep my movements slow and careful, so as not to startle it."

As he stalked across the room all I could think was: *"It"? What is this "it" and why must it not be startled?* I envisaged any number of foul beasts lurking behind me, from ghoul to byakhee to nightgaunt; yet my instinct was that the thing currently menacing me was none of those, for I had faced them all – and more – and survived. If Holmes said he had not encountered this particular creature before, then neither had I, and clearly it was of an order of magnitude worse than any other.

At the very periphery of my vision I caught sight of something small and pale twitching, like a piece of thistledown disturbed by a breeze. I turned my eyes, although not my head, and beheld some sort of insect perched upon my shoulder.

It was a beetle no more than an inch and a half long, about the size of a cockchafer but less rounded, its abdomen as thick as my little finger. Two wickedly sharp mandibles projected from its head, just to the fore of a pair of beady eyes like two minuscule ball bearings. Its antennae were tipped with tiny feathery structures that reminded me of brushes. These were what I had glimpsed waving.

It was also completely, and rather eerily, white. Its milky carapace was, moreover, partially translucent, so that I could make out the shapes of its inner organs.

The thing was busy grooming itself, using its hindmost legs to scrape its back clean. I felt a strange, hysterical laugh building in my throat. My shoulder was, to this insect, just a convenient place to alight while it conducted its ablutions. For all Holmes's intimations to the contrary, the beetle seemed harmless, no cause for concern whatsoever.

I raised a hand to flick it off.

"No," Holmes hissed. "Do not even think about it, Watson. Alarm that beetle in any way and it will obey its primary instinct, which is to seek shelter. You do not want it seeking shelter because the nearest shelter to hand is you."

I heeded the admonition. By now Holmes was back at my side, bearing an ivory-bladed paperknife.

"I am going to continue to move deliberately and unhurriedly," he said, keeping his voice low and even, "until the very last instant. The shoulder of your jacket boasts a certain amount of padding, which is good. I cannot guarantee, however, that the knife will not penetrate through, for which I trust you will forgive me. My strike, when it comes, must be fast and forthright. I cannot afford to hold back."

With a dreamlike slowness he floated the paperknife to a position above the white beetle, its tip pointing downward. The insect seemed to sense something was amiss, for it ceased cleaning itself and grew tense. The mandibles worked at the air, much as though the beetle was murmuring to itself, mouthing silent words, while the antennae quested this way and that with evident curiosity.

The paperknife descended towards the beetle in fractions of an inch. I stilled my breathing. My heart pounded in my ears.

All at once Holmes stabbed.

And missed.

Swift though he had been, the white beetle was swifter. It darted sideways as the tip of the ivory blade flashed down. Holmes had been aiming for its head, but instead succeeded only in severing one of its front legs.

He also succeeded in driving the knife through the fabric of my jacket and into my trapezius muscle.

I winced at the sudden sharp jab of pain but held my ground and my nerve. Holmes yanked the paperknife free and made a second attempt at killing the creature. It had scuttled onto my jacket lapel and was making for my shirt collar. This time the blow was a slash rather than a thrust, and again the beetle evaded, but in doing so it lost its grip and slithered off me, tumbling to the floor.

It landed just by my foot, and I, without a second thought, stamped on it.

The beetle, however, proved yet again that human reflexes were not equal to its arthropod ones. It scurried out from under my foot a split second before my heel made contact with the floor. The amputation of one leg did not seem to be hindering it unduly.

Then its wing casings parted and it took to the air, borne aloft on a blur of gossamer appendages.

"Dash it all!" Holmes exclaimed. "Now it will be harder to destroy than ever. Watch yourself, Watson. Whatever you do, don't let it near you. It will make for an orifice – any orifice – and once it is inside you, you are doomed. It will burrow in and secrete a fluid which enters the blood-stream and robs its victim of his wits within moments."

The beetle circuited the room a few times as if in blind panic before, with the appearance of sudden resolve, it dived straight for me, wings whirring. I dodged, slapping wildly at it with one hand. The creature performed an agile about-turn and dived at me again. Snatching up a book, I swung for it like a batsman who has been bowled a head-high beamer. By some miracle I caught it a glancing blow. The beetle went spiralling down towards the sofa, hitting the floor hard.

It lay on its back, legs wriggling, as though stunned. I sprang for it, reckoning I had a chance. I slammed the book down.

"Got you, you devil!" I declared.

Holmes squatted beside me as I lifted the book in a gingerly fashion.

Where I expected to see the remains of a squashed white beetle – fragments of carapace like broken eggshell around a yolk of innards – there was nothing. Nothing but pristine floorboard.

"Where the deuce has it gone?" I said.

"Under the sofa, I fear," said Holmes. "Take one arm. I shall take the other."

Holmes placed the paperknife on the floor and we stationed ourselves at either end of the sofa.

"On the count of three, we tip it over," he said. "Can you manage?"

I nodded, although I knew that lifting so heavy an object was going to play havoc with my lumbago and my bad shoulder, not to mention my recently stabbed trapezius.

"One. Two. Three!"

We heaved the sofa onto its back, Holmes immediately snatching up the paperknife.

There was no sign of the white beetle below.

"It must have—"

I broke off, spying the elusive insect clinging to the hessian on the sofa's underside.

"There, Holmes."

"I see it."

The beetle regarded us. We regarded the beetle. Its wing casings opened again.

Then Holmes darted out his free hand, the one not wielding the paperknife, and seized the beetle. The action was quick, almost inhumanly so, like a bear trap snapping shut. He clenched his fist tight and there came a loud, moist popping sound. He opened his hand and deposited the twisted, sticky remnants of the beetle onto the floor. Two legs that were still intact cycled in the air feebly. Mandibles quivered. Though the creature could not possibly still be alive, and certainly was not capable of locomotion, I brought my foot down hard on it anyway, grinding it beneath my sole until it was nothing but a pallid smear.

CHAPTER NINE

The German Connection

"*COLEOPTERA MOSTELLARIA*," HOLMES SAID.

We were seated side by side on the now-righted sofa, catching our breath after our contretemps with the beetle. My friend had helped us both to a tot of Mycroft's best scotch.

"Also known as the wraith beetle," he continued. "One of the rarest insects on the planet, it is found exclusively along the marshy banks of Lake Kwazipo in East Africa. Witch doctors are alleged to use it as part of a shamanistic ritual, as a potion containing its secretion in highly diluted form is said to induce hallucinatory and revelatory visions. Some local tribes send out their male youths to catch a wraith beetle and bring it back alive as part of their initiation into manhood. It is considered a more dangerous undertaking than killing a leopard."

"I can vouch for that," I said with feeling.

"Livingstone makes a brief mention of the wraith beetle in his journals, disparaging it as 'yet another childish native myth'. By contrast, Von Junzt, in *Unaussprechlichen Tieren*, gives full credence to its existence. It is Von Junzt, indeed, who came up with the beetle's Linnaean classification. The '*mostellaria*' derives from the title of a play by Plautus about a haunted house."

"All very fascinating," I said, "but I must ask, if this creature secretes a substance so potentially hazardous to health, were you not taking a great risk crushing it in your hand? More to the point, had you stabbed through the beetle while it was on my shoulder, might some of that secretion not have transferred itself to the knife blade and thence into me?" I rubbed my trapezius. The cut was barely a nick but nonetheless stung.

"According to Von Junzt the fluid cannot permeate through human skin. Even so, you saw me go to the bathroom straight afterwards to wash my hand, did you not? It pays to be cautious. As for you, I made sure that I was going to stab the beetle through the head. The secretion is generated from a gland in the base of its abdomen, at the other end of its body. You would have been quite safe."

"That is some relief."

"What you should really be asking is why the beetle was still alive when we got here."

"Should it not have been?"

"Usually a wraith beetle dies with its human host. Having burrowed inside a man, in most instances gaining access via ear or mouth, the female – it is always the female – releases its secretion automatically. In all animals other than *Homo sapiens* the fluid has a pacifying effect, inducing lethargy and allowing the beetle to lay its eggs at leisure. The larvae subsequently feed upon the host organism, as parasites, until they are fully grown and ready to emerge. Owing to some quirk of our physiology, however, we humans lapse into madness as the secretion spreads through the vascular system and are driven to kill ourselves. In almost every instance the beetle and its larvae perish along with the host. I imagine that is what happened with the other six Dagon Club members, whereas Mycroft proved the exception to the rule."

"Of all them, he somehow was able to prise the beetle out of his body, is that it?"

"That or, more likely, he was able to resist the deranging effects of the secretion far longer than any of the others, giving the beetle an opportunity to crawl back out before he finally succumbed to the inevitable. Mycroft must have applied every erg of logic and rationality in that mighty brain of his to countering the onset of insanity. At some point during that struggle he had the presence of mind to telephone me, doubtless in the hope of informing me what had befallen him, but alas it proved a futile exercise, since he failed to communicate anything of significance."

"The call brought you here, did it not?" I said. "So it was not entirely futile."

"True. True. But," he added bitterly, "still not in time to come to his aid."

"I know, Holmes. But let us not dwell upon that. Self-recrimination is bootless. Let us instead pay tribute to your brother's courage and tenacity, and indeed to his life – a life well lived."

We raised our whisky tumblers and clinked them together.

"To Mycroft."

"To Mycroft."

"Now," I said, "you were telling me, before we were so rudely interrupted, that the handwriting on the wrapping paper affords some clues as to the identity of the parcel's true sender."

"The handwriting and the postmark."

"Would you care to elucidate?"

"Very well." Holmes retrieved the sheet of brown paper. "There is a decidedly European feel to the penmanship. I refer you specifically to the '7' of '17 Kensington Palace Gardens'. It has a crossbar through it in the continental style. But I would go further and submit that the sender is not simply European but German."

"On what grounds do you base that assumption?"

"It is no assumption. You have known me long enough to know you should never use that word in my hearing."

"I apologise."

"A German has a peculiar way of forming certain letters of the alphabet, especially certain capitals. Here we have two prime examples, the 'I' of 'Ichabod' and the 'G' of 'Gardens'. Note how the 'I' is long and curved, looking rather like a capital 'J'. Note, too, how the 'G' is very much like a lower-case 'g', complete with descender. No Englishman would write those characters thus, nor anyone of another nationality save a German."

"Remarkable. Or should I say '*unglaublich*'?"

"I am pleased to see that your pawky sense of humour is returning, along with the colour to your cheeks," said Holmes. "A drop more whisky? Excellent. Now let us turn our attention to the postmark. It reads 'St James's', indicating that the parcel was posted not far from this very spot."

"That would have made the parcels supposedly sent by Mycroft seem all the more authentic to their recipients."

"It is arguably the case with this one from Lord Cantlemere too. Even though he lives in Kensington, his lordship is a member of the Diogenes. The St James's post office is local to the club. The postmark would not have aroused Mycroft's suspicions, at any rate."

"A diabolical trick."

"The whole enterprise is diabolical," Holmes said. "The postmark is merely the icing on a sinister cake. There is a further detail that confirms to me that we are looking for a Teutonic malefactor. The wrapping paper exudes a discernible odour of tobacco, and not just any tobacco but the particular fruity aroma of a blend used in a Dannemann cigarillo. I feel I hardly need tell you that Dannemann is a German manufacturer."

"The sender was smoking such a cigarillo while he wrapped and addressed the parcels."

"So we must conclude. As for the use of wraith beetles, that too is indicative of a German connection. Lake Kwazipo lies deep within German East Africa, in a region firmly under Imperial German control. It would not be impossible for a non-German to venture into that region in order to obtain specimens of the beetle, but it would not be easy either. A German, on the other hand, would have little trouble acquiring the relevant permits, visas and so forth. Especially a German with diplomatic influence."

"You have made another deductive leap, I see."

"Well, it is more a case of convenience than anything," said Holmes.

"I fail to follow."

"You *do* follow, Watson, in the sense that you go where I lead you."

"That cannot be gainsaid. Lead me, then."

"Scarcely a stone's throw from here – and from the

local post office branch – lies Carlton House Terrace, and on Carlton House Terrace lies…"

He left it to me to finish the sentence, which I did after some brain-racking.

"Prussia House!"

"Precisely, Watson. Precisely. The German embassy. Our culprit chose not to walk far in order to post his seven parcels. Now, if we extrapolate from the inference that he holds some position within the German legation, it is probably safe to say that he is no mere functionary. He plays rather a more nebulous, subversive role."

"A spy, you mean."

"A spy, I mean. To send parcels containing quite lethal cargo is an act emblematic of a spy. To send parcels that kill without leaving a trace similarly so. There is enough subterfuge involved here for us not to apportion the responsibility to some deskbound lackey. We must look to someone well-versed in the ways of espionage and assassination."

"That complicates matters, does it not?" I very much wanted Holmes to be able to catch his brother's murderer. I would be delighted to see the fellow hanged but not as delighted as Holmes would surely be. "Spies are by their very nature elusive targets."

"True, up to a point," replied my companion. "None of us can be ignorant of the political tension that exists between this country and certain others in Europe, not least Germany. There is war brewing. One can try to deny it, one can certainly hope it will not happen, but one cannot turn a blind eye to the situation. One would be blithe at best if one did, and at worst a fool. I myself have not been remiss in keeping a close watch on international events as they develop. I believe them to be not unrelated to another war which is already under way and of which you and I are all too cognisant."

"The war between the Outer Gods and the Old Ones."

"'As above, so below.' It is a maxim held to be true by occultists down through the ages. The earliest known recorded mention of it may be found in the *Emerald Tablet*, a cabbalistic text by the Ancient Greek mystic Hermes Trismegistus. That which occurs on the macrocosmic scale affects the microcosmic. The one realm influences the other. 'As above, so below.' Hence the conflict fomented amongst the gods by R'luhlloig is having an associated effect upon our world. On Earth, battle lines are being drawn. The unease across Europe reflects the strife which is prevailing in the – for want of a better word – heavens.

"We must recall, too, the 'world-changing future' mentioned in Zachariah Conroy's journal, as prophesied by Nathaniel Whateley while he was under the influence of R'luhlloig. R'luhlloig must have known that his war would create a contingent terrestrial analogue, and what he foretold now may be coming to pass. Was it prophecy or was it promise?" Holmes paused. "The point I am making is that I have accumulated a working knowledge of the enemy spies currently at large in Great Britain. In this endeavour I was encouraged and indeed abetted by Mycroft. It was his line of work more than mine, but from time to time he had cause to consult me on such matters. In short, there are three senior German agents operating on these shores whom I adjudge to be capable of sending the seven deadly parcels, and not just capable but so innately ruthless as to perform the deed without cavil or compunction."

"Three," I said. "That does narrow the field somewhat."

"I can narrow it yet further. I retain a network of useful London contacts, if somewhat depleted since I was a full-time resident of the capital. Through this means I keep abreast of the activities of the criminal underworld and those who would wish this country ill. I also study the newspapers religiously. Hence I am aware that two of the three German agents on my list are at the present time indisposed. One lies in hospital recovering from an appendectomy. An infection has set in and it is questionable whether he will pull through. The other is in police custody. He was arrested the day before yesterday after dishing out a severe drubbing to a man who accused him of cheating at cards."

"A pleasant fellow."

"A hypocrite, what's more, for he is notorious at the card tables for his sleights of hand."

"I am surprised someone from the embassy has not come to the Yard demanding his immediate release, citing diplomatic immunity or some such."

"He is not greatly liked even amongst his peers," said Holmes. "I imagine they are leaving him to stew in his own juices for a while, hoping it will teach him a lesson."

"That leaves just one suspect."

"It does. He is a gregarious sort who poses as a sportsman, fond of yachting, hunting, polo and other such energetic pursuits. He affects the demeanour of a country squire, but is all the time listening, nosing about, and subtly cajoling indiscretions out of the denizens of the rarefied circles in which he moves. His name is Von Bork and he is a thoroughgoing scoundrel but, by all accounts, much beloved by the company with whom he shoots and drinks and plays. I would reckon him to be the centre of half the mischief in England today, especially when it comes to gathering intelligence about our defensive strategies and naval capabilities. And…"

Holmes leapt declaratively to his feet.

"If we visit St James's post office, Watson, there we should be able to find proof that Von Bork sent those parcels."

CHAPTER TEN

The Dust of Compelling

IT DID NOT TAKE LONG TO TRACK DOWN THE POST office clerk who had served "the fellow with the funny accent and the parcels" yesterday, nor to establish that the fellow the clerk described was Von Bork, of whose physical appearance Holmes was cognisant. Yes, he had had stiff, brush-cut hair. Yes, he had been wearing a monocle. Yes, he had been smoking a cigarillo, a very pungent one.

"Prussia House next, I presume," I said as we left the building.

"On the contrary," said Holmes. "I would much prefer to confront Von Bork in his home. The embassy, after all, is technically German soil, and what I have in mind is better conducted on British soil, and in private, to lessen the chances of provoking an international incident."

"You know where he lives?"

"I will, once I have drawn upon that same network of useful London contacts I told you about earlier. It should take only a couple of hours and the price of a few telegrams to find out his home address, and then you and I can look forward to paying Herr Von Bork a pleasant house call."

Holmes spoke in a lightly arch tone that belied, I could tell, a simmering, deep-seated anger. Von Bork could scarce apprehend, I thought, the fury he had unleashed upon himself.

*

Two hours later, we were lying in wait outside a handsome Chelsea residence on the river side of the King's Road. We were watching the front door from the small park at the centre of the square on which the house stood.

Someone was at home, that much we could tell from the closed curtains in the windows on the second floor, which in most such houses belonged to the master bedroom. Someone, indeed, was having a nice, long lie-in, for it was past lunchtime. I fancied Von Bork snugly abed, warmed by the satisfaction of a wicked job well done. Imagining him thus, I would happily have throttled him with my bare hands, and I could only think Holmes wished to inflict an even worse fate upon him.

Shortly after two o'clock, a white-gloved valet at last parted the curtains. Then, some thirty minutes on, the front door opened, and across the threshold stepped a hearty-looking fellow. A cigarillo smouldered in his hand, while a smug smile split his meaty, somewhat porcine face. He was dressed in tweeds and gaiters, and a gold-rimmed monocle gleamed over his right eye. His outfit suggested someone trying to look as much like an English country gentleman as possible and, in the effort, failing.

Holmes moved like lightning. Before I knew it, he had the man by the elbow and my revolver pressed into his back.

"Invite us in, Herr Von Bork, there's a good fellow," he said, "and then instruct your staff to take the rest of the day off."

Von Bork, with an almost courteous bow of the head, complied. "Come in, indeed, gentlemen. Come in."

Once we were inside, the German duly summoned the full complement of his servants to the library. He acted coolly and calmly, for all the world as though the aquiline Englishman standing beside him was just a visiting friend and was not covertly pointing a gun at the base of his spine.

"A lovely day it is," he said. "You all deserve some time off. Go and bask in the sunshine."

"Now sit yourself down, *mein Herr*," Holmes said to him as the last servant sallied forth to enjoy the unexpected holiday. "We need to have a chat, you and I."

"It is Mr Sherlock Holmes, is it not?" said Von Bork as he took a seat in a leather-upholstered armchair. "The famous detective. Your pictures in *The Strand Magazine* do you justice. And you, sir, must be the doctor. John Watson, *ja*? That is you?"

I, the so-addressed "Chon Votson", offered a curt nod.

"Such an honour," the German continued. "Two so illustrious guests in my humble abode. But no need there was for this folderol with a gun. All you had to do was ring the doorbell and present your cards, and I would gladly have welcomed you in. What honest, law-abiding citizen could do else?"

"I think we can dispense with the bogus bonhomie, Von Bork," Holmes said. "Since you know who I am, you surely know why I am here."

"My dear fellow, I have not the first clue! The reason for your call a mystery is, and I should very much care to be enlight—"

Holmes struck him across the face with the butt of my Webley. Von Bork's head snapped sideways. He looked up at my companion almost sheepishly, rubbing his cheek.

"There was no call for that. Where is your English decency? Your sense of fair play? To hit a man without the provocation—"

Holmes struck Von Bork again. The first blow had been relatively restrained. This one was not.

"*Ach*." Von Bork rubbed his other cheek. "That was unkind. If you would but tell me why you are here, perhaps some sort of understanding we can arrive at. Otherwise, if you insist on just hitting me, how am I to help you?"

"Really, Von Bork, you must drop this pretence of bluff amiability. I know full well what sort of man you really are and what terrible acts you have perpetrated."

"Pretence?"

"You amuse others by coming across as a Teutonic buffoon. People see you affecting the airs and graces of a country squire and they think you faintly ludicrous. Thus they drop their guard and speak with indiscretion. They do not realise you are mentally logging every iota of useful data to convey back to your paymasters in Berlin."

"You credit me with a Machiavellian streak, Mr Holmes, which most assuredly I lack. I am a passionate friend of this country. I love you English and all that you stand for. I hold in high regard your way of life and the many wonderful, ingenious people that England has produced, not least yourself. An admirer of you, Dr Watson, I also am. I read all your writings. They give such an insight into the workings of British society and the British psyche. I foresee they will remain popular for generations to come."

I tried not to be flattered by this praise for my literary

efforts. It was difficult, however. Von Bork was very charming. His features, though far too swinish ever to be considered handsome, radiated a certain guileless appeal, right to the tips of his ginger hair and pale eyelashes. Had I met the man at a party, say, and known nothing about him, I would readily have fallen for his blandishments and even been willing to cultivate a friendship with him.

"And that is how you inveigle yourself into the lives and homes of the upper classes," said Holmes. "Even the cleverest of them is not immune to a fawning compliment, especially when it comes from one so devil-may-care, one who can match any man drink for drink, tennis volley for tennis volley, racetrack wager for racetrack wager."

"I do not see the harm in being sociable. Preferable it is, I would say, to hitting people with a gun."

"You do not care for being hit with a gun?"

"Truth to tell, not very much."

"How about without a gun?"

Holmes punched Von Bork on the nose with his free hand. It was a vicious, well-placed jab, and I heard the crunch of the German's nasal bone fracturing.

Von Bork let out a hapless shriek. Blood gushed down over his moustache. He rocked back and forth in the chair, cursing copiously in his native tongue.

I almost felt sorry for him. At the back of my mind a tiny doubt arose. What if Holmes's deductions were wrong? What if Von Bork was an innocent man and this abuse was wholly undeserved?

I stiffened my sinews. Holmes was seldom, if ever, mistaken. Von Bork was a spy, a master dissimulator, but soon the mask would slip and he would reveal his true colours. So I reassured myself.

"Really, sir," the German said thickly, using a handkerchief to mop up the blood that was smeared all around his mouth. "This I am beginning to think is torture for the sake of torture. Do you perhaps have something against the Germans? I know that your nation and mine are not the best of friends right now, but in my own way I am trying to remedy that. Mend fences, build bridges, foster trust, *ja*? Our future lies in co-operation, not antagonism, do you not think?"

"I think, *mein Herr*," said Holmes, "that I am going to give you one last chance to admit your guilt."

"My guilt about what, my dear chap?"

"About the murder of my brother and six of his peers. About the use of wraith beetles as deadly weapons, inflicting the most horrible of demises upon all seven men."

"Murder? Wraith beetles? What you are talking about I have not the foggiest. I was under the impression that Dr Watson recounts the truth in those marvellous tales of his, but now I am thinking otherwise. It is all very well to see on the page the words about locked rooms and messages in code and bloodstains on carpets. But when one hears about such things in person − straight from the mouth of the horse, as the saying goes − why, all at once they begin to sound absurd." He took the blood-soaked handkerchief away from his face and frowned at it. "Well, the bleeding has stopped, at any rate. How is the nose looking? Not too misshapen, I trust."

It was in fact swollen rather nastily. In addition, a

raw-looking contusion was blossoming on each of Von Bork's cheeks. He was starting to resemble some sort of garish clown.

"Very well," Holmes said. "I have been as lenient as I can, Von Bork. I have given you every opportunity to volunteer information of your own free will. You have chosen not to."

"Because I have nothing to tell you," the German insisted. "I am just a humble gentleman of leisure from Düsseldorf who enjoys very much living in this splendid nation of yours. What would you have me do? Confess to some crime of which I not the slightest knowledge have?"

"I must now resort to drastic measures."

"Drastic?" Von Bork uttered a hollow laugh. "You mean to say that hitting me is not drastic enough?"

Holmes handed me my gun. "Keep this trained upon him at all times, Watson. If necessary – if he gives you the least cause for suspicion – shoot. A flesh wound preferably. The thigh will do."

"With pleasure," I said.

From a pocket Holmes produced a silver cigarette case that held not cigarettes but an array of slim glass phials filled with various powders and liquids. He extracted one, uncapped it and tapped out the contents – an ounce or two of a dark brown precipitate that looked not unlike snuff – onto a sheet of writing paper from Von Bork's desk. He began to chant over it in R'lyehian.

Von Bork gave every appearance of ignoring what my friend was doing. Instead he addressed me, nodding at my revolver.

"A Webley Pryse top-break, Doctor. Somewhat of an antique these days. That yours is still in good working order I am amazed. You must take great care of it. Any parts you have had to replace? I imagine so. Springs wear out, do they not? They are a devil for that. I can see that the hammer looks a bit newer than the rest of the weapon. But still, a good old soldier's gun for a good old soldier. You carry it with much pride, and rightly so."

All of a sudden, Holmes leant close to the German and puffed the powder into his face.

Von Bork choked and spluttered. Quite a bit of the powder clung to the crust of blood around his nose and mouth. He breathed in and out stertorously. His chest heaved.

"What... What is this?" he gasped. "This stuff... it smells − tastes − terrible. Some of it I have inhaled. What is this you have done to me?"

"It is called the Dust of Compelling," said Holmes. "It is a magic-infused substance which forces anyone who ingests it to tell the truth, the whole truth and nothing but the truth. We should not have to wait more than a couple of minutes for it to start to work. You will shortly find yourself, Herr Von Bork, becoming the most honest and accommodating you have ever been."

"Magic-infused substance? Do you think I am an imbecile? This 'dust' of yours is nothing more than spices. Do you think I am going to fall for your ruse and suddenly feel the urge to come clean? You clearly hold me in low esteem."

"I assure you, the Dust of Compelling is genuinely

magical and it does as advertised: it compels."

"But you are a rationalist, Mr Holmes. I know it from Dr Watson's stories. You have no truck with magic. You despise and spurn the supernatural."

"Magic, I have learned, is merely another kind of science," Holmes said. "It has rules one can follow, a methodology as valid as any scientific methodology. It yields tangible, reproducible results. A certain admixture of ingredients, activated by the incantation of certain words, will have a certain predetermined effect. The idea of magic is antithetical to the spirit of our age but the *fact* of magic is undeniable, as you are about to discover."

"Really, I am losing patience with you," Von Bork said. He was blustering. "I have connections. Friends in high places, as is the phrase. I can see to it that for this behaviour you are properly castigated. But it is not too late for you to shake my hand, apologise and leave. Do so, and we shall say nothing more about what has today happened here. But if you persist in mistreating me, it shall be your ruin."

"Threats now, Von Bork? Can it be that you know you are about to blurt out every secret you hold? Soon you will not be able to keep anything in."

"Frightened I would be if I believed for one moment your dust had any kind of power. But I am not frightened. Yes. Actually, yes, I *am* frightened."

Suddenly Von Bork looked puzzled and perturbed. He had just confessed something that he would rather not have; that was the impression I got.

"*Mein Gott*, yes, you are making me afraid, Mr Holmes." He blinked several times, then tossed his head from side to side as though troubled by a bothersome gnat. "You could have kept hitting me from now until doomsday and I would not have told you a thing you wanted to know. My father raised me in strictness. 'Werther,' he used to say, 'you must never show weakness and you must never cry.' This was while beating me with a riding crop if I had done wrong, and not much did it take to make Papi angry. I learned not to cry. I learned not to give anything away, even under duress. But now… now…"

"Your childhood is of no interest to me."

"That is because it was not your childhood. I had to suffer it, not you. Oh, for heaven's sake, what has come over me? Why am I telling you about my father? My *tyrannisch* father… He hated me, did my papi. Sometimes he could not even look at me. He knew what I was. He knew the marks I bore and he loathed me for them."

"Marks?" I said. "What marks?"

"He blamed my mother," the German lamented. "He said it was her fault. He used Mutti as cruelly as he did me, if not more so, but could he not have been responsible himself? It is just as likely. Who is to say the shame came not from her but from him?"

"Von Bork," said Holmes, "the Dust of Compelling works for a limited duration only, so let us not waste time. I need you to pay attention. You sent the seven wraith beetles, of course."

"*Natürlich. Natürlich.* It was I. Those horrid little *insekten*. So dangerous it is even to touch them. I used tongs when transferring them from the little cages into the boxes. They came over from Africa in a diplomatic bag, sent by one of our great naturalists, who risked life and limb to collect them. A German thinks nothing of braving death on behalf of the fatherland. We are willing to sacrifice all for kaiser and country. Can you English say the same?"

"What was the purpose in killing those particular seven individuals?"

"*Ach*, that I do not know. I was not told." Von Bork sounded genuinely upset that he could not provide Holmes with the answer he sought. It was as though, thanks to the Dust, he wished to be as obliging as humanly possible. "I was merely given the order to kill all seven anonymously with the *verdammt* beetles. Not my usual way. Poison in a drink or a stiletto in the back or a bullet from a distance — those methods I am accustomed to and proficient in. The beetles were the chosen means, however."

"Who gave the order?"

"All my orders come from the top."

"From the kaiser himself?"

"Ultimately, I suppose. *Ja*. Our inestimable leader must be the one who dictates what is to be done, and when, and to whom. May I have a drink? Some water? I feel hot. So thirsty."

I made a move to fetch him a glass of water, but Holmes stayed me with a look of stern rebuke. I think I had begun to feel a strange compassion for Von Bork. It was clear he had invented none of those details about his awful upbringing. I pitied him for the boy he had been, in spite of the terrible crimes he had committed as an adult.

"You received specific instructions from the kaiser, then?" said Holmes.

"Not directly from him. Never. I do know that my targets were seven men of influence, from the topmost echelons of government, industry, the aristocracy and the military. Obvious are the benefits of eliminating them. Your country's strategic peacetime capabilities are significantly compromised now, and all seven appear to have committed suicide. How will that look to the public? Perhaps they were traitors. That is what people might think, *ja*? Even if such a thing is never officially claimed or denied, suspicion there will be. Maybe I shall be the one to start the rumours. 'A ring of highly placed German sympathisers,' I shall whisper in all the right ears. 'They were selling state secrets, did you know? So I heard from a reliable source. But the police were on to them. The net was closing in. They took their own lives in a single night, by mutual consent, rather than face trial.' Clever, no? That little fabrication I will spread around and England will lose some of its braggartly self-confidence."

Von Bork tugged at his shirt collar with a forefinger.

"Please," he said, "some water. I feel so hot." His face was flushed and had gained a sheen of perspiration.

"Holmes," I said, "he is not looking well. A drink can't hurt."

"I shall thank you not to be a doctor now, Watson," came the peremptory reply. "You are letting your Hippocratic oath get the better of you. Don't forget, this man has just confessed to the murder of my brother."

"He is evidently having some kind of adverse reaction to the Dust of Compelling."

"So? Mycroft had an adverse reaction to the wraith beetle's secretion. A fatal one."

"I beg you," said Von Bork. "Just a few sips. My throat is so dry."

"From whom did the order come, Von Bork? Who sanctioned the killing of those seven men?"

"I want to say, Mr Holmes. I want to! But something stops me."

"I demand you tell me."

"So hot. *Wasser, bitte. Wasser!*"

Von Bork was trembling now and sweating profusely, as if in the grip of a fever. His eyes were so bloodshot the whites were practically scarlet. A heat was radiating off him that I could feel from a couple of feet away.

"Holmes, look at him," I said. "He appears to be running a very high temperature. Something is wrong."

"Something *is* wrong," said my companion. "He should not be able to resist the Dust. Somehow he is being inhibited from revealing a crucial fact. Someone has cast a Ward of Muting over him, and its magic is clashing with mine."

"He will be of no use to us if he dies."

"He is of no use to us if I cannot exact a name from him. Von Bork! This will all be over if you simply give me what I need to know."

"I would!" the German was all but screaming. "I would! But the more I try, the more I feel as though I am aflame."

"Then try harder."

"I am. I have no choice but to. Oh, but it hurts! It hurts!"

That was when I first detected the smell of meat

cooking. Initially I thought it must be coming from the kitchen. Perhaps the cook had left a joint roasting in the oven by mistake.

Then I realised the smell was coming from Von Bork; and it was growing stronger.

"My God, Holmes," I said. "I think the fellow is burning up – literally burning up."

Uncontrollable shudders wracked Von Bork's frame. He was saying, "*Nein, nein,*" over and over, but the words were more a wail than speech.

All at once he lurched forwards in his seat. His hands clutched the armrests so hard that his fingers tore the leather. His mouth opened wide and wisps of smoke issued forth. His staring eyes clouded over, the irises turning oyster grey. The smell was now clearly that of raw flesh charring, and it was becoming cloyingly obnoxious.

I took a couple of involuntary steps back, riven with disgust and horror. Von Bork continued to burn from the inside out. The heat he gave off was as strong as any hearth fire. His lips were drawn back in a rictus of agony. The smoke had begun billowing from his nostrils as well as his mouth. His body twisted and writhed as though being manipulated by giant, invisible hands. I heard bones crack and organs sizzle, baked by the inferno within.

Then he fell back into the chair. A few last convulsions passed through him, and finally he lay still.

CHAPTER ELEVEN

The Sorrows of Young Werther

"THAT," HOLMES ADMITTED, SURVEYING VON BORK'S remains, "is far from ideal."

The German spy looked little changed on the outside, other than his glaucous eyes and the smoke smuts adhering to his face. One could only imagine the condition of his innards. I conjured up a mental picture of broiled offal, and dismissed it as swiftly as I could.

Holmes flung open windows to rid the room of the stench. The greasy miasma of fumes gradually thinned.

He returned to the corpse and regarded it with a quizzical eye.

"Who did this to you, I wonder," said he, addressing the deceased. "Did you even know a Ward of Muting had been cast on you? I suspect not. You would have said so in advance of the spell taking effect, had you known. The Dust of Compelling would have made it impossible for you not to. Whoever engaged you to conduct the seven assassinations is clearly a careful man, keen to cover his tracks. Still, I am sure there remains much you can tell us, even in death."

He bent forward and began unbuttoning Von Bork's shirt.

"Holmes…" I said.

"Squeamish, Watson? That is not like you."

"It just seems… disrespectful."

"Of a man such as Von Bork? One cannot treat the unrespectable with disrespect. It is axiomatic. And in case you have already forgotten, he did murder my brother."

"I take your point."

Having exposed the German's chest, Holmes leaned back, saying, "Ah."

"What is it?"

"See for yourself. Those 'marks' Von Bork spoke of which earned him his father's contempt. Here they are. Some might say that Von Bork senior had good cause to find his son abhorrent."

The marks in question were not, as I first imagined they would be, patches of skin discolouration such as port-wine stains or vitiligo; nor were they unnaturally large moles or warts. They were another kind of deformity altogether.

They were scales.

The scales spread across Von Bork's chest in an irregular pattern, smatterings of them here and there. They were fine and diamond-shaped, with a faint greenish tinge. They had a distinctly reptilian cast.

"He was a snake man," I said. I immediately recalled the various encounters Holmes and I had had with that subspecies of mankind during the early years of our partnership. We had first learned of the existence of a serpentine humanoid race when Professor Moriarty took us prisoner in their subterranean temple beneath St Paul's church, Shadwell, back in 1880. Thereafter a group of snake men had worked for Holmes as his secret agents in London, the Irregulars, until through my carelessness we lost possession of a Triophidian Crown, an arcane artefact which grants the wearer mastery over reptiles and which Holmes employed to make the Irregulars do his bidding. Since then, we had seen and heard nothing of them. The snake men seemed content to keep themselves to themselves and interact with people as little as possible.

"Indeed," said Holmes, nodding. "Von Bork was the rare sort of snake man that can pass for human, more or less. As long as he remained fully clothed in one's presence, one would have had no idea there was anything untoward about him. The *Homo sapiens reptiliensis* trait must have been recessive in either his father's or his mother's bloodline. There had probably been no trace of it for several generations until, by some twist of heredity, it surfaced in Werther Von Bork."

"I wonder if his being a snake man had some bearing upon his becoming a spy and assassin. From an early age he must have learned to lead a double life, concealing those scales from his schoolmates for fear of ridicule. Lying and deceiving would have become second nature to him. His father's detestation, meanwhile, would have instilled in him a very low opinion of himself and of his fellow men. From such stony soil do conscienceless killers arise."

"Your interest in his psychology is all very well but is of little advantage in our present enquiry. Von Bork was under orders to obliterate the Dagon Club. Who gave them? Somewhere on the property there may be evidence of correspondence between him and his spymasters. Are you ready for a spot of searching, Watson?"

*

Search the place we did, with some diligence. We steered clear of the servants' quarters, confining ourselves to the areas of the house Von Bork would have frequented, particularly his private rooms. We rummaged in cupboards and drawers. We pulled up rugs to check for loose floorboards. We rapped on walls, looking for false panels. We even lifted the lid of the Blüthner grand piano in the drawing room and probed its interior.

Behind a large framed photograph of the kaiser hanging in Von Bork's study we found a wall safe with a combination lock. Holmes, with deft fingers and an ear pressed to the door, was able to open it. Inside were banknotes, both sterling and marks, a passport, a passbook for Silvester's Bank, certificates for securities, deeds, and a few valuables, exactly the sort of things one would expect a rich man's safe to contain. Kaiser Wilhelm II gazed down at us as we returned him to his hook, every inch of his face reproachful, even the upturned tips of his moustache.

Back in the library we regrouped and debated. The smell from the semi-immolated Von Bork still lingered. The corpse itself, head thrown back, stared blindly up at the ceiling mouldings.

"Appearances to the contrary, I am getting senile, Watson," said Holmes.

"What do you mean?"

"I mean," he said with self-reproach, "that I am as guilty as an elderly person is of not thinking clearly. We must consider that Von Bork would not have wanted his staff to stumble upon anything suspicious. He would keep potentially incriminating letters and suchlike not in drawers or under floorboards, not even in a safe, but in a location where not even the most inquisitive servant would think to look. But where might that be? Where?"

As my companion mused, I glanced around at the books on their shelves. I was queerly pleased to learn that he had not lied about being an aficionado of my work. He owned copies of the three novels and three short-story collections I had published thus far, and they looked well-thumbed, judging by the state of their spines. Largely, however, he seemed to favour the literature of his home nation, in particular Romantic authors such as Hoffmann, Schlegel and Goethe and the philosophers Schopenhauer and Nietzsche.

A thought struck me.

"Yesterday you told me one can tell a great deal about a man by his bookshelves," I said.

"Such was the case with Fitzroy McPherson," said Holmes.

"Might it not apply here too? I see volumes of dense, difficult prose, the nature of which is wholly at odds with Von Bork's personality."

"Go on. Your knowledge of literature greatly exceeds mine and I am curious to see where this line of reasoning is headed."

"I cannot picture a man like Von Bork reading the majority of these books for pleasure or, for that matter, at all. It is likely they are just for show, an attempt to give visitors the impression of erudition."

"Indeed, or perhaps he wished to cultivate an air of intellectual insecurity. Everything the man did seems calculated to make others underestimate him."

"His servants are unlikely to peek into any of the

books," I continued. "They are all English, none well-educated, and I would be astonished if any of them had even rudimentary German."

"Watson!" Holmes ejaculated. "All those occasions when I have derided your lack of logical analysis – I take it back. A book is a perfect place to store correspondence. One simply interleaves letters between the pages. And what Englishman, casually browsing the shelves, would pull down a volume of German poetry or a Gothic novel in that same language? What German would, indeed?"

"Only one who was adventurous or foolhardy. Or," I added, "very bored."

"Did Von Bork hide his documents in plain sight?" Holmes said, studying the bookshelves. "If so, in which book or books? There are a couple of hundred before us. We could go through every one, but that would be a tedious, time-consuming process. What if we are able to single out a few likely candidates? What if…?" He chuckled, his eye alighting on a particular tome, lodged up high, out of easy reach. "Can it be, Von Bork? Can you really have been that sly?"

Standing on tiptoe, he plucked the book from its berth. It was by Goethe.

"*Die Leiden des jungen Werthers*," he said. "*The Sorrows of Young Werther*. Goethe's first novel if I remember rightly, couched in the epistolary form. Young Werther Von Bork definitely experienced a few sorrows of his own. Might we find some of the adult Von Bork's epistles within?"

He set the book down on a table, opened the cover and leafed through. His grey eyes lit up with gratification.

Practically every turn of a page revealed a slip of paper, neatly inserted. They were letters and notes, and were written in what looked like some sort of elaborate pictorial substitution code.

The average man, at any rate, would have thought it a code and found it indecipherable. Holmes and I knew better. Those abstruse, curlicued characters, hanging suspended from bars in the manner of Sanskrit, were none other than R'lyehian script.

"Oh, that is cunning," said Holmes. "Very cunning. Missives penned in a language that is unintelligible to all save a handful and unknown to most. Were these documents discovered by the police, say, or the intelligence services, there is a vanishingly small probability that those agents of law and order would be able to make head or tail of them. They would be completely foxed. As cryptographic systems go it is a simple one but virtually foolproof."

Having studied several of the letters in detail, Holmes was able to confirm to his own satisfaction that they were dispatches from Von Bork in which he passed on the fruits of his espionage.

"Look. Here is a passage concerning shipbuilding at our naval dockyards. The word '*ch'phlagmon*' translates literally as 'water-crossing', which we may take in this instance to mean 'maritime'. Here is a mention of '*flaghu ehye*' – 'boundary integrity' – that can only be a reference to coastal defences."

"And here," I said. "'*Kdag'hu hrii*'. 'Warlord followers'. That denotes soldiers."

"Where R'lyehian's ancient lexicon is lacking,

neologisms have been coined. '*Fm'latgh iugh*' means 'fire egg'. What can that be but 'bomb' or 'artillery shell'? And the '*lw'nafh*' or 'transmitter' that launches said 'fire eggs' must be a cannon."

Holmes pored over the letters further.

"Troop numbers. Development of munitions. Field exercises. Von Bork was very industrious. We have before us a comprehensive picture of Britain's military preparedness."

"Each sheet of paper is dated. They go back more than three years, the most recent from just last month. I presume these are copies of the originals."

"Von Bork was keeping a secondary record of all the information he passed on, no doubt in case any of his dispatches went astray and he should be called upon to resubmit it. You have observed, of course, how one particular term recurs with notable frequency."

"Which?"

"This: '*vlgh'ri w'gyathdrn*'."

I considered. "'Nation representative'?"

"Since R'lyehian lacks such niceties as tenses, conjugations and declensions," Holmes said, "it is not always easy to determine at a glance where a word or phrase sits in a sentence and what function it serves. One has to infer from context. In this instance, '*vlgh'ri w'gyathdrn*' seems to be employed in the vocative, referring to a person being addressed."

"The recipient of the dispatches."

"Now, who else could a 'nation representative' be, from Von Bork's point of view, but…?"

"The German ambassador," I said.

Holmes smiled thinly. "I believe, old friend, that you and I shall be paying a visit to Prussia House after all. Someone was pulling Von Bork's strings. Someone set him the task of assassinating my brother and his colleagues. Von Bork would appear to have been directly answerable to the ambassador when it came to espionage. It is at least possible that His Excellency is the mastermind behind the killings in addition to being the clearing house for Von Bork's intelligence-gathering. Where he fulfils the one shady supervisory role, why not the other?"

"Germany's ambassador himself behind the Dagon Club murders?" I was startled by the prospect and disquieted by the ramifications.

"The fact that both he and Von Bork are conversant in R'lyehian is also noteworthy," said Holmes. "And so, Watson, back to St James's we must go, although I should like to make a stop on the way."

CHAPTER TWELVE

Mufti Men

THE STOP IN QUESTION WAS AT THE CHELSEA telegraph office. I waited outside in our cab while Holmes went in. He reappeared no more than five minutes later, enough time to have composed, sent and paid for a telegram. However, when I enquired whether that was what he had done, my friend merely gave me an enigmatic look.

"I have taken a precautionary measure, that is all, Watson," said he. "I trust I shall not need to resort to it, but it is best to be prepared."

Prussia House sat on a corner of Carlton House Terrace adjacent to the Duke of York monument, with sweeping views along the Mall on one side and Waterloo Gardens on the other. Diplomatic missions seldom stint on accommodation but this great stucco-clad block, with its pediments and Corinthian columns, was more imposing than most. It seemed to have been chosen in order to offer visiting Germans a reassuring sense of their country's significance and to make indigenes of the host nation feel humbled and perhaps envious.

Holmes strode confidently through its portal into a large, airy atrium and demanded of the clerk at the reception desk that he be granted an audience with the ambassador.

"Now?" said the clerk.

"Right now."

The clerk, in precise, lightly accented English, averred that that was impossible. "His Excellency has a very full schedule. In a month's time perhaps an appointment might be made, but today? I regret that it is out of the question."

"Go to His Excellency," Holmes said stiffly. "Tell him that my name is Sherlock Holmes, and that I am here in connection with Werther Von Bork. Tell him that I have certain evidence pertaining to him and Herr Von Bork that could be considered incriminating. I will regard a refusal to see me as an admission of guilt and my next port of call will be the offices of one of our national dailies."

"Your allegations are" – the clerk groped for an adjective – "vague. I do not think them sufficient to warrant the ambassador's attention. I know this Von Bork of whom you speak. He is an upstanding member both of this establishment and the community of German expatriates. I cannot envisage him engaging in any improper activity."

"Then you are either deluded or ignorant," said Holmes.

The clerk bristled. "Sir, you are sorely trying my patience. To come in here and bandy about accusations and insults, it is most unbecoming." He cast a glance towards a couple of large, bulky men who were seated by the entrance. Both had been reading copies of the *Norddeutsche Allgemeine Zeitung* when we came in; they were now only pretending to read the newspapers, keeping half an eye on Holmes and me. They were martial in bearing, heavily muscled, with matching close-trimmed hair and neat moustaches. It was obvious that their job was to handle troublemakers, into which category Holmes and, by extension, I were rapidly falling.

"And you, young man," Holmes retorted to the clerk, "are being deliberately obstructive. I am a British citizen, a subject of His Majesty, and you, a foreigner, have no right to refuse my request."

"I have every right. While you are in this building it is you, sir, who are the foreigner."

Holmes well knew that. Furthermore, he had to be as conscious as I was of the presence of the two military men in mufti. His plan, obviously, was to provoke the clerk and thus attract their attention. He was picking a fight.

"I have never been so outraged," he said, voice rising almost to a shout. "It is true what they say about Germans. You are quite the rudest people on earth."

That brought the two mufti men to their feet. They strolled over to us and stationed themselves on either side, flanking us.

"Klaus," said one to the clerk, "are these gentlemen bothering you?"

"A little. I believe they are under some misapprehension as to how an embassy works."

"Would you like us to escort them out?"

"I think that would be desirable, yes, if they will not go of their own accord. Thank you."

The fact that this conversation was conducted in English was telling. We were meant to be intimidated.

"There is more than one way to flush out the tiger from its den," Holmes murmured to me. "How pugnacious are you feeling, Watson?"

"At present?" I looked at the two men. Each stood a head taller than I and was broader around the chest by several inches. "Frankly, very little."

"Then leave this to me."

"By all means. Be my guest."

Holmes, despite his advancing years, had lost none of his skill at baritsu. One of the two Germans was on the floor and moaning before the other even realised they were under attack. The incapacitated fellow was nursing a broken wrist and, to judge by the angle at which his lower leg jutted sideways, his kneecap was dislocated if not broken too.

His comrade came at Holmes in a grandiose boxing stance, fists upraised, knuckles towards the ceiling. He circled his arms in the air, his jaw firmly squared.

"The element of surprise is lost," he said to Holmes. "You will not find me so easy to topple."

Holmes darted at him. The German threw a punch but Holmes ducked under, getting inside his guard. He delivered three quick jabs to the ribs with stiffened fingers like knives, then stepped smartly back before his opponent could retaliate.

The mufti man let out a yelp of pain but could, I thought, have looked more distressed. That barrel chest of his could evidently soak up a fair amount of punishment. He took the fight to Holmes, subjecting him to a barrage of crosses, roundhouses and hooks. Holmes absorbed the blows on his forearms until, seeing an opening, he landed a solid uppercut to the other's jaw. He followed it up with a savage kick to the shin that sent the German staggering backwards.

"Stop! Stop!" cried Klaus the clerk, waving his arms. "This is undignified! This is not appropriate!"

His words fell on deaf ears. The noise of the fight was

echoing across the atrium and up the stairs. Heads poked out from doorways. Voices rose in agitation. Holmes's intent, plainly, was to cause a commotion. No one could deny that he was accomplishing that goal with great success and some aplomb.

"Stop!" Klaus wailed again, in vain.

"You practise an Oriental fighting style," the mufti man growled to Holmes. He could no longer put full weight on the leg Holmes had kicked. "The mark of a degenerate. No real man uses his feet in combat."

"He does if he wants to win," said Holmes, before going on the offensive once again.

As if to underscore the point, Holmes used only kicks thereafter. Toes and instep repeatedly made contact with vulnerable areas on the mufti man's body – his joints, for the most part – until the German was bent double, scarce able to stand. The fellow put up a valiant resistance to the last, but victory for Holmes had become inevitable. A final, swingeing kick to the temple sent the German keeling over, out cold. It was almost a mercy.

By now, consternation reigned in the embassy. People were out on the staircase landings, looking down and clamouring. It was only a matter of time before the ambassador himself emerged to see what all the fuss was about.

Although the ambassador's face was unknown to me, the tall, distinguished-looking man who came trotting down the stairs, barking in gruff German, could only be he. He had an air of command, and everyone else present accorded him deference.

His expression as he reached the ground floor was

complicated. He looked both indignant and intrigued.

"What is the meaning of this?" he snapped in English. "You, sir. Are you the instigator of this violence?"

Holmes adopted an obsequious grin. "Baron Von Herling, I presume. Your servant, sir. I would humbly crave a moment or two of your time."

CHAPTER THIRTEEN

Baron Von Herling

THAT BARON VON HERLING CONSENTED TO HOLMES'S request surprised me. I thought he would flat-out refuse and threaten us with all manner of dire repercussions if we did not depart forthwith. But he seemed almost amused by my friend's effrontery, and invited us upstairs to a well-appointed meeting room where he settled us into chairs and asked if we would care for refreshments. His English was so fluent as to be practically flawless. Unlike his countryman Von Bork he was not in the habit of relegating his verbs to the end of their sentences; nor did he soften his v's and harden his w's.

"Tea, I imagine, would be welcome."

"More than welcome," said Holmes. "Mandatory. I must confess myself in need of a pick-me-up after my little bout of exercise downstairs."

Von Herling pressed an electric bell button that summoned a butler.

Polite conversation whiled the time away until the servant returned with the tea things on a salver. Von Herling lamented the recent fire at the Brussels International that had destroyed the pavilions housing the British and French exhibitions. "It is always good to see nations come together at expositions," he said. "There they may show themselves off to their best advantage. It reminds us that we have more in common than dividing us and that the higher pursuits – art, science, architecture – should be our true calling. Such a shame about the fire, but I refuse to see it as an ill omen, as some have. If one is looking for ill omens, one need only consider the business of Montenegrin independence, which seems to me symptomatic of the unrest that is rapidly consuming the Balkans. Europe is fracturing before our very eyes. Somehow we must hold the continent together before it falls apart completely."

He came across as a genial, reasonable man, who wanted peace and stability. "Disruption serves nobody," he said, "other than anarchists, reactionaries and revolutionaries, none of whom should be allowed to gain a political toehold. If I and my country stand for anything, it is for cohesion and unity."

Once the tea had been poured and the three of us were alone again, the ambassador turned to the matter of our presence in the embassy.

"You have come, I take it, on an errand of some importance, Mr Holmes. That would account for, perhaps even excuse, the unruliness of your behaviour. You seek my aid? There is some crime afoot in which one of our envoys is embroiled? I will endeavour to co-operate however I can. The resources of this embassy are at your disposal."

"You are too kind, Your Excellency," said Holmes. "But let us drop the charade, shall we?"

Von Herling frowned. "I'm afraid I don't understand."

"We have played this game too many times, you and I." Holmes sounded weary. "It has become tedious. I recognise the signs now without really having to try. I am not sure what it is – an instinct, I suppose, born of experience. I see you and I know. I see *through* you. That which lies beneath the surface is never as hidden as it's minded to think."

He laid a certain subtle emphasis on the words *hidden* and *minded*.

Von Herling twitched his head. "You are accusing me of something."

"Of being a vessel and a vassal. Of carrying within you a passenger who pays his fare in the coin of worldly success."

I knew then what Holmes was implying, and I felt a dull nausea set in. Once again we were facing R'luhlloig, the Hidden Mind. Somewhere within Von Herling lurked the god that Moriarty had become, R'luhlloig's essence entwined with the ambassador's, his voice offering guidance and beguilement.

The warmth faded from Von Herling's face. It was like watching milk curdle. His features took on a darker cast. The eyes seemed to enlarge, the brow to broaden. Where there had been a courteous smile upon the lips, now hovered a sneer.

"Good afternoon, my old adversary," said R'luhlloig. "A pleasure to meet you again."

"The pleasure is all yours," said Holmes. "You had me fooled for perhaps a minute, but no more than that. Von Herling exhibited few of the traits that usually give you away. He seemed altogether too pleasant, however. The performance did not convince."

"If you are attempting to persuade me of your observational acuteness, Mr Holmes, that is all very well. I note, however, that your hand has strayed several times to your jacket pocket since we sat down. It is almost as though you have been checking something there. Some item which alerts you to my proximity, by any chance? A charm? A talisman?"

Holmes, with a sardonic chuckle, delved into his pocket and drew out a phial of liquid, one that was of a piece with the others in his cigarette case. The cloudy liquid gave off a vibrant magenta glow.

"Purbeck's Emulsion of Imminence," said R'luhlloig. "An all-purpose lodestone solution that responds to otherworldly presences."

"The light it radiates is its primary signal," said Holmes, "but the emulsion generates a small amount of heat as well when active. That affords tactile confirmation if visual confirmation is not possible."

"Your resourcefulness knows no bounds."

"When it comes to you, R'luhlloig, I take no chances."

"Do you hope to kill me? I'm sure you have the necessary tools upon your person. A gun, say. Or you could use your bare hands."

"Kill Von Herling, you mean."

"You must be tempted. You are on the warpath, are you not? Your brother's death is like a fresh, gaping wound in your soul. You yearn to lash out at any who might have been responsible, and it was Baron Von Herling who authorised the assassinations. He gave Von Bork the order. You know that, or you would not be here."

"Von Herling may have signed the Dagon Club's death warrants," said Holmes, "but at your behest. He is the glove puppet but you are the hand. I could kill him, yes, but it would not destroy the true culprit. You would simply withdraw from his lifeless body and carry on as before, unimpeded. You are like a horde of rats, R'luhlloig. For every one I kill, another springs up to replace it."

"I am damnably difficult to be rid of, am I not?"

"Damnably. But then vermin always are."

"It must be a source of some frustration."

"I cope."

"Cope? I would say you positively thrive on it. The challenges I have been setting you over the years seem to have granted you a new lease of life. When you and I first clashed in 1895 – that is, I as R'luhlloig, not as Moriarty – you were haggard and spent, a husk of your former self. Since then you have looked increasingly robust during all our encounters. I feel I should take some credit for effecting so remarkable a rejuvenation."

"You hold yourself in too high regard. I will allow, though, that you have been the whetstone keeping my edge sharp. Whenever a case crops up that betrays your influence it brings out the best in me. You choose such interesting characters to recruit as your partners in skulduggery. Count Negretto Sylvius. Giuseppe Gorgiano. Dr Shlessinger. Baron Adelbert Gruner. Josiah Amberley. What a rogues' gallery! Murderers and blackmailers and gangsters, fiends to a man."

"They are drawn to me and I to them, like to like," said R'luhlloig, "and so we forge our mutually beneficial alliances. There is a certain type of man who is susceptible to the gifts I offer. I promise power and preferment and freedom from consequence, and they lap it up. I encourage them to obey their natural inclinations, to cleave closer to their true selves, all the while coaxing them towards some eye-catching misdemeanour that will lure you into their ambit and create an opportunity to kill you. Shlessinger nearly managed it – or should I say 'Holy' Peters? That coffin at the Brixton undertakers contained a nasty surprise."

I raised an eyebrow. "I would call a ravenous zuvembie more than just 'a nasty surprise'."

"And Gorgiano's Red Circle also came close."

The Red Circle in question was a league of Italian mobsters who ruled Naples through terror, backed up by witchcraft. Their enforcers all bore a tattoo of a red circle on their chests, which could come to life and manifest as a venomous crimson centipede. I recall to this day, vividly, the horrible sensation of watching one of those creatures crawl towards Holmes and me as we stood guard over Emilia Lucca in a box room in Bloomsbury. The rippling of those legs, the insinuations of that segmented body…

"Yes, Doctor," said R'luhlloig. "That one still resonates with you, I can see."

"Brushes with death tend to," I replied.

"And Gruner, the uxoricide. He arranged for a particularly ferocious beating to be dished out upon you, Mr Holmes. Your baritsu and your prowess at singlestick were of little avail then."

"It was not easy defending myself against two Deep Ones. Those aquatic bipeds have evolved to live at a depth of many fathoms. To be able to withstand the pressures they have become endowed with great physical strength. I admit I was lucky to survive the ambush."

The Deep Ones were not quite so lucky, for Holmes had his revenge upon them, and upon their master, Gruner. Knowing of Gruner's passion for Chinese pottery, he sent him a Qing dynasty burial urn within which was trapped a *nü gui* – the vengeful ghost of a wronged woman. When Gruner removed the lid, the *nü gui* burst forth, slaughtering both of his froglike accomplices and leaving him with disfiguring injuries.

When I reminded R'luhlloig of how Holmes had rebalanced the scales of justice, he had the good grace to wince.

"Yes, it hurt, having one's face savaged by that shrieking spectre," he said. "I am not immune to the sufferings inflicted upon those whose bodies I share."

"Some small consolation," said Holmes. "I should hate to think you walk away from each of our tussles with impunity."

"Yet walk away I do, to recoup, contemplate, and devise my next scheme. So far I have come off worse in all our encounters, but there is a notable difference between us, Mr Holmes. I can lose countless times, but I only have to win once to be the ultimate victor. When you eventually lose, you will lose for good, for you will lose your life."

"Given our record, I would keep betting on myself. I feel, however, that we are approaching some sort of conclusion. Here you are in the most prominent – I might even say the most boldfaced – guise you have yet donned. Never before have you seduced quite so illustrious a figure into being your living mannequin as Baron Manfred Von Herling. You have also been keeping a low profile these past few years, which leads me to think that you have been colluding with His Excellency for most if not all of that period. Von Herling assumed the ambassadorship in 1904, not long after I deprived you of that demon-haunted gem known as the Mazarin Stone. Before then he was a mere consul, a middling diplomat with few apparent ambitions."

"You know a lot about him."

"No more than I have read in *The Times*. Only now am I divining the connotations, the story behind the story. Under your sway Von Herling has risen to his present giddy heights. He now occupies a position whereby he can influence foreign policy at home and keep a weather eye on Britain's foreign policy at the same time. Since our two countries appear to be on an ineluctable collision course, I can only imagine that you have had a hand in fomenting the antagonism and that it serves your greater purpose. For what can be more climactic than a war which, unchecked, could consume the entire world?"

R'luhlloig shrugged in nonchalant assent. "What indeed?"

"Your first move in this final assault has been the destruction of the Dagon Club."

"A few of the enemy's pieces swept off the board at a stroke."

"You must not forget that one of those so-called pieces was my brother," Holmes said with a steely glare.

"Forget? Why, it was very much the point of the exercise. You say you engineered this meeting. I rather think it was I who engineered it. The trail from your brother to Von Bork to me could not have been clearer if it had been etched in gold."

"Let us agree that we are both responsible," said Holmes. "Do you suppose I would have come here without me at least harbouring the suspicion that I was to be meeting R'luhlloig?"

"No, Mr Holmes, I imagine you knew perfectly well that that was a likelihood."

"At times it is useful to look up and meet one's opponent's eye across the board, to see what he is thinking, or what he is trying not to show that he is thinking."

"And what am I thinking?" said R'luhlloig, folding his hands across his midriff.

"That I may yet foil your plans," Holmes said. "That while I live, I pose a threat. That more than ever I need to be despatched."

R'luhlloig chortled, rather too ostentatiously, or so I judged, as if it were important that we see him amused. This may, of course, have been wishful thinking on my part. I wanted R'luhlloig to sound rattled, yet I could not escape the impression that he held all the aces and we no decent cards to speak of.

"The thorn in my side is undoubtedly overdue for plucking out," R'luhlloig said.

"I might have hoped for a less belittling metaphor than 'thorn', but I shall indulge your arrogance. You know no better."

"However, the act of plucking," R'luhlloig continued, "is not for Baron Von Herling to perform. It would inconvenience me more than a little were I simply to kill the two of you in this room. Too many witnesses. Diplomatic immunity extends only so far."

"For which reasons I decided it would be safe for us to be alone with you," said Holmes. "I would never be cavalier with my own life, and that applies all the more to Watson's. The hullabaloo in the hall was a little extra insurance, to make sure that as many people as possible in the embassy knew Watson and I were here and saw us accompany you upstairs."

"You are never short of stratagems, are you?"

"It is one of my more commendable qualities."

"Ha ha! Well then, perhaps we should send for a fresh pot of tea to toast that. Or might you prefer something stronger?" He pressed the bell. "The embassy boasts a rather fine cellar, especially if you have a penchant for sweet wines. A glass of Gewürztraminer?"

Holmes rose abruptly. "The offer is a generous one, but I feel we have stayed long enough. His Excellency's time is precious and he has many appointments to honour today. Your receptionist told us as much."

"Nothing that cannot be postponed," said R'luhlloig. "There is a certain valedictory note to this encounter of ours that suggests it ought to be commemorated. I cannot foresee that we shall have an opportunity like it again – the two of us jousting verbally, man to man, in civil fashion. We should enjoy the lull in hostilities while we can, no?"

"With respect, R'luhlloig, no." Holmes took me by the elbow, hoisting me to my feet. "Watson and I really must be going. To linger would, I believe, be a mistake."

I registered a distinct undertone of emergency in my

friend's voice. Something told me that we were in immediate danger, but I could not determine how. R'luhlloig had only a moment ago assured us that he was not intending to kill us while we were in the embassy. Had he lied?

Holmes made for the door, tugging me along with him. We had almost reached it when a second door opened. This other door connected not to the staircase but to an adjoining room. The butler had used it when bringing in the tea, so I assumed the other room was a kitchen.

This time, however, it was not a liveried servant who came through. Rather it was six men dressed in dark suits and bowler hats. They moved swiftly and with purpose, interposing themselves between the staircase door and us, cutting off our exit.

A half-dozen pairs of slitted eyes gazed balefully out from beneath the bowler brims. A half-dozen forked tongues flickered between scaly lips.

"Snake men," I breathed.

It was a while since I had last seen these creatures, and I found them no less repugnant now than before. Each of them bore a short cudgel. Each raised the weapon with clear menace.

Holmes and I put up a creditable defence, I will say that for us. Further, I will say that Holmes's defence was more creditable than mine, in so far as the snake men took longer to overpower him than they did me. He was still fighting even after I had been brought to the floor by several vicious, stunning blows from those cudgels. However, the snake men not only outnumbered us three to one but were stronger by a similar ratio. They were, moreover, armed, and although Holmes was able to draw my gun from his pocket, which would have evened the odds considerably, he was not given a chance to use it. A snake man wrested it from his grasp. In short, the outcome of the struggle was, alas, never in doubt.

R'luhlloig leaned over us as we lay supine, pinned beneath snake men. "You will be taken hence," said he. "What happens thereafter is out of my hands, but I think we all have a fairly shrewd idea of the fate that lies in store for you. If asked, Baron Von Herling will report that the two of you left by the tradesman's entrance. That at least will be true. What he will omit to mention is that you were carted out in laundry hampers by these fine gentlemen. The afternoon is already on the wane. Soon it will be nightfall, and under cover of darkness no one is liable to spot their squamous skin and unconventional physiognomies."

"You have overlooked one thing," I said.

"What, Doctor? That all you need do is start shouting at the top of your lungs, and countless solicitous civil servants will come bearing down on this room?"

"Well, yes," I said, a little crestfallen.

"But he who is unconscious is incapable of shouting," said R'luhlloig. "Now, I believe the time has come to say goodbye. If I were Baron Von Herling I would not bid you *auf Wiedersehen*, as that would imply we might meet again. Rather I would bid you the altogether more permanent *lebe wohl*, which means 'live well' but in this instance has the contrary connotation."

"You—!"

I got no further with the riposte. A cudgel descended, hard, and there was a bright flash of light, followed by utter blackness.

CHAPTER FOURTEEN

A Sibilant Interlocutor

I CAME TO AS PLEASANTLY AND EASILY AS ANYONE does from violence-induced insensibility, which is to say by slow, painful degrees, beset by sickness, dizziness, headache and a number of other no less undesirable sensations. I became aware of a small, unsteady source of light which, as my blurry vision sharpened, resolved itself into the guttering flame of a candle set into a crude clay bowl. Its feeble nimbus illuminated damp rock walls and the face of Sherlock Holmes.

The latter was sitting propped up against the wall, his forearms on his knees. He looked as groggy as I felt and disgruntled to boot.

"Ah, there you are, old friend. No, I would not advise getting up, not yet. Give yourself time to recover. It is never agreeable to be coshed; the grey matter does not take kindly to such jarring and mounts a vigorous campaign of protest when one awakens. It will pass, but you must allow it to."

I groaned a reply; I am not sure what I said, nor do I think it matters.

"If you are chastising me for being an overconfident fool, go ahead," said Holmes. "You cannot berate me any harder than I am berating myself. I should have been quicker off the mark. I should not have allowed R'luhlloig that last little bit of banter. It was the number of pushes, you see."

I somehow made my lack of comprehension known.

"The number of pushes on the bell button, Watson. Von Herling pressed it twice to summon the butler, but R'luhlloig pressed it three times. That was the signal for the snake men to enter rather than the butler. They were lying in wait in the adjoining room. One can only assume the butler was in on it, instructed to turn a blind eye to the six rather peculiar-looking individuals with whom he was sharing space in the kitchen. Possibly Von Herling told him they were sufferers of an extreme skin complaint, but more probably he simply told him not to be inquisitive. When your nation's ambassador, who is also gentry, enjoins your discretion, it is not your place as a servant to question. But still, I was a fool. A fool!"

Holmes pounded his brow with the heel of his palm. If his head felt anything like mine, this was a particularly self-punitive gesture.

I perceived, now, that we were in a small chamber, the dimensions of which were akin to those of a coal cellar. There was an aperture, roughly rectangular and big enough for a man to pass through without too much inconvenience. It was blocked up on the outside by large stones – boulders that three or four people working in concert might carry. Otherwise the chamber was bare and featureless.

I felt a stab of panic. "We have been walled in. This is a tomb."

"I cannot tell you for certain that it is not," said Holmes. "The courtesy of a candle, however, suggests otherwise. It points to this being confinement of a more temporary nature: a prison cell."

I drew comfort from his words, even if I was not able to shake off altogether the impression that we had been buried alive and were destined to remain here until we suffocated.

"Alas," Holmes added, "unlike a normal prison cell it has a door whose lock only brute strength can pick. I have tried moving the boulders and been thwarted. Together I doubt we would have any more success. We are, for the time being, trapped."

A long period elapsed during which my various discomforts began to abate while Holmes sat sunk deep in thought and probably self-recrimination too. At last I was able to manoeuvre my body into a seated position without my cranium feeling as though it was about to collapse in on itself.

"Do you suppose the snake men mean to hold us captive for long?" I asked.

"Since it would appear that we are marked for execution, who knows? It would depend on how patient or impatient they are. There is a certain pleasure to be derived from deferring gratification."

"For those doing the executing perhaps; not for those waiting to be executed. I imagine you have some plan in mind for getting us out of this."

"We do not have a gun," said Holmes. "My case of phials has been taken from me. I am bereft of tools and weapons."

"We retain our wits and the use of our fists."

"Let us hope they suffice."

"I for one will not go quietly when the time comes. I will resist to my last breath."

"Same old Watson. Spoken like the lionheart you are."

Holmes looked as though he was about to say more, but just then we heard sounds from the other side of the stony barrier that served as a door. One by one the boulders were removed, many hands grappling with them in order to lift them aside.

Once the aperture was cleared, several snake men peered in. They seemed satisfied to learn that Holmes and I still occupied the chamber and were still alive. Then they moved aside to allow another of their kind to enter.

I recognised him immediately, for he had changed little in the fifteen years since we had last been acquainted. Apparently, snake men did not age as ordinary humans did; or else their scaly hides, free from the taint of wrinkles, gave the illusion of agelessness. His black and gold markings, which banded him like a tiger's stripes, were as distinctive as ever.

It was W'gnns, he who had been the leader of Holmes's Irregulars and was, it appeared, in charge of this group of snake men and perhaps, given his dominant character, of the entire colony.

He greeted us in sardonic style: "Well, well, well. Missster Holmesss and Dr Watssson. How the tablesss are turned. Where once I was ssslave to you, now you are my captivesss, mine to dissspossse of asss I sssee fit. I cannot deny it pleasssesss me to sssee you thisss way."

"W'gnns," said Holmes brusquely, "spare us the gloating." He was speaking in R'lyehian, as was his sibilant interlocutor. "You mean to kill us, that is a given. You may even hate us, although I feel I was never less than fair in my dealings with you."

"Fair? Controlling our willsss with a Triophidian Crown isss fair?"

"It was a means to an end, and I shall not apologise for using it. I do not believe, anyway, that you and your fellow Irregulars were wholly unwitting participants in our endeavours. By helping me you helped others, and I would never have been able to force you into it, crown or not, if there were not some inherent altruism in your souls. You wanted to do good then, W'gnns, although you may not have been aware of it at a conscious level, and the same holds true now, I feel sure."

"Doesss it?" said W'gnns. "You ssseem to know more about me than I myssself, Missster Holmesss. Such perssseptivenesss!"

"You must realise that whatever agreement you have reached with R'luhlloig, it is not worthwhile. He is not to be trusted."

"What makesss you think I have reached an agreement?"

"I know R'luhlloig well. He strikes bargains. But he does not do anything that is not to his own benefit. If you and your people have allied yourselves with him, it cannot ever be any covenant of equals. R'luhlloig will want something in exchange, something of greater value than he is giving."

"R'luhlloig hasss asssked no more than that we kill you and Dr Watsssson. After yearsss of trying to achieve that resssult himssself—"

"Trying and failing," Holmes interjected.

"After yearsss of trying and failing," W'gnns

acknowledged, "he hasss commisssioned uss to disscharge the asssignment. We have a vesssted interessst in your deathsss."

"That vested interest being revenge. Revenge for the perceived slight inflicted upon you by my use of a Triophidian Crown."

"It isss that, yesss, but not only. R'luhlloig hasss promisssed usss a greater prize." W'gnns's tongue flickered across his rigid lips in an eager manner. "Chaosss isss coming to your world. Sssoon there will be dessstruction and bloodsssshed of a kind never before witnesssed. In the aftermath, opportunitiesss will arissse for thossse who have aligned themssselvesss with the winning ssside."

"What prize? I can guarantee, whatever it is, R'luhlloig will not honour his commitment to give it to you."

"It isss a prize my people have long craved and well dessserve," said W'gnns, "a prize for which we will gladly perform any tasssk. Now, enough talk. I invite you both to come with me. There isss sssomewhere we have to be. People are waiting. We musssst not disssappoint them."

He beckoned us with one scaly-fingered paw. Holmes and I rose to our feet and exited the chamber. Even though I knew we were being led to the scaffold, as it were, it was a relief not to be cooped up any longer within that cramped, airless space.

Snake men surrounded us, perhaps ten or twelve of them all told. A couple bore torches fashioned from some kind of luminescent moss wrapped around sticks. The light these crude appliances gave off was gloomy but sufficient to see by.

I noticed that one snake man was holding my revolver. W'gnns extended a hand to him and the other passed the gun over without demur.

We began to walk in a slow, straggling procession, Holmes and I in the middle with the snake men divided equally fore and aft of us. At first we travelled along tunnels that were natural in origin, part of a cave system deep beneath London's streets. It was thanks to Holmes that the colony of snake men had access to these subterranean regions at all. He had freed them from the limits of a single cavern below Shadwell and given them the run of the city's lower strata. I considered raising the point as an argument in our favour but reckoned that I would be wasting my breath. I focused instead on looking for opportunities to escape.

Soon, a distant sound of rushing water portended the juncture where the caves gave way to a different, newer habitat. By dint of squeezing through a crevice we entered London's sewer system, that grand project of Sir Joseph Bazalgette's which had rid the city of its notorious "stinks", reduced the frequency of outbreaks of cholera and typhoid almost to zero, and made England's capital an immeasurably pleasanter place to live.

Those brick-lined channels, now some four decades old, were a boon to the snake men too, affording them mile upon mile of additional thoroughfare. For myself, and doubtless for Holmes, it was noisome to wade shin-deep through foul waste water and to encounter at almost every turn hordes of sleek rats scurrying and swimming. For the snake men, by contrast, it was like ambling along a pleasant boulevard. Indeed, I saw one of them stoop, snatch up a rat and pop it into his maw with as much avidity as though he were picking a ripe plum from a tree. He munched on the rodent with relish, even as its tail, which was protruding from his mouth, flapped and coiled in all directions, denoting the creature's death throes. Revulsion is too mild a word for the feeling this sight evoked in me, yet the snake man could not have been happier about his meal or blither about its provenance. It was a reminder – as if I needed one – that here was a race which, although humanoid in some respects, was utterly alien in others.

Our journey brought us eventually to a confluence of numerous sewers. It was a vast arena, cathedral-like in its soaring proportions, based around a pool into which water decanted from several sources and drained off thence via a broad, grille-covered sluice to some further destination I could only guess at. The roar of falling, churning water was all but deafening, and the smell of effluvium, although not as concentrated as in the sewers themselves, remained strong – strong enough that it took effort not to choke. All the same I experienced a strange awe upon arriving in this cavernous tract of underground space, with its many tumbling cataracts. It had a manmade majesty that rivalled any wonder of nature.

Snake men – hundreds of them – were amassed here, silent and expectant like a church congregation. Some more serpentine than others, they clustered in the pool, the depth of which was no greater than a couple of feet. Since 1880 their ranks had swelled considerably, expanding in tandem with the increase in their roaming space. What had once been a village's worth of snake men was now commensurate to the population of a small town and, to judge by the number of very young in attendance, still growing. I spied many a child and even a few babes in arms.

Holmes and I were escorted through the crowd, who snarled insults at us, and then were steered up onto a brick structure which rose just proud of the pool's surface, near its middle. Plinth or platform or I don't know what, it lay directly below a grating down through which shone a shaft of moonlight. Into this lambent beam, like some intangible pillar, stepped Holmes and I, along with our contingent of ushers, including W'gnns with my gun.

Positioned above the crowd of snake men, and illuminated, I felt exposed and vulnerable. We were on display, and I could not help but think of French aristocrats standing in tumbrils in the Place de la Révolution, awaiting their appointment with Madame Guillotine, the mob baying for their blood. Snakelike eyes glittered, and the hissed invective grew louder.

"People," said W'gnns, his voice bringing a hush. He was, as I had surmised, now ruler of the colony. "My people. It hasss been a long, hard road for usss. Thirty yearsss ago we lossst our god. Mighty Nyarlathotep, the Crawling Chaosss, whom we had worssshipped and sssacrificed to ssso asssiduousssly, wasss taken from usss."

There were mutterings of sorrow and resentment, even from those too young to have been alive when Nyarlathotep was the object of the snake men's devotions.

"He wasss taken from usss through the actions of Professsor Moriarty and of thisss man, Sssherlock Holmesss."

The assembled snake men echoed Holmes's name hissingly.

"We lossst Nyarlathotep'sss favour, and it ssseemed that our livesss were empty and had meaning no more. Then Sssherlock Holmesss returned, bringing what sssome of ussss consssidered new purpossse. I admit, I wasss one of them. I fell for hisss liesss. I thought that by doing hisss bidding I might find a sssort of redemption. It transsspired, however, that Sssherlock Holmesss wanted only what he could get from usss. He had no ressspect for usss. He exploited usss. We were hisss 'Irregularsss'." W'gnns spoke the word with contempt. "To add insssult to injury, he employed a Triophidian Crown in order to ensssure he got hisss way. We might perhapsss have ssserved him voluntarily, had he asssked, but he did not give usss that choissse. Insssstead, he took by forssse what might have been freely offered."

The hissing of Holmes's name became both more insistent and more spiteful in tone. W'gnns was setting Holmes up as the villain of the piece, a scapegoat for the snake men's general discontent. It was classic demagoguery, delivered with the fervour of a revivalist preacher, and I found myself feeling, in spite of everything, a grudging admiration. W'gnns had come far. Since staging what was effectively a coup against Holmes some fifteen years ago – taking advantage of my inexperience with the Triophidian Crown – he must have worked hard cultivating the celebrity which that act of rebellion earned him and parlaying it into political capital. The revolutionary firebrand had become, as revolutionary firebrands are wont to, emperor.

"Now," he continued, "we have him at lassst at our mersssy, captive and humbled. It isss a great moment. He will pay the price for the abussse he heaped upon usss. He and hisss crony Watssson are oursss for the ssslaying – and the consssuming."

It should perhaps have surprised me that the snake men intended to eat us, but somehow it did not. I had already begun to suspect that this was going to be no mere execution. I knew the snake men had cannibalistic tendencies. In the past they would feed upon their own kind when other food sources ran short. Why not upon humans too?

"They will nourisssh usss," said W'gnns. "Everyone will get hisss ssshare. It isss no more than they dessserve, and no more than we dessserve either."

Those hundreds of pairs of reptilian eyes were fixed upon Holmes and me with a greed that was more spiritual than physical.

"Ressstitution," said W'gnns. "Ressstoration. Redemption. And it beginsss today, here, now."

He approached me, levelling the revolver with my head.

I tensed. I would have the gun off him if I could. I would grapple with him for it, I would seize it from him, and I would blast him to oblivion and as many other snake men as I was able. They would overwhelm me eventually, of course. They had the far superior numbers, and I only six rounds. My life was forfeit come what may, but I would sell it dearly, and I had no doubt that Holmes was of the same mind. We would show the snake men how red-blooded Englishmen lived and died.

Then Holmes said, with a remarkable calmness: "A moment, W'gnns, if I may."

W'gnns kept the gun trained on me and did not turn his head. "Yesss?"

"Might I be permitted to say something?"

"No," came the blunt reply.

"It is traditional that the condemned man be allowed a final word."

"Traditional maybe for your people. Not for usss."

"What harm can it do? There are gaps in my understanding that I would care to have filled. I would rather not go to my death with my curiosity unassuaged. You know me. I hate unanswered questions."

"Why ssshould I indulge you?"

"A good leader gives everyone a fair hearing, even his enemies. Often his enemies only damn themselves further by talking."

W'gnns considered this argument. A few of the snake men spoke up in support of Holmes. *Let him offer some mewling defence of his actions*, that was the gist of it. *Give him enough rope so that he can hang himself*. Others shouted them down. They did not want to postpone the death sentence any longer.

After further deliberation, W'gnns nodded. "Very well. Your requessst isss granted, Missster Holmesss. Do not go on too long, though. If I sssenssse that you are sssimply prevaricating, Dr Watsssson diesss inssstantly. I will give no warning. I will jussst ssshoot."

I looked to Holmes. I trusted he knew what he was

doing. Was he playing for time? Did he have some cunning trick up his sleeve for getting us out of this mess? I prayed to God he did. Yet there was a part of me that rather hoped W'gnns might shoot me. It would be a better death than being eaten alive.

"I merely wish to point out," Holmes said, "that R'luhlloig − the same R'luhlloig with whom you have thrown in your lot − was responsible for depriving you of Nyarlathotep. That was none of my doing. Moriarty usurped Nyarlathotep's godly form in order to become R'luhlloig. You have the Hidden Mind to thank for the disappearance of the Crawling Chaos from your lives, not me."

"Do you think we do not know that?" There was a crowing note in W'gnns's voice. "Missster Holmesss, we are perfectly well aware who R'luhlloig isss and how he came by hisss power. He wasss quite candid about it."

"And still you accepted his offer? From the god who destroyed your god? Is that not hypocritical?"

"On the contrary. It is sssensssible. Who isss the greater, a god or the god who defeatsss that god? Who isss more worthy of worsssship?"

"I see," said Holmes. "Nyarlathotep is dead, long live R'luhlloig. Interesting. You must think that a bold step to have taken."

"Bold but pragmatic."

"To me, it smacks of cravenness. You used to cower before Nyarlathotep. Now you cower before a god who strikes even greater awe in you. You eschewed independence in favour of another thraldom, and a worse one."

"Missster Holmesss…" W'gnns said warningly.

I was all the more acutely aware of the presence of the revolver by my head. I could see W'gnns's forefinger tightening on the trigger. I did not think my reflexes were fast enough to allow me to grab the gun from him now, before he could apply the last ounce of pressure. That flimsy shred of hope was gone and all that remained was Sherlock Holmes.

CHAPTER FIFTEEN

Ssswitsssserland

HOLMES PERSEVERED WITH EXERCISING HIS CON-
demned man's privilege.

"You mentioned a prize earlier," said he. "Would you
do me the honour of telling me what it is?"

"A country," said W'gnns. "A nation to call our own.
No more ssshall we sssnake men ssskulk underground.
After the war isss over and mankind desssimated,
R'luhlloig will bessstow upon usss a provinssse for our
exxxclusssive usss. There we may wander free and do
asss we wisssh. It isss a place you may have heard of. It isss
called Ssswitsssserland."

"Switzerland. That is your promised land."

"R'luhlloig sssaysss it hasss mountainsss and
ssstreamsss and lakesss and foressstsss and wild game
aplenty for usss to hunt and eat. All sssnake men from
around the world, our brothersss and sssisssstersss, will
migrate thither, and we ssshall live asss one and know
everlasssting peassse and prossssperity."

"It sounds like heaven on earth," Holmes observed
wryly. "A land of milk and honey, or at any rate alpenhorns
and cuckoo clocks." He used English for both *alpenhorns*
and *cuckoo clocks*, neither term having an analogue in
R'lyehian that was precise enough.

The witticism was lost on W'gnns anyway, who lacked
an appreciable sense of humour. "It isss heaven indeed,"
he said with nary a trace of scepticism, and his fellow
snake men murmured in assent. "R'luhlloig sssaysss he

hasss ssset assside a particular region of Ssswitssserland which he thinksss will bessst sssuit me and my tribe. He sssaysss it hasss sssignificansss for him and for you: the Reichenbach Fallsss."

I almost laughed. The premise that Sherlock Holmes and Professor Moriarty had engaged in a life-and-death battle atop the Reichenbach Falls was a fictitious one, invented entirely by me. It was an ironic choice of resettlement place for W'gnns and these other snake men. I imagined R'luhlloig had selected it purely as a jibe against his archenemy. Where Moriarty had met his end in my chronicles, there would Earth's complement of snake men find a new beginning.

"Well, I have visited the spot," said Holmes, "and it certainly is a dramatic cascade. Not a patch on this fine venue, but there are certain similarities."

"It isss going to be our home," W'gnns said, "and we ssshall basssk in the sssunssshine and sssport in the open air asss once our people did, countlesss generationsss ago, before the rissse of man. We have even ssseeen picturesss. Missster Von Bork ssshowed them to usss."

"Von Bork? Of course. He was one of you."

"Wasss, yesss. He wasss a friend to usss – a good friend."

"Would I be right in thinking that he acted as intermediary between you and R'luhlloig?"

"He approached usss on R'luhlloig'sss behalf."

"No human representative would have been able to gain your trust, but Von Bork had the serpentine blood in him. The ideal candidate for the job."

"He wasss our kin, and ssso we lissstened to him. And now," W'gnns added sourly, "Missster Von Bork isss dead."

"I did not kill him, if that is the implication behind your acrimonious tone. R'luhlloig may have told you I did, but Von Bork's death was solely R'luhlloig's doing."

"He would not have died if you had not activated the ssspell R'luhlloig placed upon him. You are the guilty one, Missster Holmesss. Do not ssshirk the blame. It isss yet another crime to add to the lissst of your crimesss."

Holmes gave an exaggerated shrug of the shoulders. "Oh well. One might as well be hanged for a sheep as for a lamb."

The saying did not translate into R'lyehian intelligibly. W'gnns looked perplexed and, in his perplexity, irritated. I feared the bullet would be entering my brain sooner rather than later.

"So," said Holmes, "if I have it right, killing Watson and me is your ticket to a future of ease and contentment in the paradise that is Switzerland. It is also recompense for all the offences I have committed against your people. That is the long and the short of it, yes?"

"Yesss."

"I am glad we have cleared that up. I can go to my grave with my mind at rest. Thank you, W'gnns."

"You are welcome," W'gnns said with more than a soupçon of sarcasm. "Now, by your leave, Missster Holmesss, may we commensssse the punisssshment?"

Holmes cast his gaze up high, as though beseeching divine intercession. Lowering his eyes again, he nodded to

W'gnns. "That would be fine. There has been enough of a delay. Why not get on with it?"

It took me a moment to realise Holmes had spoken these sentences not in R'lyehian, but in English. I could not fathom why he had switched languages. It occurred to me that, if he had all along been trying to cajole W'gnns into seeing reason, he had now decided it was futile and had abandoned the attempt. He was capitulating to the inevitable.

My heart sank. If Holmes was giving up, then truly we were done for. Our remaining lifespans could be measured in minutes, if not seconds.

"I hope I taste bitter," I called out defiantly to the throng of snake men. "I hope I poison you."

"Dr Watsssssss…"

The word seemed to slow, becoming one continuous hiss before petering out. W'gnns had gone stiff. He was trembling from head to toe, every muscle in his body rigid. He appeared to be suffering some kind of seizure. My revolver was still pointed at me but his finger was frozen on the trigger, mid-squeeze. W'gnns should have fired. I should have been dead. Instead, it was as though time were suspended; a moment had become an eternity.

Nor was it just W'gnns who was locked in immobility. The eager, agitated crowd had become like waxworks, albeit betraying signs of the minutest movement here and there: a pair of eyes twitching, a hand quivering.

"Don't just stand there, Watson," said Holmes. "Run!"

I did not need to be told twice. Whatever inexplicable

hysterical fit had come over the snake men, it was a blessing for Holmes and me.

I reached out to retrieve my gun from W'gnns's clutches, but the snake man's hand held it fast. Try as I might, I could not pry it loose from his fingers.

Then Holmes grabbed me by the sleeve and pulled me along after him. I felt a stab of remorse that I might never see my Webley again, but knew that whatever sentimental associations the weapon held for me, survival was the more pressing concern. I could always buy a new pistol.

We leapt off the platform and dashed through the static crowd. With the water up to our thighs, our progress was not as fast as I would have liked. I expected the snake men to shake off their strange lethargy at any moment, and knew they would have no hesitation about waylaying us and tearing us to pieces. As long as we were surrounded we were in mortal peril.

But even when we were clear of the crowd we were not safe. We had to put distance between us and our captors, and that was difficult at the lumbering rate we were going. It was like a nightmare: danger behind but one's flight impeded. Effortfully though we waded through the water, we could manage little better than walking pace.

Then a voice called down to us: "There's a ladder. Hurry! I am not sure how much longer I can keep this up."

Holmes had already been guiding us in the direction from which the voice came. I now perceived that there was a man poised at the mouth of one of the sewer outfalls, some thirty feet above our heads. He was leaning out, gesticulating wildly. I also perceived that, as this fellow had said, there was a ladder leading up to his perch – a series of iron rungs set into the wall adjacent to the torrent of water spewed by the sewer. It was not much but I viewed it as a shipwrecked mariner might a palm-fringed desert island.

Holmes thrust me towards the ladder and I started to climb. I ought not to have glanced back over my shoulder but I did, only to see the snake men stirring, gradually regaining the use of their bodies. My climbing took on a renewed vigour.

The rungs were devilishly slippery and pitted with corrosion. My shoes were sodden. Maintaining my grip on that ladder was no mean feat. To make matters worse, spray from the falling water was half blinding me. Finding the next handhold or foothold was a question of groping more than anything; securing each, a question of sheer determination.

I was aware of Holmes below me, ascending too, but my main focus was on getting to the ladder's summit. I had no fear of heights but I did have a very reasonable fear of slipping and falling. The plummet into the pool might not kill me but it would leave me sufficiently dazed and winded, possibly injured, for the snake men to finish me off easily.

Somehow, suddenly, I was at the top of the ladder. The outfall was within arm's reach, and the man standing there was extending a hand to me.

"Grab hold, Doctor. I shall help you across."

This he did, and the next thing I knew I was down on my hands and knees in the sewer's rush of water, panting hard, trying to catch my breath.

"Now you, Mr Holmes," I heard the man say.

Holmes clambered into the sewer tunnel beside me. He patted me on the back. "No time for rest, old friend. Up on your feet, there's a good fellow."

I staggered upright. I turned towards him who had come to our rescue. I knew the voice and could not contain a grin of delight as I beheld the contours of a familiar, friendly face.

"Inspector Gregson!" I cried.

CHAPTER SIXTEEN

Gregson (No Longer) of the Yard

"JUST PLAIN TOBIAS GREGSON, DOCTOR," SAID HE. "I have not been a policeman for five years now. And Mr Holmes is correct. There's no time for rest."

Gregson was as tall as ever, if a trifle stooped by age, but somewhat plumper than he used to be. Retirement obviously sat well with him.

The most signal aspect of his physical appearance, however, was the object perched upon his head. I had not seen this particular one before but I had seen its like. The design of three intertwined serpents unmistakably betokened a Triophidian Crown. Tiny veins of weird green luminosity chased along its metallic surfaces, like the embers of a dying fire.

"That's..." I began, gesturing at the diadem.

"Explanations later, Watson," said Holmes. "Gregson has bought us our freedom but I fear he has lost control of the snake men."

"Using the crown is demanding," Gregson admitted. "I had no idea. Exercising one's will over so many..."

Holmes glanced out over the ladder. "Yes. They are coming up after us. Gregson, you have a dark-lantern there. Pass it to me. I shall lead the way."

The lantern was lit but its shutters were closed, presumably so as not to have announced Gregson's presence to the snake men. Holmes opened them and aimed the cone of light ahead. Curved brick wall stretched as far as the lantern's beam revealed. He set off at a fast lick, and Gregson and I followed.

"Holmes," I said as we splashed along the tunnel, "why not put on the crown yourself? You are adept in its use. You would surely be able to forestall the snake men with it."

"In such numbers? Impossible. Not for any duration. It is a miracle Gregson managed it at all, and I would not fare much better. Fleeing is our only option. We cannot hinder the snake men, but we can, God willing, outrun them."

I was not convinced this last assertion was valid, for the snake men were already in the tunnel. I could hear their footfalls behind us and their rasping yelps of excitement, both of which seemed to be getting louder. We were in an environment that these creatures not only found congenial but were familiar with. They were, moreover, better suited than we to the conditions. I had observed earlier, while Holmes and I were being escorted to our place of execution, how surefooted the snake men were in the wet. Several times I had slithered on something soft and yielding beneath my sole, algae or some more noxious substance. I had never quite lost my balance but had come close, whereas the snake men had trodden as confidently as mountain goats. They had the home advantage, and our top speed along those slimy, sewage-clogged tunnels could never exceed theirs.

"Gregson," said Holmes, "you will have entered the sewers through some manhole or other access point. Which way to it?"

"A manhole, yes, Mr Holmes, but where it now lies relative to our position, I cannot honestly say." Gregson had doffed the crown and was carrying it under one arm. "It is a labyrinth down here. I wish I had had the foresight to bring a piece of chalk with which to mark the turns I took. I tried scoring notches in the brickwork with my penknife but could not cut deep enough to leave a tangible result."

"How did you even find us?" I asked.

"Oh, as for that, I obeyed Mr Holmes's instructions in his wire."

Gregson, it seemed, was the recipient of the telegram sent from Chelsea.

"I told Gregson to use the Triophidian Crown to home in on any unusual snake-man activity," Holmes said.

"You knew R'luhlloig would hand us over to them?"

"Not 'knew'. It seemed feasible. Where there is one snake man – to wit, Von Bork – there are liable to be more. Alerting Gregson was a prudent contingency, and happily for us this insurance policy has reaped dividends."

"The crown acts somewhat like a wireless telegraph," Gregson said. "It can be attuned to the snake men's 'wavelength'. When it picked up the thoughts of various snake men eagerly anticipating the arrival of Sherlock Holmes in their midst – a fabled figure in their folklore – I was able to follow those thoughts to their source, as though following a beacon. It led me to where they were convened. Mr Holmes kept them distracted long enough for me to implement the crown's power of mastery, and the rest you know."

"But where on earth did you come by that crown?" I said. "W'gnns took ours, and other crowns are vanishingly rare."

"Save your breath for running, Watson," Holmes chided. "There will be opportunity afterwards to discuss the whys and wherefores."

Truth to tell, I was finding it a challenge to talk and flee at the same time, and so too was Gregson, who had not so much spoken his replies as gasped them. Holmes was right. Satisfying my curiosity should be deferred until later, and there would be no "later" if we did not devote all our energies to outrunning the snake men.

With each turn we made at a junction, I trusted that the lantern would illuminate the base of some vertical shaft leading up to the surface or else that I would feel a waft of fresher air indicating the proximity of a pumping station. Instead we were confronted simply with yet more tunnel. The sewers were indeed a labyrinth, and we seemed to be penetrating ever deeper into them rather than nearing an egress. We may even have been going in circles, unwittingly retracing our steps. It was almost impossible to be sure, one sewer tunnel looking much like another.

What was undeniable was that the snake men were gaining on us. Not only that but there was more than one group of them in pursuit. They had divided their forces. Many of our diversions down perpendicular tunnels were made in order to avoid snake men intercepting us from the front, course alterations arising from necessity rather than choice, for we could hear them ahead of us as well as behind. We were desperate foxes with no lairs to run to, and the hounds were closing in.

Then we arrived at a hole in the wall, which stood at waist height and was large enough to admit a person. It looked to be the handiwork of the snake men. Bricks had been pried loose and set aside to create the entrance, and the earth beyond had been burrowed into.

"Hear that?" said Holmes, halting.

All I could hear was our relentless, ever-encroaching pursuers, but Holmes, with an ear cocked to the hole, evidently detected some other noise emanating from within that excited his attention.

"The sough of a breeze," said he. "Gregson. Quick. A match, so that we may see whether it blows towards or away from us."

The lit flame, as Holmes held it up before the entrance, bent away from the hole.

"Excellent. The airflow is the result of the difference in barometric pressure below ground and above. The air down here is cooler than the air outside, therefore its pressure is lower and the flow is inward. This is our way out."

So saying, he dived headlong into the hole. Gregson looked surprised when I baulked at following him.

"If Mr Holmes says that's the way out, that's the way out."

His faith in our companion was implicit and touchingly sincere. I, who had been in many more scrapes with Holmes than he, could be forgiven for being somewhat more circumspect. Often his solutions to crises were nearly as bad as the crises themselves.

"Oh, very well." I scrambled into the hole, and Gregson brought up the rear.

At first we could walk along the tunnel, albeit at a

crouch. Within a dozen yards, however, we were obliged to go on hands and knees. All I could see ahead was the silhouette of Holmes delineated by the swinging beam of the lantern. Stony earth dug into my elbows and kneecaps.

A cry in R'lyehian from behind told us that the snake men had discovered our route of abscondment. Seconds later they were slithering along the narrow passage too. This lent greater urgency to our movements. We went as fast as it is possible for a man to travel while on all fours. Gregson's stertorous breathing matched my own. The tunnel seemed endless, and there was no doubt in my mind that the snake men would overtake us soon.

All at once Holmes was no longer before me. There was a rough circle filled with the darting light of the lantern. An exit!

I more or less fell through it headfirst, landing in ungainly fashion on a strip of rocky ground beside a broad, fast-flowing channel of water. Gregson tumbled out on top of me. He was full of contrition as we both rose to our feet.

"I hope I didn't hurt you, Doctor."

"If I broke your fall, then the discomfort will have been worth it."

The erstwhile policeman chuckled. "You know, Dr Watson, you are truly a—"

A shot rang out. Gregson clamped a hand to his shoulder, face contorting in agony.

The bullet had come from within the tunnel. W'gnns must be leading the pack of snake men.

I caught Gregson as he sagged against me. I ushered

him away from the hole, out of W'gnns's line of fire. Blood was pouring out between his fingers. There was no time for me to assess the wound. Instinct told me it was not life-threatening, but I could not be sure. The round may have nicked the axillary artery, but if so the blood would have been bright red. This blood was, as best I could tell in the dimness, darker in hue, meaning it was venous and slower flowing; thus Gregson would be less likely to suffer fatal exsanguination.

I turned to Holmes. "The snake men will be here any moment. Where do we go from here?"

"There." Holmes indicated the turbid water. "It is one of London's so-called 'lost rivers' − the Fleet, if I do not miss my guess. Bazalgette's sewers often parallel their courses and sometimes incorporate them into the network. Being tributaries of the Thames, they all lead inexorably to that river. We simply need to swim."

"Gregson cannot swim. His arm…"

"We shall support him between us and keep him afloat. Come on. Into the water."

"No," Gregson said in a hoarse croak.

"What do you mean, 'no'?" I said.

"I refuse to be dead weight. If, because of me, you two should fail to escape… Unconscionable."

He pushed himself out of my grasp. He was wan-complexioned, in shock from the bullet wound. I had no idea how he was capable of talking, let alone remaining upright.

"Mr Holmes, Dr Watson, it has been an honour serving alongside you, in whatever minor capacity." He gave a passably policeman-like salute with his good arm. "You must live to fight another day, and it is my duty, as a one-time upholder of the law, to grant you that opportunity."

"Gregson…" I said pathetically, but I could see his mind was made up and he was not to be dissuaded.

"I am a widower," he added. "It is high time the late Mrs Gregson and I were reunited."

He about-faced and presented himself before the hole. I thought he might try to use the Triophidian Crown again. Even if it bought us just a few moments' grace, that might be enough. Then I realised that he no longer had the crown. I could only assume he had dropped it while we were running or else had discarded it in the tunnel because carrying it was an impediment to his progress.

"All right, you horrors," he said. Judging by the line of his gaze and the relative softness of his voice, the foremost of the snake men, W'gnns, was directly in front of him. "Let's be having you."

W'gnns shot him twice, in the torso, at point-blank range. Somehow Gregson did not fall. Instead he leaned into the hole and tussled with W'gnns. I do not know how he found the wherewithal to fight on with three bullets lodged in him. I do know that Holmes and I owe our lives to his courage and tenacity. I cannot state it any more plainly than that. Were it not for Tobias Gregson I would not be alive to write this and, more importantly, Sherlock Holmes would not have gone on to perform the considerable feats he shortly did.

"Watson." Holmes's face was fraught with remorse. "The river. Now!"

He did not so much invite me to dive in as manhandle

me to the water's edge and give me a shove.

Into that black, sweeping flow I plunged. I rose, spluttering, to the surface. Holmes had leapt in straight after me. Together we were borne along towards a destination I could only hope promised sanctuary.

CHAPTER SEVENTEEN

That Most Tempestuous and Unyielding Force of Nature

WE WERE IN THE SUBTERRANEAN RACE OF THE Fleet for some ten minutes, I estimate. It may have been less. It felt a great deal longer.

The water was frigid. My limbs grew rapidly numb and my breath began to come in short gasps. It was all I could do just to keep my head above the surface. I was treading water; the current was supplying the locomotion.

Every now and again some unseen projecting rock snagged my leg or buffeted my arm. Gregson's dark-lantern was long gone. There was only unending blackness all around, and the disorientating roil and swirl of the river, and the bitter cold. There was also an eerie hush. The water ran smoothly along the channel. Holmes and I made more noise thrashing our arms than did the river flowing. The turbulence we created and the lap of water were the sole aural accompaniments to our journey, save for a short, truncated scream, which echoed from far upstream, signifying the last of Gregson.

I began to perceive the dimmest of illumination, more a lessening of the dark than a brightening. Soon the rugged arch of the ceiling of the channel was discernible. We could only be heading for the conjunction of the Fleet with the Thames.

Sure enough, we were disgorged via an outlet into the body of the greater river, which felt warmer by a small margin. Close by, the fretted span of Blackfriars Bridge loomed against an overcast night sky.

At Holmes's exhortation I struck out for the bank. The Thames's current was less insistent than that of the Fleet but I was tired and I was swimming abeam to it instead of letting it carry me. Somehow I gained the shallows, and thereafter I crawled through the mud of the riverbed and the foreshore – more of an ungainly wallow than a crawl, in point of fact – until I arrived at one of the flights of stone steps that afforded access to the top of the embankment. I made it up a half-dozen steps, whereupon exhaustion overcame me and I paused to rest. So taxed was I by my exertions that I could quite happily have laid down my head and slept, for all the world as though I were lying upon a downy mattress.

"Watson, if you don't mind," said Holmes. "Some of us need to use these steps too, and there is no room to pass around you. More to the point, we are not alone."

A gunshot gave emphasis to his words. The round ricocheted off the embankment just inches from my face, gouging a chip out of the granite.

W'gnns was toiling through the muddy shallows. His expression spoke of implacable resolve. Alone of all the snake men he had leapt into the Fleet after us. Throughout his pursuit he must have succeeded in holding my revolver clear of the water so that the cartridges – of which now only two were left in the cylinder – stayed dry.

For all the immediate danger he presented, I could not help but feel a sneaking admiration. W'gnns was, if nothing else, someone who saw a job through to the end.

"Missster Holmesss, Dr Watsssson," he said, wading onto the foreshore, gun raised. No expert with a sidearm, he was moving to where he would be guaranteed not to miss. "You do not find me asss easssy to essscape asss all that. You *ssshall* die, jussst as your ally hasss. Two bulletsss remain, one apiessse for each of you. R'luhlloig hasss willed it, and ssso ssshall it be."

In that instant, something in me snapped. I had had as much as I could take. The very sound of W'gnns's wheedling voice made me sick. This upstart former Irregular had no right to kill us and he certainly had no right to do it with my revolver.

I launched myself bodily off the steps, catching him in a flying tackle. We crashed together into the mud. I was on top, and the impact of our collision had knocked the wind out of W'gnns. The advantage was mine and I belaboured him with my fists, planting blow after blow in quick succession upon that lipless, black-and-gold face. I was buoyed up by pure loathing. That was the wellspring of this surge of antagonism and newfound strength, and it served me admirably. In hindsight, I can see that W'gnns did not stand a chance. He had fallen foul of that most tempestuous and unyielding force of nature, the Englishman who has been pushed past breaking point and has nothing to lose. Against this, he simply could not win.

He may at some stage have begged for mercy. If so, I did not hear above the roar of my own blood in my ears. I pummelled him until freshets of his blood were gushing from his nostrils and he could barely move his mouth in protestation. I was still pummelling him when Holmes caught my wrists and advised me to give it up.

"He is out cold, Watson. Any more and that situation may be permanent."

"So what?" I panted. "It is just deserts."

"You are not a monster."

"He is."

"He is misguided. He is a cat's-paw. I believe you have taught him a lesson. It is fair that we give him the chance to mend his ways."

With Holmes's aid I tottered to my feet. My knuckles throbbed. My lungs heaved. My fit of passion, as abruptly as it had waxed, waned. I snatched my revolver from W'gnns's limp hand. The temptation to shoot him was there, but faint, a mere scintilla of emotion. Now that my temper was no longer up, I could not have done it, not like that, not in cold blood. I pocketed the gun.

"You get to live, W'gnns," I spat at him. "You have done nothing to earn such a reprieve but I am giving it to you anyway."

We left him lying there in the mud, broken and senseless. We neither saw nor heard from him again, or any others of his tribe.

*

Holmes and I trudged towards Marylebone in silence. All I could think of was getting home, stripping off my soiled garments and succumbing to the blissful embrace of a piping-hot bath. Holmes was doubtless keen for a similar such outcome.

Alas, it was not to be. As we turned onto my street, Holmes uttered a curse and dragged me back round the corner.

"What the devil is the matter?" I declared.

"Hssst! Keep your voice down! Did you not see?"

"See what?"

"The two men loitering across the road from your house."

I peeked round the angle of the corner and spied the two in question. They were sharing a cigarette beside a lamppost, conspicuous in the incandescent glare of its arc light. They were broad-shouldered and straight-backed and immediately put me in mind of the two mufti men Holmes had bested at the German embassy. They might as well have been members of the same family, so akin were they; brothers produced from the same mould, although in this case the mould was the military.

"Let us take the ruffians," I said. "Let us knock the stuffing out of them. Let us send them limping back to R'luhlloig to tell him that Sherlock Holmes and John Watson are alive and well and not to be trifled with."

"Or," counselled Holmes, "let us leave them to their vigil and make for Victoria station without giving them cause to think anything is awry."

"Why ever should we do that?"

"Think, Watson, think. At present R'luhlloig has no reason not to believe that the snake men have succeeded and we are dead."

"I reckon W'gnns, once he regains consciousness, will disabuse him of that misapprehension quickly enough. Him or another of the snake men."

"Be that as it may, R'luhlloig already has a suspicion that the snake men may fail in their task. Hence these two fine fellows keeping watch in anticipation of our taking refuge at your house. What he will not be expecting is that we go to ground not here but down in Sussex. There, at my farm, we may lick our wounds and gather our strength over a longer period than if we were to remain in London. It may only be a matter of a day, it may only be a few extra hours, but it is much-needed respite all the same. R'luhlloig will have spies and informants seeded throughout the capital. If we stay here, he will be able to locate us and marshal his forces against us that much more readily than if we use my farm as a bolthole. He doubtless knows the whereabouts of that too – and, if not, he will be able to ascertain it easily enough – but in the meantime we will be somewhere both less accessible and more defensible. What do you say?"

"I say your logic is sound," I admitted.

*

And so we wended our weary way to Victoria, in time to catch the last Eastbourne-bound train. Such was our besmirched appearance and the disagreeable odour our clothes gave off that we had the compartment to ourselves the entire way, although the guard nearly threw us off at Clapham Junction, mistaking us for vagabonds. Holmes suavely persuaded him that we had had the misfortune to have been roughed up by a gang of East End toughs, and this excuse and the donation of a couple of shillings – "for your trouble" – secured us a continued berth aboard the train.

"Why did you not tell me about Gregson?" I said as

we rumbled from the lights of the city to the dark of the countryside. "I thought we were doomed. You could at least have warned me he might be coming to the rescue."

"'Might', Watson," said Holmes. "That is the operative word. I could not have known for certain that friend Gregson would be able to master the Triophidian Crown, or even that he would be able to find us. I did not want to tease you with a prospect that might prove false."

I nodded, understanding if not quite forgiving. "Poor Gregson. His heroism will go forever unlauded, at least amongst the public at large."

"He was a modest soul. I should not think it will bother him."

"Speaking of that crown, where did he come by it?"

"Me," said Holmes. "I fashioned it myself, much as Moriarty did his own crown all those years ago. One never knows when one might have call for such an artefact, and I gave it to Gregson for safekeeping when I moved out of London, against the very sort of eventuality we met tonight."

"That shows some forethought."

"I like to believe I have some talent when it comes to making provision," said my friend. "And on that front we cannot afford to be idle, you and I. R'luhlloig is openly inveighing against us. Once he discovers we are alive, his next assault will surely not be long in coming. We must gird ourselves to meet it."

CHAPTER EIGHTEEN

Keeping Beelzebub at Bay

AS IT HAPPENED, HOLMES'S PREDICTION PROVED somewhat wide of the mark. What came after the alarms and excursions of our sojourn in London was a hiatus, a temporary armistice that stretched on for days. If R'luhlloig had some follow-up plan in mind, he seemed in no hurry to implement it. With every morning that dawned I wondered if today would be the day he made his move, and with every sunset I wondered if my night's sleep would be interrupted by some hostile incursion onto Holmes's property. I was on tenterhooks, as jittery as a whippet.

As time went by, however, my tension began to abate. I did not lower my guard completely, but one can brace oneself in anticipation of a blow for only so long. After a while a state of constant alertness becomes wearisome, and even in a strange way boring. I did not think for one moment that the Hidden Mind was going to leave us alone. After having gone to great lengths to ensnare and destroy us so many times, and on this latest occasion so openly and audaciously, R'luhlloig was not likely to give up just because he had failed yet again. His next attempt would, if anything, be an even more concerted effort, I was sure. I feared an offensive of such overwhelming, vindictive magnitude that we did not have a hope of withstanding it.

But it did not come, and it did not come, and still it did not come.

Holmes's and my lives settled into something of a routine. My friend would spend much of each day pent up in his study, working on various defensive stratagems and countermeasures. At the old acid-charred bench from 221B Baker Street he would sit, concocting potions and powders; or else he would pore over his extensive library of occult literature, making notes, paying particular attention to the pages of the *Necronomicon*. Sometimes I would hear him pacing about downstairs after I had gone to bed, for the study lay below the spare room. I would even, on occasion, hear him murmuring to himself. I presumed this was a habit he had got into after living alone for several years. I was prone to it myself.

His voice was muffled as it came up through the floorboards, so I could distinguish practically nothing he said in these monologues. One word, though, was audible and cropped up with some frequency: Cthulhu. I did not know why Holmes kept mentioning the name of the mightiest and most terrible of all the Old Ones, and I would have preferred it if he had not, since it evoked memories of the expedition I undertook into the lost city of Ta'aa back in Afghanistan, an episode I had tried my level best to forget during the intervening three decades but never could. The sight of that huge black marble monument to Cthulhu in the temple at Ta'aa was etched indelibly in my memory. The hulking torso, the brooding octopoid face and the bat wings that adorned the idol's back still haunted my dreams. If a mere carven effigy could awe and terrify to such a degree, I did not want to imagine what it might be like to meet Cthulhu in the flesh. It would surely be an encounter no one's sanity could survive.

When Holmes was not busy in his study he might while an hour or two on his violin. He had kept up his practice with the instrument and was still able to draw a tune from it with the customary grace and dexterity, if perhaps without much feeling, for he was always more of a technical performer than an interpreter of mood. For some reason the melodies, even the jauntier ones, seemed plaintive for being played in that remote, somewhat desolate coastal setting. It was as though, with so much emptiness around and no near neighbours, the music could not help but sound lonely.

To occupy myself – and burn off nervous energy – I took to going for long walks. There is no denying that Holmes had chosen a spectacularly beautiful corner of the world to live in, and I made the most of it, rambling along clifftop and over downland, relishing Mother Nature in all her finery. The sun shone but there was a chill to its warmth, and a faint haziness hung in the air which, at night, would more often than not thicken into mist. I enjoyed the many vistas the landscape afforded, from sweeps of close-cropped pasture to whispering copses of russet-tinged oak and sycamore to the heave and shimmer of the Channel. Yet I remained wary wherever I went, my revolver always to hand. I did not know when or where R'luhlloig's agents might spring their ambush. It could happen at any time, in any place.

One of my walks found me wandering through Crowlink – a farming hamlet in a shallow valley – and thence following a steep chalk track through herds of solemnly grazing sheep up to a crossroads. Here, at the brow of a hill, lay a duck pond and the small, flint-walled parish church which served the village of East Dean. I passed an idle hour ambling around the churchyard, examining the headstones. Many of them marked the final resting places of humble fisher-folk, while others charted generations of nobler families who had been buried close together in cordoned-off enclaves, set apart from the common masses even in death.

I was just about to leave by the lychgate when I bumped into the vicar. We engaged in amiable conversation about innocuous subjects such as the weather and the upcoming harvest festival, until the fellow, his expression turning serious, said, "If you'll forgive the impertinence, sir, you seem to have a lot on your mind. Is there anything you might like to talk about?"

"Do I give that impression?"

"You smile but it has a certain drawn quality, and there is a sombreness that never leaves your eyes. If I have spoken out of turn, pray ignore this aged, meddling ecclesiastic."

For some reason I felt the need to unburden myself, and so I did. The vicar had a kindly, trustworthy face and the look of someone who was a good listener. I told him that I had lately lost two confederates whom I considered friends. I said that both had died cruelly, but gave no more detail than that.

"Ah, it is the curse of growing old," the vicar said, full of sympathy. He was perhaps a couple of years my senior. "Members of one's generation begin to pass away, and one begins to ask oneself if one will be next to go."

"It is not that," I said. "I know that death is not far

away. Fewer years lie ahead of me than behind. I am resigned to that. I know, too, that death is as ever-present as it is inevitable. As a soldier and a doctor I have seen more than my fair share of it."

"What, then?"

"Well, Reverend, at the risk of sounding heretical, I find it hard to believe that anything lies beyond. I cannot help but think of death as a permanent end, a full stop rather than the comma that connects two clauses. Nor can I help but think," I went on, "that there is no benevolent deity awaiting us in the next world who will judge each man's soul, weigh up the value of his life and apportion reward."

"You lack faith."

"I have seen things," I said, "things that have led me to question not simply my faith but the entire notion of God. I have seen abominations and terrors, and each has progressively eroded any sense I might have had that there is some divine plan at work, that every man has a purpose, and that God bathes us in His love. I look at these graves" – I swept a hand around the churchyard – "and I think only of the mouldering corpses beneath our feet, not of the souls that once animated them. I am not even convinced any more that the soul exists."

The vicar shook his head compassionately. "Would it help if I told you that you are not alone in harbouring such thoughts? I too have had my doubts. I preach the gospel, I pray daily, I have dedicated my life to promulgating the word of God. Yet there have been times when it feels hollow; when I yearn to tear off this clerical collar and denounce my religion as fraudulent nonsense."

I must not have kept the surprise from registering in my face.

"Yes," the vicar said. "A terrible confession, and no word of a lie. But do you know what keeps me returning to my pulpit and telling my parishioners that the Kingdom of Heaven awaits them as long as they are virtuous? Because it gives them hope. Without hope, men are nothing. Without it, we are animals. Worse than that, we are monsters. Hope is what separates us from Satan. Hope keeps Beelzebub at bay."

He shrugged his shoulders and smiled.

"Granted, it is not much of a consolation," said he. "It is perhaps not the ringing endorsement of Christianity you were looking for from a man of the cloth. But if you can keep the fires of hope burning, both in yourself and in others, that is enough. And on a fine September day, in a spot as well-favoured as this, blue sky meeting blue sea at the horizon line, crows declaiming from the treetops, everything as it ought to be, well… it is not so difficult, is it?"

His words stayed with me as I headed back to Holmes's farm. I cannot say that the vicar had given me balm or allayed my misgivings. My step, however, was a little less heavy than it had previously been.

*

Holmes, it transpired, had a visitor. During my absence none other than old Tom Bellamy had called by, he who was the father of Maud, the girl we had saved from the Brotherhood of the Pulsating Cluster. She was recovering from her ordeal, he informed us, but he did not know if she would ever be quite her old self again. "She weeps uncontrollably at times," he said. "At other times she falls mute and stares at me and her brother William as though she does not even recognise us. She has a long way to go but, with time, I am confident she will get there."

He thanked us for what we had done for his daughter. "Inspector Bardle is taking the credit, but everyone hereabouts knows who really rescued my Maudie from those scoundrels. But it is not about her that I have come to see you, Mr Holmes. At least not entirely."

"No?" said Holmes distractedly. I could see he was suffering Tom Bellamy's presence out of politeness alone. He would rather have been about his labours.

"No. I seek your advice on another matter and, if available, your help."

"I am unusually busy at present."

"I understood you were retired."

"My bees are about to swarm."

"Swarming time is three months gone."

"I have a number of monographs to write."

"I see." Bellamy got up to go. "It appears you cannot muster interest in anything I might have to say. Good day, sir."

He looked disgruntled, as well he might after Holmes's rebuff, but he looked forlorn too. Recalling the vicar's homily about hope, I said, "Holmes, can we not at least hear the fellow out? I am sure he would not have come all this way from Fulworth without due cause."

Holmes shot me a look of reproof, then sighed. "Oh, very well. Resume your seat, Mr Bellamy. I am not making any promises, but if it is something I feel may be within my power to resolve, I shall do my best to oblige."

"Thank you," Bellamy said.

Holmes nodded, although Bellamy's remark had in fact been directed at me.

"It is like this," said the prosperous owner of all the boats and bathing-cots in Fulworth, folding his hands across his belly. "You know about Newford, of course."

"The town a few miles up the coast? How could I not?"

"You know of its reputation, I mean."

"I was not aware it had one, other than as a rather shabby little port which does a trade in fishing and holidaymaking, neither to any great profitability."

"Newford has more than that."

"One would not know it to look at it. It hides its charms well."

"It has history, Mr Holmes," said Bellamy. "Ancient history. There have been people living at the cove where Newford sits since time immemorial. The town's roots extend as far back as the Iron Age and even, the archaeologists reckon, the Stone Age."

"So?"

"But people are not the only inhabitants. Newford is known, at least in the vicinity, as a place where humans consort with another species."

"I take it you aren't referring to the fish the trawling nets pull from the sea."

Bellamy, being of a somewhat pompous inclination, was blithe to my friend's flippancy. "I am referring to another race. An undersea race, indeed."

"Indeed."

"I appreciate you are a rationalist, sir. You are renowned for your exaltation of fact above all else."

Holmes gave a gentle bow of the head.

"But I realise, too," said Bellamy, "that there was something in the cave to which those cultists took Maud, something science cannot easily explain. Maud has mentioned it a couple of times, in hushed, horrified tones. Some kind of jellyfish that was not a jellyfish, she says. A creature that was much more than any mere jellyfish."

"Your daughter viewed events through a prism of abject terror. Her testimony is not perhaps the most reliable."

"Whether or not that is so, I believe what happened in that cave was out of the ordinary and that you yourself must have at least sensed it, if not seen it with your own eyes. Otherwise you would not have importuned Bardle to blow up the entrance."

"Which he did, I am glad to say," said Holmes. "That place was a menace. Those deep, sheer-sided pools – a child could have drowned in one. An adult, for that matter. Closure to the public was long overdue."

"You are handing me off, I can tell. But I will persist. Newford, as I was saying, has seen repeated visits over the centuries by creatures from an undersea race. They are human-like but with the appurtenances of amphibians – external gills and such. They may survive in air, although water is their true home. It is said they dwell in a city on the seabed several leagues offshore, at a depth of some twenty-five fathoms. They come onto dry land infrequently, and only at night and when there is a mist. Some reckon the mist's moistness aids their breathing of air. Others reckon they like the cover it provides for their activities. It may be a bit of both."

"All very fascinating, as a piece of local folklore," said Holmes dully. His affectation of boredom was a ploy to preserve the image of the logical thinker. I could tell, however, by the twinkle in his grey eyes that he was becoming intrigued. "What does it have to do with anything?"

"Simply this, Mr Holmes," said Bellamy. "You will have noted that the past few nights have been misty."

"It is hard to ignore, when one looks out of the window of an evening and sees nothing but occlusion."

"They have begun visiting again. The conditions are right. Newford once more is playing to nightly haunts by the creatures."

His words evoked a small chill within me – or was it a shiver of presentiment? Did I have some inkling, even then, of the trials and tribulations that were to come?

"They are visiting," said Bellamy, "and they are abducting people."

"Abducting?" said Holmes. Now his curiosity was well and truly aroused.

"It is what they do. Not for nothing have they earned the name by which they are commonly known."

"And what name is that?" I asked.

"Sea-Devils, Dr Watson," came the reply. "They are called Sea-Devils.

CHAPTER NINETEEN

Sea-Devils

"I THOUGHT 'SEA-DEVIL' WAS ANOTHER NAME FOR the manta ray," said Holmes.

"It may be," said Bellamy, "but round these parts it means only one thing. It means amphibious beings that walk like men and venture onto land once in a blue moon to snatch unsuspecting victims from their beds and cart them off back to their subaquatic city."

"For what purpose?"

"Breeding. The Sea-Devils' females are infertile, it is supposed, or at any rate they find conception difficult. From time to time fresh brood mares must be found to keep the race going."

"Human brood mares."

"It is only ever women they kidnap from Newford, never men. Sometimes they return them a few years later, emaciated, spent, and usually quite mad from the horrors and privations they have had to endure. Mostly the women do not come back."

"That is appalling," I said.

"It is also, on the face of it, preposterous," said Holmes. "I am no biologist but even I know that it is impossible for divergent species to mate successfully."

"The Sea-Devils are alike enough to us for it to occur," said Bellamy. "One rationale is that on various occasions down through the ages women have been sent back with babies that were almost entirely human. These babies, rejected by the Sea-Devils for their lack of amphibian traits, have grown up to have children of their own, and it is their descendants whom the Sea-Devils seek out."

"Because the physiology of their bloodline is compatible with the Sea-Devils' own," I said.

"Just so."

"And these poor captive women," said Holmes, "live for years on the seabed – presumably in watertight chambers adequately supplied with breathable air – all the while being forced to give birth to a fresh generation of Sea-Devils?"

"That is how the story goes."

"It does seem more like a story than anything else. As in fiction."

"The townsfolk of Newford put stock by it."

"When was the last time such an event happened?"

"Not in living memory, that's for certain. A century ago, maybe two."

"And now it is happening again?"

Bellamy spread out his hands. "That is why I am here. Over the past week, three young Newford women have gone missing. One is the only daughter of a friend of mine, and a close intimate of Maud's: Blanche Grady."

"I am very sorry to hear that."

"I have not told Maud yet. I fear worry for Blanche might place excessive strain on her already overtaxed nerves."

"Wise of you," I said.

"Meanwhile," Bellamy continued, "wet slithery footfalls have been heard in the streets of Newford after dark. Figures have been glimpsed in the mist – silhouettes of men with gilled necks and webbed extremities.

Furthermore, several sailors have reported seeing eerie lights out at sea, beneath the waves. That phenomenon traditionally presages the arrival of Sea-Devils. The creatures are the stuff of legend, Mr Holmes, this much I admit. Until lately I would have been as dismissive of their reality as anyone. But legends tend to have a basis in truth, and it would now appear that this particular legend is one such."

"Representations have, of course, been made to the local constabulary about the missing women?" said Holmes.

"For all the good it has done. 'No evidence of foul play' is Inspector Bardle's verdict, and he will not be swayed from that view."

"He is constrained by certain practicalities of the law, I suppose. Hum!"

Holmes steepled his fingers against his top lip, the pose he was wont to adopt when concentrating. I could see him weighing up the pros and cons of the business that Tom Bellamy had laid before him. To me, it was cut and dried. If young women were being abducted, it was our moral imperative to investigate and, if necessary, find and retrieve them. I doubted Holmes felt differently. He had, after all, risked life and limb on behalf of Maud Bellamy.

"I would beg you to look into it at least, Mr Holmes, whatever your immediate thoughts," Maud's father said. "I fear that the news about Blanche might prove disastrously injurious to my daughter when she hears about it, which she surely will at some point. If you are able to use your powers to bring about a positive outcome, Maud will be all the better for it – as, of course, will Blanche and the two others."

"It could be that each of the three women has disappeared for some reason far less oblique than the depredations of manlike amphibians," Holmes said. "Perhaps in order to escape an abusive husband or father. Perhaps in order to be with some beau of whom her family disapproves. The three events occurring within the same week is coincidence, that is all; or else the decision by one of the women to make off in the dead of night has emboldened the other two to do likewise, each for her own motive."

"In the case of Blanche Grady, it is unlikely. She is a good lass, doted upon by her mother and father. Another of the three, Sarah Cummins, has a happy marriage and, what's more, an infant son. The lad was left behind. Sarah, by all accounts, loved her boy more than life itself. She would never have abandoned him."

"And the third woman?"

"Her name is Deborah Smythe, that is about as much as I know. That and she is a frail, consumptive thing who requires constant care from her mother and the doctor."

"A poor choice for a brood mare," Holmes observed. "Other than geography, are there any other common factors to link all three?"

"They are all roughly the same age, around nineteen or twenty years old."

"And all three are known to one another, I should imagine."

Bellamy shrugged his shoulders. "Newford is small.

Everyone there knows everyone else."

"So it would not be unfeasible that this is just some scheme they have concocted together."

"But to what end, Mr Holmes? To distress their loved ones? To leave kith and kin scratching their heads, half-mad with anxiety?"

"I was simply conjecturing. Conjecture, until I gather more data, is all I have."

"So you are willing to help?" said Bellamy with eagerness. "May I infer as much from the phrase 'gather more data'?"

"I am willing to give the matter my attention, Mr Bellamy," said Holmes. "Whether or not I will turn up evidence of the actions of these so-called Sea-Devils, I cannot predict, but some form of devilry is afoot, that much is undeniable, and it bears enquiry."

*

A grateful Tom Bellamy left the farmhouse, having offered Holmes a sizeable sum of money as a fee, which my friend graciously waived.

"I am glad you agreed to become involved, Holmes," I said. "I would have thought less of you if you had not."

"Clearly your chivalric impulse has been aroused, Watson."

"Three young women inexplicably missing – of course it has."

"Does it not strike you that these kidnappings, or whatever they are, have arrived somewhat conveniently? Right upon my doorstep? Now?"

It took me a moment to catch his drift. "You discern the hand of R'luhlloig in this."

"It would be remiss of us not to countenance the possibility."

"Then he is trying to draw us out. It is a ruse."

"Or a feint, to distract us while some other stratagem elsewhere is brought into play. Or the whole thing could merely be an isolated incident with no connection to the Hidden Mind whatsoever. Whether this is R'luhlloig's doing or not, we should proceed regardless, but with the utmost caution, on the chance that it is. If he has laid a trap, baited with three innocent lives, we have no choice but to spring it. We do, however, have a choice as to whether we allow its jaws to snap shut on us."

CHAPTER TWENTY

The Way of Things in Newford

HOLMES'S HOUSEKEEPER HAD A SON WHO RAN A chauffeuring business, the services of which my friend sometimes called upon. Within an hour of Holmes telephoning him, the young man was pulling up in front of the house in a rather splendid Rover four-seater with burgundy-red bodywork and copious amounts of polished brass trim. He drove us westward along the coast road, perhaps a little too fast for my liking, although Holmes seemed to enjoy the roar of the motor and the buffeting of the wind. The latter phenomenon was of particular consequence to me, for my homburg was in constant danger of being torn from my head and needed to be held in place, whereas Holmes, who had the earflaps of his travelling-cap tied beneath his chin, did not share that worry.

We passed through Fulworth, a very pretty little town with much to recommend it, including a sweeping promenade, many a tree-lined residential avenue, and not one but two golf courses. A couple of miles further on lay Newford, a place I had not visited before. It struck me as Fulworth's inferior counterpart – of roughly the same acreage and population but darker, meaner, more spiteful, as though the two were twins but their parents loved one of them more. There was about the place a rankled air, a feeling of permanent grudge. The houses huddled low, with a strip of barren, tussocky grass separating them from the pebbles of the steeply shelving beach. The fishing vessels in the small harbour swung listlessly at anchor, afforded some shelter from high seas and onshore gales by a single arm of breakwater. The inhabitants themselves went about with their shoulders hunched and, I fancied, a furtive, wary look in their eyes. They could perhaps be forgiven for their demeanour, if Bellamy's account of abductions and Sea-Devils held any truth. Newford seemed to know the miseries of a town under siege.

This impression was reinforced by the sight of a group of men gathered outside a pub. It was mid-afternoon, dusk still a few hours away, but these fellows were evidently putting together some sort of posse comitatus. All were armed – some with shotguns and rifles, others with tools such as axes and hoes – and one could only assume they were preparing to patrol the streets after dark, ready to repel Sea-Devils.

Our destination was the home of Blanche Grady, Maud's friend. Blanche was the most recent of the three girls to have been abducted, and Holmes reckoned her house would therefore be the source of the freshest clues, if there were any to be found.

Her father Samuel being the town's harbourmaster, the Gradys lived hard by the port in a two-storey cottage made of whitewashed stone. The reception we got there was, while not frosty, several degrees below warm. The atmosphere was as bereft and distraught as one might expect, and neither Grady nor his wife seemed at all convinced that intervention by the celebrated consulting detective could do anything to ameliorate the situation.

"I would not even be letting you across the threshold, Mr Holmes," said Samuel Grady, "if Tom Bellamy had not sent me a cable recommending you. He and I go back a long way, and his Maud and my Blanche were fast friends."

"You say 'were'," said Holmes. "They had a falling-out?"

"No. Nothing of the like. I say 'were' because Blanche is not coming back. I know it. My Zelda knows it." He gestured at his wife, who was sitting by the hearth in the parlour. Solemn and swollen-eyed, Mrs Grady looked as though everything inside her had been scooped out and thrown away. "Everyone knows it. It's the way of things in Newford. When the Sea-Devils come, whoever they take never returns."

"I am told there have been exceptions to that rule."

"Vanishingly few. And it does nobody any good to speculate that their loved one might be one of those few. Better to accept the loss and move on."

I did not know whether to admire or deplore such philosophical fatalism. Though childless myself, I was of the opinion that if a son or daughter were ever stolen from me, I would stop at nothing until he or she was safe in my arms again, and I would jump at any offer of help. But then I did not live in Newford.

Holmes echoed my thoughts. "Not all Newforders are so passive about the Sea-Devils. On our way here we saw what can only have been an impromptu militia forming."

"At the King's Arms?" said Grady. "Bah! They have done that the past three days running. Do you know what happens? They start drinking and by nightfall they are dead drunk. Comes the time for them to sally forth and defend the town, one by one each makes his excuses and heads home. The alcohol, rather than lending courage, diminishes it. None of them has any desire to meet a Sea-Devil face to face. They are too damned scared of the things. As are we all."

"If they were but to organise themselves…"

"You do not understand, Mr Holmes. But there is no reason why you should. You are not from here. This is something that is ingrained in us. It is in our blood. Every child in Newford is raised on stories of the Sea-Devils. We learn at our mother's knee to dread the creatures' next visit, even if it may never happen in our lifetimes. The stories get passed down through the generations. They are our history. And sometimes, as now, that history catches up with us. There is…" He searched for the word. "An *inevitability* about all this. We have been waiting for it all our lives. What you regard as passivity, we regard as simple, sensible acquiescence."

"Then you will not permit me to investigate Blanche's kidnapping?"

"No. Do so, with my blessing. But you are doing Tom the favour, not me and my wife. Zelda and I are learning to make our peace with what has happened. In time, God willing, we shall."

*

Holmes quickly ascertained the facts of the matter from Grady. The previous night, he and his wife went up to bed at ten o'clock, as was their habit. Blanche stayed downstairs, doing her needlepoint by the fire. All the doors and windows of the cottage were locked and bolted. By then the absences of both Sarah Cummins and Deborah Smythe had become common knowledge, and nobody was taking any chances. It was unclear how many victims the Sea-Devils intended to make off with in total, but until the mists stopped rolling in, no woman of childbearing age was considered safe.

Grady tossed and turned in his sleep, his head awash with fretful dreams. At around half past eleven he awoke, convinced he had heard a strange noise below. Coming down the stairs, he felt a chill breeze wafting through the house. The front door stood ajar. Of Blanche there was no sign. Her needlepoint lay on the floor by her chair, as though discarded.

Seized by panic, Grady ran to her bedroom, to find the bed not slept in. He raised the alarm. A futile gesture, he was well aware, but it had to be done. A search party of neighbours formed but they did not stray far from the cottage, not with the Sea-Devils lurking somewhere in the mist. A few perfunctory cries of Blanche's name, the odd sweep of a lantern, and everyone felt they had done their duty and there was nothing to be gained by persevering. The search party dispersed back to their own homes.

"The front door shows no signs of having been forced," said Holmes, running an eye over its frame. "How, then, did the Sea-Devils effect entry, if it was locked?"

"I do not know," said Grady. "The bolt was drawn, the key had been turned. It is almost as if Blanche herself opened it."

"Why on earth would she," I said, "knowing that

the Sea-Devils might well be abroad?"

"It is a mystery. I even warned her, before I went to bed, against doing just such a thing. 'If anyone comes knocking,' I said, 'you ignore it, girl. Come and wake me if you must, but that door stays firmly shut.' Blanche had a sensible head upon her shoulders. She would not have let anyone in. She would have obeyed my instruction." Again Grady was referring to his daughter in the past tense. He really had given her up for dead.

"The noise you say you heard," said Holmes, "what was it?"

"I cannot be sure," Grady replied. "The door opening perhaps?"

"That is all? Nothing else?"

"Music."

This came from Mrs Grady, the first time she had spoken since Holmes and I arrived.

"It was music," she said. Her voice was cracked and broken, scarcely a whisper. "I heard it in my sleep. I thought it part of my dreams."

"You have not mentioned this before, wife," said Grady, gently but with a hint of asperity.

"I did not consider it worth mentioning. I was unsure whether it had any relevance. If it was only my imagining, a phantom of sleep, why bring it up? But I believe – I am increasingly certain – that in the moments before you stirred from bed, Sam, someone outside the house was playing music on some sort of wind instrument. A flute or a fife, something like that."

"This music," said Holmes, "how did it sound?"

"Haunting," said Mrs Grady. "Repetitive. Like a lullaby. There was no tune, as such. It was more a sequence of notes repeated over and over, insistently, changing a little each time. It was quite beautiful, in a way. It felt like music I knew from long, long ago, even though I swear I'd never heard it before. That may not make sense but that is the only way I can put it." She smiled bleakly at her husband. "Now you can see, Sam, why I have said nothing about this until now. It seems absurdly fanciful, does it not? And maybe the music was, after all, just a figment. Maybe my mind was playing a trick on me." *But possibly not*, her attitude seemed to be. *Probably not.*

Samuel Grady shook his head in a noncommittal manner. "If, Zelda, you are implying that Blanche was bewitched by some flute-playing and it prompted her to open the door and go outside… well, it is hard to credit."

"Any harder to credit than the existence of amphibious men from under the sea?" said Holmes.

"Yes. Somehow, yes."

"Tell me, how were the other two women taken? What were the circumstances?"

"Sarah Cummins? She was the first. Let me think. It was just over a week ago. As I recall, she was out with her baby, pushing him along in the perambulator, trying to get him off to sleep. Some men found the perambulator and child in the street, him bawling lustily. Sarah was just… gone."

"And Deborah Smythe? The consumptive girl?"

"That was two days later. Her mother had run out of cough linctus and gone to the doctor to buy more. She could not have been away for more than ten minutes, for the doctor's surgery lies just around the corner from her house. When she returned, Deborah was no longer in her bed."

"She left Deborah alone, I take it."

"Judith Smythe is a widow, living on her late husband's pension. She has only Deborah in her life. Looking after the girl is her sole occupation. She would not have abandoned her willy-nilly, but equally there is no one she would have called upon to mind her while she was gone. She is a fiercely independent woman and trusts no one with her daughter's care save the doctor and herself."

"Was there forced entry at the Smythe house?"

"I don't believe so. A window had been left open, if I remember rightly."

"Fresh air is important for consumptives," I said.

"An open window suggests that, at that stage, security against Sea-Devils was still not a priority," said Holmes.

"Sarah Cummins was missing, and the nights were misty, and people were already beginning to mutter about Sea-Devils," said Grady, "but it wasn't by any means certain yet that Sea-Devils were actually to blame for Sarah's disappearance. It was a one-off."

"Until Deborah's disappearance made it a pattern."

"That was when we Newforders got more fearful and started locking our doors and not going out after dark. Over the next couple of nights, the Sea-Devils got bolder. They started allowing themselves to be seen, or at any rate glimpsed. People peeking out from behind a curtain might catch sight of one passing by. Just a vague outline in the mist, but inhuman in shape and bearing."

"Tom Bellamy talked of lights out at sea."

"I think fishermen from the Fulworth fleet observed them. No one from Newford did, otherwise we would have twigged sooner that the Sea-Devils were coming."

"To return to Deborah Smythe, it strikes me as curious that the Sea-Devils kidnapped a consumptive," said Holmes. "One would have thought they would choose only healthy specimens for their programme of repopulation."

"Who knows how those monsters think?" said Grady. "Perhaps it was pure opportunism. The window that was open was the window of Deborah's bedroom. They saw her through it as they went by. She was available, she was vulnerable, she was convenient…"

"She sleeps on the ground floor?"

"She cannot cope with stairs when her consumption flares up. She is too weak, so her mother makes up a cot for her in the front room."

"Still, the selection seems rather inept. Can the Sea-Devils not afford to be pickier?" Holmes said with a frown. "Well, those are all the questions I have for you, Mr Grady, for now. I should like to comb the vicinity for physical clues, if I may."

Holmes set to work examining the front door, the parlour and the area immediately outside the cottage. He did this with the customary terrier-like vigour. I watched him stoop, bend and kneel, and even go down prone before leaping to his feet again, for all the world as though he was in his early twenties rather than his late fifties. I could only marvel, once more, at such vitality in one who by rights should have been plagued by the infirmities of senescence. On the couple of occasions when he produced his magnifying glass in order to study some minuscule detail, I could only assume the detail in question could not have been viewed with the naked eye by anyone, even the most sharp-sighted; the magnifying glass betokened no lessening of Holmes's visual acuity.

Pausing at the doorjamb, Holmes busied himself collecting a sample of some substance which adhered to it at waist height. He scraped the material off with a pocketknife and inserted it in a small envelope. This action served to conclude his survey, for he then pronounced himself satisfied.

"I have seen all I need to see," he said. "I am a little the wiser, if not yet fully enlightened."

He shook hands with Samuel Grady, bade the harbourmaster and his wife adieu, and shortly he and I were back in the Rover, hurtling eastward.

"Well?" I said, shouting to be heard above the car's engine. "What have you discovered?"

"Much depends upon the results of a test of the sample I took," came the reply.

"It looked like some kind of slimy deposit."

"Some kind of slimy deposit is exactly it."

"The kind of slimy deposit an amphibious sea-creature might leave behind?"

"Just the kind of slimy deposit one would expect an amphibious sea-creature to leave behind."

"And was there anything else?"

"A footprint. A partial one. An intriguingly partial one."

"A webbed footprint, presumably."

"One that weaves a web, to be sure."

Any more than that he would not say. I pressed him but he maintained a resolute, enigmatic silence. I had forgotten how smug Sherlock Holmes could be during the prosecution of an investigation and how childishly amusing he found it to withhold his conclusions until he was ready to share them, which was often only after he had exacted the maximum perplexity and frustration from everyone around him. In that respect, just as with his physical fitness, Holmes's advancing years had not conferred maturity.

CHAPTER TWENTY-ONE

Sentinels on the Shore

WE WERE BACK IN NEWFORD THAT SAME EVENING. This time, however, we came not as investigators but as sentinels.

As the sun was setting, Holmes scouted along the beach until he found us a suitable vantage point. Just where the eastern precincts of the town petered out there lay a low promontory, a bare finger of chalk jutting into the sea, an appendix to the cliffs that rose beyond. The ridge of this feature, which stood nine feet at its highest, was just broad enough for the two of us to lie side by side. We had a view of the beach in its entirety, all the way to the harbour at the far end, and were concealed from anyone on the beach itself.

We settled in for a long wait. Holmes had warned me that our watch might last until dawn and might even prove fruitless, for if there was no mist then the Sea-Devils would most likely not appear. I had accordingly fortified myself with a hearty supper – two helpings of mutton stew and dumplings – and had brought along a hip flask of brandy to warm me against the cold and keep the blood circulating. I also had my trusty Webley with me, and Holmes was likewise armed. He did not often carry a sidearm, so this was some indication of the seriousness of the circumstances.

The sun sank from sight. Gulls wailed as though mourning its passing, then flocked to their nests. Lights flickered on in Newford's windows, frail as sparks. The sky empurpled and darkened. A grinning moon arose.

Then came the mist. It amassed over the sea, thickening at a barely perceptible rate. Everything went still. The slopping of the waves diminished to near-inaudibility. The surface of the water became millpond smooth. A hush fell, as though the world were holding its breath.

An hour elapsed, and then another. In that eerie nocturnal stillness time seemed unnaturally slow. The mist crept towards us, extending tendrils onto land like some spectral cephalopod tentatively gauging its next move. Gradually it enveloped more and more of the beach and began insinuating itself along the streets of Newford. The town's lights dimmed, windows and lamps developing gauzy haloes.

My nerves tautened. The moon, just shy of full, cast sufficient light that we could see most of the beach, but there was something uncanny about its glow. It painted the scene in flat silvery hues, like some bizarre mezzotint. A sense of unreality pervaded my thoughts, becoming stronger and less easy to repudiate as the minutes ticked glutinously by. More and more I felt as though I was watching a kinematographic display, an audience member rather than a participant, detached from involvement. I was not fully there; I was staring through the eyes of another.

The mist-muffled chimes of Newford's church clock tolled the hours: ten, eleven, midnight. Still nothing stirred. I helped myself to a nip of brandy – several nips, in fact – and shifted my leg to ease out a cramp. Holmes beside me remained as motionless as a cobra, his gaze scanning the beach keenly.

Shortly after 1 a.m. I spoke up. My voice was gravelly from disuse and the damp air. "They are not going to show. They would have by now."

"Patience, Watson. Patience. The night is still young."

"But I am not. My old bones do not enjoy lying on rocks. They ache."

"Are you not curious to observe this phenomenon? Men from the sea? I am quite enthused by the prospect."

"You, as far as I can tell, have worked up a hypothesis about the Sea-Devils and are eager to have it confirmed."

"I cannot deny it."

"Are you going to fill me in any time soon?"

"And risk appearing ridiculous if I am proved wrong?"

"You do not fear ridicule. You fear missing out on my bogglement when that which you expected, and I least suspected, turns out to be true."

"You know me so well, old friend."

"You could at least tell me what you discovered when testing the slimy deposit. I heard you cry out in your study as you were working on it – a cry of amused gratification. I can only infer that the result was all you had hoped it would be."

"It was," said Holmes. "Sometimes it is as pleasing when the outré reveals itself to be ordinary as it is when the ordinary reveals itself to be outré."

"Now you are talking in riddles."

"Then consider this, Watson. We know that subaquatic races exist. Stories abound about Innsmouth in Massachusetts, where the townspeople are said to have offered human sacrifices to certain Deep Ones dwelling nearby, in return for large hauls of fish and gifts of queer-looking jewellery made from alloys unknown to man."

"I recall that a plague in 1846 devastated the town, killing at least half the residents."

"It was no plague. It was the Deep Ones, incensed when the supply of sacrifices dried up. They inflicted an epidemic not of disease but of slaughter. However, the historical record prefers the plague explanation, the prosaic over the supernatural. Incidentally, those responsible for the sacrifices were a cult of Dagon worshippers, and it was in tribute to the way the truth was covered up at Innsmouth that Mycroft elected to call his cabal of truth-hiders the Dagon Club."

Holmes's voice caught ever so slightly upon Mycroft's name, as though tripping over an obstacle. We had been unable to attend his brother's funeral in the capital, being sequestered in Sussex. The papers had reported it as a grand state occasion, with the cortège passing along the Mall and royalty and nobles on hand to pay their respects, although it had been overshadowed somewhat by the ceremonies for the other, higher-profile Dagon Club members such as Lord Cantlemere. I wondered whether seeing Mycroft formally interred would have permitted Holmes some measure of consolation in his bereavement, the feeling that a chapter had been properly closed. It was hard to know. His intellectual life might be plainly expressed but in his emotional life Sherlock Holmes was all but inscrutable.

"I myself," he continued, "have first-hand experience of Deep Ones, as you know, courtesy of Baron Gruner. They smell fishy, by the way, much as you would expect. Quite malodorous. And now, here, we find ourselves dealing with a British equivalent of Innsmouth and some Deep Ones of our own, who doubtless will exude a similar fishiness."

"Perhaps they are related. The Sea-Devils are a racial offshoot of the Deep Ones."

"Or, for that matter, they are the exact same species by a different name. From the scanty eyewitness descriptions with which we have been furnished, there are resemblances – the gills and so forth."

"What about the music Mrs Grady spoke of? The flute-playing? What do you make of that?"

"'Music hath charms…'" said Holmes. "There is an old German violinist in Paris, name of Erich Zann, who is rumoured to have composed melodies capable of opening portals to other dimensions. If he can do that, then it is not beyond the bounds of reason that—" Holmes broke off. "*Hsst.*" A long, slender forefinger pointed. I followed its direction.

Upon the surface of the sea, some ten yards from shore, there were disturbances. In three separate but adjacent spots the water was churning like soup on a rolling boil. Something was moving below, advancing landward. And not just moving – rising. The disturbances were growing more intense as they neared the shoreline. Whatever was creating them seemed to be following the upward incline of the seabed. I could only imagine a group of three things – humanoid things – walking from the depths to the shallows in triangle formation.

"My God," I breathed. "It is them. The Sea-Devils. Here they come."

CHAPTER TWENTY-TWO

The Dead Brought Back to Life

A HEAD BROKE THE SURFACE. IT SLID SLEEKLY UP, a domed cranium, then a heavy brow ridge, then a pair of wide-set, bulbous eyes.

The creature paused, apparently taking the lie of the land. Behind it two similar heads emerged, likewise stopping when their eyes were above water.

The foremost of the trio, seemingly having established that the coast was clear, resumed its rise from the sea. Now a flat nose and a froggy mouth came into sight, along with a pair of fan-like structures, which flared back along its temples, somewhat resembling a bat's ears but most likely the creature's gills. Rounded shoulders, a profoundly humped back, and long arms tipped with webbed hands were next, until at last the thing stood on the foreshore wholly revealed, a hulking, slouching hybrid of human and amphibian. Water poured from its skin – a loathsomely glossy integument, dappled grey in the moonlight – while its chest rose and fell with slow heaviness, as though the creature was accustoming itself to extracting oxygen from air and this was a more arduous task than extracting it from water.

As the Sea-Devil's two companions joined it on the beach, I could not suppress a shudder. I had met a fair few monstrosities in my time, but these three were amongst the most hideous. Perhaps it was because they exhibited so many manlike traits. Their similarities to our species made their differences from us all the more glaring and appalling. A snake man seemed a close cousin by comparison, altogether more sophisticated and less primordial. The Sea-Devils harked back to an epoch when life was just clawing its way out of the oceans, flopping in the liminal mud to bask in the sun.

"Now, Watson!" hissed Holmes, scrambling to his knees. "While they are still getting their bearings."

"We are going to attack them?"

"Why ever not? We have weapons; they do not. And we have the element of surprise."

So saying, my friend slithered down off the promontory and began pounding along the beach, gun drawn. I, with some bemusement and no little circumspection, followed suit.

It was not until Holmes was within twenty feet of them that the Sea-Devils noticed him coming. Almost in unison they halted mid-stride and swung in his direction.

Then, to my astonishment, almost in unison they pivoted round and started making for the sea.

"Halt right there!" Holmes commanded, and when the Sea-Devils did not comply he loosed off a bullet into the air. The gun report froze them in their tracks. "That's it. The next shot will not be a warning. The jig is up. I have the measure of you, you rascals. Put your hands up now, nice and high."

The Sea-Devils looked at one another in evident consternation.

"*Hände hoch!*" barked Holmes. "*Schnell!*"

Now the Sea-Devils' hands rose, as did my eyebrows, for Holmes had just addressed the trio in German – *and they had understood.*

"Holmes," I declared, catching up with him. "What in heaven's name is going on? These three are… Germans?"

"Yes," said he with a small smile of triumph.

"Then they are not amphibious sea-creatures at all."

"In appearance, yes. In every other respect, no."

"I am…"

Lost for words was what I was. It was beginning to dawn on me that the Sea-Devils were a hoax, one of quite literally monstrous proportions. They were a hoax, moreover, perpetrated by Germans. I did not know what to make of this intelligence, but I did, if nothing else, intuit a connection between the creatures in front of me and R'luhlloig, acting through the medium of Baron Von Herling. There had been a Teutonic theme running through events ever since Holmes divined that the sender of the seven deadly parcels was Von Bork. Tonight's escapade was just the latest manifestation of that.

"Keep them covered with your gun, Watson," Holmes said, pocketing his own weapon. "I am going to see just what a Sea-Devil looks like when it is stripped of its skin. *Still stehen!*" This last was aimed at one of the Sea-Devils, who had begun taking a cautious step seaward but who, when told in his native tongue to stand still, did just that. "*Danke, mein Herr.*"

Holmes reached for the head of the nearest Sea-Devil and began to tug on it. The creature resisted but Holmes redoubled his efforts. By dint of twisting and turning, he succeeded in detaching the head. It came free in a tangle of pipes and tubes. It was, of course, a kind of mask, and its removal revealed the head of a young man with a firm jawline, a thatch of sweaty flaxen hair and a chagrined, somewhat surly expression.

"Behold," said Holmes. "The monster is a man."

The fellow growled a few words in German.

"That sounded neither complimentary nor civil," my friend said wryly.

"I have a little English," said the young German. "I can curse you in your own language if you wish."

It was then that I noticed that another of the Sea-Devils was wearing a kind of belt slung about his waist. The belt resembled nothing so much as a broad strip of kelp, complete with blister. By the way the blister bulged it seemed to serve as a pouch and held something heavy within.

The reason I noticed it at all is that, while Holmes was addressing himself to the Sea-Devil he had just unmasked, the other Sea-Devil's hand was stealing towards the pouch.

"Hullo!" I declared. "What do you think you're up to, you blackguard?"

Even as I said this, the hand delved through a slit in the pouch and came out with a peculiar oblong metal device. It was about the size of a cigar box, with a grille across one of its largest faces.

"Whatever that is, put it down," I said, thumbing back the hammer on my revolver. "This instant."

The Sea-Devil, undaunted, deftly flicked a switch on the back of the device.

After that, things stopped making sense.

*

I heard a song. It was a lullaby from my childhood, one my mother used to sing as I sat in her lap. I recalled her holding me in her arms and crooning the tune, and I recalled feeling inexpressibly contented as her hand stroked my hair and her soft breath brushed my face.

I could have listened to the lullaby all day long.

Strangely, the woman singing it to me now was not my mother but Mary. Before me she stood, as beautiful as I remembered, with that sweet, grave face and the long tumbling coils of golden hair, a vision of loveliness. She smiled to behold me, and I could only smile back, wondering even as I did what she must make of this man who was some twenty years older than when she had last seen him, greyer-headed, baggier-eyed, thicker around the middle, slower in both mind and body. Would she still love him, youthful as she was, aged as he was?

Her gaze told me she did. It was tender and forgiving. Her song said the same. Mary wished me only happiness. She longed for us to share again the joy we had known in our marriage, short-lived though it had proved to be. Here, now, we had a second chance. We might be together once more, as if our years of separation had never happened.

I knew that Mary was dead. I knew and yet it did not matter. My logic was this: if she was dead, how come she was present on Newford beach at this very moment? Therefore she must be alive. It was mystery and miracle, and I chose to discount the mysterious aspects of it and accept the miraculous.

Mary reached out to me with both arms, still ululating that enchanting lullaby. I moved towards her without compunction. The thought of enfolding her in an embrace overrode all other considerations. I would hold her and never let go. Tears had sprung into my eyes and, unmanly though they were, I let them fall rather than blinking them back. I did not know how long it was since such sentiments had last been stirred in me. It was as though I, like Mary, had been dead and had now been brought back to life.

I was within inches of her when a gunshot brought everything to a halt. It was like a hammer shattering glass. All at once there was no more lullaby and no more Mary. There was a Sea-Devil holding a broken metal box and swearing in German. There was also Sherlock Holmes standing by my side with a smoking pistol.

"Damnably clever," said he. "They almost had us. That is a radio receiver, is it not?" He nodded at the ruined device, from which wires and triodes dangled like eviscerated guts. "It is designed to pick up a signal transmitted from elsewhere – a broadcast of music, in this case. Music of a particularly entrancing nature. A Zann composition would be my guess. Is that not so, gentlemen? Erich Zann wrote this tune which warps the mind of the listener, making him see and hear things that are not really there. Yes? But while you wear those masks, the sound is filtered so that it does not affect you in the same way. Yes?"

The unmasked Sea-Devil looked nonplussed, while the thoughts of the other two, their true faces still hidden, were unknowable. None of them acknowledged or denied Holmes's assertion verbally.

"Well, I am sure I can verify it later," Holmes said. "Our immediate concern is getting you three fine fellows under lock and key. That way." He gestured towards Newford with his gun. "Yonder lies a town full of people who will be only too keen to make your acquaintance, once it has been shown to them that you are not what you purport to be."

We set off up the beach. Sorrow burned in my belly as I thought of the Mary in my vision, the woman I had lost, but this emotion vied with – and was subsumed by – the anger I felt at the Germans for using her to trick me. It felt as though my heart had been ransacked and violated. It took every ounce of self-restraint I had not to shoot them there and then.

CHAPTER TWENTY-THREE

Three Sea-Devil Suits
and a Conundrum

WE MARCHED THE SEA-DEVILS TO SAMUEL GRADY'S cottage. Since the harbourmaster was known to us and occupied a position of authority within Newford, he seemed our best bet both as an ally and as a means of convincing the rest of the townspeople that the Sea-Devil threat had been nullified.

To get his attention was no mean feat. Holmes had to importune him from outside the house for several minutes before Grady dared even to open his bedroom window. The agitation on his face shifted slowly to incomprehension then astonishment as he gazed down upon our captives, all three of whom were now unmasked.

"This... This is some joke," he said. "This cannot be real."

"As real as anything," said Holmes smoothly. "Come down and take a closer look. A terrible fraud has been inflicted upon Newford, and here are the perpetrators. See how sheepish they are now? Like guilty schoolboys lined up outside the headmaster's study. Yet night after night they have been arrogantly strutting along your streets, relying on Newforders' collective ancestral fears to give them impunity. Once you have satisfied yourself that all is as I say, you perhaps might wish to summon a constable or two."

Eventually Grady let us in, and with much marvelling and no small amount of indignation he studied the Sea-Devils.

"They are wearing costumes made of rubberised canvas," said he.

"Not unlike a diving suit," said Holmes. "In order that they might breathe underwater, their masks are supplied with oxygen from canisters built in to the suits here." He rapped one of the Sea-Devils on the back with a knuckle, eliciting a metallic ringing sound. "It is a cunning advance on the pioneering work of Messieurs Denayrouze and Rouquayrol. A diving suit normally has air pumped to it from an external source, via a tube. Here the air is kept in compressed form and carried by the user. It makes the suit its own self-contained environment. It also makes for quite a burden, as you can tell from the way these three are holding themselves, stooped forward to take the weight. They are young and strong, but even so, it is an effort. In the water they are supported. On land they struggle somewhat. That accounts for their plodding gait and also for the lack of resistance they offered when Watson and I surprised them. They knew they could not best us in a fight. The suits' bulk and cumbersomeness put them at a clear disadvantage."

I refrained from pointing out that some resistance had been offered in the form of the music from the radio receiver. I was puzzled, though, as to how Holmes had been impervious to its effects and I not.

"And you say they are responsible for the abductions," said Grady. "Including that of my Blanche."

"Not solely these three. Other agencies are in play. But they performed the deed itself. No, Mr Grady. I would resist the temptation if I were you. Unclench that fist. You are looking at underlings, that is all, men following orders. Curb your rage, justifiable though it may be. I am relying on you to set the tone for your fellow Newforders. I can foresee a lynch mob forming if we are not careful, and that would be regrettable. I ask you to keep a level head and make sure that those officials whom you muster up are of a level-headed persuasion themselves."

"If the Sea-Devils are just men, does that mean…?" Grady hesitated, the merest scintilla of optimism flickering in his eyes. "Does that mean there is a chance Blanche may be restored to us after all?"

"It depends," replied Holmes.

"On what?"

"The extent of my ingenuity and the soundness of my deductions. I would counsel you not to expect a positive outcome just yet, Mr Grady, but neither would I say that it is beyond the realms of possibility."

*

Grady left the cottage and returned within half an hour accompanied by two uniformed policemen and a couple of redoubtable-looking civilians whose trustworthiness and discretion he vouched for.

By that time Holmes and I had convinced the Germans to strip themselves of their Sea-Devil suits entirely and had bound them hand and foot with cord fetched for us by Mrs Grady. The trio now seemed utterly resigned to their fate and had begun pleading, in broken English, for clemency. Holmes assured them they would be tried in accordance with the law of the land. There would be no summary executions.

He talked one of them into demonstrating how the

suits worked. The German showed us the valve which controlled the flow from the tank of compressed air – he called it a regulator – and explained how to open and close it with a small knurled knob secreted beneath a flap on the back of the suit. There was a certain patriotic pride in his bearing, as if this apparatus, which he told us had been devised by countrymen of his, reflected well upon him by association.

With the Germans taken into police custody, Holmes and I were left with the three Sea-Devil suits and a conundrum. What to do next? It was a conundrum for me, at any rate. Holmes already had formulated a plan.

"I cannot in all conscience ask you to come with me, Watson," he said. "The risks are incalculable. I am quite willing to go it alone."

"If you can say that, then it means you still do not know me very well even after all these years."

"I did not want to presume."

"Tell me your intentions, Holmes. It will not change my mind, but it would be good to know what I am letting myself in for."

"How do you fancy, old friend, being a Sea-Devil?"

CHAPTER TWENTY-FOUR

A Hansom of the Deeps

NOT LONG AFTER THAT, WE WERE BACK ON THE beach with two of the Sea-Devil suits, which we had brought with us in a wheelbarrow. Time was of the essence, according to Holmes. The Sea-Devils would be expected to return whence they had come sooner rather than later. Suspicions might be aroused if they failed to make the rendezvous as scheduled.

As we each donned one of the diving suits, I had a few questions.

"Quickly then, Watson," said Holmes. "Keep it brief."

"First of all, how did you know the Sea-Devils were fake?"

"Feel that boot you are putting your foot into? It resembles a webbed foot, but a boot is what it is. A boot leaves a different kind of impression on the ground than does a bare foot, webbed or otherwise. The clear, sharp imprint of a heel, for one. The smooth, even imprint of a sole, for another. A bare foot does not plant itself fully. It has an arch. The toes, moreover, sink as deep as the rest of it. Yet here, with the Sea-Devil suits, the toes are immobile excrescences and barely leave a mark. In the large, unusual-looking footprint that I discovered in a patch of mud outside the Gradys' front door, the shape and the distribution of weight were all wrong for a bare foot. Therefore I could only infer the foot was garment rather than flesh and bone."

"I take it the slimy deposit was not natural either."

"Petroleum jelly, left on the doorjamb to give the illusion that a slimy creature had brushed past."

"A deliberate red herring, then."

"Funny that you should use a fish reference. I all but told you the Sea-Devils were a sham, as we lay atop the promontory. They 'exude fishiness', I said, or words to that effect. I am surprised you did not pick up on it. Too subtle? Not for a wordsmith such as yourself, I should have thought."

"I am so accustomed to the supernatural being nothing but the supernatural that you can hardly fault me, in this one instance, for failing to foresee that it might prove otherwise."

"Here we have a case where, as in one of your stories, Sherlock Holmes dismantles the façade of a paranormal-seeming crime to reveal the mundane truth beneath. I should have thought that would please you, life imitating art for a change."

"There is novelty in the bathos, I suppose," I said. "One last query. The music that the Sea-Devils used…"

"To draw their quarry out from indoors. It has a hypnotic effect, creating an alluring vision."

"As well I know. Yet you were immune to it. How so?"

"The power of the intellect," Holmes said briskly.

"Are you saying that I'm weak-minded?" I asked, half in jest.

"No, just that the emotions upon which the music preys are stronger in you than in me, and closer to the surface, making you more malleable in that respect. Now, enough shilly-shallying. We have a mission and we had best be about it. Allow me to affix your mask on, then you can return the favour. A remarkable adventure awaits us, one that normally a rare few specialists undertake. Your literary rival the late Jules Verne would have envied you that which you are about to experience."

"I only hope we have less distance to cover than twenty thousand leagues," I said with a game grin as Holmes lowered the Sea-Devil head over mine.

*

It was stifling in that mask. The twin glass hemispheres of the Sea-Devil's eyes limited my field of vision to a small fraction of its usual self, while the smell of rubberised canvas and another man's sweat were suffocating. Already it was becoming hard work remaining upright. The suit was not only heavy but badly balanced. I felt as though I might topple onto my back at any moment.

Regardless, I assisted Holmes with his mask. The webbed gloves encasing my hands made me clumsy but left me with enough dexterity to perform the task, which entailed screwing the Sea-Devil head into a threaded flange at the neck of the suit until it clicked firmly into place, much as a standard diving helmet did, then turning the knurled knob on the regulator to initiate the influx of air.

Holmes, with a gallant wave of the hand, tramped down the beach into the sea. I lumbered after him. As the water rose about me, the suit tightened. I fought down a feeling of panic. Was I really about to immerse myself fully under, reliant on air from a canister to keep me alive? What if something went wrong with the breathing mechanism? I could not swim up to the surface, not clad in paraphernalia as weighty and constricting as this, and I doubted I could shuck off the suit before I drowned. Of all the schemes Holmes had come up with in our years together, this was categorically the most hare-brained. We were not professional divers, we were rank amateurs, and it was a hazardous occupation even for the experts.

Yet, as I waded further out and the sea closed over me, I knew I was committed. There was no turning back. Where Sherlock Holmes went, there faithful Watson went too. And three young women, whether they knew it or not, were counting on us. Without us, their families might never see them again. Next to that consideration, my own cavils were unimportant.

We had set off from the same point on the beach where the Sea-Devils had made landfall. I dogged Holmes's footsteps along the muddy seabed, gradually becoming accustomed to the resistance of the water around me, which was compensated for somewhat by the support it provided. My breathing sounded loud within the mask. Excess air was expelled as from one-way valves behind the "gills", these columns of bubbles rumbling as they spiralled upward. The cold of the water was intense but, mitigated somewhat by the suit, bearable. Pearlescent moonshine filtering down from above gave us just enough light to see by, although visibility was not more than half a dozen yards. Holmes, a mere arm's distance ahead of me, was a hazy, grotesque silhouette. I had to keep reminding myself that this was my friend in front of me and no monster.

Our progress was a slow and steady trudge. The

seabed undulated underfoot but its overall trend was a downward gradient. At a depth of perhaps three fathoms my ears popped and I could hear a clicking sound inside my head, which I determined must come from my sinuses. Such, it seemed, were the physiological effects attendant upon being a merman. I wondered whether I might pen an article for *The Lancet* on the subject.

Some fifty yards out from shore, Holmes halted. He cast about, as though trying to find his bearings in the murk. I had no idea what he might be looking for, but surely it was not the Sea-Devils' fabled subaquatic city.

Then, apparently spying something, he made off again. Within moments a large round object loomed before us. It was a sphere roughly eight feet in diameter, fashioned from riveted plates of steel. It floated a couple of feet off the sea floor, tethered by anchors on the end of chains. Thick hawsers stretched away from it horizontally, out towards deeper waters. A faint glow emanated from its underside.

Holmes walked around the sphere, examining it from every angle. Then he ducked beneath, disappearing from view. Presently he reappeared and indicated that we should pull up the anchors. There were cleats to hang them on. The sphere was still tethered by the hawsers but swung more loosely in the water now. Holmes beckoned me to follow him underneath.

Through a circular aperture in the base of the sphere we rose into a hollow, air-filled interior. We climbed up onto a narrow bench, which ran in a ring around the inside. Holmes doffed his mask, I did likewise, and we drew in lungfuls of stale, salty, but breathable air. A dim electric light bulb glimmered waveringly above us.

"A marvel, this," my companion remarked. "A cosy little nook in which our Sea-Devils can gain respite and lodge their captives."

"Lodge them how?" I said. "Would the women not have to walk along the seabed in order to reach the sphere, just as we did?"

"Look above you."

Inset into the top of the sphere was a circular airtight hatch fitted with a locking wheel. Below it, three descending metal rungs were bolted to the sphere's interior.

"One can only presume the sphere is deposited here in these relatively deep waters where there is sufficient draft," Holmes said.

"For a ship to navigate safely, you mean?"

"Some sort of seafaring vessel, yes. Then said vessel retreats back out to sea, paying out the hawsers as it goes. When required, the Sea-Devils raise the anchors as we have done and draw the sphere further towards land manually, pulling it along like human dray horses. Its buoyancy in the water reduces its weight sufficiently that the feat is manageable. Once the sphere is close enough to shore that its summit is above the level of the water, the hatch may be opened and a captive made to climb through the aperture and down inside, using the rungs."

"But how does the sphere not get flooded when it is submerged?" I said, eyeing the circle of water just below my feet.

"The same way an overturned cup does not fill with

water when you place it in a sink. As long as the cup remains vertical and stable, the air inside it is trapped."

"One surely cannot stay in here for very long, though. Soon enough the air will be used up and one will asphyxiate."

"This is merely a stopgap, Watson. A mode of transportation, like a hansom of the deeps, to get us from one place to another. Observe the winding handle here."

"It operates the hawsers? To draw us along, pulley-fashion?"

"Dear me, no. It is far too small and puny for that. But I believe if I rotate it thus…" He cranked the handle through a few turns.

"Nothing is happening," I said.

"Not yet. Give it a moment. A signal has been sent along the insulated electric wire I spied, attached to one of the hawsers. Somewhere not far from here a bell is ringing or a buzzer is buzzing. If I am right, some sort of motorised winch or windlass will be churning into life, and— There! Did you feel that?"

The sphere had jerked ever so slightly.

"Slack is being taken up," said Holmes. "The hawsers are tightening. Any second now, we will start to move."

Giving substance to his words, the sphere began to shudder. I sensed a sideways tugging action. The circle of water at our feet grew turbulent, a current clearly detectable in its surface. We were being hauled along at perhaps three or four miles per hour; walking pace. Any faster, and I imagine the sphere would have been at risk of tilting or even capsizing.

For minutes on end we travelled, the sphere swerving from true every so often as an undersea current grabbed at it, before resuming its course.

"What manner of ship awaits us at our destination?" I enquired. "Do you know?"

"I have an inkling. Consider the sphere a chick. The mother hen is retrieving it."

"A larger sphere?"

"Something along those lines."

Further minutes passed, and then our speed was reduced to a crawl. The sphere butted up against another object with a muted, reverberant clang and came to a standstill.

"Journey's end," said Holmes. "I think we should put our masks back on. The longer we can pass for the original Sea-Devils, the more it will be to our advantage."

"Won't the mere fact that there are two of us, when there should be three, give away the imposture?"

"The assumption will be that we met with trouble in Newford and one of our number was apprehended or eliminated. Hence we have no captive young woman either. We are in effect returning home with our tails between our legs. With luck, that will grant us sufficient benefit of the doubt. We will be welcomed in, whereupon we pounce and take one or more hostages at gunpoint. Then we set out our demands: the three Newford women in exchange for the hostages' lives."

"It is, if I may say, a strategy not devoid of potential drawbacks."

"It is the best we can hope for under the circumstances. The odds are not in our favour, I will admit, but then we have pulled off remarkable coups in the past. Why not one more?"

As we donned the Sea-Devil masks, I felt the sphere begin to rise. There was a great thundering in the water around us, suggestive of something else rising too, something of altogether greater mass. My ears popped again as the pressure within the sphere changed. Then, at last, our ascent ended and the sphere was left swaying and rocking like a cork float that has just bobbed to the surface.

The motion settled to a gentler rise and fall, that of a boat riding a mild ocean swell. Holmes reached up and rotated the locking wheel on the hatch, unsealing it. Strings of seawater dribbled in. He then pushed the hatch open and clambered up the rungs, easing himself out of the sphere. I copied him.

The sphere was nestled alongside a far larger craft, one whose visible portion rose some five feet proud of the water and was made similarly of riveted steel. The outward-curving flank of this vessel stretched a hundred feet in either direction, with a square fin projecting on a perpendicular plane at one end and a stubby conning tower sticking up amidships, just above our heads, the sole item of superstructure.

I did not need to have seen a submarine first-hand before to know that I was in the presence of one now.

CHAPTER TWENTY-FIVE

SM U-19

LIGHTS CAME ON FORE AND AFT BELOW THE submarine's waterline, filling the sea immediately around it with limpid effulgence. A hatch opened atop the tower and a man in naval uniform climbed out. This sailor was followed by another. Both men's white blouses and soft caps betokened low rank. Their voices, as they called out to us, betokened German origin.

Holmes shouted something back in the same language. Since the Sea-Devil mask muffled his voice, the sailors appeared not to notice that he was neither a native German speaker nor one of the three men who were actually supposed to be wearing the Sea-Devil suits. They gestured at us to come aboard, throwing us a knotted rope to assist us in that enterprise.

Once we were standing on the foredeck, the sailors began bombarding us with questions. My familiarity with their mother tongue was passing at best, but I gathered the gist. Why were we just two? What had become of the third member of our raiding party? And where was the captive we were meant to have brought back with us?

Holmes patted the air in a "be patient" manner. He feigned exhaustion and defeat, more with his posture than with anything he said. I emulated him. The sailors seemed to take pity on us. It was clear to them that something had gone drastically wrong with our mission. They offered to help us out of the suits.

No sooner was Holmes's face exposed than he lashed

out at the startled sailor in front of him, catching him with a fierce uppercut to the jaw. The man fell to the deck, out cold. I launched myself at the other sailor. We grappled. My only advantage was that the Sea-Devil suit made me heavier than him. It certainly did not make me nimbler. I bore down on him until he was pressed flat beneath me, supine. He punched me in the ribs several times but the thick fabric of the suit absorbed the force of the blows.

While I struggled to keep my opponent down, Holmes squirmed the rest of the way out of his suit. He, like me, was fully clothed beneath and toting a firearm. He drew the gun and pressed the barrel to the sailor's forehead. The fellow stopped resisting straight away.

"English?" said Holmes. "Do you speak English?"

The sailor nodded. "*Ich spreche ein bisschen Englisch.*" *I speak a little English.*

"You have on board three women. Three English-women. Yes? Do you understand?"

"*Drei Englische Frauen. Ja.*"

"Take us to them. And if you call out for help, or so much as look as though you are going to, I will shoot. Do you understand that too?"

"*Jawohl. Ich verstehe.*"

"Say it in English, to prove it."

"If I call out for help, you shoot."

"Good. Then up you get."

I divested myself of my suit and we crossed the deck to the tower. So far Holmes's plan was working, and I permitted myself to think that we might just accomplish our goal after all. I had no idea how we were going to get back to dry land with the women. It was too great a distance to swim, and as far as I could tell the sphere would be no good to us. It was not independently powered. It relied on being deposited just offshore and then reeled in later, meaning we could not use it as we would a boat. We might, I supposed, detach it from the submarine and trust that the prevailing current would wash us in the right direction. Alternatively, we might attempt to commandeer the submarine itself, although I was not sure that two men could manage such a feat, even armed, given that the crew must outnumber us by a considerable factor. Perhaps there was a dinghy aboard, some form of life-raft. Holmes would be sifting through the options in his head, that much I was confident about. He would see us all safely back to Newford.

With our hostage we clambered through the hatch in the tower and descended a ladder into a cramped chamber, the walls of which were festooned with a great profusion of dials, gauges, levers and valve-operating wheels large and small. A periscope column occupied the centre of this control room, leaving very little floor space upon which to stand.

Manning their stations were just two sailors. The pair took a moment to comprehend that Holmes and I were not fellow crewmen. Their eyes widened, and one of them reached for a switch which no doubt would have set a klaxon wailing. Holmes waved his pistol at him, dissuading the man from completing the action.

Not a word was spoken. None needed to be. Leaving me to cover the two sailors in the control room, Holmes headed for'ard with our original hostage.

I waited a minute, and another, keeping a beady eye on my two charges all the while. Their faces registered annoyance and dismay. I imagined they would be in for a severe reprimand when their superiors learned how their captives had been spirited away right in front of them and they had done nothing to prevent it. I had heard that German military discipline could be fairly brutal, and I felt a little sorry for them – although, since they were part of a conspiracy to abduct innocent young women, not that sorry.

As time wore on I experienced the first twinges of misgiving. Holmes was taking inordinately long. How hard could it be to get to the women? The submarine was not that big, and it was not as if he had to search for them. The sailor with him would know exactly where they were.

Misgiving turned to unease as a further couple of minutes passed and Holmes still failed to reappear. Had some mishap befallen him? I was tempted to go after him, but I knew that the moment I left the sailors in the control room unattended, they would raise the alarm.

At last Holmes came back, and as soon as I clapped eyes on him a hollowness settled in the pit of my stomach. His expression was doleful. He no longer had his pistol. There was no sign of any women with him.

Instead, following him were two sailors armed with Mauser rifles. Following *them* was a man dressed in a pullover and a peaked cap, with an immaculately trimmed beard. The gold braid above the cap's brim denoted an officer; in all likelihood this was the submarine's captain. He was carrying Holmes's pistol.

I lifted my revolver, ready to loose off a round or two. Perhaps I could create confusion, during which Holmes and I might make good our escape.

"I wouldn't, Watson," my friend warned. "We are not only outgunned but outmanoeuvred."

He nodded, indicating that I should look behind me.

Two more sailors emerged through the control room's other doorway, to my rear. They too had rifles. I could only assume they had been lying in wait all along in the adjacent chamber.

"Put it down, sir," the officer said. "Nothing will be gained by a gunfight except your deaths."

I glanced at Holmes. His eyes said I should comply.

I laid the revolver down on the floor. At a command from the officer, one of the sailors I had been covering scooped it up. I now realised that the disgruntlement this man and the other had exhibited had been mere playacting. They had been perfectly well aware that armed crewmen were lurking next door and that more were poised to intercept Holmes when he ventured for'ard. The same went for the pair up on deck – they had been playacting too. It was all a finely executed subterfuge, and we had fallen for it.

"Gentlemen," said the officer, addressing Holmes and me. "Allow me to introduce myself." He clicked his heels together formally. "I am Captain Johann Künstler of the Imperial German Navy and I would like to welcome you aboard SM *U-19*. She is the very latest U-boat to roll out from the Kaiserliche Werft shipyards at Danzig; in fact, she is so new she may as well be considered a prototype.

Construction of the Type U 19 is not officially scheduled to go ahead until next year. In that respect, you should feel honoured to have this preview of the future of German undersea maritime transportation. Nothing in your Royal Navy even comes close, not even your C-class submarine."

"'Honoured' is, I suppose, one way of looking at it," said Holmes blandly. "Tell me, Herr Kapitän, how did you know Watson and I were coming?"

"We anticipated your arrival," said Captain Künstler. "We have been anticipating it for several days. Were there to be any anomaly during the return of our divers from land, we would know it to mean that Mr Sherlock Holmes had ascertained the truth of the Sea-Devils and was either coming in their stead or forcing them to bring him here."

"The anomaly in this case being that there were two Sea-Devils in the sphere rather than three, and no captive Newforder. Or was it perchance something else?"

"The ringing of the sphere's bell to request that it be drawn in."

"Of course." Holmes's lip curled in self-recrimination. "It was not so simple a matter as merely turning the handle. There was a code."

"Three rings. Two long, one short. You were not to know."

"I was foolish. I should have interrogated the Sea-Devils more thoroughly."

"It would have made no difference." Künstler sounded almost conciliatory. "They were under strict instruction to lie to you. They would have told you the incorrect pattern, and the result would have been just the same."

"And what becomes of the sphere now?"

"I am under orders to jettison it. It has served its purpose and will only be a drag on the submarine. We will overturn it and let it sink."

"You had this well thought out, didn't you?"

"Not I, Mr Holmes," said Künstler. "I am just a humble servant of the fatherland, doing as I am told by my betters, to the fullest of my ability. The credit lies with a passenger of mine, someone with whom I believe you are already acquainted." He glanced over his shoulder. "In fact, here he comes now. May I present…"

With an ushering gesture, Künstler stepped aside to allow someone behind him to enter the control room.

"…His Excellency Baron Von Herling."

CHAPTER TWENTY-SIX

Duty Over Self-preservation

GERMANY'S CHIEF ENVOY TO GREAT BRITAIN – AND R'luhlloig's prime spokesman on Earth – delivered a smiling bow, for all the world as though Holmes and I were longstanding friends of his whom he had not seen in some while.

I heaved a sigh. Holmes put into words what I was feeling: "I wish I could say it comes as a surprise. I had a strong presentiment that the hand of Von Herling was detectable in all this. The Sea-Devils were your auxiliary plan, in case things did not work out as they ought with our serpentine friends in London."

"Not so," said Von Herling. "Rather it was 'our serpentine friends' who were the auxiliary plan. You and they had unfinished business, and it seemed only decent to let them have a crack at you. Of course, had W'gnns and company succeeded in killing you, that would have been convenient, if somewhat dissatisfying. Here I have woven a more elaborate net in which to enmesh you."

"It does seem that organising the business with the Sea-Devils must have required more forethought than simply consigning me to the tender mercies of W'gnns did."

"Absolutely. The folklore of Newford, so close to your home, was the ideal basis for an intrigue in which you could not fail to become involved. It provided material more or less tailor-made for Sherlock Holmes, and I was happy to exploit it for my own ends."

"Well, you have us, that is undeniable," said Holmes.

"Watson and I are securely in your grasp. I would beg you, however, to release the three women whom you are detaining elsewhere on this vessel. They are surplus to requirements now. Do what you like with us old men, but those three deserve to be reunited with their families. They have lives to lead, their whole futures ahead of them."

"I second that," said I. "It does not matter about Holmes and me, but the girls have no role in this any more. Send them home."

"So noble," said Von Herling, looking from Holmes to me and back again. "So self-sacrificial. It is quite touching. It is also quite futile. Release them? Out of the question. The need for those women is not over. They still have a function to discharge."

"What, you rascal?" I declared hotly. "What on earth can you possibly want from them?"

"From them themselves? Nothing. Nothing other than their continued presence aboard this U-boat to ensure your malleability."

"For how long? You mean to kill us, it goes without saying. Why delay? Send the girls home and I swear to you, upon my honour, that in return Holmes and I will not put up a fuss. We will walk the plank, meek as anything, or whatever it is you would have us do."

"Walk the plank?" Von Herling chuckled. "A fanciful notion. We are not pirates of old, Doctor. Maybe you think we might keelhaul you as well! No, nothing so crude and barbaric is planned. Trust me when I say that."

"Trust you? Pah! I would not trust you any more than I would trust a scorpion not to sting me." I shook my fist at him, an impotent gesture but a cathartic one nonetheless.

"Really, this behaviour is most unbefitting. I might expect such histrionics from the three young ladies but not from a man of your mature years." Von Herling turned to Künstler, seemingly tired of my antics. "Captain, have your men escort our two new prisoners to join the others. A word of advice. They may look old but they are resourceful, especially when they are desperate. Take no chances."

Künstler snapped off a salute. "I shall oversee things personally, Your Excellency."

"Good man."

Switching to German, Künstler ordered the sailors with rifles to accompany him, and us, for'ard. We negotiated several bulkhead doorways, each a tight fit, with a low lintel and a high threshold. One compartment we passed through was lined with dozens of curtained-off bunks from which came snoring both soft and loud. We had to duck beneath poorly laundered clothes that hung from lengths of string draped between the berths. The next compartment along boasted several small cabins, into one of which we were invited to enter. I glanced at Holmes to see if he intended any drastic, precipitate action. As our eyes met, he shook his head minutely. There was, it seemed, to be no last-ditch fightback, at least not yet. For the time being, we were going along with Von Herling's stipulations.

The room contained four narrow bunks and not much else. Three of them were occupied by young women who blinked out at us with hollow, grey-ringed eyes; their hair hung lank and unkempt. Two appeared to be in reasonable condition, but the third's cheeks were sunken, the whites of her eyes were bloodshot, and she wheezed as she breathed. She, I could only assume, was Deborah Smythe, the consumptive.

"Listen to me, Captain Künstler," I said. "You must know that I am a medical practitioner. This girl has chronic tuberculosis. She is undoubtedly a carrier, and you have her aboard a vessel packed with human beings, living cheek by jowl. A submarine is the very definition of close quarters, and the chances of contagion are absurdly high. Half your crew could be infected already and not realise it. Do you not appreciate the danger?"

Künstler gave a shrug. "Your task, then, is to minister to the patient and guarantee no contagion happens."

"But that is preposterous. I cannot guarantee anything of the sort."

"You must. His Excellency demands it."

"His Excellency would seem to have no notion what he is dealing with."

"It is not my place to question his orders." Künstler sounded the tiniest bit rueful as he said this. It struck me that he concurred with my assessment of Miss Smythe's condition and would rather not have her on SM *U-19*. He was as worried about an outbreak of tuberculosis as I was. His sense of duty, however, overruled his sense of self-preservation. "I did raise the point when the girl was brought aboard. However, the baron dismissed my objections. He seemed to view her as an asset, not a hazard."

"Little wonder," said Holmes. "The lass will keep Watson occupied. Preoccupied, indeed. Von Herling knows my friend will do everything he can to help her, in accordance with the dictates of his Hippocratic oath and his basic human decency. That makes her a more valuable bargaining chip than either of the other two."

"The man is a demon," I said.

A brief pause from Künstler seemed to say that he did not entirely disagree. As before, however, he kept his face fixed in the placid demeanour of one who knows his place. "The baron is a greatly respected aristocrat and diplomat who has the ear of the kaiser himself. It is not for me to gainsay his decisions. Only to implement them."

With that, he shut the door on us.

I immediately went to young Deborah's side and conducted an examination. She felt feverish and her eyes did not quite follow my forefinger as I waved it from side to side in front of her, her gaze lagging a split second behind. I palpated her lymph glands to see if they were swollen – they were not – and checked her neck for scrofulous abscesses, finding none. I enquired whether she had a headache, stomach pains or any joint stiffness. She, in a faint, whispery voice, admitted to none. She was painfully thin, and while I was tending to her she was seized by a coughing fit, which lasted a full minute. When it was over, a stippling of bloody sputum bedecked the hand she had covered her mouth with.

In short, she displayed all the classic symptoms of pulmonary tuberculosis. The infection had at least not spread beyond her lungs, but that was small consolation.

One of the other girls – a pretty, auburn-haired thing – piped up. "Who are you gents?" she asked. "You are not with them, are you?" By "them" she meant the Germans.

"On the contrary," said Holmes. "We came as your saviours, and we hope to fulfil that role yet. My name is Sherlock Holmes."

"The detective? The one what lives over by Eastbourne?"

"One and the same. And this is my esteemed colleague Dr Watson."

"Him as writes stories about you."

"Him as does exactly that," said Holmes good-humouredly. "And you, if I am not mistaken, are Blanche Grady. You have your mother's eyes and nose and your father's complexion. Which means that, by a process of elimination, you" – he turned to the third girl – "must be Mrs Sarah Cummins."

"That is me," said the woman, who looked to be senior to the others by a couple of years. "Oh, Mr Holmes, what is to become of us? Five days I have been here. At least I think it's five; keeping track of time is hard when you don't get so much as a glimpse of daylight. We have not been ill-treated, we are fed, and our other needs are met. But we haven't been allowed to leave this cabin even once. I miss my husband and my baby boy. I'd give anything to see them again."

"And you shall, my dear lady, if I have any say in the matter. I fear, however, that you must reconcile yourself to the notion that it may not happen any time soon."

Mrs Cummins's eyes glistened with tears and she choked back a sob.

"What my friend is saying," I interjected, "in his somewhat tactless way, is that we cannot help you imminently but we are working on a means of getting us all out of here in due course. We crave your patience, that is all. Everything shall be well."

At that moment a loud mechanical rumbling started up, and the submarine began to shudder around us. There was the sound of rushing water, and presently I felt a sense of sinking. With a series of almighty creaks and groans the vessel tilted towards her bow. The change in angle caused both Holmes and me to reach out for support.

"They are charging the ballast tanks with water," my friend observed. "We descend."

Now came the churning of engines, a throb that travelled along the submarine from the stern and made everything vibrate.

"There go the propellers," said Holmes. "We are getting under way."

"We are travelling?" I said.

"Evidently."

"But where to?"

"I wish I knew. Some port in Germany perhaps. Bremerhaven? Hamburg? I daresay you and I should make ourselves comfortable, Watson. We are in for a long voyage."

He was right. We just had no idea how long that voyage would be.

CHAPTER TWENTY-SEVEN

Our Last Bow?

HOLMES AND I SPENT THE REMAINDER OF THAT first night at sea sitting on the thin strip of floor in the women's cabin, facing each other, his back against the outer wall, mine against the door, our legs interleaved. He invited me to take the spare bunk but I refused. It felt improper that I should enjoy relative comfort and him not. It felt even more improper for two men to be sharing sleeping accommodation with three members of the opposite sex, but we were given no choice.

I didn't sleep a wink and neither did Holmes. I watched his face. His mind was racing, I could see. He was weighing up our predicament and evaluating ways out of it, or so I could only assume.

Around 6 a.m. a sailor came with breakfast: a roll, slivers of smoked sausage, and coffee. Holmes begged an audience with Captain Künstler, who arrived shortly.

"Watson and I cannot stay here," Holmes said, indicating the cabin. "These women need their privacy."

Künstler agreed, and within an hour we were being shown to an adjacent cabin, which had just two berths.

"It belongs properly to my commander and lieutenant-commander," Künstler said. "They are none too happy to have been asked to vacate it and mingle with the ratings. I have pointed out to them, however, that I am in the same position myself. My cabin is now Baron Von Herling's, and I am relegated to whatever bunk is free in the crew's quarters. We are all of us having to make sacrifices."

"We are grateful, Captain," I said. "Might I ask what medicines you have aboard? You must have some."

"The bare necessities."

"Opiates?"

"Yes."

"Would you be able to spare a dose of morphine for me to give to Miss Smythe? Rest is what her body requires most. The strain of incarceration is not good for her health."

"I think that can be arranged."

"Fresh air would benefit her too. The atmosphere in a submarine is stuffy and none too sanitary, and that cannot be good for her lungs."

"You mean we should surface and allow her time on deck?" Künstler seemed to consider the idea before rejecting it. "Not possible, I'm afraid."

"Who is in charge of this boat?" Holmes said.

"Me, of course. Who else?"

"Then you may bring your submarine up to the surface any time you wish."

"That is correct."

"You have shown yourself to possess a streak of integrity. Can you not see that Watson's request is both reasonable and medically justified?"

"I have an itinerary I must keep to. We can and will surface when appropriate. Allowing a prisoner to roam free on deck, however, is out of the question."

"That is not your decision."

"I believe it is, Mr Holmes."

"No, you misunderstand. What I mean is that Baron

Von Herling has already made the decision for you, has he not? You are not truly master of your vessel as long as he is here. I reckon you would do as we asked if you had the choice, but His Excellency has told you to make no concessions for us."

"He permitted me to move you to this cabin."

"But beyond that, he has been quite clear: we are to be kept under the strictest regime at all times."

"And you would have me disobey him?" Künstler said stiffly. "I think not."

He turned on his heel and left. The sailor who was stationed outside on sentry duty aimed a harsh frown at us and patted the stock of the rifle that was slung around his shoulder, to show us that he brooked no nonsense. Then he slammed the door shut.

"Why did you have to antagonise the man, Holmes?" I said. "Künstler could be a useful ally. I think he resents Von Herling, although he cannot bring himself to say so. He may even mistrust him, sensing somehow the insidious entity which you and I know skulks within the ambassador. We might surely turn that to our advantage."

"Quite, old fellow. I simply wished to provoke Künstler, in order to see how deep his loyalty to Von Herling runs. It runs deep, but beneath lies a strong counter-current. In time we can tap into that."

"His sympathies will be a little harder to engage now that you have irked him."

"One should never be too obvious. Besides, in order to cultivate soil it is helpful to rake it first."

A sailor came later with morphine and a syringe. He

looked on as I injected Miss Smythe with the drug. Soon the girl was asleep and breathing more easily. I put an ear to her chest and listened to the telltale crackling noises that indicated the presence of pulmonary tubercles in the upper lobes of her lungs. These lesions would not heal unless she got plenty of rest and had good air to breathe. I resolved to press Captain Künstler on this matter, and Von Herling too if need be. Otherwise Miss Smythe's condition was going to deteriorate to the point where she would be too enfeebled to eat or drink and would waste away to nothingness.

*

Over the next four days my life alternated between being cooped up in the two-berth cabin with Holmes and tending to my patient next door. By now it was apparent that SM *U-19* would not be putting in at any of Germany's North Sea ports. Holmes had calculated that if we were travelling at the submarine's top speed of 10 knots, as the constant strenuous exertions of the engines seemed to indicate, then we would have covered the 500 nautical miles to Bremerhaven in a couple of days. Hamburg would have required a further day and a half, including the journey down the river Elbe. Since we had not called in at either, it seemed unlikely that we were bound for Germany at all. There were Baltic ports such as Rostock and Lübeck, of course, but what would be gained by sailing all the way round Jutland to get to those and doubling the length of the journey only to end up in the same country?

"No," my friend averred, "we are bound for somewhere else entirely. But where? Where?"

On the fifth day the engines' constant thrumming refrain all at once dwindled. I had grown accustomed to the sound by then, and it took me a few moments to notice its diminution. Then came an intense bubbling roar, and the bow began to lift.

"Air being pumped into the ballast tanks," Holmes observed. "We are surfacing at last."

"What now?" I wondered. "Do you think we have arrived wherever it is we are meant to arrive?"

A couple of sailors came for us and escorted us at gunpoint to the control room and thence up the ladder of the conning tower. The outside world smelled unbelievably sweet. The unventilated atmosphere within the submarine had become stale to the point of oppressiveness, thick with the reek of machine oil and men's unwashed bodies. I inhaled the new air heartily, squinting all the while against the dazzle of broad daylight, for my eyes were habituated to the vessel's crepuscular electric-lit gloom.

A half-dozen sailors were already stationed on deck; like our escorts, armed. Captain Künstler awaited us there too, sombre-faced.

To me, it looked very much like a firing squad.

"Holmes…" I said softly.

"Spain," replied he.

"I beg your pardon?"

"Perhaps Portugal. The coastline due east of us. You can just see it on the horizon. More likely Spain than Portugal, given our rate of travel, but the Iberian Peninsula definitely. Can you feel the warmth in the air? The warmth of southerly latitudes. We have navigated the

Bay of Biscay underwater, which is wise given the area's propensity for rough seas. Now in calmer conditions we may proceed on the surface, achieving greater speeds. Is that not so, Captain?"

Künstler, who had overheard Holmes's surmise, nodded.

"But," I said, "we are here to be executed, surely. Shot, and our bodies dumped overboard. How can our whereabouts then matter?"

"Shot? I think not," said Holmes. "Where is Baron Von Herling? If this were our final hour – our last bow – would he not wish to be present to witness it?"

"Doubtless he is coming up shortly to do just that."

"Well, whether or not that is the case, we should make the most of this opportunity. Let us stretch our legs and revel in the liberty we have been afforded, limited though it may be."

We strode the length of the submarine back and forth several times, our feet clanging on the steel plates of the deck, with the watchful eyes of our armed guard ever upon us. The narrow strip of coastline, from this distance no broader than a pencil stroke, was painfully tantalising. So near and yet so far.

Figures emerged from the conning tower. I expected Baron Von Herling but was surprised to see Mrs Cummins and the Misses Grady and Smythe. I hurried over to assist the last as she tottered onto the deck. She clung on to me for support, peering around her in bleary confusion.

"Just relax, Miss Smythe," I said. "Try and make the most of the clean air and sunshine while you can." I did not share with her my concern that we were all of us facing imminent death. I wanted her final moments on earth to be as pleasant as possible.

We remained outdoors for a full half an hour. As the minutes went by, my sense of ineluctable doom began to fade. Unless Captain Künstler was being unusually cruel, prolonging our agony, we were not facing execution after all. We were, rather, being shown a rare compassion.

When the time came for us to return below, I caught Künstler's eye and offered him a small nod of gratitude.

"See?" said he. "I am no monster, Doctor. His Excellency took some convincing, but I was able to make him understand that it is in his interests to keep our passengers in the best possible condition. I have been a submariner for nearly a decade. Spells outside the confines of the vessel, however brief, are precious beyond price."

"You have my appreciation."

"I do not know why it is that the baron holds you and Mr Holmes in such enmity, nor is it my place to ask. You are enemies of Germany, that much I do know. If nothing else you are responsible for murdering one of its foremost citizens, Werther Von Bork."

"Untrue."

Künstler continued regardless. "Yet it seems more personal than political between His Excellency and you. I have noted this, and it is my opinion that the two things – the personal and the political – should never be mixed. There should be a clear line of demarcation. That is all I have to say on the subject."

Back down into the bowels of SM *U-19* we went, and

shortly the submarine was on her way again. Künstler's words stayed with me. I had the sense of a deeply honourable man. He had put his neck on the line, pleading with Von Herling for us to be given the opportunity of time on deck. He apparently had no idea that he was dealing not just with an eminent national figure but with the foul, immigrant consciousness, whose advice Von Herling surely sought before making any judgement. Even so, it had been risky, simply speaking up on our behalf. I admired his bravery.

*

I resolved to push my luck with Künstler. I asked if I might be given pen and paper.

"What for?" he enquired, reasonably enough.

"I am a writer."

"I am well aware. I have read your stories, as translated by Herr Curt Von Musgrave."

"He has done a rather good job, I am led to believe."

"Your work is popular in my homeland, for all the differences that exist between our two countries. You wish to carry on writing while aboard my ship? I do not have any objection to that myself. There can surely be no harm. I will have to consult with His Excellency, of course."

"Of course."

A little later, a sailor brought me pen, ink and a blank journal with *Tagebuch* embossed on the cover in Gothic script. From the captain's own supply, I was led to understand.

I have to admit it felt good to have writing materials

to hand. There is a therapeutic effect in committing one's thoughts to paper, and the habit is hard to break. Furthermore, since it seemed that we were to be on the submarine for the duration, I thought I might benefit from having something to distract me aside from ministering to Miss Smythe.

So I began keeping a diary of the voyage, entries from which I have excerpted over the ensuing pages. In many ways, the diary helped preserve my sanity against the triple threat of tedium, ennui and dread. It was a lifeline.

CHAPTER TWENTY-EIGHT

Excerpts from My Diary of the Voyage

Saturday 24th September

We have been at sea for a week and a half now. Holmes and I have learned to live according to routine, as mariners do, and indeed as convicts do. We chart the passing of the days. We are aware of the four-hourly ship's watches. We are alert to the changing of the sentries outside our cabin. Mealtimes are another form of temporal punctuation and a welcome relief from the boredom, even if the efforts of the ship's cook can hardly be described as *haute cuisine*. Why are Germans so fond of cured meats? Even the boiled sauerkraut comes laced with slivers of bacon.

Miss Smythe is visibly improving and I am progressively reducing the morphine dosages. Sound sleeps are encouraging her body to repair itself. Still, she remains far from well. The sailors know it and shun her as though she has the plague – which is perhaps not an inaccurate simile.

Holmes, for his part, has succumbed to the lassitude that habitually envelops him when he has nothing with which to engage his mind. He spends most of the time simply lying in his bunk, at times so mute and withdrawn as to appear catatonic. One can only speculate what is going on behind those unfocused, half-lidded eyes.

Once a day, unless the weather is foul, we five captives are allowed time on deck. We are still not trusted to go up there without armed chaperones. But really, what do our captors expect? That we are going to hurl ourselves into the water and make a swim for it? Swim to where? The nearest land lies miles distant. Passing ships are too far away to hail. We remain prisoners even in the open air. The wide blue ocean is our cage.

Monday 26th September

Baron Von Herling stays in his cabin, doing of his own volition that which is imposed upon Holmes and me. Sometimes, through the partition wall, we hear him and Captain Künstler talking, although we cannot hear what is said. Otherwise we hear him move about, or occasionally murmur to himself, but that is all.

I have asked Holmes how it feels to have his mortal foe perpetually so close by. His reply: "I have lived beneath the shadow of R'luhlloig for some fifteen years, much as you have. This feels little different, merely a physical manifestation of the same."

"I would gladly throttle the rogue, given the chance."

"I would be astonished if Künstler does not have standing orders to kill one of the lasses next door in case of that eventuality. And then, with us duly punished for our effrontery, R'luhlloig would simply latch on to some other individual, lamprey-like, and things would continue as before. He might well worm his way into the consciousness of Künstler himself. Logically, the captain would be the next most suitable host for him."

"Künstler lacks the innate corruption that R'luhlloig preys upon."

"You believe he would be pure-hearted enough to resist the Hidden Mind's enticements? Well, perhaps, but even the best of us may succumb to the temptations of power and advancement. The quality of a man's probity is never assured until it is tested. My advice, Watson, is not to lose yourself in fantasies of insurgency and retaliation. Conserve your energy for when it is needed."

"But you are dreaming up ideas for rectifying this situation, aren't you, Holmes? Please reassure me of that."

"The matter is in hand, old friend."

Wednesday 28th September

I write this at the tiny fold-down desk in our cabin, shortly after midnight, during the hours of the middle watch. Holmes slumbers. I cannot. Tonight I am prey to all manner of qualms and forebodings and feel the urge to exorcise them by writing them down. I fear that we shall never see England again. I fear that Holmes and I shall not fulfil our promise to the three women to save them. I fear most of all that Sherlock Holmes has given up. He does nothing but mope and drowse. He seems worse than depressed. He seems defeated. I cajole him and chastise him, to no effect.

Has this been R'luhlloig's intention all along? To break my friend by simply numbing him into submission? If so, he may at last have hit upon a stratagem that works, and all is lost.

Thursday 29th September

Today Holmes came alive again, albeit briefly.

Early, just after breakfast, SM *U-19* slowed to a crawl

and began a series of delicate manoeuvres – turns and sideways shifts – before coming to a standstill. There followed all manner of activity both on board and off: shouts, bangs, clangs, footfalls on deck, men tramping to and fro past our cabin, the sounds of liquids gushing and sloshing into the submarine's storage tanks.

This was still going on when a sailor came to bring us lunch. Holmes, roused from his torpor for the first time in days, enquired of the fellow where we were. "We have clearly put in at port," said he. "Would I be right in thinking it is somewhere on the coast of North Africa?"

"Rabat," came the reply. The sailor in question is a young fellow called Wolfgang, a first-year cadet and the most junior-ranking person on board. He cannot be more than seventeen years old and seems a likeable sort, well-presented and well-educated, with a good command of English. I gather his maternal grandfather is a retired admiral and Wolfgang wishes to follow in his illustrious forebear's footsteps.

"Ah, Morocco," said Holmes. "Then I should imagine, because we have bypassed the Straits of Gibraltar, that we are not heading into the Mediterranean but continuing southward down the Atlantic coast of Africa."

"I do not know, sir. I think so."

"How long will we stay docked?"

"A few hours."

"And the crew will be enjoying some shore leave once they have finished loading supplies aboard, won't they?"

"Not I, but most of them, yes. I and a few others are having to remain behind, as the rota dictates. My turn will come at the next port."

"Do you miss your girl back in Hanover, Wolfgang?" said Holmes.

"My…?" The boy looked startled. "How did you…?"

"Lotte, is that her name?"

Now he looked flabbergasted.

Holmes shook his head in a kindly fashion. "You have lately written her a letter, which you have no doubt asked a fellow sailor to post for you in town. Your hand rested on the page before the ink could dry. On the outer edge of your palm a few characters can be seen, in mirror image, smudged but legible. There are two partial spellings. One is 'e-i-b-c-h', which must surely represent the bulk of the word '*liebchen*', a term of endearment usually reserved for a paramour. The other is 'Hanov', which can only mean Hanover. The inference is elementary."

"But how did you know her name?"

"There, I must admit, I cheated somewhat. The day before yesterday, I overheard two of your comrades cooing just such a name outside our cabin. They were doing it in a teasing yet affectionate manner, exactly as older men might towards a youngster in the throes of first love. I chanced my arm that the same Lotte they had spoken of was your very own '*liebchen*', knowing it was a fairly safe bet."

Wolfgang exited the cabin with the air of someone who has witnessed a marvellous conjuring trick, his enthusiasm in no way diminished by having the workings of it explained to him.

"You have made a friend," I said.

"The lad is impressionable. Even the least exercise of my powers would have an effect upon him."

"It is good to see you exercising them at all. I had begun to worry."

"I know. 'He seems defeated.' Thus did you write about me last night."

"How…? Have you been looking at my diary?" I was more ashamed than angered, but I used the anger to paper over the shame. "How dare you!"

"I did not need to look at it. I merely watched you in the act of writing. The movements of the top of a pen may reveal the words that are being written with the nib end, to one who observes carefully enough."

"Well," I said, a little defensively, "you do appear defeated."

"Appearances can be deceptive."

"For all our sakes, I hope so."

Friday 30th September

We departed from Rabat late last night, the submarine now replenished with diesel, fresh water and foodstuffs. The sailors who had been granted shore leave returned in high spirits, emitting peals of boisterous laughter and drunkenly singing songs, the lyrics of which one did not need fluent German to know were bawdy.

"Five hours, give or take," said Holmes. "That is how long an absence they were allowed."

"What of it?"

"Five hours, Watson, during which the boat was manned by a severely depleted crew."

"My goodness." I dropped my voice, for fear of being

overheard by Von Herling next door. "Are you suggesting what I think you are suggesting?"

"Against SM *U-19*'s full complement of thirty-odd men we would stand no chance, whereas against a skeleton crew of a half-dozen or so…? It is simply a question of engineering the right conditions. We will need a pretext, a distraction of some sort."

"I am all ears."

"But I need to think on it."

Holmes could not be prevailed upon to expound further. It heartens me nonetheless to know that he is seriously addressing the matter of escape, after a lengthy fallow period during which it seemed he was not. He has not given up after all. I wonder whether he was galvanised into action by learning that I thought him defeated. His pride, it would seem, cannot abide the ignominy of his best friend despairing of him.

I still have my uses!

Tuesday 4th October

Miss Smythe has rallied. Some colour has returned to her cheeks. Her coughing fits are shorter and further apart, and her sputum is now almost entirely free of blood. She is eating well. I believe the crisis may be past.

It is not my care alone that has brought about this recovery; Mrs Cummins and Miss Grady have played their part. They have been a source of constant support and encouragement to Miss Smythe. They, as much as I if not more so, have looked after her.

All three women, indeed, are proving remarkably resilient. It is something I have long believed about the fairer sex: they are the stronger sex too. I do not mean in terms of physical muscularity but in terms of stamina and mental fortitude. Women endure far more suffering and discomfort in the normal course of their lives than men do. It has equipped them with an ability to endure hardship, and rise above it, such as the male of the species can only envy. Each time I enter their cabin I find myself exposed to a camaraderie, a spiritedness that belies the grim circumstances. A bond like that of sisterhood has grown up amongst the trio and they draw succour from it.

This should stand us in good stead when we do eventually make our bid for freedom. Holmes has intimated that he has come up with the bare bones of a plan and it will require the full collaboration and cooperation of the women.

"They are our secret weapon, Watson," he has said. "While they are underestimated as 'weak, helpless females', our chances of success are increased. The same goes for our own apparent docility, yours and mine. The longer we are perceived as passive, the more complacent our captors become. The time will soon be right."

CHAPTER TWENTY-NINE

Further Excerpts from My Diary of the Voyage

Wednesday 12th October

We have rounded the rump of western Africa and are sailing across the Gulf of Guinea. The weather is sultry. The sun beats down. The interior of SM *U-19*, as she ploughs through the waves, is hot and humid and more intolerable than ever. At the height of noon it is like a tropical glasshouse in here. Condensation drips down the steel walls. The sailors move about in sluggardly, lumpen fashion. I lie sweating in my bunk and let my mind drift, too enervated to do much else.

Tomorrow, according to Wolfgang, we cross the equator. Wolfgang has become our regular bringer of meals. He has, I think, elected himself to the role, and the other crewmen are content to leave it to him. They appear fond of him and treat him as much as a mascot as a shipmate, with indulgence. Holmes seems to extend him the same sort of indulgence.

Tuesday 18th October

Our second resupply stop. We are at Benguela in Angola.

The time is not yet right for any escape attempt, Holmes says. Angola is a Portuguese dominion, not an easy place for five English fugitives to lose themselves in and seek sanctuary.

How much longer must we wait?

And how much further is the submarine going? What is the end-point of this journey?

I am beginning to wonder if there is one. Maybe the journey will never end.

Wednesday 19th October

Wolfgang did not much enjoy his shore leave yesterday. He describes Benguela as busy, dusty, and full of wretched locals pestering him, whether begging or trying to sell him trinkets and vile-looking street food. Moreover, someone picked his pocket, robbing him of money and – worse – a monogrammed silk handkerchief, a gift from his beloved Lotte. Wolfgang is not a worldly youth. He seems to have had a sheltered upbringing. This voyage could be the making of him but I fear it is more apt to be the breaking of him.

Still, he treats Holmes and me with civility and respect. Unlike his fellow sailors he lowers his guard around us and is amiable. He has told us that when he gains a commission he will ask for Lotte's hand in marriage. She is a beauty, from a good Hanoverian family. Both his parents and hers would approve of the match. I find myself wishing him well.

Friday 4th November

Terrible storms around the Cape of Good Hope. This being a U-boat, we ride them out by descending into the depths. Down here, in the sea's dark womb, we are cocooned against the buffeting of wind and wave. We cruise serenely along, immune.

Wolfgang says we were meant to stop at Cape Town but, owing to the inclement weather, we will carry on to Durban instead.

Wolfgang has become the main conduit of information between us and the rest of the submarine. He keeps us apprised of our location and he gossips about the seamen on board: the bosun who drinks too much; the helmsman who boasts he has the proverbial "girl in every port"; and the motor officer who weeps uncontrollably in his bunk at night for reasons no one knows. Through Wolfgang I feel a little less isolated and excluded; perhaps Holmes feels likewise.

When I asked Wolfgang today what he knows about our ultimate destination, he replied, "Nothing, sir. The captain has not said, nor Baron Von Herling. I think it is His Excellency who is giving directions and the captain is merely going where he is told. Our purpose is scientific, that much seems apparent."

"Scientific?" said Holmes.

"What else can it be? SM *U-19* is not, in her current configuration, a warship. Unlike other U-boats she is not fitted with machine guns on deck, and our torpedo racks are empty. Therefore we must be conducting scientific research. You two are here for your expertise, press-ganged into joining us because you would not have come of your own accord. Your talents are to be utilised to the advantage of Imperial Germany and the kaiser, whether you like it or not. The inference is elementary."

Wolfgang was clearly pleased with himself for having applied methods like Holmes's own in his appraisal of the situation. He was more pleased still when Holmes said, "You may not be far wide of the mark, young fellow. Congratulations. A sound deduction."

After Wolfgang was gone, I said to Holmes, "You sounded genuinely commendatory. Is he right?"

"He is right in as much as Von Herling doubtless expects everyone to believe this is a scientific expedition. Even if the baron has not specified as much, the crew must assume it is so. I myself reckon that R'luhlloig may indeed want something from us – expertise, or something similar."

"Having tried to kill us so often, he now needs us alive?"

"Needs it or finds it expedient."

"What if his intention is to sacrifice us again, as he tried to when he was Professor Moriarty?"

"To what end?" said Holmes. "R'luhlloig is a god now. Gods receive sacrifices, they do not make them."

"Intern us indefinitely, then. Keep us as trophies."

"There you could be on to something, Watson. Perhaps we are just spoils of war for R'luhlloig to parade before his subjects when the Outer Gods finally triumph over the Old Ones."

I raised a startled eyebrow. "You think victory for the Outer Gods is inevitable?"

"Under R'luhlloig's generalship, I fear it is. The Old Ones have not fared well. As you know, I have been doing my best to follow the conflict. At the Diogenes you asked me how it was going and I did not have the opportunity to answer. Now I can tell you that, when last I checked, it was not going in the Old Ones' favour. The *Necronomicon* may be employed as a tool of divination, like a warlock's scrying ball, by those who know how. One may commune with the book and in a dreamlike state 'see' events in the higher cosmic realms."

I thought of when we returned to Holmes's farm from London – it seems a long time ago now, not just a few weeks – and I overheard him in his study talking to himself. This must have been the act of communing he was describing.

"It sounds like a hazardous practice," I said.

"Any interaction with the *Necronomicon* is hazardous." Holmes said this airily but there was a telling graveness in his eyes. "I have used it nonetheless, and what it has enabled me to establish is that the Old Ones are all but defeated. The Outer Gods have overrun them and overthrown them. Ithaqua, Yig, Hastur, and the rest – bested, humbled and enslaved. R'luhlloig is not far from achieving his ambition of ruling the heavens. A single Old One remains standing. He has yet to be challenged, let alone beaten. R'luhlloig has saved him for last."

"Which?" I said, half knowing the answer already, for it had to be the Old One whose name Holmes had uttered several times in his study. "Which of them is it?"

"Cthulhu. Great Cthulhu. He alone remains."

Monday 7th November

We are a day away from Durban. Holmes has hinted that tomorrow we may at last stage our breakout.

He has shared his plan with me. I do not like it, for

many reasons. It leaves a bad taste in my mouth. Yet I can see its logic and believe it may work.

I have spoken privately with Mrs Cummins and the Misses Grady and Smythe during my daily iatric visit to their cabin, and they have all agreed to do their bit.

Tomorrow, our ordeal could well be over.

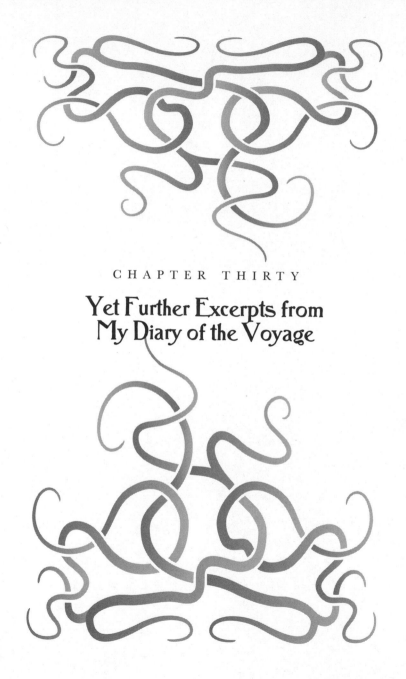

CHAPTER THIRTY

Yet Further Excerpts from My Diary of the Voyage

I write this with the heaviest of hearts. I am crushed. Never have I felt so crestfallen, so despondent.

We came close. Agonisingly close. Only to fall at the final hurdle.

Damn you, Sherlock Holmes!

No, I must not blame him. I am as much at fault as he.

I will set down an account of what happened, as it happened, with all the dispassion and objectivity at my disposal.

Docked at Durban, the crew of SM *U-19* went through the usual rigmarole of restocking and refuelling. Shore leave was granted to the majority, as ever. This gave us a period of time – five hours at most – during which the submarine was understaffed and lying tethered at port.

It was then that Deborah Smythe suffered a sudden, catastrophic relapse. A coughing fit overtook her like no other, so loud that it was clearly audible through the partition wall between our cabin and the women's. This coincided with Wolfgang bringing us our lunch.

"Gracious!" I said. "That sounds awful."

"I thought the lady was getting better, Doctor," said Wolfgang. "What is wrong with her?"

Now the sounds of Miss Smythe's distress were augmented by panic-stricken cries from her two companions.

"I don't know," I said. "I had best go and see her at once."

Wolfgang had left the door open, but there was a sailor

on guard duty outside. He barred my way with his rifle.

"Are you deaf?" I said to him. "Can you not hear? The girl is suffering. I am needed."

The guard may not have understood precisely what I was telling him, but my urgency, in tandem with the sounds Miss Smythe was making, pleaded an eloquent case. He relented and allowed me past. I rushed to the women's cabin. There I found Deborah Smythe sprawled upon the floor, wracked with coughing. When I straightened her up, her mouth was smeared with wet crimson.

"Dear God," I declared. "The infection appears to have eaten into the pulmonary artery and caused an aneurysm."

The guard, peering in through the doorway, saw the blood on Miss Smythe's face. He looked appalled and alarmed. His grip on his rifle loosened ever so slightly.

That was all the opportunity Holmes needed. He lunged out of our cabin and prised the rifle from the man's hands. Reversing it, he struck the fellow a blow to the skull with its stock. The sailor gave a sharp yelp and crumpled in a heap, out cold.

Holmes spun, aiming the gun at Wolfgang. He worked the action, chambering a round.

"Don't do anything rash, young man," said he. "Just put your hands in the air."

Meanwhile, Miss Smythe recovered her composure and got to her feet, wiping her mouth clean. Her masquerade had been exemplary, as had that of her associates. She knew well what a severe coughing fit was like and had been able to replicate one to perfection. The "blood" was in fact a passable facsimile concocted by the three women from components of recent meals – principally beetroot, ground-up potato and some kind of pale sauce. They had squirrelled away these ingredients and mixed them together according to a recipe furnished by Holmes.

"Well done, my dear," I said, and Miss Smythe offered me a little curtsey and a dip of the head, like an actress at curtain call.

I ushered the women out of the cabin. Holmes had already gone ahead of us with Wolfgang. The four of us joined the two of them in the control room. Wolfgang looked hangdog and mortified, while the couple of sailors who were on duty at their stations looked aghast.

"You will let us walk free," Holmes told them, "or the boy dies." To emphasise the point he jabbed the barrel of the rifle into the hapless cadet's spine.

"You would not shoot me, Mr Holmes," Wolfgang snarled. "I know you. You are not like that."

"Then you have no idea how highly I value my own life and the lives of my friends here, and how little I value yours," Holmes retorted.

"I thought *I* was your friend." Wolfgang's bruised, brittle tone of voice signalled a profound sense of betrayal.

"You were naïve." To the other sailors Holmes said, "So, what is it to be? Will you let us pass, or must innocent young Wolfgang perish?"

He was offering them a choice that was really no choice at all. Neither man could abide the thought of having the cadet's blood on his conscience. One looked to the other and, by mutual consent, they gestured that they would offer no opposition. Their lips were tight with barely suppressed infuriation.

Moments later we were up on the submarine's deck. Around us spread Durban's harbour, a large lagoon dotted with islets and encrusted around the edge with buildings. A blazing sun shed a furnace-like light upon wharves that bustled with activity. The air resounded with the cries of dockworkers, the clanking of pulleys and the whirring of cranes.

A gangplank connected SM *U-19* to the quay beside which she was moored. We filed down it, setting foot upon solid ground for the first time in weeks.

"You will let me go free now, yes?" Wolfgang said, both plaintive and sullen. "I am not necessary any more."

"I'm afraid you are," replied Holmes, "and you will remain necessary until I determine otherwise."

"I despise you."

"It cannot be helped. Let us keep moving, one and all."

We threaded a path through porters carrying luggage and goods, sailors ambling and lounging, and gaggles of scrawny native children who seemed to have nothing better to do than rush about laughing. Holmes no longer had the rifle pointed at Wolfgang's back, but it dangled from his hand ready in case the youth got it into his head to run. Soon we had put the harbour behind us and were negotiating a maze of busy, twisting streets.

"Where are we headed, Holmes?" I enquired. Already, in that sweltering tropical heat, I was perspiring profusely. It reminded me of my first days in Afghanistan, before my body adjusted to the climate.

"The British High Commission, of course. The ideal

place of refuge. It is an embassy in all but name, and Von Herling cannot touch us once we are there, not without inflicting serious embarrassment upon his homeland."

"Do you know where it is?"

"No, but I am sure a local can apprise us of its where-abouts."

We had just emerged onto a major thoroughfare lined with shops, Durban's equivalent of Oxford Street. The pavements were thronged with passers-by, browsing the wares in the windows.

"Him, for example?" I pointed to a beefy, khaki-clad Boer who was coming the other way. Taking the initiative, I hailed him, saying, "My good man, we are rather lost. Can you tell us where we might find the High Commissioner's residence?"

"Britishers, eh?" the slab-faced fellow said. His features settled into a sneer. "In case you don't remember, we've just fought a couple of wars against you people. Why should I help you?"

"Common decency," I said.

"The same decency your Lord Kitchener showed when he ordered Boer farms torched? The same decency that led to twenty thousand of us dying in British camps?" The man spat at my feet. "That's what you can do with your common decency. Find your own way, damn you, and be grateful that I don't give the lot of you the drubbing you deserve."

"Please, sir," Wolfgang blurted out. "These men are holding me against my will. I am a German sailor, as you can see from my uniform."

"German, eh?"

"They have threatened to shoot me. You must protect me."

Our plan was in danger of unravelling. I had not anticipated that the Boer would be quite so hostile towards us, or that Wolfgang would pluck up the nerve to throw himself on the man's mercy. Wolfgang was calling Holmes's bluff over the rifle. He knew my friend would not use the gun on him.

"Is this true?" the Boer said, rounding on Holmes and gesturing at the weapon.

"Not a bit of it. I apologise that we have troubled you. We must be going. Good day."

We moved off, Holmes taking Wolfgang gently but firmly by the elbow and nudging him forwards.

"A poor choice, Watson," he muttered to me. "You should have left it to me. I was hoping to interrogate someone a bit more sophisticated and a lot less antagonistic."

"How was I to know he harboured such a dislike of our nation?"

"A man like him, with the rough hands and sunburned complexion of a farmer? Of course he would hate the British. I would be very surprised if he wasn't amongst the guerrilla bands who harried our troops so relentlessly."

"Well, no harm done," I said breezily, looking over my shoulder. The Boer was watching us walk away, scratching his head. I saw puzzlement on his face and a growing sense that something was seriously amiss.

"Wait!" he called out.

Holmes quickened his pace, and the rest of us followed suit.

"Come back here!"

The Boer began lumbering after us. The enmity of his race towards the British disposed him to think the worst of us anyway; Wolfgang's entreaty had merely lent weight to that bias.

"Pardon me, ladies, but we must go faster," said Holmes to the women.

We broke into a run. Or at least, five of us did. Wolfgang baulked, requiring Holmes to pull him along.

"Boy," I warned him. "Come on now. Don't resist."

Wolfgang dug in his heels all the harder.

Holmes relinquished his grip on the lad. "We may as well leave him. He has outlived his usefulness."

By now the Boer had begun raising a hue and cry. Heads were turning. His fellow South Africans were becoming agitated.

"Stop them!" the Boer bellowed. "They're British and they're up to something crooked!"

Our group carried on running, now minus Wolfgang. None of us, save perhaps Holmes, could be described as being at the peak of fitness. My age told against me, as did the debilitation brought on by weeks of inactivity in the belly of the U-boat. The three women, although they had youth on their side, were similarly weakened by incarceration, and of course Miss Smythe was generally in poor shape, for all that the worst effects of her illness had been ameliorated. In short order she was out of breath, her pace faltering. Mrs Cummins and Miss Grady caught hold of her arms and bore her along with them, but she could barely set one foot in front of the other. Eventually, inevitably, she stumbled and fell.

I hoisted her upright – emaciated as she was, she hardly weighed a thing – and exhorted her onward. However, it was clear she could not go another step. Her face was white as chalk and her chest was heaving. She looked on the brink of fainting.

"Go," I told the others. "I will stay with Miss Smythe. Get to the High Commission. Fetch aid if you can."

By now the hue and cry had become an uproar. Dozens of people were following us, clamouring. A number of them were moving in to waylay us, including the owner of a hardware store who had armed himself with a rake, and a farrier wielding a large iron-headed mallet. We were moments away from being surrounded by an angry mob.

"Take this." Holmes thrust the rifle at me. He swept Miss Smythe up in his arms and we resumed running.

We diverted down a side alley. The baying crowd were at our heels, led by the Boer and Wolfgang. The latter, to judge by his feral grin, was delighted to have gained the upper hand. I imagine he was thinking it would help his career prospects no end if he helped apprehend us fugitives. Rather than being scorned for allowing himself to be taken hostage, he would be commended for foiling our escape attempt. I cannot in all honesty blame him for wanting to get his own back on us. Holmes, having cynically cultivated his trust, had then abused it in the cruellest fashion. I had gone along with the scheme, so I was no less culpable.

In the next street, which ran parallel to the one we had just been on, Holmes narrowly avoided a collision with a Negro, nearly dropping his female burden in the process.

"Quick," he said to the startled man, who to judge by the apron he wore over his suit was some kind of servant out on an errand. "The British High Commission. Which way?"

The Negro spied the mob of white men behind us and appeared to make a calculation. Assisting us would be to our pursuers' detriment, and there was no love lost between his kind and theirs.

He pointed down the street. "Far end," said he. "Go right. The High Commission is the big building just past the corner."

Off we went, Holmes thanking the Negro with a wave of the hand.

We made the turn at the end of the street, and there I beheld a Union Flag fluttering above the gate of a compound, an imposing two-storey colonial house behind. I am never unhappy to see our nation's flag but I cannot recall being more cheered by the sight of that emblem than then. We covered the last few yards to the gate and demanded admission from the soldiers standing at their posts just inside.

"We are British citizens," Holmes said. "Loyal subjects of His Majesty. We seek sanctuary."

The presence of three young women, one of them clearly ailing, aroused the soldiers' sympathies, while the pack of locals chasing us left them in no doubt that we were in dire straits. They could not ignore our plea, and so they opened the gate. I steered Mrs Cummins and Miss Grady through, while Holmes deposited Miss Smythe carefully on the ground. She tottered after the other two women, who took her hands and guided her towards the building's front door.

I made to follow them, then noticed that Holmes was showing no inclination to do likewise.

"Come on, old man," I said. "We have done it. We are safe."

Slowly and, I thought, rather sadly, Holmes shook his head.

"It is the end of it for you," he said. "Not for me."

"What on earth are you talking about?"

"I must see this thing through. I cannot leave R'luhlloig to continue with his plans unchecked. Farewell, my friend."

He turned to face the oncoming horde, and lifted his hands above his head in surrender.

"Holmes," I said. "Holmes! For heaven's sake, man, this is madness."

"We shall meet again, Watson. When I return to England, I shall call on you first thing."

Briefly I entertained the notion of shooting him. I would wing him, a nick to the meat of the leg, not a life-threatening wound but enough to incapacitate him. I could then haul him into the High Commission and he could do nothing to prevent it.

"No," I whispered, then repeated the word as a declaration of defiance. "No!" To the soldiers I said, "See to it that those three girls are looked after. One is recovering from a bout of consumption. They are to be sent back to England as soon as they are well enough to do so. My name is Dr John Watson and that lunatic over there is Mr Sherlock Holmes. Any expenses incurred will be defrayed by one or other of us. Do you understand?"

The soldiers, more than a little befuddled, nodded.

I discarded the rifle and hurried after Holmes, raising my hands too.

"I shan't easily forgive you for this, Holmes," I said as the crowd swarmed around us.

"And I shan't easily forgive you for not accompanying those women into the High Commission."

"You never intended for us to make it."

"All of us? No. The women, yes. You, perhaps. Me, certainly not."

"Hold them," Wolfgang ordered the mob. Hands seized us roughly.

It would seem Wolfgang possessed an innate authority, doubtless inherited from his admiral grandfather. It had simply taken an episode like this to bring it to the fore.

"These two are prisoners of Germany," he continued in the same imperious vein. "They are wanted in connection with the murder of a German citizen." Whether or not he had swallowed the lie about Von Bork's death, he was not above using it for his own purposes.

Around us there were angry murmurings in Afrikaans. I glanced back at the pair of British soldiers. They looked on helplessly. They were forbidden to intervene in any matter outside the grounds of the High Commission. Their jurisdiction extended only as far as the property.

Wolfgang knew he had the locals on his side. *The enemy*

of my enemy, and all that. He invited them to escort us back to the harbour.

We had not gone far before Captain Künstler appeared, along with two of the submarine's other officers.

"A crewman alerted me to the fact that you had absconded, Mr Holmes," Künstler said. "I had a sneaking feeling you and your companions might be the source of this ruckus. I never thought you would be so bold as to try something like this. Clearly I was mistaken."

Wolfgang briskly filled him in on the details of our escape, embellishing slightly – but only slightly – the role he had played in our recapture.

"The women are lost to us, you say?" Künstler asked him. "Are you sure?"

"They are beyond your reach, Captain," Holmes said. "Even Baron Von Herling would not dare venture onto what is effectively British soil in order to reclaim them. But you still have me and Watson. Be content with that. We shall come quietly."

Künstler realised that he should cut his losses. He congratulated a beaming Wolfgang and then, introducing himself to the crowd by his rank, said that he would take matters from here. He was grateful for their assistance, and South Africans should know that Germany was ever their ally, now and in the future.

I am not certain his audience was convinced by this avowal, but they at least had his assurances that the two Britons, entrusted to his custody, would face justice for the crimes they had committed. That was good enough for them.

And so Holmes and I are back once more in this accursed cabin in this accursed U-boat, which is now wending its way out of Durban harbour. There are two armed sentries outside the door instead of one. We are unlikely to be able to catch our warders off-guard again. We are here for the duration.

All because Holmes refuses to allow R'luhlloig to pursue his aims unhindered, and I refuse to allow Holmes to do it alone. We are both victims of the dictates of our consciences.

At least the women are out of harm's way. I draw consolation from that. We have done a good deed today. But at what cost to ourselves?

Thursday 10th November

As punishment for our temerity, we are being denied food. This is the second day when we have had nothing to eat and only a cupful of water each to drink.

Holmes, a hardened ascetic, seems to be taking the deprivation in his stride. I, on the other hand…

Friday 11th November

My hunger pangs are becoming intolerable. I feel the urge to pound on the door and beg for sustenance. The only thing preventing me is the desire not to let our captors know I am suffering. I refuse to give them that satisfaction.

Saturday 12th November

I seem unable to think of anything but food. I have crammed the margins of this page and the previous with drawings of cakes, joints of beef, hams, puddings, pies and other viands. My mouth waters at the thought of them.

Holmes bears the starvation with some stoicism, but I think even he is beginning to crack. I have heard him moan in the night. I have seen him clutch his belly every now and then. My own stomach cramps painfully, yearning to be filled. Hunger is like a voice howling in my head. I am constantly dizzy and feel so weak that I can hardly hold this pen. Little wonder that this handwriting is a spidery scribble, barely legible even to me.

It is a nightmare. We are human beings, and the Germans are treating us like dogs.

Sunday 13th November

Our sufferings are at an end, at last. We have been brought a meal. A bowl of thin soup and a slice of bread apiece, that was all, but it seemed like a banquet. We feasted upon it like two beggars. We were told we will be on limited rations from now on, and I suspect the reason for this is to keep us weak and remind us not to get any ideas about escaping again; but little is better than nothing.

Monday 14th November

Baron Von Herling has graced us with his presence this afternoon. I was beginning to think we would not see him until we reach our destination. I cannot say I was delighted to have him in our cabin, but at least he has assuaged our curiosity about a few things. Above all, we now know where SM *U-19* is bound. I must confess that, having been enlightened, I would rather have remained in blissful ignorance.

There he stood, hands behind his back, ever the haughty patrician. He had insisted upon the door being closed to give him and us privacy, having told the guards that he had nothing to fear from us.

"Gentlemen," said he, "I trust you have seen the error of your ways. You took a very big gamble."

"I believe it paid off," said Holmes. "Where you had five captives, now you have just two. You are the poorer for our actions, therefore we are the richer."

Von Herling flapped a hand as though swatting at a gnat. "The women were trivial. A distraction. For half of our journey you have been so focused upon them that you could not concentrate on much else."

"Half?" I said. "You mean we still have weeks ahead of us aboard this blasted contraption?"

"Six weeks or thereabouts," said the ambassador. "You cannot fail to have asked yourselves why I am bringing you along when killing you would be by far the simpler option."

"It had crossed my mind," said Holmes diffidently. "The only conclusion I can draw is that you need us for something."

"I need you as witnesses."

"Witnesses to what?" I asked.

"Why, Dr Watson, my ultimate triumph, of course."

"Really?"

"You doubt me?"

We were obviously talking to R'luhlloig now. Von Herling, as far as I could judge, had been thoroughly absorbed by the Hidden Mind. After colluding for so long together the two of them had fused into a single entity, a perfect hybrid of god and man. The voice and mannerisms might be those of the ambassador but the guiding intelligence was R'luhlloig's.

"My war is all but over," R'luhlloig continued. "You cannot be unaware of that. On the godly plane my armies have routed the Old Ones. Those so-called 'great' beings have fallen before our onslaught and now languish in dungeons built specially to hold them. I am being hailed as the supreme god of all." He preened as he said this, lifting his sleek head like a cat when its owner tickles behind its ears. "Everywhere voices rise in adulation. The name R'luhlloig is exalted. I rule the Dreamlands, the deepest gulfs of space, every corner of the cosmic realm…"

"Everywhere, in fact, but Earth," said Holmes. "On Earth, R'luhlloig is more or less unknown."

"But that will change. Earth, you see, is different. Earth is the pivot around which all turns. It is the great prize, the jewel over which the gods have contested for millennia. It will be mine eventually, once everywhere else is conquered. Surprising, really, how this humble little planet can hold a position of such importance, but then its value is not intrinsic. It is not the continents or the oceans or the icecaps that give it its worth, nor its flora and fauna, but rather the humans who have flourished across its surface. They make for such good worshippers – and such good slaves. Your race with its creativity and aspirations, its loves and hatreds, its dreams and flaws, its yearning for independence and its paradoxical willingness to be led, lends Earth a most piquant flavour. There really are no creatures in all the universe quite like humans, nothing quite as complex and contrary, and one finds them nowhere but here. You are what makes Earth special."

"You were one of us yourself, R'luhlloig, once."

"A lifetime ago. I feel no affinity for the clay I came from, for the womb that birthed me, for the caterpillar I was before I became a butterfly. I am beyond all that."

"Beyond it, yet you feel the urge to rub the noses of two particular humans in your victory. Perhaps you have not ascended as far as you think."

"You have aimed that jibe at me before, Mr Holmes. All I can say is that victory will be the sweeter for my, as you say, rubbing your noses in it. Since you are so damnably hard to get rid of, it occurred to me that I may as well have you right where I can see you, in plain sight at all times. That is especially a requisite at this most crucial stage of my operations, with things coming to a climax. I cannot have you meddling, so why not ensure it by keeping you under my thumb?"

I remained sceptical about this reasoning. It struck me as altogether contrary, not to say counterproductive. I wondered whether Von Herling had some ulterior motive for keeping us alive, having spent so many years desiring our deaths. Yet, if so, it remained opaque to me.

"Killing you and Dr Watson might be more sensible," Von Herling went on, "but humiliating you…" He sighed ecstatically, as though he had just sipped a fine wine. "*That* is true victory. You are going to understand that all your efforts to forestall me over the years have been for naught. You have wasted your time – wasted your lives, even. And with that, I will truly have defeated you."

"You seem very confident on that front."

"Oh, I am. I am. Nor will I kill you even then. I think, rather, that I shall keep you both alive, like pets. You will follow me for the rest of your days, cringing, mewling, your minds scarce able to comprehend the overwhelming magnitude of your loss. In time you may come to adore me. You will mouth my name with love, for that is all that will be left to you: love for your master who is also your tormentor."

The smile on his face was awful to behold. It conveyed such depths of sadistic glee, yet such pettiness too. It had elements of the very worst attributes of both men and gods. The same was true of the look in his eyes, the ghastly gloating glare of the lifelong bully. I did not doubt that R'luhlloig would relish visiting upon us the fate he had just outlined, nor did I doubt that he was dead set on making it a reality.

"Then there is little more to be said," Holmes averred. "You know that we will try to thwart you to our very last breaths."

"And you know that you will fail."

"Perhaps, but we can do no less. If nothing else, I believe I now know where we are going. I suspected before. That suspicion has hardened into a certainty."

R'luhlloig cocked his head. "And where is that?"

"Six weeks' journey remains to us, so you said. That could take us some considerable way out into the Pacific Ocean. Past India, past the Malay Archipelago, out to the point in the Pacific which lies furthest from any landmass, the region known as the 'pole of inaccessibility'."

"Go on."

"I believe we both know what lies there, and if I am right, then I cannot help but admire your ambition while at the same time deploring your foolhardiness."

"What is it?" I said. "What is to be found at the 'pole of inaccessibility'?"

"Come, come, Watson," my friend chided. "The information is there in your brain. You just have to retrieve it."

I did, and now I am suffused with the utmost dread. R'luhlloig has returned to his cabin, to carry on brooding, festering, meditating or whatever it is he has been doing in there over the past few weeks. Holmes and I have a month and a half of further confinement to look forward to. I do not think I can continue with this diary any more. It seems pointless. It does not alleviate the tension or provide a vent for my innermost feelings, not now. That tension is too great and those feelings too inexpressible. What use is scrawling words on paper? We are going to hell. I mean that almost literally. We are bound for the place on Earth that is most closely analogous with the pits of Hades. I know that none who go there come back, or if they do come back, they come back raving mad. I am having trouble believing that R'luhlloig truly intends it to be our destination. Then again, why not? It makes sense. He has but one major enemy left. Why not attack him in his home?

R'lyeh.

That is where we are headed for.

R'lyeh.

A nightmarish, half-ruined city, which sits atop an uncharted rocky island riddled below with catacombs where nameless monstrosities dwell.

R'lyeh.

The place where Cthulhu himself slumbers.

We are doomed.

We are damned.

CHAPTER THIRTY-ONE

R'lyeh

SIX WEEKS ALMOST TO THE DAY AFTER I PENNED that final entry in the diary, SM *U-19* found herself mid-Pacific, in seas of unusual stillness.

Our last port of call had been Simpsonhafen in Kaiser-Wilhelmsland, which is part of German New Guinea. For the crew, this protectorate being one of their nation's overseas dominions, it must have felt a bit like home. Since then we had sailed further and further east into the abyssal fastnesses of the Pacific, civilisation growing ever more remote.

At one stage we were attended by a pod of sperm whales. I did not see them, of course, but their cries were audible on board, penetrating through the hull and making the entire submarine resonate. The moans and high-pitched squeals they made were haunting and melancholy, and seemed to me a warning. The whales were telling us to turn back before it was too late. Nothing good would come of continuing on our present course.

I could not help but think that the cetaceans, these titans of the sea, were wise and that we should heed their advice. They must know of R'lyeh and give the island a wide berth during their migrations. If only the U-boat's crew could understand what they were saying…

I do not pretend that these thoughts of mine were rational. By then I had begun to lose touch with sanity. Hour upon endless hour in that cabin, subsisting on the most meagre food, had left me deracinated and sensorily deprived; a shell of myself. I had notions of ending it all.

I envisaged tearing a hole in the outer wall of the cabin, somehow using my bare hands to accomplish the task, and letting seawater gush in to drown me. Sometimes the spoon with which I ate my soup seemed as temptingly sharp-edged as a knife. Might I use it to open an artery? At the very least I might be able to choke myself with it.

I have no idea whether Holmes entertained similar suicidal thoughts. My half-unhinged state precluded me from caring much about him. I was lost to consideration of anyone's woes but my own.

Often we were brought our meals by young Wolfgang, whose countenance now evinced nothing but resentment and contempt. Not a word passed between us. Captain Künstler himself would look in on us from time to time. There was a level of compassion in his eyes, still present even after the shenanigans at Durban but buried deeper than before. Would he not have done the same thing we had, were he in our position? I thought so. But somehow he was disappointed, as though we were houseguests who had spurned his hospitality. Künstler considered himself a benevolent jailer. What he did not seem to appreciate was that even a benevolent jailer is still a jailer.

And every day R'lyeh drew nearer and nearer.

Now SM *U-19* slowed to a crawl, her engine noise subsiding to a low, thrumming chunter. Holmes and I were invited to leave our cabin by Baron Von Herling, whom I shall refer to solely as R'luhlloig from hereon, for simplicity's sake.

"Why not come up on deck and look on as we make our approach?" said he. "I feel I cannot deprive you of a single second of this momentous occasion."

What he meant was he did not wish to deprive himself of a single second of our final, total abasement.

The sea had a glassy smoothness unlike any I had ever known. It lay around us like emerald-green syrup, barely moving. Now and then a wave might swell, but it was more a blister upon the surface than anything and did not crest or break. The U-boat's bow made a greasy slopping sound as they cut through the water.

A haze hung over everything, not quite a mist or a fog, rather a blurring of the air that narrowed the scope of the horizon to perhaps a mile or so. The sun was dimmed, its light taking on a blood-red tinge.

Up on deck with us, besides R'luhlloig and Captain Künstler, were a handful of sailors. Their disquiet, although they did their best to hide it, was palpable. I observed more than one of them murmuring a prayer and Künstler himself seemed unsettled. He fidgeted, shifting his feet and tapping a hand on his bearded chin. Quite evidently none of them had encountered seas of this ilk before either. The tranquillity was eerie. Surely even the Sargasso was not as sullenly calm.

Something broke the surface with a startling splash, just off the port beam. No one quite saw what creature it was, but from the glimpse we received it was large, thick-bodied and shiny. One man speculated it might have been a seal, another a dolphin. Neither seemed convinced by his own guess or the other's.

Künstler barked out an order, which a sailor up in the conning tower relayed to the control room below. The submarine decelerated yet further until she was making headway slower than walking pace.

Then, through the haze, the island appeared. I would say it loomed, but rather it crept up on us. At first it seemed a mirage, the shimmering dark impression of an island hovering somehow just above the sea. Gradually it gained definition and three-dimensionality, manifesting as a spit of land perhaps a quarter the size of the Isle of Wight, the peak of some fathomless sea mountain. It consisted of black rock and various rough-hewn green shapes that looked manmade but which, from a distance of nearly a mile, gave scant clue as to their purpose. Edifices, one could only assume, but so monumental they surely could not have been built to house humans.

The island's most singular feature was a stone pillar, which rose from its highest point, thrusting towards the heavens like some latter-day Tower of Babel. One could not look at this monolith and think that it had been erected for any other reason than to offer a sort of blasphemous challenge. It mocked every steeple and pyramid and ziggurat man had ever raised, belittling all our architecture with its stature and its sheer, unbuttressed plainness. Even the so-called "skyscrapers" that were then sprouting in New York at a remarkable rate were dwarfed by the pillar's immensity.

As we slithered closer – for SM *U-19*'s progress through that peculiarly dense water could only be described as slithering – the contours of the buildings that lay around the foot of the pillar became clearer. Each was vast, mostly windowless and built of jade-green stone, but aside from size and colour the common factor was miscellany, since none exactly matched any of its counterparts. Some of the structures sprawled, others teetered, while yet others squatted. Nor did there seem to be a single right angle visible in their design. Rounded edges, convex and concave planes, and acute and obtuse angles there were aplenty, but no regularity anywhere nor any symmetry. They looked to have been crafted with a weird whimsicality by giants who were either ignorant of the rules of geometry or preferred to flout them.

Closer still, a ring of greasy spume skirting the island became visible, as did the slimy weed that blanketed the shoreline. No strong waves, it seemed, ever scrubbed R'lyeh's rocky fringes clean. One could only assume that this flat, stagnant calm was a year-round phenomenon, as though the island sat in a perpetual doldrums, somehow untroubled by tempests and raging tides.

We changed course so as to circumnavigate the island's perimeter, and Künstler scanned through binoculars for a suitable spot to make landfall. Soon enough he spied a crescent-shaped bay with a mud bank running along its inner rim. One could call this a beach if one were being generous. Above it rose a flight of stone steps so tall and broad as to be practically an escarpment. The height of each individual riser was difficult to gauge but could not have been less than three feet. The steps had not been built with the convenience of human beings in mind. Something far larger was meant to use them.

The submarine came to a dead stop and dropped anchor. Various parts of a wooden rowing boat were brought out from her interior and deftly assembled using screws and bolts. Within half an hour a seaworthy landing craft had been assembled, capable of holding eight.

In the meantime R'luhlloig ordered that Holmes's and my wrists should be bound behind our backs with rope. "Should the two of you attempt another escape," said he, "you will find yourselves far more constrained this time. But I suspect you at least, Mr Holmes, will prefer to remain with us, no? The island fascinates you. I see it in your eyes."

The boat was lowered into the water and R'luhlloig skipped aboard, for all the world as though he was a holidaymaker gaily embarking upon a paddle about a lake. Holmes and I were enjoined to follow his example, the request being enforced by a couple of sailors with rifles. Tied up as we were, we needed some assistance to make the transfer. The two armed crewmen also got into the rowing boat, along with three others, likewise armed. One of this trio was none other than our former friend Wolfgang. Instead of a rifle, however, he bore a pistol – my Webley, to be precise. I aimed a longing look at the revolver, my ally of more than thirty years. Wolfgang saw the look and grinned.

"I asked to be given it, Doctor," he said. "And to be a part of this expedition."

"No one will keep a closer eye on you than Wolfgang," Künstler said from the deck. "'Once bitten, twice shy' – is that not the English saying?"

"You are not coming with us, Captain?" said Holmes.

"I must stay with the ship, like a good captain should. You are in excellent hands."

"Ha! Yes!" said one of the sailors in the rowing boat. I recognised him as the man whom Holmes had knocked out cold when we stole aboard SM *U-19* back in England. So much time had passed since then, and since our abortive escape attempt in Durban. Today was Boxing Day. I had scarcely been aware of Advent or of Christmas itself, segregated as I was in that cabin; nor could I have felt in less of a festive mood. We were now in the final week of 1910, the year coming to a close.

The sailor ruffled Wolfgang's hair. "Young Wolfie will keep us all in line," he said. "Our little admiral."

The boy seemed both flattered by the attention and piqued. I could see him thinking that one day he would be in command of men like this and they would be saluting him, not patronising him.

A pair of heavily laden knapsacks, which I presumed to contain essential supplies such as victuals and spare ammunition, were handed down to the boat. Now it seemed we were ready to depart.

"Captain?" said Holmes to Künstler.

"Yes, Mr Holmes?"

"If you could kindly see your way to neatening up our cabin against our return, I would be much obliged."

Künstler frowned, while R'luhlloig shook his head pityingly. "How you can think of creature comforts at a time like this, I do not know," he chided. "Priorities!"

"Proprieties, rather," Holmes countered. "Is it too much to ask that our bunks are given new bedding and the room is aired?"

"Captain Künstler is not running a hotel."

"Really? Then why did I sign a guest book?"

R'luhlloig snorted in derision. "Your levity is unappreciated. *Mein Herr!*" He was now addressing one of the sailors with us in the rowing boat. He told him in German to push us off, then commanded two of the others to take up the oars and row.

Our little vessel swung its prow towards the island and slowly heaved in that direction. With each stroke of the oars the steel security of the submarine receded and the ominous uncertainties of R'lyeh drew nearer. A mood of apprehension grew amongst our landing party, with only R'luhlloig and Holmes apparently immune. The city, with its irrational cyclopean architecture, radiated malignancy. The very odour of the island was unpleasant, too, for we were soon within smelling distance of the mud and the weed; each was in its own way rank, but both in concert were repugnant. There was something putrid and moistly cadaver-like about that reek. It was, not to put too fine a point on it, the stench of death.

The rowing boat ran aground a few yards from the base of the steps. All eight of us climbed out, quickly sinking up to our ankles in the mud. We trudged ashore and began mounting the steps, shinning from one to the next in the manner of infants negotiating a normal-sized domestic staircase. A coating of weed made the ascent that much more awkward and treacherous, and again Holmes and I, inconvenienced by our bonds, required help. By the time we gained the topmost step we were all of us smeared with slimy greenness and to varying degrees out of puff.

Now we were confronted by buildings, none of which boasted a door upon its seaward side, nor any window slot low enough to afford entry. Huddling together, they presented a façade like that of a fortress, a blind bulwark against those who might wish to gain access to the city.

Yet R'luhlloig was undeterred. He strode confidently along the sweeping curve of the topmost step, which formed a kind of promenade, until at last he halted at a gap between two of the buildings. I could not recall seeing any such opening during our approach to the island, but neither could I swear there had been none. Everything about R'lyeh, from the scale of construction to the askew walls, induced disorientation. From certain perspectives the gap must be hidden from view, I supposed; one could see it only when standing directly in front of it. Yet I could not escape the impression that the city had surreptitiously opened up a crack in itself, in order to entice us in.

At any rate a street lay revealed, winding between beetling structures on either side. At R'luhlloig's urging we ventured inland along it, leaving behind the noisome miasma from the mud and weed. The deeper we went into the city, the greater and more menacing the silence around us grew. The oozy lapping of sea on rocks was replaced by the dull, clattering echoes of our footfalls and nothing else.

I overheard a couple of the sailors muttering apprehensively to each other in their native tongue. What they said merited a lengthy riposte from R'luhlloig. Seeing the inquisitive look on my face, he explained that the men were wondering where the inhabitants of this city were.

"The place appears deserted," he said, "yet remains in near-pristine condition. There should be people in residence, should there not? But if so, where are they?"

"A good question," I replied, looking around me. "Perhaps they are hiding." I did not like the thought that eyes might be watching us, assessing us, considering what to do about these interlopers.

"Or perhaps R'lyeh has long since been abandoned and its denizens have relocated," R'luhlloig suggested.

"Then why has it not fallen into rack and ruin?"

"You have seen how inert the sea is around the island, Doctor. The same goes for the air. The elements hardly seem to impinge upon this region. I suspect the normal processes of weathering and decay are in abeyance. Time, one might say, moves more slowly here than elsewhere. Would you not agree, Mr Holmes?"

Holmes made a noncommittal grunt.

"Come, come, sir," said R'luhlloig. "I have not brought you all this way only to have you surly and unresponsive."

"When I have a valid observation to make, I shall make it," Holmes said. "Until then I shall keep my own counsel."

"When the time comes, your counsel will be sought and it will be rendered up."

"Then that is the reason I am present? That is why, all along, you have kept me alive? So that I might be of use to you?"

"Maybe," said R'luhlloig, sounding damnably enigmatic. "Maybe."

*

On we walked, and after some while the sailors began muttering again. Eventually one of them spoke up. We appeared to be going in circles, he said. He was convinced that the narrow little plaza we had just entered was one we had crossed some ten minutes earlier.

Looking around, I could not help but concur. The buildings seemed markedly familiar. I had previously noticed a teetering edifice that resembled nothing so much as a crooked church spire. Now another of the exact same shape and proportions loomed over us, while at cater-corner to it stood a low, complicated structure as multifaceted as a cut gemstone, which I likewise recalled seeing before.

It would not have surprised me if we had inadvertently retraced our steps. R'lyeh was labyrinthine and had so many distinguishing characteristics, and these in such superfluity that it confused one's senses, in particular one's sense of direction. The nearest comparison would be a jungle in which all the trees are different but end up looking much like one another.

"Mr Holmes," said R'luhlloig, "what do you think? Have we become lost?"

"I should not like to comment," replied Holmes, "without further evidence."

Not long afterward, we arrived at a plaza that seemed the spitting image of the one before and indeed the one before that. There, again, was that crooked spire and the adjacent gem-like building.

The sailor who had first made the observation that we were going in circles swore roundly, while another let out a low, panicked moan. We appeared to have become trapped in an endless loop. R'lyeh had ensnared us in its toils, like fish in a net. We were condemned to keep tramping the city's streets, becoming ever more perplexed and adrift, until we collapsed from exhaustion and starvation.

With some difficulty, I fought down this claustrophobic dread. I turned to Holmes, seeking reassurance and, I hoped, enlightenment.

"It does, on the face of it, seem as though we are not making progress," said he. "Indeed, it seems as though the very buildings are conspiring to confuse us. Could it be that they move without us knowing? That the city subtly and silently reconfigures itself behind our backs?"

"Absurd," I said, more with scorn than with conviction.

"Absurder than any of the other spectacles we have encountered together over the years, old friend?" With a mirthless chuckle Holmes added, "Well, I do not believe it myself, either. There is one way to determine whether it is all just some artful illusion, perhaps designed to lead astray the unwary traveller, or whether there are preternatural forces at work. Gentlemen, do any of you have a knife upon your person?"

R'luhlloig relayed the enquiry in German, whereupon one of the sailors produced a clasp knife from his pocket. It was the same sailor whom Holmes had once knocked unconscious.

"Score a distinctive mark upon the ground," Holmes said.

The sailor waited until Von Herling had passed the instruction on before etching two letters into a circular flagstone near the plaza's centre. I presumed them to be his initials.

"Now let us carry on and see what happens," said Holmes.

Sure enough, minutes later we were in the plaza once more. The sailors searched around for the circular flagstone. They found no sign of it or the carved initials.

There were smiles of relief and even a ripple of laughter.

"Excellent, Mr Holmes," said R'luhlloig. "I knew you would prove your worth. There will surely be ample further opportunities for you to exercise those much-vaunted mental powers of yours. I would advise you to make the most of them while they remain to you."

*

We did not re-enter the plaza a fourth time. It was as if we had passed a test and R'lyeh was allowing us to go on unimpeded. I was thankful for that, but still cursed whoever the diabolical architects were who had dreamed up that deceitful illusion. Were they – or more likely their descendants – at this very moment looking down on us from some lofty perch, hugging themselves in their amusement, their eyes alight with cruel glee?

Presently the street we were on, a broader thoroughfare than any previous yet still lined with those terrible, extraordinary buildings, began to incline upwards and to turn a long bend at the same time. It appeared to be leading us up the slope of the island, albeit in a roundabout fashion. By this point I was becoming weary, my feet sore, my legs aching. The ropes about my wrists were starting to chafe, too, and my arms to cramp from being forcibly maintained in one position for so long. All in all I was succumbing to a misery, both of body and mind, from which I found it increasingly hard to rouse myself.

R'luhlloig, for his part, seemed full of boundless energy. "Yes," he said, pleased with his own prowess, "I knew that if we kept heading inland, we would come eventually, inevitably, to the other side of the city. We are in, one might say, the suburbs, and this road would seem to be a major artery, affording access to the island's interior."

"How clever of you to be able to navigate this landmass without a map," Holmes averred drily.

"Who needs maps when common sense will suffice? Besides," R'luhlloig added with a demonstrative sweep of his hand, "that pillar yonder serves as an unmistakable landmark."

"And that pillar is our final destination."

"Quite so. Where else?"

Whether one could describe this area of R'lyeh as the suburbs was debatable, but there was certainly a less cloistered, more rarefied feel to it. We were now passing statuary shaped like beasts and demons, and again the sailors began muttering anxiously amongst themselves. Each cavorting carven grotesque was more intimidating and alien than the last. Bas-reliefs adorned the sides of many of the buildings, too, showing scenes of abominable rituals and indescribable depravities. Everyone who had a weapon clutched it close to him, drawing succour from its cold metal and its promise of death-dealing. I had not the heart to tell the sailors that guns were effective in a place like this only up to a point. If the city was inhabited, its denizens were apt to be creatures that were impervious to bullets or else would attack in such swarms that our stocks of ammunition would run dry long before their numbers were exhausted. This was true, at least, if my own past experiences were anything to go by.

We pressed onward, upward. Ahead the pillar towered ever taller, ever more imposing, a great beckoning beacon towards which the sinuous street seemed to be feeding us inexorably. A feeling of nausea arose in me that I ascribed to fatigue and the prolonged lack of exercise and a proper diet, until I saw it reflected in the faces of most of the sailors. The statuary and the strange geometries in tandem were having a cumulative sickening influence. It was as though the mind could bear only so much of those inward-turned corners and the surfaces that looked to be angled both away from and towards oneself, let alone those grim graven images. Beyond a certain level of exposure these things upset some essential inner sense of rightness, and the mental disturbance of equilibrium translated into a physical one. A couple of the Germans doubled over and ejected the contents of their stomachs. I came close to doing the same.

It may have been two hours after we came ashore, it may have been somewhat longer, but eventually we arrived at a second flight of steps, this one narrower than the first but no less outsized: a series of oblong blocks that climbed clear of the city outskirts and rose to the island's summit. We hauled ourselves up these steps as we had the last ones, Holmes and I requiring assistance, until we came to the foot of that vaunting, sky-piercing pillar.

Inset into its base was a door. And what a door! Its dimensions would have suited a barn – a generously proportioned barn at that – and it was fashioned from some kind of metal that had both the pitted texture of cast iron and the subtle gleam of bronze.

Etched into this portal was a portrait of Cthulhu, a stern-browed melange of squid, dragon and human, gazing balefully down upon us. This large and fearsome rendering of the greatest of the Great Old Ones gave the sailors pause. I remembered my own first sight of an image of Cthulhu, in Afghanistan, and knew the thrill of primordial horror such a thing could evoke in the unwary. All of the sailors quailed before it, and at least three of them looked ready to turn tail and flee.

R'luhlloig offered them soothing words in German. I am not sure exactly what he said, but I heard "marks" and could only assume that he was pledging some sort of financial incentive for carrying on. The prospect of money from Baron Von Herling's pocket stirred the men to bravado. All at once they were disparaging the image on the door and laughing at their own timidity. Wolfgang laughed louder than anyone, but then he, as the youngest, had the most to prove.

Surrounding the door was an arch shaped like an asymmetrical "M". It was studded with square stone projections, each of which was engraved with a different symbol. A few of the symbols I recognised – there was an Elder Sign and a Seal of N'gah amongst them – but the vast majority were unknown to me. Did they constitute a message? An admonition perhaps, like Dante's "Abandon hope all ye who enter here"? Or were they mere ornament?

Holmes eyed them with interest while R'luhlloig, with no less interest, eyed Holmes.

"Well, Mr Holmes?" R'luhlloig said. "What do you make of it?"

"From what I have read about R'lyeh, and specifically about the pillar before us, we have reached the entrance to the house of Cthulhu – the subterranean abode that is variously called his lair and his mausoleum. How we gain ingress is another matter. Abdul Alhazred and Friedrich Wilhelm Von Junzt, our primary sources for such information, are both reticent on the subject. One cannot simply knock and expect Cthulhu himself, or failing that some pageboy or butler, to come and answer. The door itself is solidly built and too heavy for us to push open. Even assuming we had the manpower, I see no hinges. A lack of hinges moreover suggests that the door does not open by conventional means. A lack of any obvious lock suggests some form of hidden mechanism. How am I doing so far?"

R'luhlloig nodded. "Your inferences echo mine."

"Can it be that you yourself are unsure how to get in?" Holmes cocked an eyebrow. "Surprising. I would have thought that the all-powerful Hidden Mind knew everything."

"In this company you are to refer to me as Baron Von Herling or His Excellency," R'luhlloig said sharply. "Anything else may cause confusion."

"Of course, Your Excellency," Holmes said in an ironical tone. "The men must not at any cost be confused.

Those of them who have sufficient English, that is."

As it happened, none of the sailors had been following the foregoing exchange of dialogue. All were too busy outdoing one another in expressing ribald contempt for the picture of Cthulhu.

"It would seem to me," Holmes continued, returning his own attention to the door, "that the stone projections on the arch serve some other function than simply to decorate. I would go so far as to state that they might prove instrumental in opening the door."

"Keys of some description?"

"Precisely." Holmes went over to the one nearest him and nudged it experimentally with his shoulder, exerting the lightest of pressure. "Yes. There is give. It moves. The tiny striations we see on the sides, which all the others have too, have been caused by it sliding in and out, its edges grinding against the slot in which it sits. These projections are, I would submit, somewhat akin to a typewriter's keys, and also to the dial on a safe. If depressed in a certain sequence, they will trigger a mechanism and the door will open."

"I agree," said R'luhlloig. "I had already drawn the same conclusion but I was curious to see whether your thinking aligned with mine."

"I shall have to take your word on that."

"Believe what you like, Mr Holmes. As ever, you overrate your importance in the scheme of things. What I must establish – and you may provide input if you wish – is the correct sequence. To me the symbols seem an entirely random selection, with all manner of different provenances and very little commonality. The number of possible permutations verges on the infinite. We could be trying them from now until the end of time without success."

"That could be the point," I said. "We are not supposed to enter. No one is."

"Spoken more in hope than expectation, Doctor," said R'luhlloig. "I am not one to give up so easily. I mean to get inside and I shall. I believe, in fact, that I have just divined a thematic thread linking several of the symbols."

"I see none," said Holmes.

"That only proves which of us possesses the keener intellect."

R'luhlloig then spoke to the men, asking for a volunteer. As far as I could gather, he wanted someone who was a good climber.

A hand went up. The fellow, whose name was Pfaff, hailed from Bavaria and had in his youth done plenty of mountaineering in the Alps. R'luhlloig instructed him to scale the stone projections, using them as handholds and footholds, and press certain of them in an order that he, R'luhlloig, would call out.

Pfaff scurried up the left-hand column of projections with the agility of a monkey. He seemed eager – as well he might – to show off his climbing prowess to the man he thought of as Baron Von Herling. Impressing the ambassador might well lead to a commendation, perhaps even a promotion.

At the top of the column he paused, looking back over his shoulder. His forehead creased in a frown of bafflement. He said something about things not seeming right. He was looking down... but also up.

I saw him sway, but then he shook his head, blinked a few times, reaffirmed his grip on the projections, and appeared to recover his composure.

R'luhlloig drew Pfaff's notice to a projection to the right of him, a short way along the diagonal downward stroke of the top of the "M". He advised him to press that one first.

Pfaff moved sideways along the lintel, hand over hand. Now he was leaning at an angle, suspending himself more or less with his arms alone. The toe of his left foot was just touching the projection it was on, while his right leg hung free. He made the feat look effortless. The strength in his upper body must have been tremendous.

Letting go with his right hand, he groped for the projection to which R'luhlloig was directing him. As he did so, I noted a certain tight-lipped anxiety upon Holmes's face. It was more than mere concern for Pfaff's welfare. It occurred to me that my friend disputed R'luhlloig's choice of symbol but was refraining from saying so.

Pfaff managed to press the projection.

At once, every single one of the projections sank inward simultaneously, and Pfaff, with nothing to support him, fell.

But he did not fall downwards. He fell *sideways*.

Flailing, screaming, he hurtled twenty feet towards the right-hand jamb of the door. He fell just as a man would if plummeting vertically, except in his case it was horizontally.

He hit the jamb with a sickening crunch. His body

rebounded bonelessly away, and now the gravity that his fall had thus far defied took him and he dropped to the ground.

If the first impact had not killed him, this second one did. Pfaff landed head-first, and the sound of cervical vertebrae snapping was as loud as a gunshot.

I hastened over and took his pulse anyway, but it was never in doubt. Pfaff was dead.

Then the door began to open.

CHAPTER THIRTY-TWO

Gibberers in the Dark

THE IMAGE OF CTHULHU WITH ITS GOATISH EYES seemed gleeful as the metal portal into which it was etched slid slowly upward. This raising was accompanied by a great deep tumult, as of unseen cogs turning, ratchets creaking and chains clanking. The ground underfoot trembled.

Shocked though the sailors were by the door's sudden opening, they were altogether more shocked by Pfaff's demise. What set the mind reeling was not so much the unexpectedness of the tragedy as the unnaturalness of it. His fall had contravened the laws of physics.

The crumpled body lay before what was now a cavernous, yawning aperture, with nothing but darkness beyond. The door had risen wholly out of sight, and the mechanism that was drawing it upwards abruptly ceased to operate. Echoes of its rumbling resounded for a while afterward.

R'luhlloig's expression spoke of a transport of delight so intense it bordered on ecstatic. The sailors, by contrast, were fearful and verging on mutinous. Tempers flared. An argument erupted. The exchange was too rapid for me with my limited German to follow fully, but the gist was clear. Given what had happened to Pfaff, and *how* it had happened, the men advocated that we should head back to the U-boat with all due haste.

R'luhlloig was of the opposite view, and he found a seconder in, of all people, young Wolfgang. The lad, never one to miss an opportunity to gain preferment, sided with

Baron Von Herling, even to the point of saying he would shoot anybody who left as a deserter. The sailors did not take kindly to the threat, least of all because it came from a callow youth, the most junior amongst them.

The debate grew ever more heated. R'luhlloig asserted his superiority over his subordinates simply by barking more loudly and authoritatively than anybody else. He invoked the name of the kaiser – a personal friend, he was careful to remind everyone – and renewed his offer of significant sums in coin of the realm for those who held their nerve and stayed the course. A combination of loyalty to their emperor and love of lucre brought the men back into line.

As the discord was being settled, Holmes said quietly to me, "R'luhlloig lied, or else was bluffing. There is no solution."

"You mean pressing any of the symbols would have unlocked the door?"

"Yes and no. It seems that the key was not the stone projections. A blood sacrifice was required. R'luhlloig may well have intuited as much, and he, the scoundrel, wittingly sent poor Pfaff to his death."

"Did you know as much yourself?"

"Not with any certainty."

"If you had, you would surely have said something, and R'luhlloig would have had a much harder time securing a volunteer."

"He would have overruled whatever protest I made. That is his way. And Pfaff, or another, would still have died."

"It never ceases to amaze me how callous and cold-hearted he is."

"To R'luhlloig, any and all of these sailors are expendable. I would not be surprised if, before this day is out, we see more of them used and tossed aside like rags."

"And we? Are we expendable too?"

"That remains to be seen."

"Should we not at least warn the men about what they are getting into? They have already had a taste of the island's threats, and there can only be more, and worse, ahead. If we were to give them some idea of what lies in store, they might become less compliant towards R'luhlloig, and that in turn would make it more difficult for him to—"

"Doctor?" said R'luhlloig, cutting in. "You and Mr Holmes seem to have much to say to each other. Would you care to share what concerns you so?"

Before I could answer, Holmes said, "Watson and I were merely speculating on the mechanism by which the door was opened. A system of counterweights, I believe, with sand filling buckets on chains attached to spindles."

R'luhlloig seemed satisfied with this reply. I, on the other hand, was puzzled why my companion appeared unwilling at least to try to undermine further the confidence of the men under R'luhlloig's command, which would be to our advantage. It was almost as though Holmes was as keen as the Hidden Mind to pass through the door and learn what lay beyond.

For all my reservations, I resolved to follow his lead on this, as I had on many another occasion. I trusted he knew what he was doing.

The attenuated sunlight was not strong enough to penetrate far through the doorway, but the sailors had brought electric torches with them. At R'luhlloig's behest they switched them on and trained the beams inward. The outlines of a vast, smooth-walled chamber were revealed. It occupied the entire base of the pillar, its ceiling too high for the torches' light to reach.

In we went, making our way towards the chamber's sole feature: a circular depression dead centre of the floor. This proved to be a shallow pit from which a spiral stone staircase descended. As elsewhere in R'lyeh, the staircase's proportions were inhumanly immense, each wedge-shaped step as large as a cathedral altar.

"Down?" said Holmes to R'luhlloig.

"But of course!"

So we embarked upon a long, winding trek downward. Whereas the others had all four limbs free in order to lower themselves carefully from step to step, Holmes and I were obliged to make the descent in a series of slithering leaps. The toll this took on my knees and ankles was heavy. I begged R'luhlloig to allow our wrists to be unfastened, but he merely sneered. Our discomfort seemed to give him a petty pleasure.

In no time we were beyond reach of natural light. The torches' darting beams were our only source of illumination amidst a darkness so profound that it oppressed the very soul. The courage which the crewmen had summoned earlier rapidly evaporated and once more they were fretful and given to muttering and cursing. The financial incentive R'luhlloig had offered them was again losing its lustre.

R'luhlloig regained their acquiescence again, this time by saying that the deal was conditional. The sailors would get paid only if they *all* stuck it out to the bitter end. Should just one of them quit, the money was forfeit. Now the men were committed to seeing the expedition through. None of them was going to turn back, for fear of being the one who queered the pitch for the rest. R'luhlloig had preyed successfully upon their competitiveness and their fear of ostracism.

For my own part, I felt a similar trepidation to theirs. We were venturing towards the actual vaults below R'lyeh where sleeping Cthulhu was reputed to lie. We were going where few men had and where no man in his right mind should. It was beyond folly; it was downright madness. According to all the texts, whenever Cthulhu awoke, disaster followed. I did not anticipate that we would emerge from the cavern, and in the unlikely event that we did, we would be so traumatised by the experience that we would not know peace of mind thereafter.

Yet, for all that, I cannot deny that I felt a modicum of curiosity as well. A certain dark fatalism had overcome me, as perhaps it had overcome Holmes too. Thirty years on from the city of Ta'aa where I first heard the name Cthulhu, there was every chance that I was about to meet the god himself. No idol this time but the living original, in the flesh. Would I stand firm or would I collapse, quivering in abject, cowardly terror? There was a sense of things coming full circle. This escapade seemed the fitting, inevitable conclusion to the past three decades during which Holmes and I had braved horrors beyond imagining. Cthulhu had been a constant background presence in our lives, so much the epitome of the aloof, malevolent cosmic entities whose influence we had fought to mitigate that his name had become more or less a byword for all of them. To face him was the ultimate test, the capstone of our careers, and I would not even have considered doing so had I had a choice, but since I had no choice I was resigned to it. In fact I was perversely excited about it.

I cannot say how far we descended on those stairs. It may have been as much as half a mile. At their bottom the air was thick and clammy, seeming to clog the lungs like cobwebs, and the temperature was that of a cold winter's day, which made me think of London. There snow might even now be falling, blanketing a city where the euphoria of Christmas had yet to abate, where families would be gathered by the hearth, children playing with their new toys to the sound of church bells pealing across the rooftops...

I shook my head to dispel this reverie. Thoughts of home were of no use to me in the present circumstances. They would only demoralise me, for it was a home I had precious little hope of ever seeing again.

The sailors shone their torches far and wide. We were in a cylindrical chamber, a vestibule like the one directly above us at the summit of the staircase but somewhat smaller. There were open doorways leading off from it at irregular intervals around its perimeter. Disquietingly, these doorways did not appear to be fixed in place. One might be picked out by a torch beam, only to be not there when the same or another beam was aimed at the spot a moment later. The men were of the view that this phenomenon was an optical illusion, like the recurring plaza in the city, and I hoped it was so.

"Well, Mr Holmes," said R'luhlloig. "What now? We appear to have an embarrassment of choices when it comes to routes."

"We do, and I wonder if I should continue offering my help. Perhaps I should leave you to fathom out this little conundrum yourself."

"Don't be like that, sir. I would hate to have to offer some drastic incentive, such as instructing Wolfgang to put a bullet in Dr Watson – something I'm sure the youngster would willingly do."

"I would," Wolfgang said with ghastly eagerness.

"I thought it might come to that," sighed Holmes.

"Civility gets one only so far," said R'luhlloig.

"And then barbarism rears its ugly head."

"I prefer to think of it as expedience. So? Your thoughts?"

"Holmes…" I began.

"No, Watson. I will not have you sacrificing yourself. Your life is more precious to me than anything."

Rare was it that Holmes expressed sentiments of affection towards me. I took it as a mark of how dire our predicament was that he resorted to it now.

"In my view, Von Herling, there are two possibilities. On the one hand, each door leads to its own distinct route. On the other hand, they all lead to the same place."

"In other words, it makes little difference which way we go. All roads lead to Rome, eh?"

Holmes nodded. "What appears a multitude of beasts is in fact one: a hydra whose many heads attach to a single body. Cthulhu does not encourage visitors to these catacombs and would deter them at every turn. Making it look as though things are more complicated than they are is one means of accomplishing that."

With a feigned air of decisiveness R'luhlloig told the sailors that he knew which doorway we must take. He invited them to direct their torches at one I could tell he had selected at random. We headed through it into a tunnel along which an elephant could have comfortably trodden, with room to spare.

For all that it was spacious, that tunnel felt oppressively close-confining nonetheless. We were deep under R'lyeh, well below sea level, and I was conscious both of the colossal weight of rock above us and of the ocean pressing in on the island from all sides. The tunnel seemed endless and I began to worry that we might walk down it forever and never reach anywhere, and likewise that if we turned round we might never get back to its beginning. What if, now that we had gone far enough into the tunnel that we could no longer see the entrance, the doorway had not just moved but had vanished altogether? What if this shaft had swallowed us up like a python and we were now sealed in its gut, entombed?

Not long after these misgivings started to assail me, it became clear that we did not have the tunnel to ourselves.

At first it was simply a few rustling footfalls that could have been echoes of our own. Then it was the odd high-pitched titter, which again might have been an echo or else was a trick of the ear, something born of the tunnel's acoustics.

More and more, however, the sounds became distinct, obviously unconnected in any way to the noises we were making. The torches swung this way and that as the crewmen aimed them towards where they thought the sounds were originating. The beams lit up just bare rock... but occasionally there was the merest glimpse of *something* flitting out of sight, so quick and evanescent that one might dismiss it as a stray shadow or some vagary of the tungsten filament bulbs' incandescence.

The tittering continued, growing louder and somehow more confident, and now was interspersed with bursts of a chattering, liquid kind of speech. If it was a language, it was one without an appreciable grammatical system, a jumble of vowels and consonants really only describable as gibbering; but for all that, its tone was patently full of scorn and mockery. I judged that it was coming from at least a score of different throats, and there was a primitive call-and-response pattern evident. One gibberer would make a statement and others would mimic it several times, then another gibberer would offer some comment which the rest would take up and replicate, and so on.

The first gunshot was as ear-splittingly startling as it was predictable. The sailors were close to panic – and I was not far off it myself – and someone could not resist the urge to fire his weapon. The intention, I am sure, was more to scare than to harm, for there was, after all, nothing of substance to fire at.

The gibberers responded with chimpanzee-like howls of alarm and outrage. There was a flurry of activity, audible but invisible, and when it subsided we were a man down. He – a swarthy fellow with a cataracted eye – had been snatched from our midst in the dark. One moment he was beside us, the next he was gone, abducted by unseen forces.

The other sailors called out his name: "Schneider! Schneider!" But Schneider was either out of earshot or dead. Whichever it was, we never saw him again.

He had been taken without even managing to scream. That was perhaps the most chilling aspect of it. Nor could it have been coincidence that it was Schneider who had loosed off a round at the gibberers.

We all made the connection but Holmes was the one who extrapolated what it might signify for us.

"Von Herling, tell your men not to shoot again. It would appear that these things react to threat. They are trying to goad us, in order to excuse a retaliation. Whatever happens, whatever the provocation, we must ignore them."

Easy to say, hard to do. Damned hard. As we continued along the tunnel, the gibberers taunted and harassed us. At times it was as though we were martyrs being harangued by an angry mob on our way to the pyre. The sailors gritted their teeth and kept their forefingers on their triggers. At any moment I thought one of them might snap and start firing off a volley, whereupon the others would surely join in. Then we would, every one of us, be as good as dead.

The cacophony of gibbering reached a crescendo, and then one of the sailors let out a cry. He had been struck in the back by some hard object, something that had been flung at him. It had felt somewhat like a football, he said.

Torch beams roved the vicinity until one of them alit upon a roughly spherical shape on the ground. It was Schneider's head. It lay on its side, mouth agape, peering up at us almost quizzically with its one good eye. The stump of the neck was a ragged bloody mess, showing evidence that the decapitation had been carried out savagely, using claws, or possibly teeth.

The next moment, a hand reached out from the darkness towards the head. It was a smooth, pallid thing, halfway between human hand and animal paw, its stubby, thick-knuckled fingers tipped with wickedly curving talons. The hand caressed the head insinuatingly, as if to draw attention to Schneider's hideous fate. The taunting had reached a new level. The gibberers were trying once more, desperately, to incite further violence.

"Steady," advised Holmes. "Steady. For God's sake, men, if you value your lives, keep your cool."

Von Herling did not need to translate. The sailors may not have understood Holmes's words but his tone of voice made their import clear.

One of the torch beams roamed the length of the gibberer's arm, coming to a rest at its face.

All of us, as one, recoiled. The face was loathsome in every degree. The features were broadly simian, from the heavy brow to the flattened nose and jutting jaw, yet hairless and as pale as the moon. There were sockets for eyes but they were empty, puckered hollows, a vestige of true eyes. The thing must have belonged to a race of subterranean creatures who were ignorant of daylight, wholly blind. It did not even know a torch was shining in its face.

Slobbery fat lips peeled back from rows of peg-like teeth, leaking drool. The gibberer made a soft, hooting sound, which could almost be construed as mischievous.

That was when the full horror of it hit me. The gibberers were a deadly menace, yes, but to them this was all just play. They were challenging us to participate in a game with them – a game of assault and maiming which they considered entertainment but which was liable to cost us our lives. They wished to toy with us, as vicious as cats with their prey, yet some weird code of honour forbade them from doing so unless they were attacked first.

Once again the gibberer nudged Schneider's head, causing it to roll over onto its nose. Wolfgang let out an involuntary whimper, while another of the sailors ground his teeth in indignant fury. Everybody, however, continued to heed Holmes's admonition.

A full minute ticked by, until eventually the gibberer realised that its invitation was being rebuffed. None of us was offering himself as another Schneider, for the amusement of this creature and its fellows. The gibberer gave a sigh that was childishly deep and heartfelt, then about-turned and sloped off down the tunnel, its broad back hunched over. It called out to the rest of its troop as it went, its tone unmistakably one of disappointment. The others answered in kind, and we heard their chattering voices growing more distant as they retreated back whence they had come.

"As dull-witted a monster as any we have come across," Holmes said, "yet no less dangerous for that. I would not be surprised if we have just met the erstwhile inhabitants of the city above, R'lyehians by any other name. At some point far back in time they descended into the dark and, down here, over the eons, evolution robbed them of their intellect as well as their pigmentation and their eyesight. These blind, albino cretins are the remnants of a once-thriving humanoid populace, regressed to a primitive state. A salutary lesson in how even an advanced civilisation may crumble and decline."

"Your analysis is intriguing," said R'luhlloig, "but the matter need not detain us any longer. We must forge on."

And, our number now reduced by two, we did.

*

By and by, the tunnel came to an end. We were disgorged onto a broad ledge that overlooked an enormous open space, a cavern of such magnitude it boggled the mind. The torches afforded a glimpse of neither its bottom nor its roof nor its far end, and had no hope of doing so. However, simply by the just-perceptible curvature of the walls that extended to either side of us it was possible to build an impression of the overall dimensions of the place; by the faintness of the echoes of our voices, too, for sounds were swallowed up by that vast emptiness like breadcrumbs disappearing into the maw of a leviathan. The cavern, I reckoned, could quite easily have housed a large town, perhaps even a small city. By comparison the one in which Ta'aa was situated seemed paltry.

The men asked permission to rest, which R'luhlloig reluctantly granted. The knapsacks were opened and water canisters were passed around and pieces of cold sausage shared out. Holmes and I were invited to partake, and our hands were untied long enough for us to do so, but this felt like no mere charity. We and the men had all just run the same harrowing gauntlet together and, as with soldiers after a battle, we were equals now, irrespective of rank or background, for enduring a sustained attack by a shared enemy is the great leveller, erasing all differences. Only Wolfgang seemed still disenchanted with us Englishmen, for he objected, albeit in vain, when his fellow sailors gave us food. The lad could nurse a grudge.

Towards the end of this period of respite, Holmes drew R'luhlloig aside for a quiet word. I eavesdropped.

"I feel we do not have much further to travel," Holmes said. "Our quest's objective draws nigh. A few questions, if I may, while we enjoy the lull before the storm."

R'luhlloig made an obliging gesture. He could afford to be magnanimous, with victory practically within his grasp.

"You have elected to fight the decisive battle of your war on two fronts, is that not so? On the cosmic plane and here in the mundane realm."

"A double-pronged attack, you might call it," said R'luhlloig with a nod of acknowledgement.

"That certainly would seem a logical tactic. Cthulhu is simply too dangerous a foe to leave anything to chance. Your Outer God troops are even now gathering, preparing to launch a massed psychic assault upon him. Meanwhile, down here, you are going to unleash a physical assault at the same time. A rather incendiary one."

"What makes you say that?"

"I caught a glimpse of sticks of dynamite in one of the crewmen's knapsacks just now. No amount of explosive will be enough to destroy Cthulhu's bodily form, however. The *Necronomicon* tells us that he is able to reconstitute his flesh after any injury, no matter how severe. Therefore the dynamite can only be intended as a diversion."

"Very good, Mr Holmes. Yes, to annihilate Cthulhu corporeally would take a weapon far more potent than any man has yet devised. Not even a direct hit from a howitzer would suffice. But then I don't need to do that. I only need to cause him enough pain and distress that his mental defences will be compromised. By the same token, the Outer Gods' attack will render him easier for us to lay siege to down here, for he will be distracted, his attention divided."

"Marvellously devious."

"Why, thank you. It all comes down to timing. I am ready to give my forces the order. They are poised, waiting. Once we have located Cthulhu's exact position, then it is a simple matter of my issuing a mental command. Thereafter events should unfurl precisely as preordained. And you, of course, cannot do a thing to stop it."

"Not even by throwing you off this ledge?"

"You would have the two of us wrestle, as Dr Watson depicted in his story? Holmes and Moriarty above a precipice, locked in a death struggle?" R'luhlloig chuckled condescendingly. "Real life is never as straightforward as fiction. There are stalwart Germans over there armed with Mauser rifles and keeping a close eye on you. They would intervene the moment you tried anything untoward."

"I was joking."

"No, you were not. At least not entirely. But I have, as I say, made provision in case you should attempt something rash. When it comes to a matching of wits, Mr Holmes, you will not find me wanting."

Holmes glanced over at the rim of the ledge, beyond which lay a drop of unguessable depth. Perhaps, for a moment, he was seriously contemplating making good on his threat, and to hell with the consequences. If he should perish while killing the body that R'luhlloig was using, that might be an acceptable price to pay. Eliminating Von Herling would at the very least put a crimp in the Hidden Mind's plans, even if it did not ruin them altogether. Equally, Holmes might just be throwing his life away for naught, if there was any truth in R'luhlloig's assertion that he had a countermove already in place.

I tensed, all set to weigh in on Holmes's side. Were I able to catch Wolfgang unawares and relieve him of my revolver, I might then shoot the sailors with rifles before they could use them on my friend. I might also get shot myself for my pains, but the situation was so desperate that such an outcome was justifiable and, to my mind, acceptable.

The moment passed. Holmes and R'luhlloig exchanged gentlemanly nods. There would be no physical confrontation between them, not for now.

CHAPTER THIRTY-THREE

The Resting Place

WE MADE OUR WAY DOWN A MEANDERING PATH that wound downward from the ledge, cutting back and forth in a zigzag. On one side was sheer cliff-face; on the other, sheer nothingness. The path was a good ten feet wide yet still felt precarious. One misstep, the merest stumble, and a fatal plunge awaited. I cleaved close to the rock wall. To add to my woes, my bonds had been refastened, as had Holmes's, and already my wrists were chafing again and my arms beginning to cramp.

The cavern floor, when we finally got there, was strewn with boulders and horribly uneven, a series of ridges dotted with crater-like hollows, much how I imagine the surface of the moon to be. I had lost all sense of how far below the Earth's surface we now were but it was deeper, surely, than any miner or speleologist had ever gone. We must be near the lower limits of the planetary crust, with an ocean of boiling magma not far beneath our feet. I say this not least because it was very warm down on the cavern floor, the atmosphere dank, humid and hard to breathe. There was a sulphurous tang to the air, too, that singed the nostrils.

Without hesitation R'luhlloig sallied forth across the cavern, weaving a course around the sundry obstructions. Holmes was close behind him, while the rest of us followed at the rear like ducklings straggling after the parent birds.

Every now and then we would pass a towering column as thick around the middle as the rotunda of the Albert

Hall. These glistening masses of sediment, bulbous and sinewy like melted tallow, were either stalagmite or stalactite or a conjoining of the two. One could scarcely calculate how many eons it must have taken them to form, drip by drip. The cavern was as old as time.

Our hike across that hypogeal plain was a long gruelling succession of ups and downs, our feet crunching on gravelly soil. One by one the torches' batteries gave out, but somebody, doubtless R'luhlloig, had had the foresight to bring along spares.

It felt as though we had been walking forever — and would continue to walk forever — when all at once R'luhlloig lofted a hand, inviting us to halt. Some way ahead lay a glow, which came from a series of football-sized crystals perched on plinths. They shed their wavering green effulgence upon a large stone structure that had something of a temple about it and something of a crypt. Multiple porticoes rested upon a slab-like base. Between the columns a polygonal dais was visible within and, lying athwart this, an enormous supine form.

The eerie will-o'-the-wisp light from the crystals also revealed numerous humped, rounded objects, which were arranged outside the structure in concentric circles. The nature and purpose of these mounds were hard to determine. Roughly ovoid, they looked not unlike big, misshapen eggs.

Yet my gaze kept being drawn back to the figure inside the building. Although it was a mere green-tinged silhouette — an impression of fleshy bulk — I knew that it could only be him. Cthulhu. There was that flattened brow; there a coil of mouth-tentacle; there the scalloped edge of a bat wing. I fancied I could even make out a slight rise and fall where his chest must be. Cthulhu was breathing slowly and steadily. Cthulhu was sleeping.

Dread came over me then, a dread such as I had never known, a dread so all-encompassing that it ousted every other sensation from my body. I could not have been more terrified were I in the presence of Satan himself. In many ways I was, for there could be no more tangible a personification of evil than Cthulhu. Even the Devil of the Bible must acknowledge that here in this Old One he had a close rival, if not a superior.

A muffled gunshot roused me from my stupor of fear. I whirled about in time to see one of the sailors crumple to the ground. His rifle tumbled from his limp hands. The back of his head was a jagged wet ruin.

It was perfectly apparent that the fellow had turned the Mauser around, placed the end of the barrel in his mouth and blown his brains out. The same dread that had suffused me was, for him, too much to bear. Instinctively, at a visceral level, he had known what the slumbering figure in the temple-cum-crypt was and what it represented. His reaction had been as automatic as it was drastic. In a way I admired the deed, envying him the oblivion he now enjoyed.

That left just five of us: me, Holmes, R'luhlloig, Wolfgang and the sailor who had used a clasp knife to carve his initials into a flagstone back in the city. His name, I had gathered, was Dörper. The name of the man who had just committed suicide I never learned.

R'luhlloig seemed little affected either by the sailor's self-inflicted death or by the dread which proximity to Cthulhu engendered. We ordinary humans were ashen-faced and glassy-eyed – even Holmes looked unsettled – whereas the face of Baron Von Herling exhibited nothing but a breezy resolve. R'luhlloig was here to conduct his business and was not going to let anything interfere.

At his urging we made towards the building and those strange ovoid mounds with which it was girt around. I could not help but think that we must be at the centre of the cavern now, and never had I felt further from civilisation or remoter from the world of the everyday. If Holmes and I died here today, which was not a distant possibility, who of our acquaintances would ever know? No one. No one would find our bodies. No one back in England was likely to discover what had become of us. We would have almost literally vanished from the face of the earth. It was a desolate thought.

Arriving at the outermost circle of mounds, we soon perceived that they were organic. Although they lay inert, there were faint tremors and pulsations visible within them that suggested respiration. All were of a uniform size, roughly that of a prostrate adult human, and all were orientated the same way so that their tapered ends pointed toward, and their blunt ends away from, the resting place of Cthulhu.

Holmes, a slave to his own curiosity, knelt beside one to examine it.

"Some sort of sac," he said, brushing fingertips lightly over the opaque, membranous covering. "A caul or cocoon enclosing a living being." The thing inside twitched in response to his touch. "I would say these are creatures who have entered a torpid state, a form of self-induced syncope, having first fashioned a protective casing around themselves. Would you not concur, Watson? Watson?"

"Syncope, yes," I said vaguely. I had too much else on my mind to be very interested in biological study just then.

"Come on, old man," Holmes urged. "Buck up. I need my Watson wholly with me. In my opinion," he continued, resuming his inspection, "what we are looking at is a clutch of Cthulhu's acolytes."

"Are they the same creatures as the simian things in the tunnel?"

"They do not have quite the same proportions, and no mammal I know of forms a cocoon around itself. One can also glimpse leathery skin through the casing, which would suggest these are, rather, beings of a reptilian or amphibian nature, or possibly insectile. They may be native to the cave or they may have migrated here from elsewhere. I am inclined to favour the latter."

"How so?"

"Observe how they are arranged around the dais. Does their attitude and positioning not strike you as that of worshippers in the act of idolatry?"

"I suppose."

"Might it not stand to reason, then, that they are likely to have accompanied Cthulhu hither? And for a very specific purpose."

"As attendants."

"Or, as I said, acolytes. Acolytes whose devotion is

so profound that they have put themselves into a kind of enforced hibernation. While their lord and master sleeps, they sleep, and no doubt when he awakens, they will awaken too, ready to serve him."

"Or feed him," said R'luhlloig. "Has it not occurred to you, Mr Holmes, that a god, like a man, emerges from slumber hungry? Cthulhu requires a convenient source of sustenance after his long periods of repose."

"So they are not servitors," said Holmes, "but meals."

"Willingly they make of themselves a sacrifice to him. They live to quench his appetite. But that is not to say they will not defend him if he is attacked. We must tread with caution and do our best not to disturb them unduly. They are watchdogs as well as fodder."

"Incredible," said Wolfgang, joining in the English conversation. Although evidently as appalled as any of us by the horrors and revelations being visited upon us in the course of this expedition, somehow he was managing to keep his wits about him. I could only ascribe it to the resilience of youth. "I never realised there could be things like this. Baron, in your daring you are truly a tribute to German breeding."

"You too are a good German, my boy," said R'luhlloig, "and will no doubt go far. But now we have work to do. Dörper?"

The other remaining sailor snapped to attention.

R'luhlloig, in German, entrusted Dörper with the task of laying the dynamite around the building in such a way as to bring it down upon its sleeping occupant. The aim was to cause the maximum possible damage both to the structure and to the being within.

Dörper, sticks of dynamite in hand, picked his way through the rings of hibernating creatures. There was a distinct tremor in his step as he neared Cthulhu's resting place. He kept his gaze averted from the huge, slumbering form as he moved around the building's periphery, placing the dynamite in bundles at strategic points. He attached fuses of varying burn rates to the bundles and linked them together so that they culminated in a single main starter fuse. He used his clasp knife to trim the pieces of cord to size. As far as I could judge, the lengths and timings of the subsidiary fuses were calculated so that the sticks of dynamite would all detonate simultaneously.

It was the work of half an hour, and by the end of it Dörper was a shambling wreck of a man. He was operating much nearer to Cthulhu than we were, and it seemed that the Old One's malign influence, like heat from a furnace, was that much more devastating in close proximity. How he remained compos mentis long enough to complete the job, I have no idea. It was a miracle. As he re-joined us, unravelling a long coil of starter fuse behind him, his expression was haggard and wild. He kept muttering a single word over and over − *unbekannt*, "unknown" − while saliva dribbled from the corner of his mouth and his eyes swivelled in their sockets. He sat down on his haunches, rocking back and forth, still repeating "*unbekannt*" to himself in a childish singsong manner, until all of a sudden he went stock still and fell silent; and then, abruptly, he keeled over sideways, collapsing to the ground like a sack of coal.

He was, to judge by the absolute immobility with which he lay, quite dead. The sudden, precipitous lapse into lunacy had robbed Dörper of not just his senses but his life. It was as though his brain had become so thoroughly deranged that it had forgotten how to run his body.

R'luhlloig was phlegmatic. "He did what he had to and he did it well."

"That's four now." I would have shaken a fist at him, had I been at liberty to do so. "Four men who have died to get us this far."

"Four heroes of Germany," said Wolfgang.

"And you can shut up, whelp!" I growled. "I've had enough from you. You are no better than R'luhlloig."

"I take that as a compliment, Doctor," the lad said blithely.

"Insolent little—!"

"Restrain yourself, Dr Watson," said R'luhlloig. "Keep your voice down and your temper in check. Do you wish to wake the sleepers? I would not have thought that wise."

I withheld the insults that were on the tip of my tongue. I let my hunched-up shoulders drop.

"Much appreciated," R'luhlloig said. "Now, everything is in place. All that remains is for me to contact my allies elsewhere…" He paused, savouring the anticipation. "And then the end may begin."

CHAPTER THIRTY-FOUR

The Fall of Cthulhu

BRIEFLY, R'LUHLLOIG'S GAZE LOST FOCUS. HE WAS communing with the Outer Gods in their astral domain.

I shot Holmes a beseeching look. Was there really nothing we could do at this juncture to turn the tide of events?

Holmes nodded towards Wolfgang, who had us both covered with my Webley. The lad was completely, hopelessly in thrall to the senior German. He may have had only the vaguest inkling what was going on and no clue as to who Baron Von Herling really was, but he sensed the momentousness of it all and was eager to play a part.

I had the impression that my friend was suggesting one of us should rush at Wolfgang and attempt to disarm him. I thought it through. Even if I could reach Wolfgang before he shot me, what would be the use of it? I was hardly in a position to wrestle him to the ground, tied up as I was, let alone prise my Webley out of his grasp. However, I might at least bear down on the youngster with my greater bulk, preventing him from firing at anyone else. If I took a bullet for my pains, so be it. There was a chance it would give Holmes an opening and, although his hands were likewise bound, he might be able to take action against R'luhlloig. Even with his capacities limited, Holmes was not without means.

I tensed, ready to follow through on this plan. It was a mark of the desperateness of the situation that I was prepared to risk everything in return for the slimmest possibility of defeating R'luhlloig. Any advantage we could get, though, was better than none.

Then I caught sight of Holmes shaking his head. He had inferred what was going through my mind and was warning me against it. Now I understood that he hadn't been advising me, with his original nod, to attack Wolfgang. Quite the opposite. He had been trying to forestall any such precipitate action on my part. He must, I assumed, have something else up his sleeve. I prayed he did.

"There," said R'luhlloig, returning to us. "It is done. And see? Already Cthulhu stirs. He is uneasy in his sleep. What troubled dreams my troops are bringing him! Each in turn is delivering a mighty psychic blow, bit by bit eroding his power."

The figure on the polygonal dais writhed. A low, deep moan issued forth, reverberating through the cavern.

R'luhlloig stationed himself beside the starter fuse with a matchbook in hand. His face was agleam with exhilaration.

"I want you fully awake, Cthulhu," he said. "I want you to appreciate how adroitly you have been outmanoeuvred and how helpless you are."

Around us, the creatures in their sacs began shifting restively. I backed away from the one nearest, putting a judicious distance between me and it, and also between me and the resting place with its freight of dynamite. My attention, however, was fixed upon Cthulhu to the exclusion of almost all else. The god was lashing out with his arms as though fending off unseen assailants. He was still asleep but the utterances he was making were becoming more voluble and less thickly slurred. Gradually he was surfacing towards consciousness.

All of a sudden he leapt up from the dais, his feet slamming thunderously onto the base beneath. In the green lambency of the crystals his eyes flashed like two emeralds, their vertically slitted pupils widening. A roar of rage and anguish escaped him. He cast his terrible gaze about, seeking out the enemy whose presence he sensed close by.

His sheer enormity was matched by his sheer repellence. Tentacles of varying lengths and thicknesses sprouted from beneath his nose, which was itself a drooping, ribbed proboscis with long, flaring nostrils. All of them coiled and writhed disgustingly, like dozens of octopuses crammed together and squirming. His head was flattened at the top and divided into ridges and folds with a central fissure, so that it resembled in no small way a brain. Two short tubes projected from recesses in his temples. From the way they dilated and contracted, I could only assume they were breathing siphons.

As for his body, it was bulky and muscular but with a certain sagginess, reminiscent of the physique of a boxer past his heyday, now gone to seed. His batlike wings drooped either side of him, their membranes tattered and gashed here and there, indicative perhaps of past conflicts. His rugged hide was likewise scarred in places, all of which served to make him seem a more, not less, daunting proposition. He was, it seemed, a veteran of wars which he had survived while his foes had not.

Worst of all were those eyes. No effigy or image of Cthulhu I had seen could do justice to those malignant orbs. They glowed with a loathing unmatched in all of history. Nobody bore as much hatred for the world and all that was in it – all that was good, all that was proper – than Cthulhu.

"Here I am!" R'luhlloig cried in R'lyehian.

Cthulhu turned his huge head and gazed down at him.

"Yes, in the form of man, but so much more! You know me, Cthulhu. You have heard of me even in your sleep. I am the general of the army that has laid low your relatives one after another, including your half-brother Hastur. Say my name. Say it!"

"*R'LUHLLOIG!*"

The sound, more earthquake than speech, emerged from a beaked orifice between flaring tentacles. Cthulhu's brow furrowed in a terrific scowl. He flexed his wings and pointed an accusatory, talon-tipped finger.

"*R'LUHLLOIG!*" came that voice again, a rumble that shook me to my bowels.

R'luhlloig, in answer, let out a laugh that was stuttering and high-pitched like a hyena's. He tore a match from the matchbook and struck it. As the match head flared, he picked up the fuse.

"*R'LUHLLOIG!*" said Cthulhu a third time, venomously, and he began to stride forth from his resting place.

But he did not get far. He staggered as though caught by a violent gust of wind. A hand went to his head, clutching it. His eyes creased up in pain.

"That's it," said R'luhlloig. "Stay there. The Outer Gods are stepping up their offensive. It hurts, doesn't it? And how weak you are feeling. Look at you. You can barely stand."

Cthulhu tottered, slumping back onto the dais, catching himself with an elbow. It was sobering, almost disturbing, to see this much-vaunted Old One suddenly so enfeebled. I was far from feeling compassion for him but there was nonetheless something pathetic about his plight. He was like a baited bear being brought down by hounds.

Splits appeared in the sacs containing his acolytes, like eggs starting to hatch. I registered this fact, but only abstractedly. I could not tear my gaze from beleaguered Cthulhu.

R'luhlloig brought the tip of the fuse to the match flame – a tiny flicker of light that heralded huge consequences. The fuse caught and he dropped it. A sizzling, sparkling burst of fire hurtled like a shooting star along the length of saltpetre-impregnated cotton cord. In no time it reached the junction where the starter fuse split off into several strands. There it ramified into a half-dozen discrete fire-bursts, which raced at varying speeds towards the bundles of dynamite sticks.

All I could do was press my hands over my ears and wait for the detonation.

Multiple eruptions of orange light blazed, dazzling in the cavern's gloom. The concussion was so great I was nearly knocked off my feet. Porticoes crumbled, the roof of the resting place collapsing in upon itself. Cthulhu was trapped beneath falling masonry. He bellowed grievously as several tons of broken stone engulfed and buried him.

As the rolling echoes of the explosion dwindled and the haze of dust cleared, all we could see was a demolished ruin. Chunks of stone lay about in heaps. One solitary column remained standing, albeit sheared to half its former tallness. Of Cthulhu himself there was no sign.

"I have done it," R'luhlloig declared. I could just about hear him above the ringing in my ears. "Cthulhu lies crippled, powerless to resist. While his body struggles to repair itself, the Outer Ones may continue to wreak merry havoc upon his mind, unimpeded. Even if he is able to put himself back together, his intellect will have been decimated and his will broken. There is no coming back from this. Cthulhu has fallen!"

He brandished a fist in the air.

I turned to Holmes.

My friend had sunk to his knees, not far from the body of Dörper. At first I thought he was praying. His head was bowed and he was murmuring to himself.

R'luhlloig was under the same impression. "What's this, Mr Holmes? Are you calling upon God to deliver you in the hour of crisis? How unlike you."

Now Holmes began swaying back and forth.

"Really!" R'luhlloig snorted. "This behaviour is most unbecoming. Could you not at least have the decency to act as the circumstances warrant? You have always prided yourself on your rational approach in all affairs."

The ringing in my ears was beginning to fade. "It is yours," I heard Holmes say.

"Eh?" said R'luhlloig.

"I return it to you." Holmes intoned the words much in the manner of a priest leading communion. "Your gift has served me well but now is the time for you to take it back. Receive that which you lent. Your need is greater than mine."

He shuddered from head to toe, seized by a paroxysm whose origin I could not fathom. His eyes rolled up in his head and his mouth gaped. From deep within him a keening cry arose, growing louder and shriller as the spasms that were racking him intensified.

It was some kind of fit, I could only assume. A fever of the brain had stricken him, brought on by recent deprivations and exertions. That, or this was simply a piece of theatre, Holmes indulging in sensational dramatics for reasons I could only guess at. To misdirect R'luhlloig, perhaps, while he pulled off some last-minute coup, a masterstroke that would reverse all our fortunes.

In the event, it proved to be a little of both and a lot else besides.

CHAPTER THIRTY-FIVE

Toadies

THE HILLOCK OF RUBBLE STIRRED. ALL AT ONCE A hand shot forth, groping upwards. Then, with an almighty heave, Cthulhu burst free from his prison of debris. He rose to his full height, shrugging off hundredweight lumps of stone as though they were flinders. The detritus fell around him in a clattering cascade.

The only word I can think of to describe how he looked then is reinvigorated. His eyes gleamed with purpose. If a mouth consisting largely of tentacles can be said to grin, his was doing so.

Sherlock Holmes, meanwhile, had collapsed in a swoon, and at some level I understood the two phenomena to be related. The one was somehow the causation of the other. There had been some form of *exchange*.

I ran over to my friend, even as Cthulhu strode intently towards us. Holmes was still conscious but his face was pallid and his eyelids fluttered feebly. With my hands tied behind my back there was little I could do in the way of tending to him. Scarcely had I felt more impotent.

R'luhlloig stood his ground, glaring defiantly up at the gigantic, hulking form of Cthulhu. If he was taken aback by his enemy's unexpected recovery, it barely showed.

Cthulhu pointed to him, then to himself.

"You would battle me here, is that it?" R'luhlloig said. "In gross hand-to-hand combat, like two street brawlers? But, as I am now, you could crush me with a single blow. What would that gain you?"

"Meet him on his own terms," said Holmes in a hoarse croak.

R'luhlloig flicked a glance at him. "Why should I?"

"Because you can. You know you can. Invest that body with your full godly power and you will be equal to Cthulhu's challenge. Will it not be satisfying to best him one-on-one? Will that not be the ultimate vindication of your greatness?"

Holmes was appealing to the vestiges of Professor Moriarty which lingered somewhere within R'luhlloig, the part of him that was still prey to human foibles such as vanity.

And it seemed that, despite all his boasts to the contrary, R'luhlloig had not transcended his mortal origins altogether, for he nodded in agreement.

"Yes. Yes!" He looked back up at Cthulhu. "You always have been a crude god, and so you should be beaten, not with finesse, but crudely. You are doomed anyway, but how much more fitting will it be, how much more crushing, to deliver the final blow here on this plane of reality – to feel with my own hands your bones and organs shattering and the life ebbing out of you."

With that, the body of Baron Von Herling began to transform. I can scarcely relate without an involuntary shudder and a certain incredulity how it grew and expanded, becoming grotesquely swollen as R'luhlloig imbued it with every ounce of his essence. The limbs distended like gnarled tree trunks. The torso twisted and bloated, ripping to shreds the clothing that enrobed it. The head became something almost unrecognisable, a spherical mass with squashed, globular features, which bore not a trace of Von Herling's urbane good looks. Flesh had become putty, reshaping itself to contain and express the immense raw power suffusing it. R'luhlloig had begun his life as a god by usurping the shape-shifting formlessness of Nyarlathotep, the Crawling Chaos, and now he was demonstrating a similar plasticity as his physical host warped into a being that looked every bit Cthulhu's equal in size, bulk and strength.

The two gods squared off against each other, eye to eye. Cthulhu flapped out his wings to their fullest extent – an intimidating sight given that they spanned some fifty feet from tip to tip – and bellowed at R'luhlloig. The huge sprawling abomination that R'luhlloig had become, and which hardly resembled a man any more, bellowed back. They were monsters as much as gods, primordial giants driven by the most basic of urges: to fight, to conquer, to destroy.

It was then that I noticed that Holmes's hands were free. Rope still encircled his wrists but loosely, severed ends dangling. Clutched in his palm I spied a clasp knife – Dörper's – the blade still open. Holmes had manoeuvred himself close to the fallen sailor so that he might retrieve the knife from his person. At what point he had used it to cut through his bonds, I was not sure. It must have been prior to him swooning, whereupon he had kept his hands hidden so that R'luhlloig would not know that he had freed himself and would not suspect anything was amiss.

Holmes was too enfeebled to do anything but direct his gaze meaningfully towards the knife. Not that I needed to be told what to do. I sat down in ungainly fashion with my back to him and groped for the knife. By dint of levering it up between my wrists, I was able to start sawing through the rope. Dörper, God rest his soul, had kept the blade keenly whetted, and in surprisingly short order my bonds slackened. I dropped the knife and shook my hands free from the rope.

At that moment Cthulhu and R'luhlloig ceased their posturing and threw themselves at each other. They came together in a clinch like a pair of wrestlers in the ring. The collision made the cavern floor shake underfoot.

I stood and pulled Holmes to his feet. There was no point in us remaining in that place a moment longer. Events were out of our hands. Cthulhu and R'luhlloig were in the grip of rampant bloodlust, and we were liable to be trampled if we did not get out of their way.

Besides, the sacs around us were all nearly open, the creatures within toiling harder than ever to escape their self-imposed confinement. I saw a hand tear through the sac nearest us. Its fingers were tipped with flat pads like a frog's. From an adjacent sac a head bulged, straining to break the tension of the membranous casing. The head stretched the material so thin that it became partly translucent, and I could discern goggling eyes and blubbery lips that were froglike too.

Holmes was almost incapable of staying upright. I draped his arm around my neck, put mine around his waist, and lodged a shoulder under his armpit.

"Walk, Holmes!" I urged him. "I can take some of your weight but I cannot carry you. Walk, damn it!"

Cthulhu and R'luhlloig reeled apart from each other, then re-engaged. As body struck body, chest to chest, another booming tremor shook the cavern.

This seemed to galvanise Holmes and he began to walk.

Wolfgang was staring up at the grappling gods, dumbfounded.

"You too, boy!" I yelled at him. "Don't stand there gawping, not if you want to live."

"No, not him," Holmes murmured.

"Yes him," I replied. "We cannot leave him behind. Whatever our differences, whatever we have done to him and he to us, he does not deserve to die here." Holmes made a few further flimsy protests, which I ignored. It seemed quite unlike my friend to deny aid to someone who was guilty of no crime save having been misled. I ascribed it to his overall parlous state of health. He was not thinking clearly. To Wolfgang I said, "We must go, boy. Now!"

My cries served to break the spell of awe that held the youngster mesmerised. It helped that, at the selfsame moment, a sac just a few yards from him burst completely open. The creature that had been cocooned within staggered upright from its prostrate position, sloughing off the ribbons of sticky skin-like film adhering to it. It was, I now saw, more toad than frog. It had a flabby, bulging throat. Its belly was pale and soft while the rest of it was rugged and wart-festooned. It stood like a man, if with a stooping hunch to its upper back. In all, it was as repugnant a being as any I had beheld, the more so when a fat purplish tongue lolled from its mouth like a balloon inflating. It was probably just a reflex response but it looked as though the creature was licking its lips avariciously.

Wolfgang took one look at this horrid servile thing – which I cannot help but dub a "toady" – and his astonishment turned to disgust. The toady, in turn, let out a croaking yelp, crouched down on its hindquarters, and sprang at the lad.

Wolfgang ducked out of its way, hurling himself prone, and the toady's leap carried it over him. The creature about-turned immediately, however, and came at him a second time. Wolfgang scuttled frantically away on all fours, but the toady alighted upon his back, pressing him flat to the ground. I could not think how the creature might possibly harm him until it opened its mouth wide and I saw that there was a fringe of teeth around the interior, each as thin and sharp as a nail. These it meant to sink into the boy's neck.

In his panic, Wolfgang had dropped my revolver and so he had nothing with which to defend himself. However, Dörper's rifle lay just within my reach. Still supporting Holmes, I bent down and snatched up the Mauser. I rested the butt against my chest and fired one-handed. The recoil sent a jolt of pain through my ribs, but the bullet went where it was supposed to. The toady's head exploded in a spray of fleshy gobbets. The creature slumped on top of Wolfgang, and he, with a groan of revulsion, shook off its dead weight and rose up.

More of the toadies were hatching. At the same time,

the fight between Cthulhu and R'luhlloig was becoming more tumultuous and bestial by the second. The two gods belaboured each other with savage blows, their every footfall sending out terrific rumbling vibrations. Cthulhu caught R'luhlloig with a swipe of one taloned paw, rending a series of parallel gashes in that near-featureless face. R'luhlloig retaliated by shoving Cthulhu backwards so that he crashed onto the rubble that had been his resting place.

Cthulhu seized the last column standing and, plucking it from the ground and brandishing it like a quarterstaff, swung it at R'luhlloig. The column shattered against the Hidden Mind's shoulder with such force that fragments of stone rained in all directions. We humans were lucky not to be hit, but a couple of the toadies did not go unscathed. One was brained by a chunk the size of its own head, while the other was struck in the small of the back and knocked flat. To judge by the way it squirmed on the ground, its spine had been severed.

R'luhlloig himself was nearly toppled by the assault but regained his balance and charged at Cthulhu, roaring in fury. The force of his lunge sent Cthulhu sprawling, whereupon R'luhlloig started pounding at his opponent's head, which rippled like jelly at each impact and eventually split open. With a grunt of agony, Cthulhu threw R'luhlloig off him. The fissure in his head sealed itself as he delivered his riposte, bringing both fists, clenched together as one, down upon R'luhlloig's chest repeatedly.

All this I observed while beating a hasty retreat. Holmes limped along beside me, still leaning heavily on me. Wolfgang was with us too, now thoroughly eager to leave the scene following his close shave with the toady. He had at least had the common sense to pick up my revolver first before fleeing.

Some of the toadies lolloped after us in pursuit. The majority, however, were more concerned with the battle between their master and his enemy. Without seeming to think twice about it, they launched themselves into the fray. They swarmed around R'luhlloig, clambering up his legs, biting him. He swatted them off and stamped on them, squashing them beneath his soles like insects. Yet they persisted, blithely surrendering their lives in the name of their god.

We hurried onward. Every so often I turned and took a potshot with the rifle at the toadies behind us, fighting a rearguard action. Hampered as I was by keeping Holmes upright, I fired more in hope than expectation. Yet, though my aim was lacking, I nonetheless scored several bullseyes.

Alas, the remaining toadies were not deterred by seeing their cohorts die. They came on after us, leaping and bounding, chasing us with a mindless obstinacy that would have been laughable were it not so much to our disadvantage.

All the while the battle between the gods raged on, and the entire cavern quaked with the intensity of it. At one point an enormous chunk of the ceiling broke loose and fell to earth, dislodged by the tremendous forces being unleashed elsewhere. It landed just ahead of us with a deafening boom. Cracks were appearing in the floor, as well, and I wondered whether the place was not about to come tumbling down around our ears.

The toadies caught up with us eventually. There were

only a handful of them left, and by now the magazine of the Mauser was empty. I set Holmes down and ran at them, holding the rifle by the barrel and wielding it like a club. Wolfgang, belatedly remembering that he had my Webley, shot three of them dead. The rest, numbering just two, I despatched with ferocious swings of the gun. I batted them until they fell to the ground, dazed; then I hammered them on the head with the butt of the Mauser until their skulls broke and the brains poured out. I was in a frenzy of loathing. I did not care about the blood and the lumps of grey matter that spattered me. I cared only about making sure those toadies were put down in such a way that they never got up again.

I gathered up Holmes and on we went, Wolfgang leading the way with a torch. The sounds of divine combat continued unabated, but dimmed to the volume of a distant cannonade, for the gods were now out of our sight. I had no way of telling which of them was winning, Cthulhu or R'luhlloig, nor did it much matter to me. I was interested only in getting out of that cavern and, if possible, off the island. This goal seemed an almost inconceivable one, taking into account how far we had to go yet and how the cavern appeared to be in imminent danger of caving in. Yet I clung to it ardently, for the alternative was simply to stop in one's tracks, give up and wait for the inevitable.

Somehow we found ourselves at the foot of the cliff, and somehow, even more remarkably, not far from the zigzagging path. Up this we breathlessly scrambled. Holmes had regained some of his lost energy and thus was not so great a burden on me, yet still it was, in every sense, an uphill struggle. I recall little of that section of our journey, and likewise of our subsequent foray through the tunnel of the apelike gibberers. Thankfully those haunters in the dark left us alone this time. Doubtless they were too perturbed by the commotion of the battle raging below to wish to resume their "playful" games with us.

At last we came to the spiral staircase, and I began to believe that we might actually make it back to the surface after all. A surge of delight revived my flagging stamina.

"This is it, Holmes," I said to my friend. "Not far now, old man. We have it in the bag."

"Not quite, Doctor," said Wolfgang, and the click of a revolver being cocked had me cursing my overconfidence. "There remains one last score to settle."

CHAPTER THIRTY-SIX

Phantoms in the Sky

"WOLFGANG..." I BEGAN.

The young German mariner looked pityingly at me down the barrel of my Webley. "I think you have gone far enough. I cannot allow you to leave here alive. Not after all that has transpired."

"Really now, Wolfgang, don't be foolish. I know there is bad blood between us, but it is not worth this. Shooting us in revenge will gain you nothing. If it helps, I am sorry that we used you the way we did. Please accept my apology, which I tender sincerely, and put the gun away."

"Not just Wolfgang," said Holmes. "I tried to warn you but you would not listen."

"What?"

My friend fought to get the words out. "R'luhlloig said he had made provision. In case I attempted something rash. Who would be the likeliest candidate to replace Von Herling if he perished? Someone with ambition and feelings of rancour. And Wolfgang didn't bat an eyelid when, earlier, you referred to Von Herling as R'luhlloig. The name was not jarring to him. Because he knew it already. Because he is not Wolfgang, not entirely. Look at his eyes."

The lad's eyes were wide and fanatical, but there was something else in them, an added element, a gleaming glint I knew all too well.

"R'luhlloig," I said, half sighing. "You have R'luhlloig in you."

"Just a scintilla of him," said Wolfgang, "but it is enough. He is speaking to me even now, just as he has been speaking to me since Durban, and he is telling me I must slay you. It is only right. You must be punished for the inconvenience you have caused."

"Don't listen to him," I said. "R'luhlloig is nothing but lies and hollow promises. He will use you and use you until there is nothing left, and then he will spurn you without a second thought. I speak from experience. I know what he is capable of."

"But I know him personally, and I trust him."

"Think about Baron Von Herling. Think about what has become of him back there in the cavern. Do you reckon there will be anything left of him after this, regardless of whether R'luhlloig wins or loses against Cthulhu?"

"I have a bright future," Wolfgang said with a dogmatic air. "R'luhlloig is going to ensure it. He has vowed that I will receive everything I could wish for. And the price is negligible. Merely your life and Mr Holmes's."

"I beg you. This is your last chance to turn your back on him. Kill us, and you will be his forever. Refuse to obey him and there is still hope for you."

"Incorrect, *Engländer*. Hope for me lies in your deaths. There are still three bullets in this gun. I need not worry about resistance from Mr Holmes. The first bullet, then, is for you."

"Wolfgang, listen to me—"

A shot rang out. I flinched. Wolfgang had fired from point-blank range. There was no way he could have missed. I was dead.

The lad looked down at himself in mild perplexity. The revolver drooped in his hand. Upon his chest, dead centre of his sternum, a blot of blood oozed outward, becoming a poppy-sized stain.

He returned his gaze to me, and his expression was piteous, as though I had somehow betrayed him a second time.

Then his legs buckled under him and he sagged to the ground.

I glanced round. Behind me, at the foot of the staircase, Captain Künstler lowered the rifle in his hands. With him were two of his crew, also armed.

"Doctor?" said he. "Are you well?"

"As – as well as can be expected," I stammered.

"And Mr Holmes?"

"He has been better. How…? What…?"

"What are we doing here? Why have I killed Wolfgang?" Künstler looked grim. "I am not sure of my reasons myself. Let us just say that I am not sure I have been on the correct side in all of this."

The ground trembled and granules of dust rattled down from on high.

"What I am sure of," Künstler added, "is that the island seems to be experiencing some sort of seismic activity and it might not be wise to remain here much longer. I take it you are the only survivors of the expedition."

"The three of us." I glanced down at Wolfgang and amended, "The two of us, rather."

"Then without further ado, we should go."

"You will have no argument from me on that front."

Künstler instructed his men to relieve me of Sherlock Holmes and carry him between them. I bent a knee by poor Wolfgang's corpse, said a small prayer for the boy's soul, and prised my revolver from his limp hand. Then, straightening, I joined Künstler and the others, and we mounted the stairs.

*

Daylight – a sight I had thought I might never see again – blinded me. Our party wound down through the outskirts of R'lyeh, making haste because the tremors were worsening. The statues rocked on their pedestals. Fractures were appearing in walls, carving lightning-like lines through the bas-reliefs, and every now and then a morsel of a building would crumble away and crash to the ground.

By the time we were passing through the main part of the city, the entire island was convulsing like a patient in the agonies of fever. Deep below, the contest between Cthulhu and R'luhlloig must be escalating yet further. Heedless of anything but each other, they seemed oblivious to the wider repercussions of their actions.

The rowing boat sat in the mud, closer to shore than where we had left it. We climbed in, and the two sailors shoved the boat out into the shallows and clambered aboard, then took to the oars and began hauling us away from the island. The water was agitated, rising to small peaks. All around us marine animals beyond description cavorted near the surface, seemingly in response to the subterranean disturbances. There were things with too many teeth and too many fins, and things that were both gaudy and ugly, and things that belonged only in nightmares.

As we lumbered towards the submarine, Künstler explained that he had sent a man out from the submarine to retrieve the boat. The fellow had swum all the way and rowed back, a brave undertaking in those waters, thronged as they were with unknown beasts. Künstler and another two sailors had then taken the boat over to the island once more. He knew where he might find us, since he had been scanning the island through a telescope since our departure and had seen our party arrive at the base of the pillar.

There had followed an arduous journey through R'lyeh. The layout of the city's streets that so foxed our expedition had proved almost as baffling to Künstler, the difference being that the old seadog had resorted to a compass and dead reckoning when his sense of direction began to fail him; and these navigational skills, and not a little luck, had seen him and his companions safely through.

What the captain would still not vouchsafe is why he had come looking for us. I had the sense that he was trying to make amends, but what had prompted the change of heart?

No sooner had we gained the lee of SM *U-19* than Künstler leapt onto the deck of the larger vessel and ordered the engines to be started. I supervised the transfer of Holmes onto deck, then nursed him through the process of climbing down the conning tower ladder.

I remained on the conning tower with Künstler as the U-boat turned hard to starboard and began to chug away from the island. As we watched, the buildings of R'lyeh started shaking as never before. Several of them collapsed in on themselves or tumbled against their neighbours. The pillar that marked the entrance to the catacombs fell. The entire island was overcome with paroxysms of shuddering.

Then, above it, we glimpsed hazy shapes in the sky. Two gargantuan figures were locked in a life-or-death struggle. They were gauzy and diaphanous, like spirit forms, shadowy projections of reality. One was clearly Cthulhu; the other, R'luhlloig.

"You are seeing this too?" Künstler said in half-disbelieving tones. "It is not some trick of the light?"

"It is there," I said. "It is real enough."

"What are they?"

"You could call them gods, but gods of the profanest, obscenest kind."

"I have never…"

Künstler could say no more. He could not summon the words.

As SM *U-19* gathered speed, the phantom battle reached a climax. Cthulhu had the upper hand. He was holding R'luhlloig in a remorseless grip, flinging him to and fro like a terrier with a rat. All at once R'luhlloig came apart in his hands, sundered in twain.

This was accompanied by the mightiest upheaval to afflict the island yet. The whole place gave a tremendous rising surge, then started to fall to pieces. Bit by bit, segment by segment, from the edges inward, the spit of rock sank beneath the sea, taking the ruins of R'lyeh with it. The sound of its death throes was a long, sonorous roar, so loud one's ears could hardly make sense of it.

Cthulhu raised his arms aloft in triumph while what was left of R'luhlloig dissipated like dust blown away by a strong breeze. The Old One beat his chest and howled to the heavens. At the same time, what was left of the island – a scattering of rocky shoals here and there – was inundated by an enormous inrush of water.

Then the image of Cthulhu was gone from view. The effects of the cataclysm, however, continued as a huge surging wave rippled outward from the spot where the island had stood. There was no hope of SM *U-19* outrunning the wave or diving fast enough to escape it. We could only ride it out.

Künstler and I grasped the sides of the conning tower as the wave swept towards us. I looked at him and, in answer to my unspoken question, he assured me that the U-boat could survive what was coming. He sounded certain, but the whiteness of his knuckles and the set of his jaw told a somewhat different story.

We were caught by the wave as though being scooped up by a vast hand. It bore us along at stomach-swooping speed with the submarine canted towards her bow. The buffeting was horrendous. For several awful seconds I thought the U-boat might be pitched stern over prow, swamped and capsized. All I could hear was seething water and the squeals of protesting metalwork.

Then the turbulence subsided. SM *U-19* righted

herself. The wave rolled beyond us, smoothing out, losing force. We bobbed about wildly in its aftermath, but the worst was over. The danger was past.

Künstler and I took one last look back. Aside from an expanse of frothing, churning ocean, there was no sign of the island, not a glimpse of Cthulhu, not a trace of the city of R'lyeh. All was lost beneath the waters.

For good, I hoped.

CHAPTER THIRTY-SEVEN

Time and Sherlock Holmes

OVER THE NEXT FEW DAYS I TEASED THE TRUTH out of both Holmes and Captain Künstler. The latter was the more readily forthcoming of the two. Although hesitant at first, he soon revealed what had compelled him to venture onto the island after us.

"Your diary," he said. He and I were in his cabin, formerly Von Herling's. "I read it. Mr Holmes all but invited me to. Do you not recall how, just as you were departing in the rowing boat, he asked me to tidy your cabin and spoke about signing a guest book?"

"I thought he was being facetious."

"As did I, but it ignited a spark of curiosity in me. The comment seemed so incongruous, so unlike him, that I could only think he was hinting at something. I went to your cabin and found your diary under your pillow and I was moved to open it. Initially I was sceptical about some of its wilder assertions, particularly those pertaining to Baron Von Herling. They struck me as quite possibly the ravings of a madman."

"You might well be forgiven for thinking that. What changed your mind?"

"Though quite outrageous and implausible, what I was reading nonetheless made a kind of sense. There was always something about His Excellency that I could not quite put my finger on. That is the saying in English, is it not?"

"It is."

"Something about him did not sit right with me, and there you were, writing about him being possessed by the power of a strange god with an unpronounceable name."

"R'luhlloig."

"Just so. I am not a fanciful man, Doctor. I put my trust solely in things I can see and touch. Yet at the very least I knew that Von Herling had a dark side. He did not act as a normal, moral person should. What if that wickedness came not from within him but from elsewhere? I did not doubt for a moment that you believed this R'luhlloig existed. The way you wrote about him was so precise and so matter-of-fact that I was driven to ask myself if it might not have some basis in the truth. To that end I entered this cabin, which then was still given over to occupation by Von Herling, to see if I might turn up any evidence that would support your diary's claims."

"And did you?"

"At first, no," replied Künstler. "The cabin was meticulously tidy, not a thing out of place. I resolved to investigate further and tried the various drawers, cupboards and cubbyholes, of which you see there are quite a few. The man's personal effects were all neatly stowed, nothing untoward about any of them, until I found something which did pique my interest."

"Namely…"

"A book, Doctor."

"A book?"

"Your concealed book led me to another concealed book."

I fancied the second book he was referring to must be

the sort of esoteric tome that Holmes, for one, was wont to consult in his pursuit of the unearthly and the uncanny. Had R'luhlloig even owned a copy of the *Necronomicon* itself? It would not be unlikely.

In the event, the book that Künstler produced − fetching it out of a drawer of the desk at which he sat − was a rather unexceptional-looking little volume. It was battered and worn, its cloth binding threadbare in places, its spine heavily creased.

Upon the cover were the words:

THE DYNAMICS OF AN ASTEROID
by
PROFESSOR JAMES MORIARTY

Seeing this, I let out something that was halfway between a laugh and a gasp.

"Good grief," I declared. "Moriarty's one and only published work, unless you count his treatise on the binomial theorem."

"When I saw the author's name," said Künstler, "I recalled immediately that you had mentioned a Professor Moriarty in your diary. You wrote that he had become this R'luhlloig entity, who in turn was inhabiting the form of Baron Von Herling. It struck me as a curious coincidence, to say the least, that Von Herling should have a copy of a book by the same Professor Moriarty. Look inside."

I opened the cover. The first few pages of the book, from flyleaf to title page to indicia page, were unblemished, if somewhat dog-eared. Where the book proper began, however, there were countless instances of underlining and crossing-out, along with swathes of scribbled marginalia. Often every scrap of available space on a page was covered with scrawled notes, which were in a mixture of English and German, with here and there a smattering of R'lyehian runes. There were complex mathematical and physical formulae, and sketches too, some seemingly abstract, some of nightmarish creatures. In the last category were renderings of snake men, lizard men, ghasts, nightgaunts, and byakhees, along with other beasts I did not recognise and various of the Old Ones and Outer Gods.

From what I could discern, R'luhlloig had been painstakingly going through *The Dynamics of an Asteroid*, adding a commentary on the original text and expanding upon the ideas expressed by Professor Moriarty. It was as though, in all the years since Moriarty published his little-understood, generally maligned magnum opus, he had been unable to forget its poor critical reception and the indifference of the reading public towards it. The wound still festered, and even in his new incarnation as the mighty, godlike Hidden Mind, Moriarty had remained obsessed with improving the book. He could not help including aspects of the knowledge he had gained since becoming R'luhlloig, so that his rather abstruse scientific dissertation had developed, after all, into a sprawling, chaotic cosmology. The book was now perhaps even less comprehensible to the uninitiated than its forebear, and yet, as far as its creator was concerned, more noteworthy.

"I can only imagine," said Künstler, "that Baron Von

Herling spent days of his life, weeks, maybe even months toiling away, filling the book with what appears to be nonsense. What few of his additions I could make head or tail of, I took as evidence of a sorely deranged mind. That was when it began to dawn on me that there may, all along, have been truth in your writings and that Von Herling was both less and more than he seemed. I had watched him drag you and Mr Holmes off to that island, and now it was apparent that I had entrusted you to the mercies of a lunatic. Worse, I was in the employ of a lunatic and was blithely doing his bidding. I already had my misgivings about Von Herling. Now they seemed warranted."

"So you elected to follow us to the island," I said, "even though it entailed risking the lives of your men and yourself."

"A wrong needed rectifying, no matter the cost."

"I am glad you did, and I thank you." My own voice sounded husky with sincerity.

"You should really thank Mr Holmes," said Künstler. "He was the instigator."

"You arrived in the nick of time, too. How did you know that R'luhlloig had got his hooks into young Wolfgang as well as Von Herling?"

"I overheard you and Wolfgang talking. Again that name came up: R'luhlloig. Wolfgang was about to shoot you, an unarmed man, and that was most uncharacteristic. It was clear the same madness which had infected Von Herling had likewise infected him. I had only seconds in which to act, and there seemed no alternative but to shoot him before he shot you."

He paused, a shadow passing across his face as he thought of the boy and how he had ended his life.

"It was no easy thing to do," he said eventually.

"But it was the right thing to do," I assured him.

"All the same, it will be on my conscience for a long time to come, perhaps forever. Similarly what I saw above the island as it was destroyed – that too will remain with me for a long time to come."

"What would you like done with this?" I indicated the obsessively annotated copy of *The Dynamics of an Asteroid*.

"I have no desire to keep it," said Künstler. "Take it, please, with my blessing. Do with it as you will. Burn it would be my recommendation."

I did not burn it but disposed of it in no less permanent a manner, tossing it overboard the next time SM *U-19* surfaced. The book floated for a minute or so, bobbing on the waves. Then, as its pages became waterlogged, it sank slowly into the Pacific depths, vanishing without trace.

Holmes had been right about R'luhlloig. For all that Moriarty had transcended his own humanity, there had still remained a great deal of his old self in him – so much so that it had, in the end, proved his undoing.

I only wished it were as simple a matter to rid myself of the memory of the evil he had done as it was to drop that book in the ocean.

*

As for Holmes, he was too weak to talk at first. He lay in his bunk, motionless and all but insensible. Now and then he was able to sit up and take a sip of water or a bite of food, but largely he spent the time hovering in that halfway house between wakefulness and sleeping.

He looked old all of a sudden. The youthfulness and sprightliness that had marked him over the past few years, in defiance of the rigours of time, had abandoned him. His hair was distinctly greyer and his aquiline features more gaunt and wrinkled than before. No longer would one mistake him for anything but a man in his late fifties. He looked his age and indeed much older.

Time, it appeared, had caught up with Sherlock Holmes at last. It had been held in abeyance for a while but now was back with a vengeance.

Finally he was well enough to speak and I was able to get him to admit that which I already suspected.

"It was Cthulhu, wasn't it?" I said. "You struck a deal with Cthulhu. He bestowed upon you some small fraction of his power, in return for which you gained a vitality that allowed you to prosecute your campaign against R'luhlloig all the more energetically, to the fullest of your abilities."

"Even asleep, Cthulhu knew," said Holmes. "He knew R'luhlloig would be coming for him eventually. I knew it too, and so I communicated with him via the *Necronomicon*, offering him my services. His slumber was not due to come to an end yet. I needed him; he needed me. We reached an agreement. I became his agent."

"Was it thanks to him that you were able to resist the hypnotic effects of the Zann music the Sea-Devils used to such effect?"

"It was."

"Not 'the power of the intellect' at all, as you

claimed. And your allegiance to Cthulhu was why you did so little to hinder our expedition from entering the vaults below R'lyeh."

"So that I might render back to him that which was his, at the appropriate time."

"Folly!" I ejaculated. "Utter folly, all of it. You must have known how hazardous it is to have dealings with any Old One, let alone Cthulhu."

"I deemed the risk acceptable."

"And now look at you. You're half dead."

"Is that a considered medical opinion?"

"Dash it all, yes. Cthulhu took from you as much as he gave, if not more."

"I shall recover."

"Will you? I wonder."

"You are angry with me, Watson."

"And rightly so. Of all the reckless, inconsiderate, idiotic…!"

"It saved us in the end, did it not?" said Holmes placidly. "The threat of R'luhlloig has been negated. Cthulhu, with the return of the power I had borrowed, was able to rise up and destroy him. You yourself have told me how you witnessed his annihilation. And without R'luhlloig at the helm, the Outer Gods' war will surely founder. In the absence of his leadership they will lapse back into anarchy and infighting, as is their wont. It is over."

"So you say."

"I am certain of it. We have won, Watson. We have won at last."

I frowned. "But at what cost?" I said.

"Do not look at me like that. I am not dying."

"Nor are you in good health. I do not have to be a doctor to know that. Your constitution seems irreparably damaged from the undue exertion you have placed upon it, living for too long beyond your natural means. Cthulhu's power has been worse for you even than cocaine. Your dependence on it has harrowed you from the inside out. If you do not take care…"

"You will keep me going, old friend. I have faith in you."

"I shall try," I said. With a snort of derision, I added, "Sea air and honey."

"Sea air and honey?"

"You told me those were the source of your rare good health."

"And you fell for it."

"It seemed barely credible, but yes, I fell for it. But why lie? Why keep your association with Cthulhu a secret from me?"

"Would you have approved?"

"No."

"Then there is your answer. You can be quite the nag, you know, Watson. You would have never ceased berating me. I regret keeping you in the dark but I felt that on balance it was the better option. Besides, what is Sherlock Holmes if not the man who withholds the truth from Dr Watson until the last possible moment? Would you have me behave in a manner inconsistent with the character in your fictions?"

He began to laugh, but the sound devolved into a dry, dreary coughing. Soon after, he fell asleep again.

*

Scarcely did I leave his side, all the way home. Captain Künstler deposited us at Pitcairn Island, where we boarded a schooner that brought regular supplies to the inhabitants of that tiny British dependency. By the time we sailed into Tilbury Docks, Holmes was showing marginal improvement but only marginal. We repaired to Sussex, and there I stayed for the next few months as Holmes's permanent physician, he my resident patient.

There were good days. There were bad days. Sometimes Holmes seemed firmly on the mend, only to suffer a relapse. There was no one particular ailment that he suffered from, just a general ongoing malaise as though all the illnesses he had been spared through Cthulhu's auspices were amassing in him at once. It might be his lungs that were the problem, or it might be his heart, or his liver, or a bout of arthritis, or a touch of gout. The nature of the sickness changed almost daily. I treated him accordingly and clung to the belief that all would be well in the end. I could do no less for my oldest, dearest friend.

It was late summer of 1911 before there were distinct and incontrovertible signs of an upturn. Holmes left his sickbed and was able to go about his daily affairs much as before, although he tired easily and even a brief, none too brisk walk would leave him lightheaded and short of breath. He was, simply put, a frail old man. Premature senescence had him in its teeth. I would watch him from the window as he ministered to his beehives, and his movements were pitifully unsteady and slow. Sometimes he could not remember a certain word or had trouble keeping track of where he was in the book he was reading. I recalled the sharp-witted, sturdy individual he had been, and it made me want to weep.

Holmes had given so much of himself to the cause, and sacrificed so much; the penalty was heavy.

Was it worth it?

I still cannot say.

EPILOGUE

AS I TYPE THESE FINAL PAGES, I VEER BETWEEN relief and regret. I have needed to set the words down on paper and divest myself of the truth. It has been pent up within me for far too long. Now I am shriven. I feel lighter in my soul, if perhaps not any cleaner. It does not matter that nobody will ever read this trilogy. My own satisfaction is enough. I have not laboured for naught.

War came to Europe regardless of Holmes's and my efforts. The continent was devastated and a whole swathe of British manhood wiped out. Events, it seemed, had gone too far to be reversed. The hostilities that R'luhlloig helped set in train gained their own unstoppable momentum. Even now, almost a decade on, England has yet to get over the trauma, and there remains a sense of unfinished business. The old political tensions still simmer away. The cracks have been papered over but continue to spread. Will the twentieth century be a century that knows no peace? If so, that is a legacy R'luhlloig can be proud of.

I have, too, heard recently from my correspondent

and fellow author H.P. Lovecraft. His latest letter from Providence, Rhode Island, carries news that is bleak indeed. R'lyeh has, he says, reappeared above the waves, at the exact same map coordinates where we found it: S. Latitude 47° 9', W. Longitude 126° 43'. Its discoverers, according to Lovecraft, were the crew of a yacht, the *Alert*. He has not revealed to me the specifics of the incident but he intends to publish a full report about it in the next few months, correlating it with a quantity of other Cthulhu-related data, which he has gleaned from the papers of George Gammell Angell, a professor of Semitic Languages at Brown University. Lovecraft says he will dress up his narrative as fiction, putting his words into the mouth of a non-existent Bostonian by the name of Francis Wayland Thurston. Thus he may make the truths he exposes palatable to a mass audience.

Yet the dire fact remains. The island has resurfaced, somehow intact, and the city that rests upon it has rebuilt itself. Cthulhu has bided his time but now rises again to menace mankind. By awakening him, R'luhlloig struck another blow against our race's security, one whose effects are belatedly making themselves felt. He may well have cursed us to a future of unrelenting terror.

I know I shall not live to see these ominous forebodings become reality. I am old, my faculties are failing, and lately I have felt certain inner pangs and exhibited certain symptoms that point ineluctably in only one direction. My days are numbered.

Sherlock Holmes has preceded me into the embrace of the hereafter, and I will not be long in following him. As ever, loyal Watson trails in his companion's wake. Holmes has encountered the greatest mystery of all, and I wonder if he has solved it yet. I wonder, too, if he will be there to greet me on the other side of the veil, smiling in his usual sardonic way, offering me a pitying shake of the head and telling me to keep up.

"So slow, old friend," he may say. "Do I have to explain *everything* to you? Especially a matter as elementary as this."

Then we shall stride off together into whatever awaits us. The miseries of life will have been left behind. The terrors we faced and fought against side by side will be in the past. The many tribulations and vicissitudes we have known will fall away, forgotten.

As the vicar said to me in the churchyard all those years ago, hope is all. One must have hope, for otherwise existence is meaningless madness. Hope steers us clear of the void.

Therefore I hope. It is the only thing I can do. In the twilight of my days, with my heart uneasy and my mind plagued by ghosts of memories, I hope. R'luhlloig will not have won after all. Victory will not be his from beyond the grave. Fate will prove kind to humanity. This is what I hope.

AFTERWORD
BY JAMES LOVEGROVE

WITH THAT EMOTIVE, PLANGENT VALEDICTION, DR Watson's typescript concludes. And my involvement in bringing this trilogy to light ends too.

It's been a labour of love, preparing and editing the books for publication. I won't deny that. It's been hard but rewarding.

It's also been troubling. I haven't had an easy night's sleep since I started working on the project. My dreams have been fraught with strange imagery – glimpses of places I have never visited yet somehow know; things I have never seen that still seem familiar; and worse than any of that, hints of great crawling evil and intimations of darkness. I have not mentioned this to anyone, not even my wife, but it's as if my subconscious has somehow become infected by the words I have been transcribing from paper to screen. Daft, I realise, but that's how it feels.

Not only that but every once in a while, and increasingly, I've been convinced that someone is watching me. I have sensed the gaze of eyes on me – stern, pitiless, inhuman eyes.

In fact, I'm sensing them right now, as I sit in my office at my desk with my computer tower whirring beside me and my dog curled up in her basket at my feet. It is late. The dog is whining in her sleep, her claws scratching at the basket's wicker sides. A wind off the Channel is rattling the windowpanes of this draughty old house of ours. My family are all upstairs, tucked up in bed. I'm tired. I should be with them. But deadlines loom, publishers are tapping their feet impatiently, and I hate to let anyone down.

Still, I'm certain that I am not alone. *Someone* is present in this room with me. I'm telling myself that it's only my imagination. (I'm a writer, y'know. I have one, and it's nothing if not overactive.) I'm telling myself that prolonged exposure to these *Cthulhu Casebooks* is getting to me. I'm a man in my early fifties. I'm reasonably mature and sensible. I shouldn't be jumping at shadows like some nervy adolescent who's just watched their first scary movie.

Odd thing, though. My computer screen has just started misbehaving. Stuttering on and off. Jagged lines of interference fizzing across it.

Ph'nglui mglw'nafh Cthulhu R'lyeh wgah'nagl fhtagn

I swear to God I did not just type that.

Ph'nglui mglw'nafh Cthulhu R'lyeh wgah'nagl fhtagn

There it is again, and I didn't even touch the ruddy keyboard. Some software glitch maybe?

Ph'nglui mglw'nafh Cthulhu R'lyeh wgah'nagl fhtagn

Maybe a virus has got into the system. Maybe that's it. Or someone's pranking me. Yes. This is some hacker's idea of a joke.

Ph'nglui mglw'nafh Cthulhu R'lyeh wgah'nagl fhtagn

Those damn words. "In his house at R'lyeh, dead Cthulhu waits dreaming." Not so much a statement of fact as a warning. A threat.

Ph'nglui mglw'nafh Cthulhu R'lyeh wgah'nagl fhtagn

Okay, that's it. Enough of this.

Ph'nglui mglw'nafh Cthulhu R'lyeh wgah'nagl fhtagn

For the record, I've just hit Control-Alt-Delete three times and it hasn't made a blind bit of difference.

Ph'nglui mglw'nafh Cthulhu R'lyeh wgah'nagl fhtagn

I've now tried pressing the power button. Again, nothing's happened. Computer won't turn off.

Ph'nglui mglw'nafh Cthulhu R'lyeh wgah'nagl fhtagn

I've unplugged the machine. The screen is still on. The hard drive is still going. I'm not kidding. What the hell is happening?

Ph'nglui mglw'nafh Cthulhu R'lyeh wgah'nagl fhtagn

Great. Now the dog's upped and scarpered out of the room, whimpering, her tail between her legs. That's all I need.

Ph'nglui mglw'nafh Cthulhu R'lyeh wgah'nagl fhtagn

Oh God. Eyes. There are eyes looking straight at me. Staring out from the screen. *His* eyes.

Ph'nglui mglw'nafh Cthulhu R'lyeh wgah'nagl fhtagn

Straight at me. Staring.

Ph'nglui mglw'nafh Cthulhu R'lyeh wgah'nagl fhtagn

No!

Ph'nglui mglw'nafh Cthulhu R'lyeh wgah'nagl fhtagn

Nonononononononono

Ph'nglui mglw'nafh Cthulhu R'lyeh wgah'nagl fhtagn

Ph'nglui mglw'nafh Cthulhu R'lyeh wgah'nagl fhtagn
Ph'nglui mglw'nafh Cthulhu R'lyeh wgah'nagl fhtagn
Ph'nglui mglw'nafh Cthulhu R'lyeh wgah'nagl fhtagn
Ph'nglui mglw'nafh Cthulhu R'lyeh wgah'nagl fhtagn

PUBLISHER'S NOTE

IT'S MORE OR LESS COMMON KNOWLEDGE THAT James Lovegrove suffered a nervous breakdown earlier this year, shortly after completing work transcribing and editing this, the last of Dr Watson's three *Cthulhu Casebooks* manuscripts. He was found in the small hours of the morning, prostrate on the beach at Eastbourne, staring out to sea with his body angled in a south-easterly direction. According to eyewitnesses, he was mumbling the very phrase – *Ph'nglui mglw'nafh Cthulhu R'lyeh wgah'nagl fhtagn* – that recurs in his afterword to the text.

Police and paramedics were called, and at first it was thought that James had had a seizure, perhaps a stroke. It was soon determined that he was fine physically but had been the victim of some kind of psychotic episode. For his own wellbeing, he was sectioned under the Mental Health Act.

Since then, James has been receiving treatment and is said to be on the road to recovery. The cause of his illness is believed to have been stress brought on by extreme overwork. All of us here at Titan Books wish him well.

The decision to publish this final book in the trilogy has not been taken lightly and was arrived at only after much debate in-house and following extensive consultation with James's family. We have chosen to reproduce the text just as it was found on his hard drive. We like to think this would be in accordance with his wishes, but we shall never know until he regains the capacity for coherent speech, which, we hope, will be soon.

Read on for an excerpt from
James Lovegrove's

SHERLOCK HOLMES

CHAPTER ONE

The Case of the Purloined Pearls

"AH, THERE YOU ARE, WATSON. COME QUICKLY. WE must hurry."

Scarcely had I disembarked from the train at Eastbourne than Sherlock Holmes was accosting me with these words.

"What, no hello?" I said. "No handshake? No greeting whatsoever?"

"Yes, yes, remiss of me," said Holmes. He clasped my hand for the briefest span of time conceivable. "How are you, old fellow? Well, I hope. You look in good health."

"And how was my journey?"

"Are you wanting me to tell you or entreating me to enquire?"

"The latter, although I've no doubt, you being you, you could manage the former."

"Then how was it?"

"Very agreeable. The compartment was not too crowded, and there is that very scenic view from the Ouse Valley Viaduct just north of Haywards Heath when one can look out of both sides of the carriage and see for miles in either—"

"Good," said Holmes. "Good, good. That's quite enough pleasantries. Come! No time to waste."

We hustled across the station concourse, I lugging my leather portmanteau which held toiletries and changes of clothing sufficient for a week's sojourn in the country. It was notable that my friend had not subjected me to the customary list of deductions about my recent doings and circumstances based on close scrutiny of my appearance. This had long been his habit since he abandoned London for a rural idyll and he and I saw each other far less frequently than we once did. It would amuse him to assess, with his usual uncanny accuracy, in what ways my life had changed – both for better and for worse – during the intervals between my visits.

That he had refrained from the practice today told me that he was greatly preoccupied. But then I could also infer it from the brightness in his lively grey eyes and the agitation with which he moved. I knew Holmes better than any man, I daresay better even than his own brother, the late Mycroft, had. I knew his character and moods intimately.

"Holmes," I said as we emerged from the station building, "if I'm not mistaken, you are on a case."

"Watson, you read me like a book."

"I don't need to be Sherlock Holmes to understand Sherlock Holmes. You are behaving exactly as you did when you were resident at Baker Street and had just caught the scent of some intriguing and seemingly intractable problem which you felt deserving of your energies and attention. My only quibble is, I thought you were no longer in the consulting detective game. You have, have you not, forsworn the gloom of London for that soothing life of Nature you so often yearned for. Your own words, Holmes. 'That soothing life of Nature.' Yet here you are, quite evidently in the throes of an investigation."

"Not in the throes, my friend, not yet. We are, as of

this moment, en route to the scene of the crime. I have not assimilated a single clue, nor formed a single theory. I am coming to the case as fresh as you are. We are both equally *tabula rasa* in this instance. All I know is that I received an urgent summons less than an hour ago. By sheer happenstance I was just leaving my house to come and meet you. I thought to myself, 'I shall pick up Watson on the way and together we shall peruse the evidence and identify the felon, just as in the old days.'"

"This is hardly what one would call retirement, old chap."

"Shall I tell you what retirement is, Watson? Retirement is a balm to the weary soul, a respite from quotidian cares and stresses, the contented evening after a hard day's toil – and also at times extremely tedious. I have found myself feeling particularly under stimulated and restless of late. The novelty of beekeeping has worn off. The allure of penning monographs has waned. Life has lost a little of its savour."

"You're bored, in other words."

My friend turned to me, amusement twitching the corners of his mouth. "Bored stiff, Watson. Bored almost to tears. And when a case presents itself, however trifling it may seem…"

"You jump at it."

"What can I say? Detection, like any addiction, is a hard habit to break."

We proceeded down Terminus Road, which connected the station directly to the seafront. Eastbourne's main commercial thoroughfare was bustling at this midmorning hour, full of housemaids fetching the daily groceries, matrons eyeing up the garments displayed in windows, and children spending their pocket money on sweets. All the shops had their awnings down against the surprisingly strong late-September sunshine. We had just endured a dismal summer, but as if in compensation for the weeks of unseasonal wind and rain the autumn of 1913 was glorious, bathing England in a mellow amber warmth.

An open-topped motor charabanc clattered raucously down the road, bearing a party of my fellow travellers from the train to their rooms at one of the town's many hotels. Since its inception in the mid-1800s Eastbourne had grown and flourished to become one of the country's most popular seaside resorts. Year round, visitors flocked from the capital and further afield to enjoy its health-giving sea air and the delights and diversions of its promenade, as well as to bathe in the refreshingly bracing waters of the Channel.

"Not far now," Holmes said with an "onward" gesture.

His strides were rapid and long, and I would have struggled to keep pace even if I weren't burdened by my luggage. I was two years' Holmes's senior and at that moment was feeling every day of it. His vitality seemed little diminished, for all that he was just shy of his sixtieth birthday. Mine, by contrast, was a shadow of its former self. The vigour of my youth seemed a long way away, a far distant memory. I had slowed and thickened as I inched towards senescence, whereas my friend retained most if not all of the nervy energy which had rendered him so lively and dynamic in the past.

We were waylaid outside a branch of W H Smith by

a cloth-capped ragamuffin who was doling out handbills to passers-by.

"Final day, sirs," he said. "Last chance to see the marvels and miracles before we strike tent and move on."

Holmes peremptorily brushed the boy aside, uttering an airy "Not now. Busy. Shoo!"

I, stricken by a twinge of pity for the lad, though he appeared unbothered by Holmes's brusque rebuff, took one of the proffered handbills.

"You won't regret it, sir," the urchin said. "Matinee or evening, the show's a wonder. You'll never see the like. Never mind you won't believe your eyes – you won't believe any of your senses!"

The handbill advertised a travelling circus that was ensconced somewhere just outside town. I glanced at it long enough to glean that much information and no more, before promptly stuffing it into my coat pocket and hurrying to catch up with Holmes.

Presently Holmes halted outside a jeweller's shop, Barraclough's, which appeared to be closed despite this being a Saturday, surely the busiest day of the week for such an establishment. The blinds were drawn and the sign in the window invited customers to return during business hours.

Holmes rapped hard, and the door was unlocked and opened by a bewhiskered middle-aged gentleman whose choleric complexion and glassy stare spoke of anxiety verging on panic.

"You Holmes?" he barked. "Detective fellow?"

"I am he. You, I take it, are Gervaise Barraclough, proprietor of these premises."

"Yes. Enter. Quickly." Barraclough was in such a state of discombobulation that he did not query my presence, or for that matter acknowledge it. "I hope you're the genius everyone says you are."

"If I'm half as clever as I am imputed to be, not least by my esteemed biographer here," replied Holmes, "then I'm sure I shall be more than adequate to the task. What is it I can do for you, Mr Barraclough? The messenger you sent to me was short on specifics. All he would tell me was that there had been some catastrophe at your shop and that, with a promise of remuneration for my services, I was to come as quickly as possible. I have done so, and would be grateful if you could enlighten me."

"It's a disaster, sir, an absolute disaster," Barraclough wailed. "Robbery. My prize goods, the cream of my collection, gone. Gone!"

I looked round the shop. The shelves and cabinets were bare. Velvet-lined ring trays contained no wares. Display boxes showed indentations where bracelets and necklaces should have been.

"You do seem to have been completely cleaned out," I observed.

"This? No, no, you've got it wrong. This is how the shop normally looks first thing of a morning. We remove all the jewellery overnight and stow it in the cellar. Otherwise thieves could smash the windows and pilfer as they pleased. The cellar has safes large enough to store all of our stock. They're Chatwoods, moreover, with intersected-steel coffers and unpickable, gunpowder-proof locks. Nobody should be able to steal from them."

"Yet somebody has."

"A thousand pounds' worth of stock has vanished. And that's a conservative estimate."

"My goodness," I said with a whistle.

"A sizeable sum," Holmes allowed.

"Including," Barraclough went on, "a dozen beautiful Tahitian black pearls which I took receipt of only last week, almost perfectly spherical and worth more than diamonds, along with a choker of domed cabochon emeralds, a truly exquisite piece which caught the eye of the Duchess of Devonshire, no less, on a recent stay in the town, and which Her Grace requested me to lay aside with a view to purchasing it on her next visit." He wrung his hands. "Oh, Mr Holmes, you must know how influential the Devonshires are in Eastbourne. Why, they more or less built this place from the ground up. Near enough every street name commemorates them or some piece of land they own. If I were to lose the duchess's patronage, if it were to become public knowledge that I had let the family down so grievously…"

His expression finished the sentence for him. He was contemplating the prospect of a sullied reputation, of abject ruin.

"There, there, Barraclough," my friend reassured him. "No need to fret. I shall recover these gems for you if it is at all in my power to do so. Now, show us these safes of yours. Let us see what we can see."